More praise for *Catching Heaven*

"Flashes of heart and soul . . . There is something achingly sad about these sisters' realization that some things in life have simply passed them by. And it's that simple truth that makes *Catching Heaven* a nice catch."

—*New York Post*

"Hall describes with wit and insight the personal growth of a compelling group of people who develop into an alternative family."

—*New Age Journal*

"Ms. Hall writes with a genuine gift for how we (humans) sound, and for sensing how we feel and think in our everyday lives. But she also seems to intuit what happens *between* these realms—between the said and the thought and the felt. As Octavio Paz wrote, what's 'in between' is where the poetry lies. And so it does in *Catching Heaven*."

—RICHARD FORD

"With fluid, elegant prose and a watchful eye for detail, Hall has crafted a compelling novel about love, loss, and hope."

—*The Sacramento Bee*

"[An] elegantly crafted first novel . . . This is a complex story, messy as real life, and told in a most compelling way."

—*Booklist*

"Hall's first novel meticulously details Southwestern life and the rancor of middle-aged sibling rivalry."

—*Publishers Weekly*

CATCHING
HEAVEN

CATCHING
HEAVEN

SANDS HALL

BALLANTINE BOOKS

NEW YORK

A Ballantine Book
Published by The Ballantine Publishing Group

Copyright © 2000 by Sands Hall
Reader's Guide Copyright © 2001 by Sands Hall and the Ballantine Publishing Group,
a division of Random House, Inc.

www.ballantinebooks.com

Library of Congress Cataloging-in-Publication: 2001116904

ISBN 0-345-44000-5

Manufactured in the United States of America

First Hardcover Edition: August 2000
First Trade Paperback Edition: August 2001

10   9   8   7   6   5   4   3   2   1

THIS BOOK IS FOR MY PARENTS
—AND GREAT FRIENDS—
BARBARA AND OAKLEY HALL

LATE SEPTEMBER

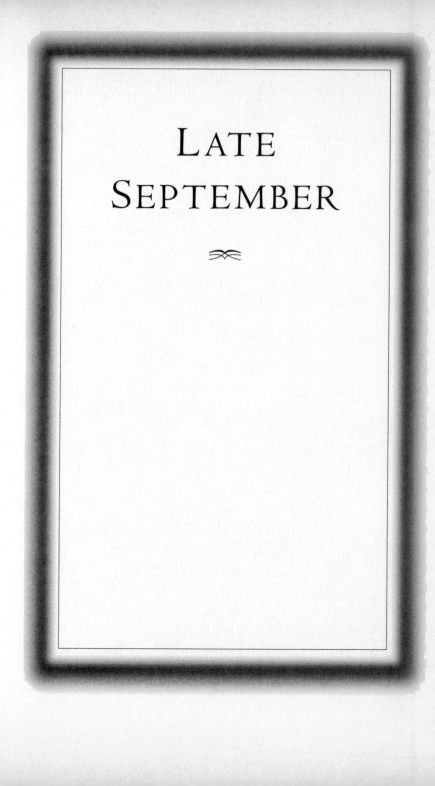

CHAPTER 1

MAUD

I have been studying how I may compare
This prison where I live unto the world
                    —RICHARD II

The sky was still dark when Maud closed the motel door behind her. Shivering, she crossed the street to the twenty-four-hour restaurant and bought a cup of coffee from a yawning waitress. She'd left the freeway late the day before, turning east onto a two-lane highway. Now it unfurled ahead of her headlights, which she kept on high beam except for the rare times a truck or car approached. She thought how like eyes the bright lights coming at her were, and how easy it would be to swerve into their oncoming glare.

An hour after dawn, a small town rose like a mirage out of the Arizona desert. Maud passed the flickering sign of a burger stand, a gas station, a battered motel before pulling in at Maria's Trading Post, whose attractions—GAS! MUTTON! NAILS! FLOUR!—were advertised on a hand-lettered sandwich board at the edge of the road.

The gas tanks were round-topped, old-fashioned. There seemed to be no expectation that she pay before pumping the gas. The latch on the trigger was broken. As Maud leaned against her car, holding the nozzle in the fill hole, she had another wince of memory. Actually, it was more than a wince, the rearranging of her shoulders she'd had to do when images of the Cheesios audition, of Miles, of Nikos' acting class leered towards her as she drove. A fragment of one of the days she'd worked on *Tucker's Larks* pushed at her. When she'd filmed her short though vital scene with Tucker, the actor hadn't actually been present. He was in Chicago playing baseball for a handicapped children's benefit—they planned to film his lines later. "Virtual Tucker," a crew member joked. In the sterile, muted space of a police interrogation room that was the set, Maud emoted her half of the scene to the plaid shoulder of the cameraman. Off to one side, the script girl read Tucker's dialogue in a flat, nasal voice. "Wait a bit after each line," the director coached Maud. "I know that's tough, given the, like, highly charged context of the scene, but we can't have any overlap."

The trigger beneath her finger clicked. Maud pulled at it a few more times, watching the numbers on the gas pump inch by. This isn't acting, she'd wanted to tell the people gathered in the room, wielding boom mikes, lights, makeup brushes. She replaced the nozzle in its slot in the gas pump. *I will not keep this form upon my head,* Constance, pulling at her hair, tells King John just before she exits and goes mad, *when there is such disorder in my wit.*

The wind pushed out of the desert, flattening her skirt against her legs. Maud closed her eyes before its chafing warmth, holding her hair back from her face with fingers that smelled of gasoline. *'Tis an unwanted garden*—no, that wasn't right—*'tis an unweeded garden that grows to seed. Fie on't, ah fie.*

A large yellow car with fins, parked askew, guarded the door to Maria's Trading Post. Its back seat was filled with newspapers. Both taillights were broken, and the paint above the tire wells badly rusted.

The screen door screeched as she opened it, activating several buzzing flies. A man leaned against the counter, watching a woman hack with a cleaver at a glistening haunch of meat. On his cheek was a constellation of pockmarks—a swirl, a small galaxy of indented scars. The door slapped shut.

"Sorry," Maud said, using a French accent.

The woman gestured with the cleaver. "But get that car to Sara anyway."

It took a moment for Maud to realize that this instruction was not meant for her. The man leveled dark eyes in her direction, then went back to brooding on the skinned carcass. Maud made out angles of marbled fat and blood that might have been part of a leg, cut off above the knee. A cowboy hat sat beside this on the counter, jaunty, incongruent. She turned away, into an aisle, walking past huge cans of chili and hominy, cellophane packages of HoHos, boxes of cornflakes and saltines, loaves of Wonder bread. She stared at a shelf that held polyester shorts and sneakers, wondering if this man and this woman held their pockmarked faces against her, her and her kind.

"Need help?" the woman called.

Desperately, Maud thought. "Merci," she said. "I am just looking." She didn't know why she'd started with the French accent but she didn't know how to stop now. She stared down into hunched burlap sacks of flour, beans, dried corn that stood at the back of the store. After searching for an apple or an orange, she settled for a package of sunflower seeds from a dusty display next to the cash register. She handed a twenty to the woman. "I would take this, please. And I put the fifteen dollars of the gas in the car." Her ability to use a French accent had always been rather dismal. The woman looked at her sharply before lifting a cash box up from beneath the counter.

"That car of yours is packed up pretty good," the man said. He'd put his hat on. Leaning against the counter, hip cocked, looking back at her from under the brim, he reminded Maud of an advertisement for jeans or male cologne in a hip fashion magazine. Sexy, definitely. Black hair looped over one shoulder fell to his waist. "You coming or going?"

For a moment she thought he meant the idiom: *you coming or going?* Was it so obvious that she was indeed *at sea?* that she was *at sixes and sevens, all balled up?* But his eyes were black, opaque, unamused.

"Well, I am coming, I guess." She straightened, as if her shoulders had been rounded by the weight floating around her, as tangible, as encompassing, as a long black veil.

"Where from?"

"Hollywood."

The air in the room shifted. They were impressed by and at the same time dismissive of this admission—which was what Maud felt it was. "Los Angeles, I mean," she amended.

"L.A." The man stated the letters as if something vast were connected to each one.

"Well, you sound foreign," the woman said. "Don't she sound foreign, Driver?"

Maud opened her mouth in a silent laugh, wanting to let them in on the joke: Hollywood *is* foreign. She wanted to convince them of this, as if this would give her defection validity. Hollywood is another *planet*. Instead, ashamed of having started the absurd charade, she accepted her change with a muttered "Merci." As she pushed the bills and coins into the pocket of her jean skirt, the man straightened and stepped away from the counter. Startled, she met his eyes and noticed again the nebula of scars on one cheek. She wondered how many women had reached a finger to trace the precision of that spiral; it was intriguing, oddly attractive. Although he wasn't as tall as she'd expected from his broad shoulders and length of torso.

The screen door slapped again behind her. "Sorry," she called. "Pardonnez-moi."

A phone booth leaned against the wall outside the store. Maud closed herself into it. It had been easy, yesterday, not to call Miles. When the car was in motion, on the freeway, calling him involved waiting for the next exit, the next town, pulling over, looking for a phone. Each time the urge struck her there had been lots of time to talk herself out of it. She'd called last night before she went to sleep, but he was at the studio. Of course. She hadn't left a message. Let him worry when he got home. But she'd slept fitfully in the double motel bed, waking up again and again to stare into the darkness that encased her, while Joni Mitchell mourned that the bed was too big, the frying pan too wide.

She pressed the series of buttons that added up to his phone and her calling card numbers. But of course he did not answer. When no one else had rented the studio he often worked there until morning, sometimes through the next day. Unless he was sleeping. His machine picked up.

"Hey there! This is Miles! Leave a message, and I'll be in touch, real soon. See ya!"

"Miles." Her voice was shaky. "Are you there?" She had argued with him over the use of that word, *real*. "It's *really*," she'd told him, as if by changing that one word she could change the tone of the whole message and by extension some aspect of their life together. But as he had pointed out to her, they had two separate phone lines; he could say what he wanted on his.

"Miles?" The idea that he might be lying in the next room, listening to her high, tight voice, made her pause again. "I can't do this anymore. So I've gone." A short laugh, the breathy one, the one that irritated him. "Which you'll figure out."

A dog, ribs showing through patchy fur, one leg lifted under its belly, limped through the trash at the side of the road, stopping to sniff at a curl of abandoned retread. Tears filled Maud's eyes. She listened to the hum of long-distance wires, the tape full of silence spooling onto his answering machine. She held the phone more tightly. "It's just that I had wanted—"

She'd used the past tense. The past perfect tense, to be precise. As her father had long ago informed her, using *had* before a verb was far more final than not using it. Plain old past tense could imply something ongoing; past perfect meant the thing being discussed was perfectly, as in completely, over and done. Because she had at various times pointed this distinction out to Miles, he would notice.

She wished she could change the message, even delete it. But there it was, a blinking red light that would alert him to listen as soon as he got back to the apartment. He would hope it was a producer, be disappointed that it was Maud, be baffled and then irritated that she'd placed his phone and his machine on the floor. The phone table, a long-ago gift from her mother, was one of the first things she'd packed into her car. "I'm sorry. I'm—" She imagined his pursed lips, his flared nostrils, the shake of his head as he knelt to punch the rewind button on his machine. "I'm sorry."

She watched the dog halt its way across the road. Behind her the screen door of the store slapped. The man named Driver stepped down the cement block that served as a stair. Heeled boots emphasized strong thighs. He turned to look at her. He'd tilted his hat forward, shadowing his eyes. She smiled, suddenly nervous. He stared a few moments longer, then stalked to the battered yellow Chevrolet. Gravel shot from beneath its wheels as he spun out onto the highway.

The car seemed to drive right into the sun, diminishing in size along the gray ribbon of highway. Just beyond Maria's Trading Post, the town stopped as abruptly as it had begun and then the distance started, a greenish gray and brown distance, dotted with scrub and an occasional blowing, bouncing tumbleweed. A semi came into view, leaping through the flaming hoop of the sun, growing huge in size and sound, shifting down noisily for the short trip through town. The driver lifted a hand. She raised hers in return, sucking in her belly, closing her fists, praying to the gods that the dog would not be hit, exploded, turned into a bloody carcass tumbling along the road, a sign that would be too much to bear.

The truck blared by. The dog lurched its way along the opposite side of the road. Maud offered thanks.

She checked the top rack—the blue tarp covering the load, frayed from the constant buffeting wind, and the multitudinous criss-cross of rubber cords that held the load in place. No one, she thought, no one in the world, knew where she was at this moment. She hadn't told Miles she was leaving; she hadn't told Lizzie she was coming. If the impossible should happen: if Cheesios should call Danielle and say they'd loved Maud's brief, bizarre, cud-chewing appearance and would she please take the commercial; if her parents should eat bad sushi during the Tokyo symposium and die; if her other agent, Scotty, should suddenly receive the perfect script with the perfect role for her; if Miles discovered he couldn't live without her; if she herself should decide to join the Navajo nation, or the Hopi tribe, or otherwise disappear into the space between worlds she sometimes thought was the best place for her, could her trail be traced? She'd used cash to buy gas along the road, purchased Diet Cokes, coffee, had spent the night in St. George. She wondered if she could be found on the basis of those stops, and this one, here at Maria's Trading Post, where she purchased sunflower seeds and spoke in a French accent to a man with a pockmarked face.

"For you have but mistook me all this while," she told her windshield as she started her car. A feather and a turquoise bead, tied to a leather shoestring, dangled from the rearview mirror. She set the bead swinging as she adjusted the mirror, angling away the slice of exhausted, wrinkled paleface staring out at her. She imagined highway patrolmen, search-and-rescue teams, paratroopers combing the highways, asking for news of a white Toyota with a skewed bumper, looking for a woman of her description. She hoped the descriptions would include the detail that she was thin—would she be remembered as thin, or at least, slim?

CHAPTER 2

LIZZIE

NOTES FROM BENEATH THE MAGNETS ON LIZZIE'S FRIDGE

Southwest Ink—call
closet doors
Sparky re engine
Hannah—new leotard
Patricia—car pool Tues
SAM

Lizzie painted in a wooden trailer that stood not far from her house. The trailer had come with the property. Even then its exterior was a faded green, cracked with age. The wheels were gone, and long ago earth had risen up to fill the space between ground and floorboards. From its window, a large one above the sink, she could watch the hunched peak of Fable Mountain as it brooded its way through the seasons.

Over the years she'd equipped the trailer, which had been her first home on this land, with various amenities. She'd let years pass before she installed electricity, finally replacing the kerosene lanterns and woodstove. Hot running water came with the birth of Hannah. After Summer was born, about two years after the contract with Southwest Ink came through, she built the big house. About that time Sam helped her install a skylight at the trailer's north end, and ever since she'd used it only as a studio.

She stood at the sink and used her thumb to urge the white, green, turquoise paint from between the coarse hairs of her brushes. The watery colors spooled together, a pleasant enough aquamarine, on their way down the drain.

The voice of Sam calling, "Luna," hanging long on the *u*, made her look up. Through the window she watched him move up the path towards his old caboose at the crest of the hill. He had always been a big man, but there was something about her perspective— below him, gazing upwards—that made him seem shorter today, his barrel of a chest somehow diminished. A plastic bag hung from one wrist. He'd been to the store. His gray braid dangled like a dead snake down his back. Halfway up the path he turned and waited for Luna, who shambled up the path towards him. One hand on the dog's head, the wind flapping his shirt, he stood looking down towards the house and the studio.

Lizzie wrenched the spigot closed and shoved the brush in with the others in the large Skippy peanut butter jar. From the studio door she called, "Sam!" and jumped the two steps. Sam watched her come. She stopped in front of him, panting from the trot up the hill, swiping hair out of her face that the wind kept flinging back. "Where the hell have you been keeping yourself lately?"

He gazed at her, smiling a little. He did look thin. "Where I always keep myself, Lizard."

He did not, he would not, ask the obvious question in return. She couldn't have said when or why he'd stopped treating her house as his own, or why she no longer traversed the path to visit him, taking him vegetables, corn bread, soup.

"You didn't come the other night," she said. "You missed Maud being a homeless person on television."

"I hear she was killed. Lots of bullets, Summer said."

"Summer thought she'd really died. She wouldn't stop crying until we'd called and talked to her in person."

"Well, now, I'm both sorry and not sorry I didn't see all that." He turned to set out again. Luna hitched herself to her feet and lumbered up the path behind him.

"I miss you, Sam," she called after him.

He waved a hand.

She walked back down the hill, past the goddamned engine Sparky still hadn't gotten out of there. It looked like a plant from Mars, the way it had taken root. She would have to move it—Sparky never would. And it was clear that Summer, only seven, had inherited his tendency to procrastinate.

She headed across the driveway, up the stairs, stooped to listen to the intercom system that connected her studio to Theo's room. The intercom was turned up high, making Theo, rolling over in his crib, sound like a horse wading through high grass. Lizzie squinted at his whimper, but it died away. When she heard the rattle of Jeep's car coming up the long gravel driveway, she slid the pile of student journals she'd finished grading that morning off the table and onto one hip and pulled the studio door closed. The sky, laced with ragged, racing clouds, arced above her.

"Theo awake yet?" Jeep called. She wore her usual jeans, torn extravagantly at the knee and beneath one buttock.

"Nope." Lizzie crossed the driveway and dumped the journals through an open window onto the back seat of her own car. "But that doesn't make you not late."

"I got a phone call."

The note of defense in her voice made Lizzie look at her sideways. "Was it Rich? Jeep."

Jeep pulled a Tonka truck from the back seat of her car. Wisps of blonde hair, escaping the ponytail on top of her head, blew across her face. She held up a pile of picture books, a miniature baseball cap. "Spoor of Theo."

"Repeat after me," Lizzie said. "I will not talk to Rich. I will not talk to Rich. I will not talk to Rich."

"It's not like I'm going back to him or anything," Jeep said. "He's a bastard."

"He's a shit." Lizzie stomped up the stairs to the front door. She found her wallet in the pile of papers on the counter, her keys beside a sprawl of Theo's toys. She grabbed a banana and aimed this like a gun at Jeep, who'd followed her into the house. "He treated you like shit."

Jeep shrugged and began to run water over the dishes piled in the sink. "He says Jake is back."

Lizzie kept the banana in firing position. "Is that supposed to mean something? Does that mean something?"

Jeep's ponytail moved from side to side. "I guess not."

"I didn't get to the dishes. And I might be late. I keep promising to have a drink with a colleague." She put this word in quotes. "Patricia's doing my car pool. The girls will be home from gymnastics around six."

"Just so I get to my AA meeting at seven." Jeep gathered cereal bowls off the counter and slid them into the sink.

"Yeah, yeah." At the door Lizzie stopped and aimed the banana again. "And don't call Rich."

Jeep stopped scrubbing, her back a statement of injured reproach. "You're not my mother."

"Well, I should have been."

Lizzie headed down the stairs and across the gravel driveway, wondering why she would be so angry, why her hands on the steering wheel would shake at the thought that Jeep might call Rich, why she would shift gears too quickly, grinding into reverse with a horrible sound at the idea that so-called love must always make these stupid, *stupid* efforts to reconnect.

CHAPTER 3

JAKE

love me any way you choose
handle me with kid gloves
light me like fuse
love me

Jake bought a newspaper on his way into Joanie's. Sat at the counter. Lunch was over, the café empty. Joanie's had added a brew pub while he'd been gone. He wanted a beer—he'd spent the day tangling with software at the new job. Thought he might order something called Red Coyote, but settled for coffee. Had rehearsal later. Wasn't so much fun anymore to be even a little muddled while figuring out chord changes and the logistics of harmony. One of many things that had changed.

The waitress behind the counter looked vaguely familiar. Wide-apart brown eyes. Pert nose. She smiled, poured coffee, turned to keep scrubbing at the hot plates of the coffeemaker. Pushed at her bangs with the back of her hand and then untied the strings of her apron, which had slipped low on her hips. With deft fingers, behind her back, she tied another, tighter bow. Emphasized her waist.

She met his eyes in the mirror that ran the length of the wall behind the counter. "I heard you were back."

Jake nodded, resumed his study of the box scores. She brought the coffeepot, topped off his cup. "Everyone says you went to Nashville. To sell your songs, they say."

"That was the idea." Jake wondered who "everyone" was.

"Wow, Nashville." She leaned a hip against the counter, coffeepot dangling. Jake stared down at the newspaper.

"How long were you gone?"

"A little over a year. Almost two, maybe."

"I knew it! See, I'd just started working here when you left town? My name's Tina?"

"Ah!" Did his best to look like he remembered.

"You still have that band of yours? Did it fall apart?"

"Could have. But didn't. We got it back together." He clinked his spoon against his coffee cup. Keep her from seeing how much this fact still had the power to move him.

"So it *is* you that's playing at Farquaarts next month! You guys're my favorite dance band."

"Thanks."

"They were telling me you used to live in Nashville."

They? "Years ago."

"Why'd you go back?"

He held his hand over his cup to stop another onslaught of coffee. "Seemed a good idea. Worked once." He heard Minerva: *Can't step in the same river twice, buddy.*

"But it didn't work this time?"

Jake shook his newspaper. If this went on any longer Tina would think he was flirting.

She didn't take the hint, leaned in further. "I've always wondered— Oops, just a sec." Flashing that sweet grin, she headed towards a man who'd sat at the counter several stools down. Jake nodded at his nod, short tip of the chin. Stood and fished in his pocket for change. Along with the coins came a piece of paper. His own scrawl:

> coffee!
> milk
> paper towels
> o.j.
>
> Withheld hearts
> No more of this (these?) withheld hearts

starts
parts, darts

bread
toothpaste
Ajax

call Willy and Sue—Johnny's Birthday!

I fell in love with all of you
~~how can I love just part of~~
do I only get to

how do I love apart from you
how do I love just part of you
your withheld heart

    Tina returned. Jake tucked the scrap of paper back in his pocket. "As I was saying," she said. Scooping coins off the counter with a swipe of that deft hand. "I've always wondered why it is you call yourselves Jake's Blakes. At first I thought it was a typo. Like it should be *blokes*."

    "Well, you're close."

    "I don't get it."

    "You're on the right track."

    Tina shook her head at him. "Come *on*."

    He tapped the newspaper on the counter. "Gotta go. I have rehearsal with those blokes."

    "You do?" Tina clasped her hands between her breasts. "You *do*? That is, like, so cool."

    Jake shook his head in appreciation. Started away, came back. "Any thoughts on what to buy a nephew who's nine?"

    "You have a nephew?" Hands still clasped between her breasts. It had been a mistake to ask this.

    "Thanks anyway. I just thought of something."

    The man down the counter stared straight ahead. Fork, napkin on one side of folded hands, knife, spoon on the other. Waiting. Lizzie had once told Jake that coffee shops were the home kitchens of the lonely. Where else can they find the aromas of Mom? Toast, coffee, casserole with tomato sauce. Where else can they hear people sounds? Fork against plate, laughter, talk.

Lizzie.

Jake offered the guy the newspaper.

"Thanks, man."

He paused at the pay phone on his way out to call his sister. Willy answered. "You've taken your sweet time about getting over here to say hi in person."

"Job keeps me busy. Like you pointed out the last time I saw you, Willy, I can't just go on being a goddamn *artiste* all my life."

"Yeah, well. I was drunk."

Which was as much of an apology as Willy would muster. Jake accepted it with a grunt. "I want to drop something by for the Jellybean before rehearsal."

"We're not going anywhere."

Jake headed down the sidewalk towards Elmer's Mountain Music. Paused to take a look at Fable Mountain. She glowered above the slanted roofs of Marengo's houses. Crook-backed, familiar as a children's story, raising her bald and jagged peak. Invitation. Threat.

Your withheld heart.

CHAPTER 4

L I Z Z I E

NOTES FROM BENEATH THE MAGNETS ON LIZZIE'S FRIDGE

The hunter stands beside the tree in the storm and the lightning and when the hunter raises his rifle to shoot at the deer the tree whaps the hunter with a branch and the hunter falls down and the deer is safe and he says thank you old friend to the tree and the tree leans down to pat the deer with another branch I love you, Ma.

SUMMER

In Lizzie's afternoon Life Class, Sara Roantree held her arms over her head in a position that was a crouch, about to spring. Or warding off an expected blow. Or kneeling in agonized prayer. The erect spine and bowed head, the twisted fists, the angle of harsh cheekbones, managed to convey despair, pride, supplication. What was it in this combination, Lizzie wondered, that reminded her of her sister?

She checked her watch. "Three minutes," she said, and ignored the groans of her students.

Her own fingers itched for a piece of charcoal. As she wandered through the forest of drawing pads propped on one knee, clipped to an easel, held in a lap, she saw few students capturing the arrogance, nor the entreaty, the pose implied—the appeal to some power larger than self, and, at the same time, the self's ability to withstand what the gods might deliver. Again she thought of Maud. In one of the last moments of the episode of *Tucker's Larks*, the searchlight of a hovering helicopter had leached all color from the scene. Caught in that fierce light, Maud jerked and swayed in a barrage of bullets meant for a gang member. Blood bloomed from her mouth. Lizzie, admiring the Gorey-esque color scheme—black, white, red—did not realize Summer was weeping, hysterical. "She's dead, Ma, she's dead!" As it turned out when they called, Maud was not dead, but she was also not fine. She was in yet another questioning-our-relationship crisis with Miles.

She checked her watch. "That's it. Sign your sketch. Close your notebooks."

The class moaned. Sara rubbed her upper arms, blinked and yawned. Lizzie draped a kimono over her shoulders. "Great pose." She turned to the class again. "I said, that's *it*. No pissing and moaning. And no erasing—" She snapped her fingers. "Yvette, I said no erasing."

Yvette writhed in front of her easel. "But it's terrible. You'll flunk me for sure."

"Probably not," Lizzie said, and earned a fiery, grateful look from beneath the black beret. Yvette's attempts to look like an artist living on the Left Bank in the thirties amused Lizzie. In addition to the beret, slanting across a marble-white forehead, the girl wore a jumper, tights, clogs—all black. On the official student roll sheets her name was Ellen.

"Those who didn't hand in your sketchbooks last week, and you know who you are, get them on my desk, now. You'll get them back next Tuesday."

Yvette reluctantly closed her notebook and stood in line to deposit it on Lizzie's desk. One student still gazed at the pad clipped to his easel. "Aaron." Lizzie snapped her fingers again. "Now."

"Okay, okay." Aaron, closing the large leaves of the sketchbook, paused as Sara made her way across the studio towards the changing room. Lizzie turned to see what he saw. Splayed bare feet, almost as wide as they were long, shaped by years of walking barefoot. Kimono tight around the roll of large hips. Pendulous breasts straining the kimono's silk. Aaron whistled softly. "Some boobs!" he said to the student standing next to him.

Hands on her hips, Lizzie walked towards him, wrinkling her nose against his cheap and tangy cologne. "Boobs, Aaron? Did you really say *boobs*?"

Aaron stepped back. His eyelashes drooped like a beauty queen's. They were long, black and feathery, reminding her, with a mental lurch, of Jake.

"Be careful of the words you choose," she said. "They are just like lines of charcoal. Each one has the potential to convey as much about you as about your subject." She sounded exactly like her father. Sententious, Maud called it, behind his back. She gathered up the pile of sketchbooks and pushed with hip and shoulder against the heavy classroom door.

The hallway was lined with stripped canvases, sculptural attempts, discarded found-art objects ready to be re-found, gunmetal tables and cabinets that looked as if they'd been used as palette and as canvas. Even the floor was dappled with daubs and spots of paint. She breathed in the beloved smells of clay and turpentine.

"Mrs. Maxwell?"

Lizzie turned, supporting the notebooks on a hip. Aaron sped towards her down the corridor. His shoes flashed—he'd painted the inner half of his high-topped Keds neon red, the outside purple. "Mrs. Maxwell!" He slid to a stop, face open and flushed. His skin glowed.

"It is not *Mrs.*," she said. "We've been over that."

He ducked one shoulder and took a deep breath, as if running down the hall had emptied him of all oxygen. "When can I get my journal back?"

"What did I say in class?"

Aaron shook his head. "I didn't hear you. I was, you know, so into—" He swiped a hand through the air, up towards the sky, as if he could summon whatever ambiance had been hovering around Sara as she posed. His hair, composed of a million black, loose ringlets, reminded Lizzie of a younger, thinner version of Jake. But it wasn't just the eyes, or the hair. It was the slanted, humorous I-can-see-through-you gaze, and the sense of boundless energy he carried with him.

She felt her lips fold into a straight line. "Is that all?"

Aaron waved at the pile of notebooks. "Could I borrow mine back? Just for a sec? I want to write down what you said. About a line of a drawing and a word—I liked that."

A number of students used their sketchbooks as diaries, and

Lizzie sometimes puzzled over the quotations, thoughts, scraps of poetry scribbled in and around their drawings. "It can wait until Tuesday." She sounded unbearably prim, even to herself. "If you find it a really valuable piece of advice, it'll stick with you until then."

In front of her office door, she squeezed two fingers into a pocket to get at the key, managing to balance the notebooks until the door opened. They slipped out of her hold and sprawled onto the floor with a series of loud thumps. "Fuck it!" She slammed the rest of them down on her desk, amazed at her sudden desire to burst into mad weeping. She wasn't yet forty. Was this the first sign of the peri-menopause crap she'd heard too much about from the other soccer moms? Her father would say it was just one more excuse for female displays of emotion.

"I think you dropped something." Cal, the art history teacher, crouched in the doorway, gathering notebooks. "Here you go." He deposited them on her desk, pushed his glasses back up his nose.

"Thanks, Cal." She sounded brusque. Cal's goofy, lopsided grin irritated her. She often had to overcome the impulse to move be-hind him, place her hands over his rounded, obsequious shoulders, a foot in the middle of his back, and pull, hard. "Thanks a lot."

He crossed one arm in front of his waist and one behind and bowed. She chuckled in as appreciative a way as she could muster. "Madam," he said. "Is today the day we finally get to have that drink?"

"Oh, Cal." A margarita sounded good, a Bass sounded great. And she had promised. But not with him, not today. "It's my day to car-pool." It wasn't a complete lie. It had been, until she'd asked Patricia to do it for her.

Cal shook his head, blinking rapidly.

"We'll just be damned sure we do it, okay? Maybe next week?" Lizzie looped the straps of her bag over her shoulder, slid her grade book into it, gathered up the pile of sketchbooks.

"Sure, sure." His wide front teeth made him look like a cartoon character. "We had it in the book, though. Want me to carry those?"

"I'm fine, really." The heels of her red cowboy boots echoed down the corridor. She heard his office door close. The quiet click reproached her.

Sara's bulky figure undulated in the heat rising from the black asphalt parking lot. "Sara!" Lizzie called, and trotted towards her. She let the notebooks fall onto the hood of Sara's huge yellow car. "Too fucking hot."

"Hot for September, sure. The seasons are crazy. Sam says they're changing for good." She screwed up her face. "I've been filling out forms."

Sara's distaste for anything bureaucratic stemmed from her experiences with the Bureau of Indian Affairs. Lizzie could hardly blame her. From the stories Sara had to tell of living on the Reservation, it seemed nothing got done whether you did or did not fill out all the necessary governmental papers. Sara hated anything to do with paperwork and had modeled all of the previous semester without being paid. It was only by accident that Lizzie'd found out about it.

"I'll work you a lot this semester, if you like."

"You just want to use me because I got some boobs." Chuckling, Sara lowered herself into the driver's seat. The back of the car was filled with newspapers. Lizzie couldn't make out whether it was an ongoing recycling attempt, which she rather doubted, or—and this seemed far more likely—a bed for some itinerant relative.

"That young artist looks like that friend of yours that was."

"No. You think so?"

Sara started the engine and spoke over its roar. "Except this one thinks too much of himself already. Get those things off the front of my car."

Lizzie scooped up the notebooks. "Want to see what you look like?"

"Not through those eyes." Sara put the car in reverse. "Tell Sam there's a powwow this weekend. He should come."

"He never goes to those things."

"Well, he should. Won't admit he's lonely, but he is."

"He has us," Lizzie said, stung.

"Sure. He has me, too. But when does he actually come over for a meal? He sure don't with me. You seen him lately?"

"Just today. He's coming to dinner." Lizzie slapped hard at a non-existent fly. "Probably. Your taillights are broken."

Sara shrugged. "At some point one of us'll get stopped and get a citation and then we'll fix 'em. You seen Jake since he's been back?"

Lizzie shook her head.

"He looks good. Sad, though. Eyes like one big bruise he's so sad. That place weren't good for him." She began to back out again and called, "Powwow's down in Chinle. Saturday. Sam won't come. But tell him anyway."

Lizzie used the pay phone at the edge of the parking lot to call Jeep. "Wow," Jeep told her. "Theo's like definitely teething. You having fun with your 'colleague'?"

"Decided not to. Listen, stay for dinner. I'm asking Sam down."

"I have AA."

Lizzie watched Aaron and Yvette emerge from the Art Building and lope their way down the outside stairs, carefully, too carefully, not touching. "Shit," she said.

"What?"

"One day at a time," she said, her voice pinched, snide.

Unexpectedly, Jeep laughed. "Don't knock it till you've tried it. Oh, and Miles called."

"Miles?"

"Something to do with Maud, he said. He left a number."

"It's probably about the other night. They're always fighting. Why she just doesn't leave I can't figure."

"It's not always so easy." Jeep sounded as if she were crouched in a cave—distant, sad and alone.

"They've turned into people who are bad for each other. I know all the signs, believe me."

Lizzie kept an eye on Aaron and Yvette making their way through the rows of cars. They seemed almost drunk, wavering towards and away from each other, weak magnets beginning to find true north. Young love. She sniffed, and as she crossed the parking lot, she went out of her way to walk by them. They stood talking next to a beat-up Honda. "Hey, you two."

Aaron raised his eyebrows. "I'm choosing my words with care, Ms. Maxwell," he said, riding hard on the s of Ms. His brown eyes managed to both admire and mock her.

"You do that."

She wished Sara had not told her that Jake was sad. "His fault," she said, starting her car. After dinner she would turn on the lights out in her studio, rework the painting of the bare-breasted, long-haired woman in a swirly gypsy skirt. Arms out, almost frantic, the woman rushed towards the clean-cut man dressed in a white linen suit.

His eye's one big bruise he's so sad.

She turned on the radio. Turned up the volume. The marching martial music that introduced *All Things Considered* filled the vacant interior of her car.

CHAPTER 5

MAUD

When to the sessions of sweet, silent thought
I summon up remembrance of things past,
I sigh the lack of many a thing I sought,
And with old woes new wail my dear time's waste
                              —SONNET 30

Even as she sped along the narrow road that cut across the desert, Maud imagined herself snail-like. She traveled with her house on her back: the small table, boxes of tablecloths and plates and glasses, books, clothes, two lamps, even a chair. She couldn't see out the back window. The seat beside her was crammed with bags, her purse, a small basket with food, a box of cassette tapes.

She slowed as she approached a pickup truck dawdling ahead of her, broom handle stuck into one side of its tailgate, shovel in the other. Two young girls riding in the back sat up to peer at her. Maud waved. Giggling, they ducked out of sight, then popped up again and waved. When Maud waved back, they collapsed behind the tailgate again.

Sucking salt from a sunflower seed, she tangled with another wince of memory. Cheesios. "It's a new snack product, hon." The voice of her commercial agent, Danielle, coming through the answering machine. Maud was still in bed. On the other side of the bed Miles dozed, curled away from her. "I know it's early, but hustle your little butt on down there. You're a mom, kids in school, housewifing away."

Maud moved her shoulders, blew the shells of sunflower seeds out the car window, sang along with Bonnie Raitt about finding love in the nick of time. Changed the tape.

"They want slacks, sweater knotted over your shoulders," Danielle's cheerful, high voice continued. "You know the look. Call me to confirm."

"I do not 'know the look,' " Maud said.

Miles slid an arm across the expanse of mattress that separated them and patted her. "Mom, eh?"

"Is that supposed to be funny?" Maud flung the covers back. She showered, pulled on jeans, knotted a sweater over her shoulders, did not wake Miles, who had fallen back asleep, before she left the apartment. She put her makeup on in the car. No script waited at the casting office. Instead, the clients had provided a cartoon: Large set of lips. Tongue curling out at one corner. Nose designated by two dots. Barbie-doll eyes. Arching eyebrows registering astonishment and appreciation. The copy was easy: "Mmmm, good!!!" Five women, wearing jeans, sweaters knotted over their shoulders, sat on folding chairs. They slid and curled their tongues into the corners of their lips. "Mmmm, good!" they whispered. "Mmmm, *good!*" "*Mmmm*, good!"

Maud groaned and snapped a sunflower seed between her teeth. Waving wildly, the girls in the pickup popped up in unison from behind the tailgate, as if they'd counted down before sitting up. Maud waved wildly back. Mouths wide in laughter, they dove out of sight.

The cameraman wore a baseball cap turned sideways. "Hiya!" he said. "I'm Billy. Have a seat on that stool."

An assortment of cracker boxes and bags littered a table beside the stool: Triscuits, Wheat Thins, saltines, Goldfish. Billy plied the bill of his cap up and down. "Okay, honeybunch, we got to drop that sweater. The clients decided a little more homey, a little less sporty."

Maud unknotted the sweater, lowered it to the floor.

"Okay," Billy said. "You're lounging on your couch. I know you can't really *lounge* on a *stool*, but anyway. You've got all these crackers to choose from, boxes and boxes. You nibble this one, that one, you finally try a Cheesio. Your face lights up. This is *the* snack cracker."

"Enlightenment in a cracker."

Billy's eyes widened. "Whoa! Right. Ha! All your life you've been searching and finally, *wow*! You say—"

"Mmmm, good?"

"Ha! That's it exactly. Use Goldfish for the Cheesios—they aren't on the market yet. We have to *imagine*, you have to do some *acting*." He chuckled. His head disappeared as he checked Maud through the camera's viewfinder. "Just one more thing. After you say, 'Mmmm, good,' the clients want this little peep of tongue. Sex sells, I don't have to tell *you*. Just slide it over to the corner of your mouth—"

Maud attempted this.

"A little more curl? A little more? A little more? Yeah! That's about it." He wiped a hand beneath his nose and hummed as he adjusted a light, took off his cap, scratched at his hair, put the cap back, sniffed. "We just want a slate, usual thing, and we'll just take it from there."

Maud slanted her legs to one side, so her thighs wouldn't look squat, foreshortened, to the men who would view this tape in a boardroom somewhere in America.

"Slate."

"Hello!" Maud spoke into the round eye of the camera. "My name is Maud Maxwell? I'm represented by the Cromwell Agency?" She smiled as punctuation.

"Good!" Billy whispered. "Now, you're lounging, yearning for that perfect cracker. Lounge and yearn, that's it."

Triscuit in hand, Maud leaned back, hooking the arches of her feet beneath the rungs of the stool. She nibbled the cracker's salty edge, imagining her home in suburbia, the housecoat and slippers she'd put on that morning to get the children off to school. Surrounded by crackers, she could relax now, in her recliner—bought on credit—as she watched her favorite soap opera on the not-yet-paid-for TV. She wondered what it would be like to have a life where part of what you did with your day was evaluate your snack food.

"Such a *boring* cracker!" Billy prompted, whispering.

She made a face, put down the Triscuit, picked up a saltine, nibbled, sighed, looked dissatisfied. She raised her eyes, shook her head: would the heavens answer her prayer?

"Yes, yes!" The camera whirred.

She picked up the Goldfish bag, looked at it with interest. Eyebrows raised, she drew out one of the orange fish and examined it. She put it in her mouth. It stuck to her tongue, then glued itself to her hard palate. She was reminded, forcibly, of the time she'd attended a Catholic service and been inspired to follow the others kneeling before a stern-faced priest, who'd placed a Communion wafer on her tongue. Should she suck? Was it all right to chew? She tried to smile, to convey the wonder attached to this amazing cracker, but the Goldfish seemed to have used all available saliva. Her lips stuck to her teeth. "Mmmm, *good*," she said, through the cud of dampened gauze. She tried again. Orange flakes sprayed on the word *good*. She giggled. The rest of the cracker whooshed out of her mouth.

"Cut, cut." Billy switched the camera off. "Goddamn. I keep *asking* Cora to get some water in here. You okay?"

Maud held up a hand, unable to stop laughing.

"Let's try it again. It was pretty good up to there."

Still giggling, Maud worked her tongue around her gums. She pulled her lips back, placing her front top teeth against her bottom teeth. "Anything show?"

Uneasy, Billy leaned back, peered, pointed. "A little orange, there."

Eyes seeping tears, Maud scraped a fingernail across the tooth he indicated. She might have to spew laughter until she died, but was afraid that in fact she was about to cry, and once she started she'd never stop. "I have to leave." Her voice sounded as if it came from the other side of the room.

Billy stared, one hand on the camera. The silence stretched. Maud felt very serious. Dreadfully, awfully serious. In the context— this was about *crackers*—this struck her as hilarious. She began to laugh again.

"You're leaving?" Billy dragged the back of his wrist beneath his nose.

She picked up her sweater. "I have to leave." Leave, she thought. Leaf. Leave. Leaves. *That time of year thou mayst in me behold, when yellow leaves, or none, or few, do hang upon those boughs.*

"L.A.," the man with the pockmarked face had said.

"Well, you sound foreign," the woman had remarked.

"This thou perceiv'st, which makes thy love more strong," she lectured the girls, who were waving at her again. She emphasized her points with her forefinger. "In this case, Sonnet 73, Shakespeare begins with 'yellow *leaves*,' a reference to the autumn of his life. The sonnet ends with the instruction 'to love that well, which thou must *leave* ere long.' Pretty clever, don't you think?"

But the pickup's turn signal was blinking. The truck slowed almost to a stop before lurching onto a rutted road. The girls waved. Maud felt bereft. She wanted to follow, wanted to see where the road might lead: a trailer and its hogan, the smell of lard, of rice and beans, the clang of a bell around the neck of the pet goat, the warmth of lamplight that would soon begin to glow out of small windows.

CHAPTER 6

LIZZIE

NOTES FROM BENEATH THE MAGNETS ON LIZZIE'S FRIDGE

MARENGO STATE COLLEGE
Faculty Senate Meeting
Wednesday, October 3
THE VOTE YOU'VE BEEN WAITING FOR
Adjunct Faculty representation!
All staff urged to attend. Let your voice be heard!

Lizzie parked behind Sam's battered Galaxy pickup. He never drove it anymore, always walked the mile to Artie's general store. Hannah sat on the top step of the porch stairs, bent over a book—since starting sixth grade she'd rarely had her nose out of one. Summer used her belly to balance on the railing. When Lizzie yelled at her to get down, Summer gave her a baleful look and took off up the path towards Sam's. "Homework first!" Lizzie called.

Jeep came out onto the porch, carrying Theo on a hip. "Miles phoned again."

"Summer!" Lizzie called more loudly. "Tell Sam to come for dinner. I've got a message for him from Sara."

"Mami!" Theo put out his hands.

Jeep allowed him to spill from her arms into Lizzie's. "He said if you don't reach him at home, try him at the studio."

30

Hannah followed them indoors, carrying her gymnastics bag. "I always like it when you're here, Jeep," she said as she opened the door to the basement. "It's the only time the house gets clean."

"Hannah!" Jeep said.

"Cleanliness has recently become an issue." Lizzie got herself a beer. "God knows whose genes those are."

"They're Blair's," Hannah called from the basement. Lizzie heard her set the water to running into the washer. "He's tidy, same as me. Can I go up to Sam's too?"

"Go, go, go. Just get your homework done. And make sure Summer does hers."

Jeep pointed to the notepad next to the phone. "Those are his numbers. This time he said it's kind of urgent." She kissed Theo on the head. "Goodbye, pumpkin."

Lizzie walked her out to the porch. Jeep stopped at the top of the steps, looked out across the driveway and the field beyond. "I've thought about what you said. About school. I'm saving. I'm waitressing at three places now. If any of the waiters at Harmony House ever leave, I've been promised their shifts, and then I can quit the Red Garter. I hate that place, but it's good money." She started down the stairs. "Sometimes I think I'll never make it. I see a new backpack in a catalogue, a pair of skis on sale, a six-pack. But so far so good. One day at a time."

"Yeah, yeah, yeah." Lizzie waved her off, dumped Theo in front of the TV with a video, and tried Miles at home. His number was different from Maud's. He answered on the first ring.

"Miles?"

"Maud!" Miles said, an exasperated *at long last*!

"This is Lizzie."

"You sound just like her. Have you seen her? Has she called?"

A pause flickered. "What's up?"

"This is so weird. I get home this morning—I had a late night in the studio—and I sack out. Wake up midafternoon. I'm trying to get this demo tape done? Anyway."

There was the sound of a match being lit, a quick inhale and exhale. "A lot of times she's not here—out on an audition, rehearsing a scene for acting class. But I'm having some coffee and it dawns on me—the house looks different. Pillows missing from the couch. Rug gone from the wall. And my answering machine's on the floor! This little table she lets me use, she says you have one too? Anyway, it's gone."

Their mother, always careful about fairness, had given each of them one of a set of three nesting tables. Lizzie wondered why she'd busted up the set, since the point was they were supposed to nest. Maud offered that maybe it was so that each of the Maxwell households—"such as they are," she'd said with that high, forced laugh—would have one.

"Maybe you'll think I'm a little dense here." Miles cleared his throat. "I was thinking she was just using all this stuff as props—she does that, for scenes she does for that acting class of hers. Then I listen to my messages." Another long exhale of smoke at the other end. "She says she 'had to go.' Doesn't say where she's calling from. I look around. Manoman. What it looks like, is that she's, like, left. Or something."

Lizzie sat down, took a long pull at her beer.

"She's taken a lot of things out of the closet. Some couch pillows. Photographs. Manoman. Those candlesticks your mom gave her. At least she didn't take her piano. It looks like she's left the house, but she's taken the home away."

Lizzie was touched by this.

"Yeah," Miles said, "she left the house, but she took our home away."

Maud had told her once, in the early days with Miles, that she *thrilled to hear their love transmuted* into lyrics and music. Those were her words. *Thrilled. Transmuted.* Lizzie, still with Jake then, had said, "Jake ever tries such a thing, he'll be out on his ear."

"Lizzie?"

"You guys have a fight or something?"

"We've had far worse fights than the one we had last night, night before last. I mean, it wasn't even a fight."

"The night *Tucker's Larks* was on?"

"Or maybe it was that audition. Her agent sent her out for some commercial that was a bust. And she was pissed about the size of her role on *Tucker's Larks.* I tell her she should be glad she's working, but she keeps talking about how it used to be. She took the plates! No, here are the white ones." Lizzie heard the sounds of cupboard doors opening and shutting, drawers yanked open and closed. "Left glasses. Took the wooden spoons. She headed your way, you think?"

Since moving to Los Angeles Maud had come to visit Lizzie often. But never before had she arrived with candlesticks, a Navajo wall hanging, wooden spoons.

"I'll let you know if I hear from her, Miles."

She wandered out onto the porch and stared up at Sam's trailer. She'd relied on Sam a lot, in the early days. He was the steady father her girls had otherwise never had. She used to talk to him about everything, and she was tempted, now, to climb the hill, ask him what she should do if Maud was indeed heading her way. But she couldn't face what that trailer would look like after all these years of neglect, that bed where she'd had some happy times with Sam, years ago, before she'd met Blair, and had Hannah. It all went so fast. *Life is what happens while you're busy making other plans,* John Lennon crooned in her ear. She sighed. Everyone had assumed she would live in Paris, wear black, paint huge canvases, become famous. But instead of fame she had children. Instead of Paris she had Southwest Ink, whose prestige and marketing savvy turned her paintings into lucrative greeting cards.

Sometimes Lizzie wondered if she and Maud had gotten mixed up in the womb, some Maud-ish sperm implanting the seed that was intended to be Lizzie, and vice versa. Maud should have been the homemaker, the teacher. Instead, she'd stayed in the kind of motion to which Lizzie aspired. Theater in Seattle, a mime troupe in New York, Shakespeare in San Francisco, Colorado, Oregon, even a tour of Europe, and, after she'd moved to L.A., guest-starring roles on television that sometimes took her to exotic locales. All that time, Lizzie slogged through the banal details of life in Marengo, the details Maud so admired when she visited, raising the kids Maud wanted, building the home Maud longed for, while Maud lived the life Lizzie was made to have.

But in the midst of success, in the depths of failure, Maud continually questioned the tentative, ephemeral, scary business of her art.

You have your paintings, Lizzie! They take up space in the world. No good
to tell Maud they were fucking greeting cards, tossed in the waste-
basket when all was said and done. *The paintings exist. People can hang
them on their walls. And you have your children.* After Maud moved to
L.A., it had gotten worse. She mourned to Lizzie about how unset-
tled life was with Miles, and the irony of driving the freeways and
avenues in and around Hollywood in search of jobs that would last
three days, a week, two months at most, jobs that would allow her to
go on living in a town she hated, in a career whose validity she questioned. *And your life, Lizard, your life is so settled, so sane, so lovely.*

Lizzie went back inside and checked on Theo, who was caught
up in his favorite video, all about earth-moving equipment. Before
she started in on the next batch of journals, she placed the phone
where she could easily reach it, when Maud called.

CHAPTER 7

MAUD

What country, friends, is this?
—TWELFTH NIGHT

The sun tottered on the edge of the horizon, a yellow lamp blazing through Maud's window. Huge rock formations loomed out of the desert, from one angle looking eerily like one thing—a troll, hunched and laughing, a ship in full rig sailing across sand—but as her car hurried her along, becoming something else altogether.

And then the lamp in her side window disappeared, extinguished. Pink, orange, red oozed out along the distant edge of the earth.

She glanced out the window again and again, watching the seep of colors shift and change, darken. She felt a prickle of excitement, a surge in her belly, as she imagined Miles discovering just how completely she was gone. The living room had looked decimated, bleak, when she walked out the door, but would he notice? She'd been driving for most of two days, but wasn't sure he'd even been home yet. All the afternoons and evenings the living room had been empty when she arrived home—it would be his turn to wander through the house, wondering where she was.

Or would he, as she rather thought, be relieved?

She swerved, slamming her foot onto the brake. A jackrabbit, a gopher—*what was it?*—shot out ahead of her car. A box stowed behind her slid forward, pressed against her head. A lamp slipped between the seats, making it impossible to downshift. Her open purse and basket, cassette tapes and cases, skidded off the seat beside her. "No," she said. "Please."

She pulled to the side of the road. Leaving the engine running, she walked back along the highway, squinting through the gathering dusk, looking for a curved, bloody shape. In the middle of the highway she spotted something dark. Hand held against her mouth, she walked towards it. It was hard to imagine anything worse than having to decide what to do with a small creature who would die, suffering terribly, whether or not she killed it all the way dead herself. She squatted to look. Not for the first time she wondered why, if this was one of her greatest fears, she had held on for so long to the wounded life she led with Miles. She stared at the shape on the roadway, her relief enormous; this carcass had been there a long time. Dried, desiccated, its original shape hardly discernible, it was an irregular patch of skin, a sheen of mashed bone, almost one with the pavement on which it lay.

The day's heat rose from the asphalt, pulsing against the backs of her thighs. In the distance a mound of mountains glowed a sullen purple. She felt minuscule, squatting on the roadway beneath a dome of sky. Like an inverted pottery bowl, it shaded from light gray above her to deep blue where the rim rested on the horizon.

Breathing in the smell of heated tar, exhaust, the scent of sage, she waited—for the distant growl of a car, for the sound of a human voice, for a bleat or faint cry that would let her know that she had not been let off the hook. But the night was still. She walked back to her car and restowed the things that had shifted, fished the cassettes and the contents of her purse off the floor. She had not known she was chilled, but in the warm interior of the car she began to shiver, and she scavenged for her sweater.

It took her a while, driving, to realize why it was so dark. Expelling a breath that was only partly a laugh, she turned on the headlights. Without their light she might not have seen the man at the side of the road. He did not raise an arm to flag her down, but stood as if he were expecting her. His hair was long over the shoulders of a fringed jacket. He wore a cowboy hat. She weighed the pros and cons of leaving a hitchhiker alone in the darkness against the potential dangers of picking him up. She passed him, slowing, debating, and then pulled over. *You are too full of the milk of human kindness,* Lady Macbeth mocked her.

She got out, peered back through the darkness. "I don't have a lot of room," she called. A breeze with a hint of chill wafted towards her. "But if you don't have far to go . . ."

Scuffing steps approached. She thought of bolting, wondered if he had sent the nonexistent jackrabbit to slow her down, if he was indeed the jackrabbit.

It was the man from the Trading Post, Driver. She watched him come, feeling like an actor in some demented but corny low-budget film. She kept her eyes low—on his jeaned legs scissoring towards her, on his booted feet placing themselves so carefully along the faded line at the edge of the highway.

CHAPTER 8

JAKE

you are the one who said to me
we sail our boats alone upon the sea

The only way into and out of the front seat of Jake's Volvo was through the passenger door. For a long time the driver's-side door merely screeched when it opened. But about a year ago, right after he'd arrived back in Nashville, right after he'd seen Minerva after thirteen years, right after she'd told him he still wasn't facing his ancient bullshit—actually she'd called it karma—it stopped opening at all.

What it is you're locking out, buddy? Minerva would have asked. *Or closing in?* Or, *Why's it so hard to get to the driver's seat, buddy?*

No answer. He took what would have been Lizzie's approach: "It broke. Fix it." Promised himself, again—tomorrow he'd call Lester at the Volvo place.

He clambered over the gearshift, holding the package for Johnny. Elmer had wrapped it in brown paper. He stood for a moment on the sidewalk outside Sue and Willy's house. Stood on a street full of houses that were all made out of ticky-tacky and that all looked about the same. Welcome-mat-sized lawns. Here an awning. There an open garage door. Toppled bicycle on the sidewalk, tricycle across the street. Red wagon chauffeured by a teddy bear. Smell of barbecue. BBQ. Distant laughter, then a call—"Joey, you git yer butt home double quick!"

Hoarse voice. Beer-slurred. Like his own dad's. Snoring away on the Naugahyde couch too early in the evening, TV babbling at the otherwise empty room.

Jake let himself in. Greeted by the bright gab of TV talk, canned laughter, smell of roasting meat. For a minute, surprised it was Willy, not his dad, who sprawled in the armchair reading a newspaper.

"So you're back," Willy said. Can of beer sweating on the table next to him.

"I am."

"Nashville not what you cracked it up to be."

"Nope."

"Told you."

"You did." What Willy had said, actually, during that dismal farewell supper, was that Jake's being an *artiste*—his word—was not an excuse he could use the rest of his life to keep from facing up to the normal goddamn things that normal goddamn people had to face up to. "Where's Sue?"

"Outside. She's tired. Janie called in sick. She had to work today." Willy slapped the tips of his fingers against the top of the newspaper, making it stand to attention. "Seen this crap on the new Supreme Court justice?"

"Is that the Jellybean watching TV? I'll just say hello." Jake waved his package.

"What you got there? Chopsticks?"

But Jake, following the noise of the television set into the den, didn't stop. In general he agreed with Willy's politics. But you didn't want to get into a conversation with him. For one thing, it wasn't a conversation. Whenever Willy indulged in one of his long, didactic discourses on how everything in the nation was going to hell, it depressed Jake so much that he drove around for days thinking about moving to Australia.

Johnny sat cross-legged in front of the wide-screen TV. Hands folded, spine rounded, staring upward, rapt.

"Ho! Jellybean! Venerating the Great God Tube, I see."

Johnny jerked, scrambled to his feet. "Uncle Jake!" Thin arms went around Jake's waist. "You've been gone so long."

Jake tousled Johnny's hair. He'd been back a month. He could have come over sooner. John Wayne's chaps flapped in a desert wind as he rolled with his seaman's gait along the main road of a frontier town. "Your mom told me you had a neat birthday party."

Johnny's eyes were eager. "So cool. We threw water balloons!"

"What's this one make you, nineteen?"

Johnny butted Jake's ribs with the side of his head. "Nine. And I'm going to be a Martian for Halloween."

"You already are a Martian!" Jake held his head against his side with his elbow. Johnny yelped in delighted protest. "Nine Martian years old. I owe you a present. Here. Picked out that special wrapping paper myself."

Johnny gleamed a little look up at him. "Nice choice, Uncle Jake." The little hands ripped the tape, unrolled the brown paper. "Drumsticks! Oh, Uncle Jake!"

Jake knelt for the hug. "That okay?"

"Okay? Mom! Look!" Johnny ran out of the room.

Jake followed, pausing to watch a bottle of laundry detergent dance across a washer and a dryer, and then bounce, slow motion, into a folded pile of clean diapers. *Signs are everywhere, buddy, if you want to see them,* Minerva had always said. He argued he didn't want to. *Maybe you didn't used to want to,* Minerva had told him in Nashville. Tabby purring beneath beringed fingers. Geraniums blooming on the windowsill. Crystals spinning above the kitchen sink, sparked by sun. Same crystals. Different sink. Different window. Same sun.

He found Sue and Johnny in the backyard. Sue stopped spraying the hedge and hugged him, smelling of soap, cleanliness, order. Johnny straddled a picnic bench, using it as a drum. Moved his shoulders to the sound of a huge internal rock band. "Good present, Uncle Jake," Sue said.

"One of the few times I've remembered. It better be good." Jake adjusted Johnny's fingers around the drumsticks. "Keep 'em loose. Let the drumhead do the work for you."

Johnny beavered away on the picnic bench. Sue smiled at him. "Willy tells me you decided to join the rest of mankind."

Jake nodded. "It's not so bad. I make my own hours. Pay's good. Nice place to work. Sometimes the projects are even fun. Not unlike music—multiple harmonies, anyway, sorting out all the available routes something can follow."

Johnny paused in his drumming, worried. "But you're still Jake's Blakes?"

"That won't change." Sue hugged Jake again. "I know you were hoping Nashville would work. I'm sorry it didn't. But I missed you. I'm just so glad you're home." Her voice shook.

"Home. Yeah. Well."

"Home. Yeah, well." She picked up two empty gallon buckets, pointed at shrubs with a trowel. "Did you know this? I didn't. Things grow faster if they're planted in the fall."

"That doesn't make sense. Things die in the winter."

"Perennials, anyway. I don't pretend to understand." Sue handed him the hose. "Finish up that last stretch for me. Johnny, will you let me have a few minutes with Uncle Jake?"

Johnny made a face but went inside. Sue sat on a step, untied her muddy Keds. "Phew! Life makes more sense when I know you're around."

Jake made the spray arc, shimmy, curve. Drops catching the last of sunlight. Falling rainbows, miniature prisms. "Willy says you were at the clinic. Makes this a long day."

Sue's high blonde ponytail flounced. "Up since five. A group of Operation Rescue types from Illinois are making things pretty tense. Janie freaked out. Anyone would, after two days of hymns and posters of chopped-up babies." She traipsed towards him through the water on the cement walkway, began to coil the hose. "I wish they'd give us credit for the work we do that's patently helpful. But don't get Willy started. I've had as much rhetoric, on either side, as I can stand. Can you stay for dinner?"

"I have rehearsal."

"Well, you can stay for one more minute. Let me just get my cigs." She looped the hose expertly over a tin arm that stuck out from the side of the house and disappeared through the sliding glass door into the kitchen.

Jake sat at the picnic table. Details like that—tin arm ready for a hose—just snuck up and floored him. That his sister and Willy had bought a house in the first place. Dealt with mortgages and renovations, poured cement walkways, bought a furnace. Gone about creating a child on purpose and, after Johnny was born, wallpapered a room. Moved him into it along with sheets covered with dinosaurs, pictures of the Wild West. Bought hoses and a tin arm to hold them. Planted flowers, thought about the growth rate of shrubs. Had friends over for dinner, went to church. Sue was three years younger. Why had he consistently kept from doing these things?

Come on comeon comeon. Minerva's face, surrounded by its crinkly triangular mass of black, rose up to grin at him. Arms lined with clinking bracelets angled upward in a yawn and stretch. *Buddy. You know.*

The first time he lived in Nashville, twenty-odd years ago, he and Minerva shared a tiny apartment. Ate out of cans, rarely remembered to sweep the kitchen. Never grew beyond that stage, although when Jake's songwriting career enjoyed its first spate of attention they'd gotten married one drunken afternoon in Las Vegas. Rented larger and larger apartments, eventually a house. But they'd never purchased real estate. *Real* estate. The rocking chair, the pewter platter, the kitchen table at which he sat struggling with the divorce papers. "Is this *real?*" he'd asked Minerva, sliding a palm over the table. She was standing in front of the cracked mirror in the kitchen, lining kohl beneath her already dark-as-coal eyes. She nodded. Their sad eyes met in the mirror. "But real isn't just what we touch. Or can sell." She tapped her forehead with the eye pencil, pointing to all the pictures there. "We can't say who gets to own these."

Sue stopped in the doorway. "Beer?"

He shook his head. "Thanks anyway."

She sat across from him, lit a cigarette. "Seen Lizzie since you've been back?" Shaking the match out, trying to be casual.

"Nope."

"How long's it been?"

He shook his head.

"Come on, tell me. A year?"

He looked at water drops clinging to leaves nearby. "Two. More than two. Jesus."

She exhaled a long plume of smoke. "Since before Theo was born."

Jake found a splinter of wood on the edge of the picnic table, pressed the tip of his finger against it hard enough to hurt.

"Why are you and Lizzie being such jerks? You've never answered me."

"It's complicated." He didn't see how he could confess to anyone. At the time it had seemed a small thing. But the more time that passed, the worse it got. Thinking about it made him feel like a skewered worm. He could move, buck, stretch, yearn. No way to detach this hook. No way to escape.

Sue put out the half-smoked cigarette on the bottom of her shoe, stared at the mangled butt, and promptly lit another one. "You want to know what I think?"

"You're going to tell me."

"I've stayed pretty quiet. You've got to hand me that."

"I hand you that."

"No matter what went down—she screwed someone else, or you did, *whatever*—go talk about it. Just go *start*."

He stood. "I should get going. Need to clean my living room. Our rehearsal space downtown got purchased by somebody planning another Ye Oldey Shoppey, so we're at my apartment upsetting the neighbors until we find something else."

"Okay, okay, sit down, I'll drop it."

He didn't sit. The distant noise of cars on the freeway designed to circle the historic town of Marengo sounded like wind through trees, waves on a beach. The smell of something sweet wafted towards him. "You know what's scary?" he said. "If I met someone tomorrow, how much work it would be. At eighteen, you only have to catch up on eighteen years. At forty-odd, it's impossible. How do you ever know? Know enough that you think you could spend a life together?"

"You never do." Sue ground out another cigarette. "How could you? That's what marriage is *about*." She scrubbed at her forehead with the heels of both hands. "These days, it's too easy to . . ." She stopped.

"I saw Minerva in Nashville. Ready for this? She's a therapist."

"*Minerva?*"

Jake nodded. "That's all her card says. *Minerva*. She went back to school. Her practice includes meditation and Wicca as well as co-dependent guidance. Don't laugh. She's wise, all right. And I don't just mean because she's got her license. It's in her eyes. She *knows* things."

"A therapist." Sue sat with her eyes closed, forehead scrunched. "Is she seeing somebody?"

"I didn't ask. Sitting there with her I realized I still love her. It startled me, after so many years. But we hardly even hugged. I sat in her kitchen. Sun pouring in these big windows." He smiled. "The table is this one we bought at a garage sale together. Round, oak, I'm sitting next to the burn mark from the Camel she left on the edge of the table too long. And this black circle where she put the hot spaghetti pot down. I mean, I remember those moments. So much of our life was spent at that table. Eating, drinking beers with friends, me writing songs, her casting everyone's tarot and I Ching. Our *life* was in that table, and it's still around. But without me. I'm not saying this well."

But Sue was listening.

"Walking out of her house—it's like a storybook, Sue, you'd love it. You go through an arbor, roses, vines, flowers everywhere, overgrown, rambling, bursting with life. She walked me to my car. It would have been easy to hug."

Sue scrubbed at her forehead again.

"Could we have made it, if we'd hung in there?" He shook his head. "We've both changed so much. She went back to school, got her degrees. It took me years to get out of Nashville, stop screwing around in every sense of the word. Came here, moped around, started a band that finally works—" He stopped short of mentioning Lizzie. "Maybe I'm no good at it. Minerva. Lizzie. Maybe we were just keeping each other from going where we needed to go."

"But *anyone* could say that!" Sue smacked a hand on the table. "You don't *keep* each other from doing anything. You make adjustments because you love someone so much you can't imagine doing anything else. No. Sometimes you don't love them. And you can *certainly* imagine doing something else. You choose not to. And you hope love comes back."

Jake lowered his head. *You hope love comes back.* "I have to go."

"Well, come to dinner one of these days." Responding to some tacit agreement not to move through the living room, where Willy sat, she followed him out to the street through the gate at the side of the house. "And if you see Lizzie, tell her we send love."

"I won't. But if I do, I will." He kissed her cheek, waited for her to finish waving, made sure she had shut the gate before he strolled around to the Volvo's passenger side and bumped his way over the gearshift.

You hope love comes back.

We took a wrong tack. It was my lack, I have this knack. Your withheld heart. Bring it back.

CHAPTER 9

LIZZIE

NOTES FROM BENEATH THE MAGNETS ON LIZZIE'S FRIDGE

Ginger did everything Fred did—
only backward, and in high heels.

Dusk. Maud still had not called. Lizzie stepped out on her porch and yelled for the girls. She would not tell them. Hannah would insist on staying up all night if there was the slightest chance her beloved Aunt Maud might be arriving.

The door to Sam's trailer opened. "He says thanks anyway but he's already eaten." Hannah's voice floated towards her.

She had left it too late. Sam knew the invitation was an afterthought. And while he might say he had already eaten, the meal would have been saltines. Perhaps a can of soup.

"Luuuuna," Summer shouted. "Goodbye, Luna. See you tomoooorrow." She ran holding her arms outstretched, making hooting noises and zigzagging back and forth down the hill and up the kitchen steps. Hannah followed more slowly.

"I'm an owl," Summer said, and hooted again.

"I thought that's what you might be. Do owls wash up?"

"Owls *hate* water."

"Well, wash up anyway. You too, Hannah."

Hannah headed for the sink. Summer clambered onto one of the stools beside the counter. "Sam says can he take a rain check."

With Theo perched on one hip, Lizzie stirred the beans with such force that some of them flew out of the pot. "Times like this I wish he had a phone. Dammit!"

Summer held a hand to her mouth in a parody of shock.

"Want me to run up and ask him again?" Hannah asked.

"He knows he's welcome. Summer, wash up, please."

Summer slid from the stool onto the counter and sat there grinning.

"Down, you monkey." Lizzie ignored the tongue Summer stuck out at her and ladled beans on top of Hannah's rice and to the side of Summer's. Summer, sitting cross-legged on the counter, stared down at her plate.

"Your homework done?" Lizzie asked. Hannah nodded, forking rice and beans into her mouth. "Summer?"

"Didn't have any."

"You did too. She did too, Ma. She did it. Sam helped."

"Shut up." Summer poked a bean with a tine of her fork. "I hate this stuff."

"Last week it was your 'favorite thing,' " Hannah said.

"Shut *up*. I could take this up to Sam. He's always hungry, Ma."

"That's a good idea. You eat yours. I'll take some up to him after I put Theo down."

"But *I* want to."

Lizzie kept Theo on one hip as she unbuttoned her shirt, unhooked her nursing bra, fretting about Maud. It was unlike her to stay out of touch.

Summer eyed her. "You keep saying you're not going to do that anymore."

"Do what?"

"For weeks and weeks and *weeks* you've been saying how you're not going to nurse him anymore."

"I have every intention of weaning him. It creates a lot of tension and tears I'm not ready to deal with yet."

"No, you just don't want to stop having him suck on you," Summer said, and then lowered her eyes in triumph.

Lizzie stared, wondering if the time had finally come to smack her. Something about this thought must have shown in her face. Summer picked up her fork. "I'll *eat* it, Ma."

"You do that." Lizzie smoothed Theo's hair. This petty warfare was all too similar to the battles she'd had with Sparky over the trucks and cars and exhaust pipes and driveshafts that wound up in her driveway, upon which Sparky insisted he was going to work his magic and never did. After a while it had been hard to remember why she'd fallen in love with him, why she'd wanted to make a baby with him.

Theo's eyelids began to droop. "I'm putting Theo down," she said, and left the kitchen. She rolled him into his crib, grateful, as she often was, for his good nature, which allowed him to sleep easily and under most circumstances. She stared down at him for a moment, trying to remember if that quality was or was not like his father's.

When she came downstairs, Summer's plate was clean. Lizzie shook a finger at her, too tired to check the garbage disposal. "You ain't foolin' me, girl."

"Ma!" Summer protested.

Hannah said, "Told you so," which caused them to begin the did-not-did-so ritual. The sound of jangling collar and tags interrupted this. "Luna," Summer yelled. "Sam!"

The dog wagged towards her, followed by Sam. Summer sank to her knees beside Luna. "Hello, you old thing," she said, her voice muzzled in Luna's fur. "Hello, you fat old dog."

Lizzie felt a knot loosen she hadn't known was in her chest. "Sam," she said.

"Hello, Lizard." Sam's hair was slicked back into a tight braid. Lizzie was reminded for the second time that day that Sam had been her lover. She had traced with a gentle finger the parentheses that framed his lips, wrinkles that tonight looked as if they'd been laid in by a painting trowel, nose to chin. And he was pale. Thin. She turned away.

"We were talking about bringing some dinner up to you." She adjusted the flame beneath the pot of beans.

"And here I am. But no dinner for me. I ate."

"I'll do it, Ma!" Hannah pushed in beside her at the stove as she spooned rice and beans onto a plate.

"No," Sam said, waving a hand, but he took the plate and sat at the counter. "I just thought Luna and I'd stop by to say good night the way we haven't done in a while."

"We're so glad!" Hannah said. "Ma! Aren't we glad?"

"We are. Just in time for bed." She averted the storm of protests by saying, "Brush your teeth and get in your nighties, and maybe Sam will come up and say good night."

Sam nodded. The girls made a beeline out of the room. Summer reappeared and squatted down next to Luna, who had settled in next to Sam's stool. "Good night, you stupid old dog," she said.

Sam put down his fork. "Well, now. She's not so stupid."

"About as stupid as me?"

"About as stupid as you. And we know how stupid that is."

Pleased, Summer ran from the room, arms stretched to either side, hooting. Sam pointed. "Owl."

Lizzie nodded. "Sara says hello. She's modeling for my Life Class again this semester."

"That's good."

"She says to tell you there's a powwow down in Chinle. This Saturday."

Sam hunched over his plate, mashing beans into the tines of his fork.

"She thinks maybe you'd like to go?"

He chewed, staring thoughtfully at his plate.

"I assume she'd drive."

Sam shook his head. "Don't know no one."

Lizzie waited.

"Well." Sam crossed his fork with his knife. "That was good. How's your painting?"

The phone rang, just as Summer and Hannah yelled, "We're ready!"

"I'll go," Sam said as Lizzie reached for the phone. Luna shook herself to her feet and followed him out of the room.

"I know you said you'd phone if you'd heard from her," Miles said without introduction. "But I just thought maybe she'd arrived and you were deep into girl talk and had forgotten to call me."

"No."

"How long's it take to get there from here?"

"A very long day, if you drive straight through. Eighteen hours. Twenty. She's stopped for the night, Miles."

"She stopped for the night last night. She's been on the road for two days already. She'd call, wouldn't she?"

Lizzie, who thought exactly that, stayed silent. She tucked the phone under her ear and walked across the living room to sit on the lowest step, beside Luna. The dog, unable to climb after Sam, whimpered at the bottom of the stairs. Lizzie pulled at the dog's ears, hearing at the other end of the line the scratch and then hiss of a lighter. "I'm sorry to bug you. I don't know who else to call. Your parents are out of the country again, and—"

"Whatever you do, don't get hold of them! They worry enough about her as it is. Mom would fly right back home, Tokyo or not. Yikes, what an awful thought."

"I keep noticing things that are gone. She wouldn't take things and then, like, do away with herself?"

"Jesus, Miles!"

"I keep thinking how she died on *Tucker's Larks*. All that black-and-white helicopter stuff, and her jerking when the bullets hit her. The blood in her mouth, so red."

He sounded as though he'd memorized these lines. "I've got to go, Miles," Lizzie said. "It's the girls' bedtime."

"What do I do, Lizzie? I keep imagining all these straws, falling down on Maud-as-camel, forgive me, she's a beautiful camel. Which straw was it—was it mine?—that made her feet go sprawling, that cracked her back, that sent her out of here? Will she be back?"

Lizzie shook her head at the new song she could hear in the making. "I'll call when I hear from her."

Sam sat on a chair beside Summer's bed. Hannah was curled under the covers of the twin bed opposite. Summer looked up at Lizzie. Her gaze leapt like blue neon across the space between them. "Sam found *snake eggs* up near the ditch! He's keeping them warm under a lamp. He showed me. And now he says when they hatch I can have one!"

"He said *if* they hatch." Hannah shook her head. "And you are not keeping it in our room."

"It's my room, too!"

Sam touched Summer's cheek. "I'm going, little one."

"Thanks for putting us to bed," Hannah said, gravely, as he hugged her.

Hannah often made Lizzie feel as if she were living in a television special, the kind of film Maud, having acted in them, referred to as *Scenes From Mostly Nonexistent American Family Life*. With Summer it was the exact opposite.

She followed Sam down the stairs. He placed each foot with deliberation. "Maud seems to be on her way here," she said to his back, surprising herself.

Sam paused, turned a stiff neck to look at her. "Coming here?"

"Miles called. Said she packed up a lot of stuff and took off."

After a long silence Sam nodded. "She weren't happy in that place. So that's good." He emphasized "that."

He negotiated the next stair. His hand was white where it clenched the banister. When had he lost all that weight? His shirt was faded, almost threadbare in places, and a stale smell lingered in the air behind him. At the bottom of the stairs Luna heaved herself to her feet and stood panting. The dog's eyes were rheumy. The white half-moons of cataracts slowly covering each eye were getting worse. Lizzie felt something tighten in her chest.

"You know what I hate most about teaching?" she said as they headed, a slow threesome, towards the front door. "That I have to say goodbye to all those students. Every semester. Just when you get to know them. I tell them not to bug me. 'Get out of here!' Why on earth does anyone need to say goodbye?"

Sam stopped to look at her, his smile etching deep parentheses into the skin around his mouth. "My Lizard."

"You and Maud. You're the only ones who call me that."

"Thanks for the dinner which I wasn't going to eat but ate anyway," Sam said. "You've got the cumin right at last."

"I have?" she said, surprised, gratified.

He nodded, scratching Luna's ears. "You have lived away from your clan as long as I have lived away from mine, Lizzie. Now there is someone coming to join you in a world that has been only yours."

She had known he would understand.

He put his arms out to either side. Was it meant to be a weak version of throwing his hands out in despair? Or was it welcome? Be open? He wanted a hug?

But if he hugged her she would cry. She saw him down the porch stairs. Luna wagged along behind him until the two of them merged into a black shape against the darker black of the hill. She looked up at the billion stars above her, wondering where under those stars Maud might be. High on the hill the light of the kerosene lantern glowed through the window of the trailer. As Sam opened his door, the light yawned open, the golden entrance of a fairy tale. Silhouetted against this light, he raised an arm to her. She moved hers in response. The rectangle of light narrowed to a thin line and then to black. She tried to imitate that odd opening of arms. Above her the window glowed, a small square of gold, holding the spirits of darkness at bay.

CHAPTER 10

MAUD

O time, thou must untangle this, not I;
It is too hard a knot for me to untie.
—*TWELFTH NIGHT*

Driver sat stiff-backed beside her, his profile dimly lit by the green lamps of the instrument panel. The passenger seat, pulled forward as far as it could go to accommodate the boxes in the back seat, forced his knees to butt up against the dashboard. His feet and calves were surrounded by the items Maud had been unable to stuff anywhere else in the car. Nevertheless, with his lifted chin, his straight back, he managed to look regal, distant, superior.

They had driven in silence for what seemed like hours, although perhaps it had only been miles. Maud cleared her throat, trying to think of another stick of conversation she could proffer. "Where are we headed?" had received a wave of a hand signifying somewhere forward and to the left of the road. "What happened to your car?" had been answered by "Friend has it." Her cheerful attempt to talk about coincidence—that she'd seen him at Maria's Trading Post, that there he was by the side of the road—got no response at all, although after a long pause he'd said, "You slow down enough, you can find synchronicity in everything." She'd been mulling this over for the last twenty minutes, wondering whether Driver thought this a good thing or a bad thing.

"I'm sorry there isn't more room." She'd dropped the French accent. He hadn't commented.

Driver made a noise that was either assent or disagreement. Silence closed once more around them. The headlights funneled into the darkness. Driver shifted, pointed. "There'll be a dirt road up ahead. On the left."

Maud put on the blinker, although there were no headlights behind her and she had not seen another car for well over an hour. "Where is it I'm taking you?"

"Maggie's place. Slow down. Turn here."

Maud braked, wondering yet again how smart it was to be driving down deserted country roads well after dark with a total stranger. But it would be unkind to drop him now. She wondered where, in a hundred-mile radius, there might be a motel, a telephone, a place to sleep.

The road was hugely rutted. The feather hanging from her rearview mirror bounced and swayed; the bead clacked against the windshield. Driver put out a hand to hold it. She slowed even further. Driver took his hand away but flicked a finger at the swinging ornament. "Look how you take our signs," he said. "But you see only the surfaces of these things."

"Pardon me?"

"You make this?" He crooked a long forefinger around the dangling leather and bead, the feather that had landed at her feet the taut, sad day after the night in the Taos hotel room. In a wince of memory, quickly shrugged away, she thought of Miles' desperate, whispered "I *can't*."

"You make this thing?" Driver asked again.

"Made. Found. I tied a knot or two in a piece of leather, is all."

The lights on the dash glowed, eerie and green. She was aware of the length of jeaned thigh beside her, of the fingers he tapped on his knee. "You go for a two-week retreat and learn how to make a spirit drum. Sit in a sweat lodge and chant words you don't understand and think you know something? You don't have a clue."

Maud looked to see if he was trying to be funny.

He stared ahead. His eyes were dark sockets. "You think by reading Frank Waters and Castaneda and *Black Elk Speaks* you can learn our ways? Lynn Andrews betrays our trust and our religion in her books which are very silly in any case, you hang dream catchers from your ceilings and feathers from your rearview mirror and think you know *anything?*"

Maud peered in several directions, hoping for a lighted house, a neon sign, anything that hinted at civilization.

"You come to the Southwest, a bunch of wanna-bes. You want to touch our gods. *Our* gods."

Maud cleared her throat to tell him this was not, in her case, true. But he would be sure to ask what, then, she was doing there. They jounced over a few more ruts. "Can you blame them?" Maud said carefully, not wanting to set another rant in motion. "Can you blame us, if we see something in your path that we find lacking in our own?"

Driver heaved in his seat to face her. "But our gods belong to *us.* They run in our blood."

Maud was glad the darkness hid the shock she was sure showed on her face. She tried a sound that could be taken as a chuckle, in case he was inclined that way.

"I'm serious. It's genetic. We can know our gods. You can't. You need to know your own. Go find them."

"Well," Maud began.

Driver leaned towards her, one hand braced on the dashboard. "What *you* bring is a twisted body of a man on a cross, his eyes rolled back in pain. All your lessons about what's bad, bad, bad on this earth. You drink your so-called savior's blood, you eat his body—"

"I don't," Maud said, and thought of the orange cud of Cheesio.

"Don't be literal. I'm talking, here. So of course you want the Navajo's walk in beauty. Or you want what the Hopi know beyond the perceivable world. You've tried to force your suffering on us. You want us to forget our laughter, to see the world through dark eyes. And you have almost succeeded."

"Some of us might agree with you," Maud offered. "Maybe this is why people turn to your ways."

He slapped the dashboard. "Then find your own way, find your own gods. You have so many—Greek, Roman, Norse. They run in your blood. What's your last name?"

Startled, Maud said, "Maxwell."

"That's easy. Scottish. You have a clan, you have a plaid, all your own. You have all those Celtic deities."

Dancing in the darkness outside the car Maud saw blue-faced naked warriors, jabbing spears in the air. The last play she'd done, two, or was it three, years ago, had been a modern story based on a Scottish legend. At the opening-night party they'd asked a guest to take a photograph of the cast and crew: all of them sitting on one couch, jammed in together, arms slung over shoulders, laughing, grinning, raising glasses to the camera. Family. Clan.

"Ask those ancestors to speak to you. Stop usurping ours."

He sat beside her in a steaming silence. After a few moments she cleared her throat. "How far do we have to go?"

"You want it now, you want it quick," he exploded, slapping the dashboard again. "Fast-food spirit. You haven't put in years and centuries and blood and sinew and *souls*. Instead you develop new gods. The one of science. The ones of doctors, and drugs. The one of psychoanalysis. Which is based on a Catholic premise, you know. You've done wrong, go talk about it, say you're sorry, you're absolved. Then go do it again."

This made Maud laugh.

"It's true!" He waved at the night around them. "How is it possible for you to imagine that you are at the center of the universe when our dust is the same? We are the same particles, given life, come around again." He reached to still the swinging feather. "We're about there."

It took Maud some time to translate an odd, oblong glow off to one side of the car into the shape of a trailer. She wondered about the source of the silvery light it emanated until she saw a bright coin of moon, low in the opposite sky.

Following Driver's instructions, she pulled past the Airstream and parked beside a mobile home. A number of additions and extensions had turned it into a ramshackle building. A dim yellow light shone through one window. She turned off the engine. Driver extricated himself from the items around his knees. Maud, opening her own door, was greeted by a silence so profound it resonated. Some glowing, distant light must exist beyond the dark material that was night, she thought. The stars were pinpricks in that canopy stretched high above her.

Driver mounted the step in front of the trailer. Before he could knock the door opened. "Hey there, Driver."

"Hey, Maggie."

"Who's your friend?"

Maud introduced herself to a woman who was a short and rotund shadow. "Nice of you to give him a lift," Maggie said as she waved them in. The aromas of spice and meat assailed Maud. "For someone named Driver he sure do need a lot of rides."

Driver made a strangled sound and headed for the stove, where he lifted and banged the lids of several pots.

"Beans," Maggie told Driver's offended back. "And take your hat off." She wore a long skirt and a plaid flannel shirt. Her black and gray hair was pulled back tight into a silver barrette. In the light of the lantern on the table Maud saw that she was probably not Driver's girlfriend, but perhaps his mother. "I just ate. They should still be hot."

Driver pulled bowls off a shelf, yanked a troublesome drawer open for spoons. He held a bowl in Maud's direction. "Want some?"

"Do you have a phone?"

Maggie shook her head. "Nearest one's back down the road you just came up on, then another thirty-forty miles either direction."

"Would I find a motel there as well?"

Both of them seemed to find this amusing. Driver pushed aside papers and cups and ashtrays and matchbooks and a carton of cigarettes, and slung a loaf of white, sliced bread in a cellophane bag onto the table. He ladled beans into a bowl. "You want some?" he said again.

"I've got to figure out where I'm staying, what I'm *doing*."

"There's a bed out back." Maggie gestured with her chin. "You're welcome to it. Get on the road again in the morning."

"That's so nice of you, but—" Maud wondered if Miles was worried yet. "I don't *know*." She rubbed at her forehead with both hands. "I don't know."

"Eat something." Driver banged two steaming bowls onto the table, sat in front of one of them. "You look like you're about to fall over."

Maggie nodded. "Eat a little, sleep a little, things always look better. Hat off, Driver."

Driver put his hat on a chair, pulled his hair through a rubber band he pulled from his jeans pocket. Maud didn't know what was in those beans, how much lard or butter had been used to cook them. But she moved towards the table. Driver pushed the bread in her direction. The lantern light made the angles of his face sharp, emphasized shadows beneath his eyes, made the scars on his cheek disappear. He was handsome. He looked tragic. Maggie sat in a chair next to him. "And where've you been, Mr. Doctor of Philosophy? You abandon your little project out there?"

An aggrieved look took hold of Driver's face. "Sick of it."

Maggie shook a cigarette out of the pack lodged in the pocket of her shirt. "I thought you were supposed to be reporting to a high-up mucky-muck at that school of yours."

Driver shrugged. "Changed his office hours. Hell if I was going to hang out an extra day, waiting. And Sara needed the car."

In this context he seemed substantially less forbidding. Maud found she was disappointed. In the casting of the romance film she'd done as they drove, he was supposed to be difficult and harsh, and she, with sensitivity and love, would change all that.

The soup, a kind of chili, was delicious, with a hint of flavor Maud couldn't place. "What is this?" she asked.

"Beans," Driver said, resorting to the kind of *duh* face that had gotten Maud in trouble, as a child, for making.

Maggie poked his shoulder with a bony forefinger. "Don't be rude. Anasazi beans."

"And what's that spice?"

"Cumin, probably. There's others too. Coriander."

"You heard of them? Anasazi?" Driver paused with the spoon halfway between bowl and mouth. His nose had a little bump in it. "Of course you have. I bet you've been to Mesa Verde, seen the Spruce Tree House and Cliff Palace, heard the know-it-all round-eye rangers tell you all about how it was fear of invasion that drove them into those cliff dwellings?"

"Driver," Maggie said, blowing smoke.

"Well," Maud began, ready to talk about drought, which was the explanation she'd most often heard.

"Bought yourself a pair of Kokopelli earrings, then ran on down to Canyon de Chelly to gawk at Spider Rock for ten minutes, then slid on down the Navajo sandstone to look at the cliff dwelling there, White House. Then buzzed on over to Hovenweep, climbed a wooden ladder into a kiva and imagined you were touching the ancient ways?"

"I did go to all of those places."

"And then you string a bead and a feather onto a shoelace"—he bracketed the last word with an aural leer—"and go back to 'L.A.' and let everybody know how hip you are. And of course you visited Chaco Canyon."

"Yes."

"That's out of the way," Maggie said. "And maybe we don't need to hear your whatever-you-call-it, discutation, right here and now, Driver."

"Dissertation." Driver lowered his spoon again. "And maybe you heard from Erich von Daniken how the Anasazi were helped by creatures from outer space or how else could they have built straight roads and high houses, not to mention a solar marker that measures the solstice, the equinox, and the nineteen-year cycle of the moon? Native Americans couldn't possibly have dreamed up the Sundagger by themselves—no, they had to have help. Ever wonder why so few of the rangers are Pueblo? Zuni? Acoma? Afraid to find out that all those 'wise' archeological theories are so much bunk, that's why."

"Oh, go sit in your excavation." Maggie stood up.

Driver gulped soup, one eye on Maud, who, aware of his gaze, watched Maggie walk towards some shelves at the far side of the kitchen. She returned with a huge milky-white plastic jar, the kind in which one would buy mayonnaise or pickle relish in bulk. She reached into the jar and put a fistful of its contents into Maud's hand. "Anasazi beans."

Maud turned them over in the palm of her hand. They were mottled purple and white, quite beautiful. "All that color cooks out," Maggie said. "Then they just look like regular beans, pintos, maybe."

"Anasazi. Enemies of Our Ancestors. Is that right?"

"Enemies of Our Ancestors." Driver repeated this, mocking, and sat back with his arms folded.

"One way of looking at it," Maggie said. "And don't mind Driver. He don't know how else to get his point across yet. Others might say that 'Anasazi' means The Ancient Ones. Depends on your perspective."

Driver disappeared after eating a third bowl of chili. Maud assumed he'd bedded down somewhere in the trailer. Exhausted, as much from sidestepping Maggie's kind questions as from the long day of driving, Maud accepted her offer. She fetched her toothbrush and a T-shirt out of the car. Maggie escorted her to the Airstream, leaving her with a kerosene lantern and some matches, an extra blanket, and a roll of toilet paper. "Pee outside," Maggie said. "If it's otherwise, use the toilet in my place."

The lack of a phone postponed for a number of hours the need Maud was beginning to feel that she should let someone know where she was. She was glad her parents were out of the country. She tossed from one side of the narrow mattress to the other, mashing the single pillow into a multitude of shapes, wondering if Miles was worried yet, if he missed her. The T-shirt of his she'd brought with her was clean; there was no lingering scent of him.

The moon emerged in a corner of the trailer's high, rectangular window, bright as a flashlight beam. She sat up and scrubbed at her forehead, holding her face in her hands. Miles had accompanied her only once to the Southwest, on one of the visits to Lizzie he called her "pilgrimages." Maud wanted to show him Santa Fe, Taos, Chaco Canyon, but they'd flown into Marengo and had no car. Jake Arboles, Lizzie's boyfriend at the time, offered to loan them his Volvo. Miles had been reluctant. He seemed to be enjoying the sniping conversations he was having with Jake about the similarities of and differences between the music scenes in Nashville and Los Angeles. The tension between them made Maud gushy and overenthusiastic. Lizzie had just disappeared into her studio. When Jake made his offer, Maud seized it, grateful.

As they drove towards Taos, she brought up the idea of moving to the Southwest, laughing so Miles would not think she was serious.

But he knew she was serious. "How am I supposed to get a record deal in Santa Fe?" he said, adjusting the rearview mirror. "Or in Albuquerque? Or Fairfield?" He waved at a sign that told them Fairfield was sixty-five miles away. "Or Marengo, for that matter?"

Maud allowed minutes of barren landscape to pass by before saying, "Jake's a musician, a songwriter. He got a record deal."

"I *knew* you would bring that up." Miles slapped the gearshift. "That deal fell through."

"He's put a band together. He makes money doing that. He sells his songs."

"He *used to* sell his songs. You heard him—that hasn't happened in a while. You can't live forever on residuals. And anyway, *if* he sells any songs, it's because he did his time. He *established* himself. Like I'm trying to do. Jesus, Maudie. Whatever this picture is you have of life here, it doesn't seem to include me. What in hell do you expect me to do for a living, bag groceries?"

"There's always something."

"Something is not a career."

They'd eaten green chili at the Taos Inn, a delicious soup so hot it made their eyes run. They'd drunk margaritas and gone back to their hotel room and undressed.

"Is it safe?" he whispered as they stood beside the bed.

Safe. It was as if pregnancy were a disease. Or her womb was itself diseased. Or she was, riddled, oozing pus with her longing. He began to rock against her, his cock lifting and hardening. "No, I'm not *safe*, Miles," she whispered, in a hot torrent of words, "but can't we please make a baby?"

Miles stepped back and sat on the edge of the bed. She followed, needing connection, stumbling on a small throw rug by the bed. She let herself sink to the floor. "Can we just this once see if it *happens*?" She was almost crying. "Just go for it? If it doesn't, we'll take it as a sign from the gods or whatever and I'll make sure I'm safe every time again. Please." Her words were muffled, face pressed against the knobbly hotel bedspread. Her hands, clasped together, stretched out across the distance that separated them.

The bed creaked as Miles lay back. He lit a cigarette and placed a hand on one of her outstretched arms, as if he too felt a need for connection. She heard the sharp *ssss* of burning cigarette paper as he inhaled, and the long exhalation of smoke seconds after. Finally he said, "Really, Maud?" The question caught in his throat.

Rain began to rustle the leaves outside the window. The damp exhalation of the earth, the smell of the ground as it readied itself for growing things, made her womb ache. Sometimes she thought of it, her womb, as a beautifully furnished room, waiting once a month for its occupant to arrive. It was done all in earth colors, with a preponderance of dark reds, draped in soft silks and satins, velvet. Her period, each time it came, was accompanied by such severe cramps that she imagined miniature hands clawing at her innards as these furnishings bled out, a voice bleating, *Don't let me go, don't let me go.*

She stayed kneeling, her arms stretched across the bedspread, the position one of such supplication she felt both ashamed of and awed at herself. The rain hissed down and splattered against the flagstones outside their window. She imagined living in this land of surprising landscape and huge sky. She would be close to Lizzie and Hannah and Summer. She would have a house with a terra-cotta floor and Navajo rugs, where she would walk barefoot and pregnant, or nursing an infant. Light would fall through tall windows. She would grow sunflowers and basil and tomatoes and peppers. She would have a pair of big chairs next to a fireplace with ottomans and good reading lamps. She would hold candlelit dinners for friends. Her vote would count in a runoff for mayor, and in favor of library funding. She would live in a place long enough to observe the coming and going of seasons, and she would mark, each year, the highest and lowest points of the rolling sun on her wall. She would finally know the continuity provided by living in awareness of things, such as the growth of perennials, and the hardy nature of geraniums.

She was startled, thrilled, when Miles lifted her up beside him. But at the last moment he pulled out. "I can't, Maud," he moaned as he jerked against her. "I just *can't.*"

He sounded so terrified, so sad, so young, that she found herself stroking his shoulders, patting the small of his back, trying to give him comfort. She lay for hours, sleepless. *Can't what?* she wanted to ask. But she had been unable to form the words.

Maud lifted her face. The moon had moved out of the frame of the trailer's window. She stared at the rectangle of starry sky. For almost two years she and Miles had made love, if that's what it could be called, with the Taos memory lurking in the back of her mind. The smell of rain, the tin ceiling of the hotel room, the question of what it was he *couldn't*. She had never—and why hadn't she?—alluded to it. From this distance her passivity seemed extraordinary.

She stood, panic gnawing at her chest, then sat again on the edge of the bed. She wrapped the blanket around her, wishing she could make some chamomile tea, something that would help her towards the sleep that she knew would now elude her.

Lizzie had always just done it, gotten pregnant when she felt like it. Why had Maud always felt she needed to ask permission, that it was something the two people involved should decide together? It had gotten her nowhere. It had gotten her nothing. She hated that she would feel the power, the ugliness, of the word *barren*.

She pulled on her jean skirt and sandals, wrapping the blanket around her. As she opened the trailer door she let out a tiny whoop of fright: Driver stood below her. Moonlight gleamed, a ghostly white, on his face and bare torso.

Maud drew the blanket up over her shoulders. "I was going to my car. To get something to read."

"I've been doing what Maggie told me to do," Driver said. "Sitting in my excavation. Want to see it?"

CHAPTER 11

JAKE

on the lam from love
fleeing down that long and lonesome road

Jake propped open the door to his apartment, lower story of a two-story duplex. Light spilled into the darkness. He carried Pasqual's congas down the walkway to Santiago's van. Roy followed with one of the keyboards, went back inside to get his sax. Randy wandered out. Without her boots. "You should fix your outdoor light," she told him. "What if one of us fell with a load of expensive equipment?"

"It just needs a new bulb." Jake went to get the guitar stands.

When he came back out she'd placed herself beneath a street lamp. Light spilled over her waterfall of blonde, turning it pale silver. She watched them load Pasqual's percussion paraphernalia into the van's carpeted interior.

"Pretty damn good." Santiago grunted as he moved the other keyboard into place.

Pasqual nodded. Roy nodded. Jake nodded. Randy flipped her horse-tail length of hair over one shoulder. "Hardly room for Santiago's keyboards with all Pasqual's shit."

Beside her, Roy hugged his sax case, rocking back and forth. "Hmmm, hmmm," he murmured. "Hmmm, hmmm." Managed to imply agreement as well as a sense of impending doom. Sang, "Looks like we're in for nasty weather."

Jake eyed Randy's stockinged feet. She'd been giving out signals all through rehearsal. No way to avoid the tête-à-tête she clearly wanted.

"You still haven't forgiven Jake for not hiring that friend of yours." Santiago placed the last of Pasqual's Guatemalan bags, jingling, clacking, in the back of his van. Moved across the sidewalk, put an arm around Randy's shoulders. "Just because you're the best goddamn female bass player on the planet doesn't mean we have to believe he's God's gift to the world of percussion. Let it go, senorita."

Randy shrugged herself out of Santiago's embrace. But as she pulled her hair back, holding it in a fist high above her head, she looked mollified. Jake sent a look of intense thanks in Santiago's direction. Santiago chuckled.

"What're you laughing at?" Randy demanded. Looked at Jake. "What are you two laughing at?"

"I gotta go," Roy said. "I'm gonna split. I'll see you later, sometime, tomorrow, have a nice life." Loaded his sax case into his red Buick and drove off.

Santiago was still laughing. His big belly shook. "We're touchy today. You on your period, or what?"

Jake had been wondering the same thing. He'd known Randy longer, but wouldn't have asked.

"Slimebag. That's a sexist assumption," Randy said.

Pasqual laughed. "If feminism has you on their side, they don't need masochists."

"Misogynists, stupid," Randy muttered.

"Or masochists either. C'mon, pobrecita," Santiago coaxed. His grin was big and white. "Give us a smile."

"Anyway, Ran," Jake said, "a month ago you were sleeping with him. Now you're not. Wouldn't that have gotten a bit complicated?"

Randy flipped her hair again. "Who knows what might have happened if he'd landed this gig?"

"If he loved you for your connections, you don't want him," Santiago said.

Randy ignored this. "And percussion's one thing. We need a *drummer*."

Amidst the laughter, Santiago shook his head at her. "Sometimes you are one transparent tomatillo. Now come on, before Joanie's closes or, Dios forbid, runs out of green chile enchiladas. You'll feel better after you eat."

Randy eyed him. "You haven't known me long enough that I'm going to let you talk to me that way."

"This is *respect*, woman. I'm trying to indicate my concern for your welfare."

"You coming?" she asked Jake.

Jake shook his head. "One of these nights I've got to unpack. I've been back three weeks and look at it in there."

"You've been back for over a month. What's another day?" Randy's lower lip moved out. "Come on to Joanie's. Please."

"I'm bushed, Randy. I've worked all day."

"He's gotta finish that song," Santiago said. "And you don't want him to come to Joanie's. Tina tells me she's got the hots for him."

"Oh, *man!*" Randy put her hands on her hips, glared at Jake.

Jake began to sputter. Santiago howled with laughter.

"You left your boots inside," Jake said. "Want me to get them?"

Randy lowered her head, strode up the cement walk.

"Uh-oh, poor Jake, Randy's pissed." Pasqual laughed. Lean as a weasel, when he shoved his hands in his pockets he looked like he might take his pants right down to his knees. "But then Randy's always pissed at you."

"Unrequited love." Santiago ducked into the driver's seat.

"No," Jake said, but it was too complicated to explain. "See you tomorrow. Setup's at eight." Waved them off.

Randy greeted him at the front door of his apartment. One boot on, the other in her hand. "What?" he said.

"You told me you were over her." Randy pointed. The offending snapshot was propped up against some paperbacks.

"What's it *matter*, Ran?" Jake almost groaned.

Randy flopped on the couch. Put a long, slim leg high in the air to pull on the second boot. Looked triumphantly at Jake. He nodded. She did have a fabulous body. Curious that their brief affair had been largely unsexual. There had been few frantic couplings. He was still touched when he remembered how her small back had moved against his chest, how she'd pulled his arms around her. The perfection of her long legs had only served, most of the time, to make him miss the slightly bowlegged quality of Lizzie's. "Look, Ran, you have the best legs in the world, you're a fabulous bass player—you got that from Santiago himself. What else do you want to hear?"

Pouting, Randy pulled her hair over one shoulder. Fingers moved quickly, braiding a blonde rope. "I just want someone to love me, Jake-ie."

He sat, looped an arm over her shoulders. "I do love you. Just not the way you want. But you don't love me that way either."

"That's true, I don't."

He searched for the little lines at the corners of her eyes that would tell him she was cheering up. "You are something else, you know," he said. "Flashing that bass of yours around up there next to me, those legs of yours driving the guys wild. Swinging your blonde mane—"

Randy drummed the heels of her boots into the floor. "Okay, okay. Stop with the syrup, already."

"And what would I do without you to hustle me away from the backstage chicks—"

She hissed. "Women."

"When'd all this start, Ran? I go out of town for a few months and you get your consciousness raised?"

"I've just been talking to a few people, is all."

"Look. I'm just not in the mood to be with anyone. If it ain't you—"

"No," she said, twisting up her mouth, "if it ain't *Lizzie*. Lizzie, Lizzie, Lizzie."

But she felt better, Jake could tell. She zipped up her waist-length, fake-fur-trimmed jacket. Sauntered back down the pavement towards her car. He stood in the doorway and watched her go. Now that they weren't sleeping together, neither one of them seemed to mind if people thought they might be. He took time to admire the high, round attraction of her rear end, smiled. Already she was looking around to see who else might be noticing it.

He went back inside. Maybe he'd finally unpack the boxes in the bedroom, use the shelves he'd bought two weeks ago and had yet to assemble. On his way through the living room he picked up the photo of Lizzie from the bookshelf. While they were together he'd meant to get it framed. After they split, it hadn't seemed appropriate. The snapshot, curled at the edges, was a close-up of her grinning face. Uneven bottom teeth, tousled cap of red hair. Darling.

He'd had it angled up against some books before he moved to Nashville. Unpacked it into a similar place in the depressing apartment he'd rented there. Here it was again, propped up against probably the same two Tom Clancy paperbacks. He left it where it was. Headed for the kitchen to get a beer.

Looking through drawers for a screwdriver, he did his imitation of Don Henley getting down to the heart of the matter. *"But I think it's about . . ."* He sang as he peered into the drawer closest to the wall, and closed his eyes to finish the line. *"Forgiveness."* A tilt of emotion made him pause. Matchbooks. Warranty card for the coffee-maker. Batteries—AA and AAA. Flashlight. Keys. Plastic vegetable bags. Rubber bands. Corks. The motley assortment, so quickly assembled, made him feel that he was, what? Home? Not quite. But something. *"Even if, even if,"* he wailed, *"you don't love me anymore."*

CHAPTER 12

MAUD

KATE: *Let him that moved you hither*
Remove you hence. I knew you at the first,
You were a movable.
PETRUCHIO: *Why, what's a movable?*
KATE: *A joint-stool.*
PETRUCHIO: *Thou hast hit it: come sit on me.*
KATE: *Asses are made to bear and so are you.*
PETRUCHIO: *Women are made to bear and so are you.*
—THE TAMING OF THE SHREW

Driver led the way past Maggie's trailer, then past the octagonal shape of a hogan. He wore no shoes. The moon gleamed on his bare back and silvered the scrub and sagebrush around them. Several times Maud had to break into a jog to keep up with him. With the blanket dragging behind her, she felt absurd, a caricature of a squaw, wearing a costume created out of a limited dress-up box.

Suddenly Driver dropped from view. A fissure—a canyon—opened where there had seemed to be solid earth. On the other side of the canyon the silvery scrub continued, but beneath her the moon lighted a path that zigzagged down the wall in a series of hairpin turns. Driver did not slacken his pace, and Maud slipped and slid in her sandals over the slick rock.

Driver waited at the bottom. The temperature had dropped as she descended, and Maud pulled the blanket high on her shoulders. Above them, a cliff bulged, rising like an enormous, unwrinkled forehead. She wanted to speak to the age and the size of these canyons, the power of water and wind and sand. But it had all been said, and would sound trite.

"Okay?" he asked. She nodded, and he set off again along the sandy bottom of the canyon. After a short distance he veered right and began to climb.

"We're going back up?" Maud knew she sounded plaintive.

Driver pointed at the soaring rock. "There's steps carved into that if you prefer. We took the easy way down."

She trudged after him, wrapping the blanket around her neck like a huge muffler so she could use her hands to clamber over fallen boulders and maneuver the steep places. From somewhere above her Driver said, "Here, toss that up to me." Arms outstretched, he stood on a shelf that jutted out from beneath the brow of rock. Maud tossed, and scrambled on all fours to join him.

The light of the moon, working its way down the canyon, hinted at ruins tucked into the angle where shelf and overhang met. Some walls still stood, easily ten or even fifteen feet high, with the small doorways Maud recognized from her tours of Mesa Verde. Elsewhere, walls had fallen, but the rubble she would have expected had been swept away.

Driver grinned at her astonishment. "Come on." He led the way along the cliff shelf, up a few stone steps, and stopped beside a ladder protruding from the edge of a large pit. He handed her the blanket and clambered down the ladder. He looked up, his face and torso smudges of white in the dark, a circle above a broad V. "Toss."

But Maud hugged the blanket to her, shy; entering the kiva was like entering a church.

"Come on."

She had to clear her throat. "May I?"

"Nice of you to ask."

She negotiated the smooth tree limbs of the ladder. She recognized the few elements of kivas she'd come to know: the fire pit, right behind it the slab of stone that acted as an air break, above that the ventilator shaft. Niches had been built into the wall at intervals. A low stone bench ran the circumference of the circle. The floor was swept clean.

She nodded with appreciation. When Driver smiled, he looked young and the taut anger that characterized his face disappeared. She knelt beside the small hole called the sipapu. "Why is this called the Place of Emergence?"

He told her what she'd already heard—that it was the place where The People had emerged from the previous world into this one.

"But is it a metaphor? Like our Garden of Eden? Or like our Flood?"

"Omi*god*." He dropped his jaw in a parody of shock. "Is the Flood supposed to be a *metaphor*?"

"Ha ha. Did some version of Emergence really happen? Or is it just coming across the Bering Strait or something?"

The whites of his eyes gleamed. "How much we both want another world," he said. He pulled twigs and bark from a pocket of his jeans and knelt beside the fire pit, laying these in a careful circle. "The Bible, Gilgamesh, the Navajo, the Hopi and Acoma—lots of creation myths have a flood in them. Something happened. Something dire." He layered larger twigs and branches stored in the kiva onto the pile, then lit it with a match. He blew in strategic places, a dark, lithe shadow moving in the dim, growing red light. His legs were stocky, his back long and lean, an unexpected combination. Muscles moved beautifully beneath his skin. She felt her belly soften and warm.

The fire crackled. Maud pulled the blanket more closely around her. "If a person studied hard enough," she said, "and knew the proper ways, and had the right blood running in her veins—" He looked at her sharply, but she did not smile. "If you had all that, could you go back through the sipapu if you wanted to?" she asked. "Could you vanish?"

"You mean like you are trying to do?"

She laughed. "Is that what I'm trying to do?"

They watched the flames flicker and then catch. The spurt of energy that invested their first few minutes in the kiva disappeared, but they both knew they had not come there to talk. She helped him spread the blanket so they could lie together upon it. "Is this all right?" she whispered.

He raised his head to look at her.

"To sleep with you in this place?"

He put his lips to the skin of her throat.

Maud found herself with her mental eyebrows raised at herself, watching behavior she didn't recognize as her own. She watched her mind skip away, merry and coy, from how quickly this had happened, from thoughts of disease, the betrayal of Miles—in their eight years together she'd slept with no one else.

Driver was firm, not at all gentle, but she found she did not mind. This act seemed to be a gift, a necessary gift. Bestowed by whom? He moved into her with a huge, shuddering sigh and took the rest of his pleasure with little attention to hers. She did not come before he did; usually this meant she would not come at all, but she found herself burrowing towards climax with a selfish attention foreign to her. Her period was due in a few days; if she could be fertile, it was unlikely to be now. Nevertheless, she thrilled and panicked at the idea that she might, with her impulsiveness and her vigor, be pulling a child into her.

It seemed to her that Driver wept. "Driver?" she said, but he would not raise his face. She stroked a hand over the incredibly smooth skin of his back. He sniffed. "Why is your car so packed up? Why are you leaving L.A.? Why did you speak with an accent and now you don't?"

She shifted so she could see his eyes, but found no mockery there. There were so many things she could say, so many reasons for all those things. She didn't want to talk about Miles. And even if she could explain the necessary inanity of commercial auditions, that was only part of it.

She touched a finger to the constellation on his cheek. He tensed, but let her trace its curve. "Someone told me that I needed to get out of my head."

"Get out of your head," he repeated, and sighed. "Me too. Who told you to do that?"

"Nikos."

"Ah."

"No. Not like that. He's a teacher. My acting teacher."

"Teacher," Driver murmured. "Say that three times, it's an odd word. Tell me the story of how you were told to get out of your head."

She told about Nikos first. How exciting it had been to be accepted into his master class.

"What does that mean, 'master class'?"

"Supposedly it means that the people in it are good. They're 'masters.' They work a lot. Not me, though."

"Why not?"

"I don't know. That's all part of it. I don't know."

"It doesn't matter. Go on."

"The class is held in a theater on Saturday mornings. There's a stage and rudimentary lights." All this detail was too much. But how could she convey what it had been? She tried to match her breathing to his. Perhaps they would fall asleep. The warmth of the fire was pleasant against the bare skin of her legs. Beyond that she didn't want to think.

He pulled the edges of the blanket up and over them. "Go on. I like stories."

She described the scene she'd chosen, told him about her scene partner, Damien. "I didn't know he was gay when I asked him to work with me. I just thought he was right for Beau."

"Beau?" He laughed. "What a name. As bad as Driver."

They'd worked hard on the scene. The night before their scene was up, she'd gone to bed early, had risen early and worked out, wanting to be thin, taut, streamlined. But halfway through the scene she lost track of where they were, forgot her lines. "It was terrible," she told Driver, "but I kept going."

She hooked a heel over the rung of a stool, leaned against the makeshift bar, pushed her shoulders back, offering cleavage and a glimpse of lace beneath her dressing gown's plunging neckline. Damien—Beau—held the Jim Beam bottle by its neck. "Of course I'm going to be hitting bars," he said. "Picking up other women." His hand shook as he filled his shot glass. Maud held hers out, but he ignored it. "I mean, look at you. You're a joke. You keep telling me you're leaving, but all you do is sit around all day in your fancy underwear."

Maud tipped her glass and then her chin up, and in testament to

Emma Bovary, flicked her tongue to gather the last drops coating the bottom of her glass. Her lips decorated the rim with a semicircle of Flamingo Red. Her fingernails were painted a purply red, the color of new blood. She crossed her legs and let the robe fall open, revealing, just as she'd planned, a stretch of shiny thigh.

"I couldn't remember what came next," she told Driver. "All I knew was when he shouted I was supposed to turn over the coffee table. I don't know what lines I dropped before that."

Damien yelled. A puff of white feathers waved at her from the tops of her heeled slippers. She stood, and wobbling on three-inch spike heels, watched red fingernails on what appeared to be someone else's hands disappear under the edge of the coffee table. She lifted, shoved. Magazines slapped to the floor. The thump of the table followed.

Damien grabbed her arm and pulled her to him. Minuscule drops of sweat beaded the muscled planes of his bare torso, the wings of his nose, his upper lip. Maud wondered if the bronze of his skin was the product of a tanning booth and then shook her head, concentrating on the heat of the Delta outside, the buzz of mosquitoes, the smell of gardenias, something that would anchor her before she floated away.

"You ain't goin' nowhere." He held her by her upper arms too tightly, but she could use that. "Beau. Honey-darlin', you're hurting me!" She writhed a little, trying to escape.

He turned her into the curve of his arm. They stared out. On the fourth wall, against the yawning dark of the auditorium, they had placed a window. During rehearsal they'd agreed the panes were dirty and the curtains yellow. Maud locked her eyes on the space where the valance would be, glad that the bright lights glaring down at them from the back and sides of the theater kept the faces of her classmates invisible. Nothing, however, could keep her awareness from floating towards Nikos, sitting in the front row. The light spilling from the stage caught his white Reeboks. He bent to scribble something in his notebook.

"You make me laugh," Damien's lips moved against her ear. "You'll never leave. A woman never leaves when she's gettin' it good." He slid his hand into the top of her dressing gown.

It was time for the moan. She'd worked on it endlessly. "Ooooh," she'd tried. "Aaaah." Over and over, alone in her car on the freeway, when she was in the shower and the noise of running water would drown her out, when Miles was working on a song in his study with earphones on. "Oooaaah." In spite of her efforts, Miles had several times asked, "What? Maud, did you say something?"

She closed her eyes and dropped her head back on Damien's shoulder. "Oooooh," she breathed, trying to convince the audience, convince herself, when all she felt was the pull of Damien's damp hand across her skin. "Ooh, honey." His fingers touched, backed away from, the edge of her bra. "Beau, don't."

He pulled her closer. "You'll never find what I got, babe. Not what I give you, huh? Not anywhere else." Hand along her jaw, he pulled her face towards him. Her neck twisted, awkward with the effort to get her mouth into a position where he could reach it with his. His lips gleamed, then pressed against hers. His eyes stayed open for a moment too long, staring into hers, glazed with fear.

"Go on, go on," he muttered. He pulled her around to face him, so her back was to the class, and supported her as her hands slid down his chest. She knelt in front of him. She moaned again, feeling inutterably foolish.

"Go *on*," he said.

Maud pulled at the leather belt, its sudden erect flap slipping out of the buckle. The false fingernails she'd applied for the scene made it awkward to draw down the zipper of his fly. Silence hung over the stage, over the auditorium. She knelt there, staring at the triangle of his red silk underwear until he took a breath and said, "End of scene."

"Jesus," Driver said. "Sexy stuff. Is that the sort of thing people usually do in an acting class?"

"Not at all. Nikos had asked me to work on revealing myself. So that's what I was concentrating on. It was awful. He got us up on stage and made us try it again."

The wood of the stage beneath the lights was warm against her bare feet as she walked towards Damien and placed herself inside the niche of his arm. An acrid scent rose from him, a smell of poisoned sweat, a smell of fear. In a high voice Damien said to Nikos, "You want me to do that part where I feel her breast again and everything?"

Nikos' eyebrows swarmed across his forehead like large anten-
naed beetles. He raised them, pushing his head back to examine
Damien. "You don't need to hide your sexual preferences from us,
Damien. Or protect them. But what we're doing here is called acting.
So act."

Maud tapped a finger against Damien's hand where it lay beneath hers, although she felt in no position to give reassurance.

"And you, Maud." Nikos shook his head. The leko lights above
the stage highlighted the white woven in among his black hair. "What
am I going to do with you, Maud?"

Maud swallowed. She would not cry this time.

"All this stuff." Nikos reached out and pinched a bit of the gauzy
gown between finger and thumb. "When I suggested you find a
scene in which you could work on revealing yourself, I wasn't talking
clothing."

Driver's belly moved against hers as he laughed. He raised his
head to look at her and shook his head.

"Exactly," she said. "It's so obvious. What was I thinking? And yet
the costume had been the only place I could think to begin." She did
not fill Driver in about her choice of underwear. She'd worn a flesh-
colored thong, so she would look naked beneath the silk robe. A
saleswoman had helped her find a bra with underwiring and pad-
ding. "Now that's nice," the woman had told her, head cocked to one
side, assessing. "Your breasts look pert. He'll like that."

She'd never shown Miles, to see if he'd like her breasts pert or
not. And the bra had stayed behind, in the top drawer of her dresser
in L.A.

She had even painted her toenails for the scene. The drop deco-
rating her little toe stared up at her.

"Maud?" Nikos waited for her to look at him. "Hanging out
over the abyss, getting out on that limb, revealing your guts, turning
your insides out for others to see, is something you *must* demand of
yourself. It's what this is all about." His gesture took in the stage, the
auditorium, the lights overhead. "We are working—so hard! It takes
so much work!—to create a moment that is gone, poof, the instant it
is created. But the reason we work so hard, Maud, is so that moment

will *live*." He tapped his head. "Up here, in their minds, where anything worthwhile stays. Yes?"

Out in the theater the heads of the class bowed. Maud heard the scratch of pencil put to paper. She wanted to be out there, writing these words of wisdom down, instead of standing up on stage resisting them. She had written so many things in her own notebooks: petitions, prayers, invocations, to entice the work that didn't come. These mental excursions and epiphanies, these promises and resolutions, had not worked. She had thought perhaps a padded bra and a flesh-colored thong might provide the answer.

"Okay. Take it from your line, Damien. This time, Maud, let me *feel* him turn you on. Let me feel a throb between my own legs, you know? That little sound you made, first time through, was like you'd found gum in your hair or something." Nikos made his way down the stairs and sat. "Let's have it."

"You'll never leave—" Damien began.

"Take a breath," Nikos said. "Find zero. Start again."

"You're never gonna leave . . ." Damien sounded as if he expected interruption.

Nikos tipped the bottle of Evian to his lips. Maud dragged her eyes away from him, forcing herself to concentrate on Beau, on the narrow life of her character, delineated by sex and booze and the stench of garbage in the cobbled streets of New Orleans.

"A woman never leaves when she's gettin' it good." Damien lowered his hand into Maud's bra, this time, for the first time, pushing his fingers all the way under the lace and curving them around her breast. His fingers trembled. She wanted to cry with how much she loved his bravery—she had a good idea just how hard this was for him.

And yet it was all so *absurd*. She tried her moan.

"Again," Nikos said.

She moaned again.

"Breathe, Maud! Think back to your last orgasm. This cry comes from your belly, your G-spot, clitoris, solar plexus, belly chakra, whatever it takes, Maud, *give it to us*! Please! Let us have some of what I know you're capable of."

Tears rose. She resisted them, breathing, breathing. The moan came out breathy, false, absurd. She wanted to die.

"Again, Maud. Give an erection to every man in this room."

She felt her mind grinding on several levels: the one that processed that command and tried to do something with it, and the one that wondered what the ability to give every man an erection had to do with revealing herself. Or for that matter what it had to do with acting. Or with life. Or with anything she wanted to do with her life. But she tried the moan once more. Her voice caught in her throat. Damien's hand twitched a little, his fingers damp against her breast.

"I don't know what else—" Maud said. "I can't—"

Nikos stomped back up the stairs. Damien slid his hand away. "Get out of your head, Maud!" Nikos said.

Maud breathed in and then out as slowly as she could, blinking. She wanted to put her head back and howl, and knew Nikos would respect her if she did exactly that. Instead she sucked in her cheeks and held them with her back teeth.

"Maud," Nikos said, "you're looking confrontational."

"I'm *feeling* confrontational."

The class laughed, a loud, spontaneous gust of sound that swept like a cleansing wind through the room. A movement of Nikos' arm stopped the sound dead. It was a parody of a king's sycophants: laughing on cue, hushed on command, but she too responded to the downward slash of Nikos' hand. She let her cheeks out from between her teeth and straightened her head.

"You're paralyzed, Maud. Stuck."

Nikos talked on, but all she heard were synthesized words, words put on reverb through a piece of Miles' recording equipment. *Stuck-uck-uck. Paralyzed-alyzed-yzed . . .*

"Paralyzed with fear." She caught up with what he was saying. "That limb I was talking about. You're nowhere near it. You're clinging to the trunk of the tree so hard you can't *move*." He held his hands in front of him, palms up, pleading. "You've got all the tools. The intelligence, the face, your hair, the body—" He stopped. "Maud."

"No tits." She got the laugh she wanted from the class.

Nikos raised both fists in the air and shook them. "Zeus!" He got an even louder laugh. He turned to the class. "She's asking for a rant on the stupidity of the average American audience, how you pander to them, allow their idiotic obsessions to become your own. But I'm bored of this subject. Get out of here. Ten minutes. Maud, you stay."

"Uh-oh." Driver lifted his head to look at her. "Now you'll get it. Sounds like a graduate seminar, teachers letting you know what a moron you are and how smart they are, insisting on their pet crackpot theories."

Maud shook her head. "He said we could rework the scene, bring it back in a month or so. Or we could drop it, work on something else."

Nikos crossed his arms, muscular, covered with black hairs, over his chest. "But these things, I think, are not the answer."

She looked at him, feeling sulky, recalcitrant.

"You need to examine what you're doing here."

"In this class?"

Nikos pursed his lips, a moue of distaste. "Maud. Don't turn literal on me. Usually you are one of the few who understand my metaphors, although 'reveal' seems to have passed you by." He waited to see that the compliment landed, then reached a finger to flick the lace of the bra that, Maud knew, peeked above the edge of the dressing gown. She found time to wonder how such an invasive gesture could be so kind.

"Do you know why you're doing this?" He picked up one of her hands, examined the fingernails, the polish. "You don't like this, Maud. You don't feel good about doing it. Why put yourself to the trouble? If you like to act, or if you love theater, it is for reasons other than this."

The tears pushed forward; Nikos' face blurred.

"Look at that. Look at that. I've said something that is either very right or very wrong."

Maud held a sleeve of the dressing gown to her eyes.

"It is not your talent, dear heart, that is in question."

His Reeboks squeaked as he disappeared between two high black velvet curtains. Maud heard the pneumatic stage door sigh open, then closed.

Driver seemed to have fallen asleep. His weight was beginning to grow uncomfortable, though it kept her warm. She looked past his

shoulder, above the curve of the kiva's top edge, to the stars that
pricked the sky, thinking of Mercutio's lines to Romeo about Queen
Mab: *This is the hag, when maids lie on their backs, that presses them and
learns them first to bear.* So many meanings an actor could jam into that
one word, *bear.* And the Nurse, too, to Juliet: *I am the drudge, and toil in
your delight, but you shall bear the burden soon at night.*

She slid her hips from beneath Driver's weight.

"And where do you think you're going?"

Where did she think she was she going? And why? What was it,
exactly, that had made her pull the first dress from its hanger, wrap a
wineglass in newspaper? She saw herself talking to the plaid shoulder
of the cameraman while Tucker played baseball in Chicago. Picking
her sweater up from the floor in the Cheesios audition. Billy's *You're
just going to leave?* Summer's voice on the telephone: *Are you dead,
Aunt Maud?* As she'd driven Highway 10, then 5, her car had turned
into a cartoon of speed—a lopsided trapezoid, lines sparking off its
rear end—in her desire, once she had made the decision, to *get out.*

"Don't go." Driver burrowed in beside her, pulling the blanket
around them hard. After a moment he groaned. "Do you believe in
the drought theory or the invasion theory?"

"Drought?"

"That drove the Anasazi into cliff dwellings? Or do you sub-
scribe to the alien theory?" His voice had gone hard again, cold.
"Maybe it was fear of little men in spaceships that made them live at
the tops of ladders?" He stayed quiet for a moment, groaned again. "I
don't want to *think* about this. Tell me another story. Are you a famous actress?"

Maud laughed. "Very famous. The last part I had I was on-screen
for a total of five minutes."

She told him about the *Tucker's Larks* episode, leaving out the ar-
gument with Miles that had followed. She told him about talking to
her mother on the telephone, about crying so much that she could
dampen an entire dishrag with tears and snot—

"About what?" Driver asked.

"About the fact that it's too late for me to have what most
women have by now. That I can never catch up."

She told him about the postcard her father had finally mailed from Sydney, Australia, where one of his think tanks had been meeting. *Buck up,* and printed in his firm hand beneath this, the motto of the Maxwell clan: *Despair is base.*

"Buck up," Driver said. "Pretty sympathetic."

That led to telling him about the acting technique of Michael Chekhov: find the right action and the emotion will follow. As Nikos said: "Having a hard time getting angry? Pound the table and see what happens." She told him other wisdoms of Nikos: "Think about the last fight you had with your loved one. Was it really about what it was about? Really?" He'd waited for chuckles of recognition. "This idea is what you must bring to your scenes. A good scene is always about much more than what the dialogue says they're about."

"This way of thinking makes life complicated," she said to Driver. "Everything is always about something else and something more. Unstated, hidden."

But he was asleep. Gray light hovered above the canyon. The fire was out. She had used her jean skirt for a pillow, and its metal button pressed against the back of her head. She folded back the blanket. For a moment Driver looped a leg over hers, then let her go. "You like my excavation?"

"I do." She slid into her skirt and pulled on Miles' T-shirt, missing him suddenly, acutely. Her underpants were back in the Airstream.

Driver rolled himself into the blanket. In the pale light he looked doleful. Maud was tempted to put a hand to his cheek. But she got to her feet.

"So," he began, but didn't finish this thought.

She fastened her sandals and swiped with the jean skirt between her legs at the leak of come. As she moved towards the ladder she was aware of Driver watching from his cocoon of blanket.

"What if we made a little half-breed?"

She turned to look at him. "It isn't likely."

"Because if we did, I don't want to hear about it."

She shook her head. "Just about the time I begin to think you might be sort of all right—"

"Well, I don't." Driver sat up. "There are enough mongrels in the world. There is enough watered-down blood."

"Oh, go sit in your excavation. Cliff dweller."

His eyes gleamed with humor, quickly extinguished. "So I'm a cliff dweller. You're a past-dweller."

Stung, she started up the ladder.

"You'll stay in the past until you figure out why you're in the present," he said. "Believe me, it takes one to know one. But I liked your stories."

She began to climb again.

"You ask me about the sipapu. You ask me about blood." His voice, low and desperate, stopped her. "I can tell you what I think, what others think. But how can I *know* what flowed through the veins and brains and minds of the Ancient Ones? How can I ever know?" He lowered his head. His bare back rounded beautifully out of the brown cornucopia of blanket, until his forehead touched the floor of the kiva.

Maud was tempted to go back, kneel beside him, put a hand on that lovely, smooth back folded between the peaks of his knees, offer comfort. Kiss his scarred cheek. But before she could think too much about why and how she'd come to be there, or why and how she was leaving, she moved swiftly up the ladder. She clambered through the tumbled boulders to the canyon floor, found the path and, almost running, zigzagged her way back to the top.

Smoke rose from the hogan. In the Airstream she rolled Miles' T-shirt around her toothbrush, pulled on her tank top, sweater, watch. She tore a piece of paper from her notebook in the car and wrote a note to Maggie, thanking her. She left this, weighted with a rock, on the top step of the trailer.

"If it were done when 'tis done, then 'twere well it were done quickly," she told the raw sun that blared through her windshield. "In these cases we still have judgment here." Her laugh was harsh, almost a croak.

THE
FALL

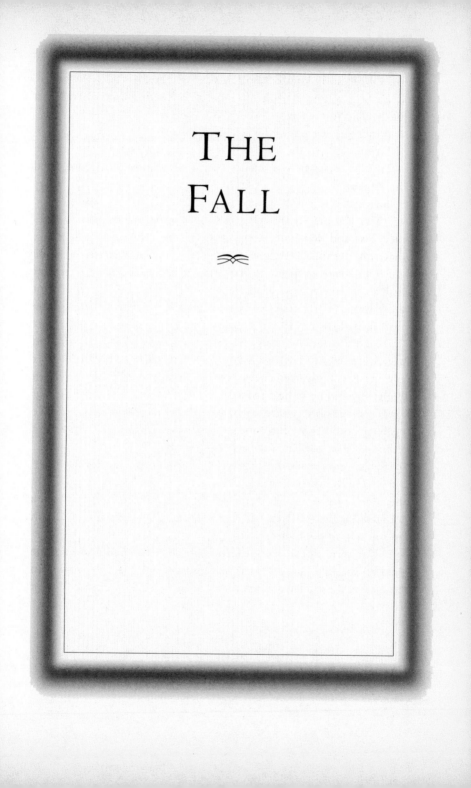

CHAPTER 13

JAKE

leaning into loneliness
elbows on the bar
staring at my empty glass
wondering where you are

Jake avoided Sue's invitation to dinner as long as he could. With Willy, things were always tense. And walking into his sister's house was eerily similar to coming home after school to their parents' house. Same smells. Same moods. He'd moved away from the shag carpeting, the ranch-burger layout, vowing never to have a life that remotely resembled theirs. Although the glossy Sears furniture, nutty aroma of baking potatoes, nonstop gossip of the television, even the knowledge that an army of cans and slope-shouldered bottles of beer lined the lower shelf of the refrigerator, still held a nostalgic and peculiar appeal.

Sue, talking on about some project of Johnny's at school, gave him a beer, checked the roast, handed him flatware, napkins. Put her head around the door to the living room. "Willy. Would you let Jello know it's time to wash his hands?"

Jake heard the rustle of newspaper, the squeak of the recliner. "Jellybean!" Willy shouted. "Hands!"

Sue and Jake raised their voices to a high whine. "If I'd wanted to yell, I could have done that myself!"

"All Mom's stuff that I swore I'd never say or do." Sue handed him two long forks, held the platter while he hoisted the sputtering wad of beef onto it. Willy, rubbing at his eyes, got himself another beer. Johnny hefted himself up into the chair opposite Jake.

"I like it when you're here," Johnny said. Sue inspected his fingernails.

Jake eyed Willy. "Thanks."

Willy blessed the table, began to carve. Ominously silent, he wrestled with knife and roast beef. Belly protruding like a pregnant woman's. Thighs bulging the seams of new jean overalls. He caught Jake staring, passed him a filled plate. "Your grits."

"Thanks."

Willy used the serving fork to lift a scrap of meat to his mouth. Chewed, bland eyes carefully avoiding contact. Air humid with all that was not being said. Their father all over again.

"Tell us about Santiago," Sue urged.

Tension gathered at Willy's end of the table. Tornado brewing, the air as thick, as yellow. The meat, perfectly cooked, stayed in Jake's mouth like a cud of chewed gum. He swallowed. "He wanted to leave Nashville for the same reasons I did the first time. The emphasis is all wrong. You start to question why you're playing music at all. All tack and trash and flash. The worst aspects of moneymaking, not to mention music making. He starts asking what Marengo's like. I get homesick telling him. Two days later he's talked to his wife and kids, we're all packing up. It's like he's always been part of the band. Took a while for Randy to warm up to him, but now he's her best pal. Funny how things work out."

"If we just let them," Sue said.

Willy said, "New Age horseshit." Nudged Johnny's arm. "Don't sit there with your mouth open. Eat."

She put her fork down. "Lizzie's sister's in town."

Jake held his knife and fork poised above his meat.

"That's what I heard." Willy nodded. "The actress. From Hollywood. Got herself a job at the Red Garter. Barney was in the store. Said she's skinny as a beanpole but pretty."

"I just hate how we've fallen so out of touch with Lizzie," Sue said. Jake was grateful when Johnny began to drum his feet against his chair. "She was a lot of fun."

His forehead felt like a knot of rope, bunched up, black as tar.

"Barney said she's moving into that old miner's cabin on Emerson," Willy continued. "Those sack-of-shit hippies that were in there fell behind on the rent. Took Norma six months to evict them. Then along comes Lizzie, says her sister needs a place. Everybody's happy."

"It's so small," Sue said.

"Big enough for one."

"Do you know her, Jake?"

"Met her once or twice. Her name's Maud."

"Yeah, Maud." Willy nodded. "That's what Barney said."

Jake and Lizzie were still living together when Maud dragged her boyfriend, Miles, on one of her treks to the Southwest. Told them over dinner that Miles was an invented name. Grumpy, animated, Miles admitted he'd been Jon Marcus in what he called "a previous lifetime." Miles was a songwriter too. A coincidence that Maud found remarkable and Lizzie dismissed. Miles kept Jake up late two nights in a row talking about "The Biz." Which meant Miles told anecdotes demonstrating the astonishing number of big-time producers and record executives he knew. That Jake recognized few of their names seemed to gratify and disappoint Miles in equal amounts. Against his better judgment, encouraged over breakfast coffee by Maud, Jake played CDs of some of the various artists who had recorded his songs. Miles offered commentary. Urged by Maud, he fetched his own demos. It had been a contest, a duel, seeming to delight Maud in proportion to the degree it irritated Miles. Lizzie, pale and strained-looking, unusually quick to blaze to anger with Jake and the girls, spent her time in her studio. When Miles and Maud began to bicker about renting a car to visit Taos, Jake offered his Volvo, delighted to get them out of his hair.

Johnny thumped his feet against his chair again. Sue reached to fold one hand over his. "Jello. Be considerate of others at the table, please. Uncle Jake loves drummers, but I'm sure he hears quite enough of them."

Johnny looked at Jake from under thick eyelashes, a legacy from his grandfather. Jake had them too. "Mom's promised me a drum set when I turn ten! To go with my sticks!"

"What have I started?" Jake bent a look of utter sympathy towards Sue, who raised her eyes heavenward.

"Ten months! But I have to practice." Johnny pointed with his fork. "I'm going to be the best drummer in the world. I'm going to be in your *band*! One of your Blakes!"

"All riiiight, Johnny!" Jake beat a brief tattoo with his knife and fork on the tablecloth.

"Yeah." Johnny did a fair rhythm break of his own.

"Johnny," Sue said.

They all watched Willy. He chewed, swallowed, wiped the back of his hand across his lips. Triangulated his knife and upside-down fork so that their tips met at the edge of the plate. "When'd you decide all this?"

"Come on," Sue said. "Ten months is a long way away."

"I should be consulted, don't you think?"

Sue stared down at her plate. The tip of her nose was red, which meant, Jake knew, that she was dangerously close to tears. "Can we, just *once* when Jake is here, have a nice dinner?" Her voice quavered.

"Just mentioning how I think I should be kept informed."

Sue shook her head imperceptibly. "If you *were* ever here, Willy, we'd talk to you about it. If you were ever 'here' when you are here, you might find some things out. But you're so much more interested in how your rakes are selling and if the price of nails is going up or down and what that means for your *stats*. Or if it isn't that, how the country is going to hell in a handbasket, which seems to be much more important to you than what's going on in your own home." Cheeks red. Breath coming fast. Her chest heaved. "When I do ask you to take some time and sit down and talk something over with me, there's always, *always* something more important. So one way or another we don't have a chance to discuss these things, do we?"

She crumpled her napkin, put it next to her full plate. "You're missing all his growing up. Do you know that? Every *day* he's changing—" She waved a hand at Johnny. "Get down, Jellybean. I'm sorry I'm yelling."

Johnny slid out of his chair, out of the room. Silence like glue settled over the table. Willy cleared his throat.

"No," Sue said. "Let me finish."

From the den came the music of *Jeopardy*. The last phrase made Jake want to sing, *Just tip me over and pour me out.*

"You missed his ones and his twos—you were getting the business off the ground. And then you had to *expand*. So you missed him being three and four. Then employees had to be trained. Always, *always* something else more important—" She pressed fingertips against her lips. "So now you don't know your son. You don't *know* he wants to play drums, that it's his *dream*. He's been talking about the Blakes for years. Even Jake, who's been *gone*, knows more about this than you do."

Jake executed a complicated maneuver with his shoulders—to convey to Sue that yes, he did know about Johnny's dream, to let Willy know he was sorry he had to hear this.

"Of course I know about his goddamned attraction to percussion," Willy said. "I also happen to know it's just misplaced adolescent sex drive." Leaned back, poured what was left of his beer down his throat.

"We'll talk about it later," Sue said, in a faint voice.

"You're right. We will talk about this later." Willy stood, crumpling his beer can in a large fist.

He left the kitchen. Moments later a door slammed, an engine started up. Sue sighed. "He'll go drink boilermakers for hours down at Old Joe's, that awful awful place, and come in at two A.M., crying and apologizing." She stood, began piling plates, sat again. "You're not finished."

She used her shirt to dab at her face. Jake saw brown skin where she hiked the shirt up, white fabric of a bra. Glanced away—responding to the ancient insistence he "not look" when they had to share the tent on camping trips, change clothes in the back seat on a long-distance car ride. "He's bad enough as it is, but every time you're over— 'Adolescent sex drive.' For pity's sake." She shook her head.

"Forget it."

"Mom." Johnny stood in the doorway.

"Hello, Jello." Sue moved to squat beside him. "I'm sorry I yelled."

"Can I have some ice cream?"

"You bet. Want some, Jake?" She opened the upper half of the refrigerator. "The nominees are—Rocky Road! Peach Yogurt! Chocolate Chip! And the winner is?"

"Rocky Road," Jake said.

"Me too." Johnny clambered up on a bar stool next to the counter. "And chocolate chip too."

Jake perched on a stool next to him. Sue placed bowls in front of them, licked the serving spoon.

"Aren't you having some?"

"Mom never eats ice cream." Johnny waved his spoon. "She eats that yogurt stuff, though. Have some yogurt, Mom."

"No, thanks."

Jake worked at his ice cream, loosening chunks of marshmallow and walnut. Thought of Willy, sitting at a different kind of bar.

Johnny kicked at the board beneath the counter. Jake joined him, creating a counterrhythm. They ate their ice cream, feet swinging in and out. "Will we leave scuff marks?"

Sue shrugged. "Go ahead. I'll have them framed."

Johnny began to syncopate the steady two-four beat.

"All right, Johnny." Jake tapped spoon against bowl. "*And.* One two *and* three—*And* one two *and* three—"

"Whoa!" Johnny used his spoon against the countertop to tap the missing *"FOUR!"*

"Good. *And* one two *and* three—"

"FOUR!"

Jake leaned over to grab a wooden fork out of the dish drainer, grinned at Sue. She smiled back, though her eyes stayed sad. He used the fork to add yet another counterrhythm. Whooped. Johnny tried the sound, coming up with a feeble "Wuu!" Across the kitchen Sue whooped too. Took a spatula from the canister beside the stove, joined the steady one-two beat Jake was keeping with his feet.

"All right, Mom," Johnny said. *"FOUR!"*

᪥

Sue got Jake to read a story to Johnny, then walked him to the door. "You know what you ought to do?"

Jake groaned. "Call Lizzie. It's not that easy, Sue."

"Well, I wish you would. Convince me that men aren't all either assholes or scaredy cats. But I was going to tell you to go climb Fable

Mountain. You haven't done that in a long time, and you always come back feeling all cleaned out."

"I don't have time. I have a real job now, you know."

"There's always the weekend. Like *normal* goddamn people."

He smiled, loving her for that. "Weekends I gig."

"Figure it out. It'll be good for you."

He didn't head home. Found himself making the turns that would take him to Main Street. Neon bar signs flickered, store windows glowed cool blue over moccasins, cowboy hats, jewelry, Southwestern clothes, pseudo–American Indian junk. For Halloween, the ubiquitous red-pepper lights had been temporarily replaced with strings of small plastic skeletons, lit from within.

"No more of these withheld hearts," Jake sang, revving his engine at a red light. To a different but related tune he sang the bridge to the song: "Hope against hope that love comes back." Santiago had created a great running counterpoint, all on keys in the upper register of the piano. It had turned into a good song.

He looked around for the lit cubicle of a phone booth. But he couldn't call Lizzie. Not tonight. Maybe not ever. Easier to climb Fable Mountain.

Across the street a couple emerged from Farquaarts. Arms looped around each other's waist, heads angled together. The light turned green. Jake released the clutch too fast. Tires squealed. He lifted a hand in apology, though he knew they couldn't see it. Ahead of him, the sign for the Red Garter glitzed its way over the edge of a rooftop. Neon garter, including rosette, stretching and then snapping back to a brilliant red circle. The hotel/saloon existed just outside the historic district and in spite of a great deal of community uproar had gotten away with the flashy neon sign.

He parked, pushed through the swinging saloon-style doors. Stood just inside. Squinted against darkness and cigarette smoke. Never been in before. Not his kind of place. Cow-horn hat racks. Brass foot rail beneath the bar. Shiny spittoons-cum-ashtrays, also brass, well polished.

Waitresses strutted and hovered, uniforms some absurd cross between historical sexy and Playboy bunny naughty. Black fishnet tights socketing into high-cut satin legholes. Fringe shivering over round rear ends. Necklines plunging, breasts bulging. Jake found himself mesmerized, repulsed, aroused with the kind of desire he knew left you wondering, even when spent, if there wasn't something more exciting, somewhere else, with someone else. He'd lived with it in Nashville, in the heyday of his successes. It had wasted his marriage.

It *had?*

"Can I help you?" A waitress in green, full-busted, wide-hipped, stood in front of him, tray proffered. A mass of carrot-colored hair exploded around her face.

"I'll sit at the bar, thanks." He watched the flip of black fringe across her rear end, the rear end itself, as she sashayed away. That would not be Maud, unless she'd gained a lot of weight and dyed her hair a carroty parody of Lizzie's.

Rich Pack sat at the bar. As Jake walked towards him he tilted his cowboy hat up, let it drift low over his forehead again.

"Rich."

"Jake."

Rich stretched his long legs out. He rented the trailer and half acre Jake owned out on Dead Horse Hill. Buying it had seemed a good investment at the time. Now the rent barely paid the mortgage and taxes. Rich was two weeks late with it. As usual. Not that he couldn't afford it. Every summer he made three thousand a week, easy, working as a guide—read gigolo—for a dude ranch outside town. Rich had told Jake about his "rides." Flush and horny divorcées he had to "manage." Rich's girlfriend, Jeep, who used to baby-sit Lizzie's girls, put up with his philandering. Perhaps because he made enough money to allow both of them to glide through the winter skiing, drinking, and taking recreational drugs.

Jake ordered a draw. Slouched with his back against the bar. "Still got that job?"

A nod. "Packed 'em in again this year."

"How's Jeep?"

Rich shrugged. A salmon-colored beam spilled onto a woman playing the piano. No one appeared to be listening.

"Omigod, Jake!" A blonde waitress, dressed in shiny pink, stopped dead in her tracks, almost upsetting the drinks she had perched on her tray. "What are you *doing* here? I *heard* you were back."

"Jeep!" Jake slid off the bar stool to give her a hug. "I was just asking about you."

Jeep moved backwards, shaking her head. A beaded headdress spangled in the dim light. "No fraternizing," she whispered. "Barney'll kill me. I'll just drop these drinks."

"Fraternizing?" Jake said, but Rich had turned away. Jake was accustomed to seeing Jeep in shorts, jeans. The high-cut legs of the leotard and the high-heeled boots made her athletic, even chubby thighs look almost lean.

The woman at the piano drew out chords to end a song. Jake prepared to clap, but she segued into another tune without a break. He sipped his beer. Jeep returned, made a show of mopping the bar with a tiny white rag she carried coiled on her tray.

"You look great, Jeep. You been working here long?" Keeping himself from asking about Lizzie.

"It's a factory. But the tips are great."

"You come in just for the sheer pleasure of looking at her?" Jake asked Rich. He sat with his back to them, brooding over his empty glass.

"Sure is different—" Jeep started, speaking low. "Hold on. Back in a sec." She darted off towards an arm waving in her direction.

"We broke up," Rich said.

"Ah."

"She's going to AA. Changing her act, so she says, and that includes me. Going back to school. Says she's going to graduate this time."

"Ah," Jake said. Although even that seemed like too much, and a betrayal of Jeep. The woman at the piano sang about love having no pride. The first time he'd heard Linda Ronstadt croon that lyric at him out of a car radio he'd thought it was pap. He took a long swig of beer. Over the years the song had grown on him. *And I'd do anything to see you again.*

The woman's voice tremored on the high notes. Wasn't much of a player, either. Most of her tunes had easy chord changes. Skinny.

Backbone knobbling up the shiny material of a turquoise corset. She'd piled her black hair on her head, topped it with a ridiculous ornament that looked like antennae. Jeep was wearing one too.

He downed the last inch of beer, left several bills for the bartender. "Rent," he said to Rich, who nodded, once.

Jeep stopped him at the slatted swinging doors. "It's so good to see you, you don't know."

"Careful, now. You fraternizing with me again?"

"Stupid Barney. Rules, rules, rules." Jeep pushed her red-painted lips into a pout. Her cheeks were round the way a child's were round. She was too young to wear the tarty uniform, the rouge, the heeled boots. "He's in the back bawling out Veronica for spilling a drink. If the money wasn't so good, none of us would be here."

Jake jangled his keys in his pocket. "Rich told me you guys split."

"I had to, Jake. I was just going nowhere, so fast, you wouldn't know. I hit bottom, joined AA. 'I am an alcoholic.' " She laughed. "Don't look so shocked. Or irritated, whatever it is. You and Lizzie. Sometimes I think she drinks twice as much beer as she used to just to get my goat."

Something must have appeared on Jake's face. "I'm sorry," Jeep said. "I forgot you guys . . ."

Jake shrugged. The piano player sang Joni Mitchell's song about being able to drink a case of her lover and still be on her feet. "Jake?" Jeep looked upset.

He patted her arm. "It's fine."

"Anyway. I'm just determined to work my way out of this." The wave of her arm took in the bar, the streets outside, her life. "Lizzie says—" She stopped. "So part of it was I called it quits with Rich. Months ago. I don't know why he comes in here. To bug me, maybe, or to watch the new piano player. Omigod! You probably don't *know*!" She pointed. "That's Lizzie's sister. The one playing the piano. She's moved here, did you know?"

Jake recognized her now. She played the last slow chords of a song, pulled the mike towards her. "I'm taking a little break here." She'd adopted a bit of a southern drawl. "But I'll be right back."

"She's real nice," Jeep said. "Want to say hi?"

Jake stepped backwards. "No, thanks. Not tonight."

Canned music began to blare from speakers behind the bar. Jeep pressed his arm. "You take good care." Wobbled on the high-heels as she headed towards a table filled with empty glasses. From the bar, Rich stared balefully at him from beneath the brim of his ridiculous hat.

Jake slapped his way back out through the fake saloon doors. Cursed at the red lights that slowed his way down Main Street. Sue was right. He should climb Fable Mountain. But right now he needed his guitar, needed to hold the sleek, round, breasts and hips woman of her, needed to give to her and pull from her the song he could feel coming, something about loneliness and neon, the terror of love.

CHAPTER 14

MAUD

Grief fills the room up of my absent child,
Lies in his bed, walks up and down with me,
Puts on his pretty looks, repeats his words,
Remembers me of all his gracious parts,
Stuffs out his vacant garments with his form:
Then have I reason to be fond of grief.
　　　　　　　　　　　　　—KING JOHN

Her first morning in the little house on Emerson Street, Maud lay face up on the futon she'd borrowed from Lizzie, willing away the all-too-familiar feeling of loosening and seepage within her womb.

Her period was four weeks late. She'd held this knowledge to herself, vibrating between hope and fear, elation and tears. Her father once told her that the root of the word *hysteria* came from the Greek word for *womb*. This fact had always irritated her. Now it made sense.

She had welcomed Lizzie's encouragement to find a house of her own, mostly because of the faint possibility that there might be a child to share it with her. But she felt the flux descend, feeling the way the movement of lava down a mountain looked. And it would be that red, though not as hot. She moved to the bathroom, peed, wiped herself. There it was: the scarlet rose of blood on white tissue. Sign, signal, emblem that once again her womb had rejected what had been offered it.

In these five weeks since she'd slept with Driver he had never been far from her mind. If she was pregnant, it was his; it had been a long time since she and Miles had made love. She stared at the faint yellow of her bathroom wall, remembering Driver's belly moving against hers as he laughed, seeing him as she'd clambered up the ladder: his naked torso the color, and it had seemed to her the opacity, of wood smoke in the dawn. *Perhaps we made a little half-breed.*

"We didn't," Maud told his memory. She found a tampon, debated taking an aspirin. One of the many deals she tried to make with God, the universe, the Powers That Be, was that if she forced herself to bear the cramps of menses, then might she, one day, be allowed to bear the pain of childbirth?

She stood in the living room, rubbing her eyes, staring at the pile of boxes and the odd pieces of furniture Lizzie had loaned her. When Lizzie'd heard about the house, she'd run by to see it and came home describing it as "miniature." She was right. From the outside it looked like something a benevolent uncle might build to house the doll collection of a spoiled niece: a tiny kitchen, a bedroom barely big enough for a double futon and a bureau, a living room with just enough wall space for a rented piano. Miles had promised to ship hers. That phone call was the last time they'd talked. "Sounds like you're not planning to come back here anytime soon," he said, with that ironic lilt in his voice that at one point she'd loved. "I don't *know*," she said. He closed the conversation then: "Well, if you decide you do know, give me a call."

In a kind of terrified astonishment she watched herself taking step after step, plodding mulishly away from the path she'd walked and planned for a decade. The job at the Red Garter. This house. And even now, as she dragged a box into the kitchen and began to unpack plates and bowls from their beds of wadded *L.A. Times*. Some force kept driving her away from the life she had envisoned, into this one, which seemed almost as familiar—as if all this time she'd been living a dual life and had simply jumped tracks.

The shelves in the kitchen were hand-built, bookshelves rather than cupboards. She wondered if her dishes and glassware would gather dust. In Los Angeles, anything left uncovered developed a kind of sticky dark grime, its texture similar to the paste that kept labels on jars and as difficult to scrub off. This gluey-grime had come to represent L.A., the creeping, insidious darkness that seemed to have infested, infected, every pore of her being.

She cleaned the kitchen with the energy and certain degree of fury her period always brought. She tried to ignore the cramps that coursed through her abdomen, that odd, mostly nonlocalized pain that sometimes forced her to bend over in pain. She gave in and took an aspirin: God didn't seem to be interested in the barter anyway.

In the living room, the various boxes sat where they'd been dumped during the hectic move-in the day before. Lizzie, carrying boxes, had marveled at how much Maud had managed to fit into her car. *That car of yours is pretty packed up.* Driver. *You coming or going?*

Maud knelt beside a cardboard box marked MISC. Would that be kitchen misc., bedroom misc., music misc.? "Sheet music?" she said, pulling at the flaps. "Sheets and towels?"

"Who are you talking to?"

A little boy stood in the doorway, one hand on the knob. Behind him the unwatered lawn stretched more gold than green in the afternoon sun.

Maud's fingers moved to her throat, clichéd gesture of fear. But this was not L.A. She did not have to be jumpy about unexpected voices and turning doorknobs. "Hello."

The boy assessed her, lower lip pushed out. He was perhaps four or five years old. His face was round, his cheeks quite red. "Who are you talking to?"

"God?" Maud pushed one of the boxes with her foot so that it slid across the floor.

The boy stepped farther into the room and then retreated to the doorknob again. "What are you doing?"

"Unpacking. Do you live around here?"

The boy nodded. His shorts came down all the way to his knees, emphasizing sturdy calves. His bare feet were dirty.

"What's your name?"

"Noah." He watched her for a moment and then, as if it came up often, said, "It was raining."

"I see."

Noah watched as she tugged open the MISC. box. Folded tablecloths and napkins, candlesticks, packages of Trader Joe's candles, never used.

"Do you have something I could drink?" he asked. "Do you have pop?"

Maud straightened, pushing hair out of her face. "I'm sorry, Noah. I haven't been to the store yet."

"Oh boy," Noah sighed, as if this were the last straw.

"I'll get you some when I do go." She lifted a tablecloth, matching napkins. "Where should I put these?"

Noah advanced into the room and placed his balled-up fists on his hips. "Did you bring any kids?"

"I didn't, Noah."

Noah screwed up his lips and looked off to one side, as if this disgusted him. "Why?"

"Now that, Noah, is a good question."

"It's not so funny." His eyes grew shiny; his upper lip trembled. "Who am I s'posed to play with?"

He disappeared off the front steps. Stroking the tablecloth she had over one arm, Maud looked after him. Someone with children had lived here, then moved away, taking Noah's friends with them. Leaving him desolate, the first of many partings life would bring him. She wadded the cloth into a ball, pulled it against her stomach, and sat. She put her elbows on her folded knees, pressed the palms of her hands against her eye sockets, the half-packed boxes around her an atrocious, unbearable metaphor. "Miles," she whispered.

She needed at these times to remember why she'd left. The night she was on *Tucker's Larks*, the first work of any size she'd done in over a year, he'd been at the studio, and came in the door after the show had started, his briefcase leaking its usual assortment of lead sheets and chord charts and the demos he sent out again and again to record companies. These CDs, marked MILES! in speedy italicized letters, made him sound as if he had a huge band playing behind him. In reality, it was only himself and his prodigious talent. She didn't know why she wanted to hold this against him, but the lack of an actual band struck her as false advertising, misrepresentative. Although she couldn't particularly say that her career was—had been?—any more honest, any less false, whatever the words might be.

His blond hair was pulled back in a leather thong, straggly, un-kempt. "I tried, Maud. I really did." As he always said.

The distance guy, Nikos called him once, when he couldn't re-member his name. It wasn't a fair moniker; Miles was, in fact, capable of tremendous intimacy, as he'd proved over and over again, all the many times they'd broken up.

"No big deal. It's not as if I'm starring in the thing."

"Don't start." Miles got himself a beer and leaned against the kitchen door jamb. Maud kept her eyes on the television, although she knew he was watching her. The commercials ended. "You plan-ning to watch?" she said, because she needed to say something.

Miles sat on the arm of the couch. "So, who are you?"

"I told you about this when I was shooting it."

Miles shook his head.

"Yes I did. I'm the subplot. I'm a mom who doesn't want, can't keep, her baby—I know I told you about this."

"No."

"You said, 'Typecasting,' and laughed."

"Well, I don't remember. I'm dense, I'm forgetful, I'm thought-less, I don't listen when you talk to me. These are things we've estab-lished. You want to tell me, or not?"

Maud watched his profile for a moment. "I'm homeless. Can't support my baby. So I ditch her in a Dumpster."

"At least this time they didn't saddle you with some cute Marl-boro man who does his best to get in your pants."

Maud closed her eyes and took a deep breath. *Anyway.*

"Joke, Maud. Yoo-hoo." He waved his hand as if she were leaving on a train and he was right next to the window. "You take things so literally."

"Fuck you." Nikos: *Although "reveal" seems to have passed you by.* "I do not."

Miles closed his eyes and rubbed his head. Maud stared at the television. Colored shapes and figures advanced and receded. Tears welled up. "I'm sorry, Miles. I'm sorry. God, I'm just so tired of it all."

Everything sounded like a script. A bad script, written by a bad writer who relied heavily on clichés. She reached for the remote and pushed the volume up. After a moment, Miles placed a hand on her thigh. It was an awkward transition. As an actor she would never buy it. She would want to run the moment again until they got it right. *Suit the word to the action, the action to the word.* . . . Obedient to something she couldn't name, she placed her fingers on top of his. It was what the acting technique of Michael Chekhov would encourage—by doing the action associated with an emotion, you make the emotion come.

But their hands were like two blocks of wood, one on top of another. Under the pretense of dimming the volume on yet another round of gunfire, she took hers away. And then there she was again, lit by a bright helicopter light, eyes large and black in a bleached-white face. "You look awful," Miles whispered.

"I'm supposed to," she said. "All hope is gone." She stood, arms stretched to either side, in a fusillade of bullets. She stared in the direction of the camera. A petal of blood, garish in the bright light of the hovering helicopter, drooled from a corner of her mouth. She collapsed, jerking from the onslaught of bullets.

As the music of *Tucker's Larks* swelled, the phone rang. "Let your machine get it," Miles said. "It's your mother, calling to say you're wonderful, your talents are squandered, what are you doing with a man who doesn't deserve you."

"Miles." Maud stopped. She was holding fingers to her forehead in what she realized was the parody of someone with a headache, the gesture of someone who has had *just about enough*. She pulled her hand away and looked at it. "I wouldn't mind if someone were calling me, you know, to say congratulations," she said. "Or that they thought my work was good. Something." But she'd let the machine turn on.

Past-dweller, she heard Driver say. She stood up, refolded the tablecloth. She was a kite on a string. Or maybe a fish on a line. She kept swimming, feeling like she was getting away with something, fearing and hoping the jerk would come that would reel her back in; she would be yanked towards a past she knew she didn't want anymore but was terrified of leaving behind.

It was also possible that no one had hold of the line. She might be the fish; she might also be the fisherman.

Her mouth dry, heart beating too fast, she roamed the house. But the phone would not be installed until Wednesday. In any case, she told herself as she peered out windows she had to stoop to see through, found her purse, how could she call Miles? Call him only to let him know that she missed him upon occasion with a sensation that felt like a metal gum wrapper against a silver filling.

She set out to walk the few blocks to a market she'd spotted the day before. Noah was playing in the yard of the house next door. She waved, but he peered ferociously away from her. *But love is only chance,* Cyrano said, so much anguish layered into that word, *chance.* Once she'd tried to explain to Miles how sad that idea made her. "But of course it's chance," he'd said. "What, you think two people wander the world until they find each other?" She pulled her mind back to the houses, all in need of paint, that lined the streets of the neighborhood.

At the market, Maud found a phone booth and dialed Lizzie's number. There was no answer, and she didn't leave a message. "Buck up," she told herself. She stared at the phone, but finally just called her own machine in Los Angeles, checking her messages. She wondered if Miles might be standing over the phone, listening as the messages replayed, tempted to pick up. Her agents, Scotty and Danielle, accepted that she was out of town "on family business," so there were never any auditions. If she didn't return, what would they do with the hundred photographs she'd given them only a few months before? One of these days she would have to let them know, and cancel her phone, but she couldn't do it yet. Nor had she been inspired to contact her few L.A. friends, wax enthusiastic about what she was doing in a small town in the middle of nowhere. "Working in a bar," laugh laugh laugh. "It's called the Red Garter, do you believe it? No, not waitressing—I play the piano. I even slip in a few of my own songs now and again. No one listens, the pay's abysmal, but the tips are good." None of which addressed how quickly she had come to depend on the job, the meaning it gave her existence. What was she *doing*, at the age of forty-one, almost forty-two!, having pulled up the pathetic little roots of her life to play an upright piano in a bar, dressed in some demented designer's image of women in the

1890s? She looked forward to—depended upon—seeing Jeep, the red-haired Ginger, the bartender Bart.

The bulletin board outside the store was crowded with flyers, ads for apartments, roommates wanted, skis for sale, massage therapy. A long, bright orange poster advertised a series of bands at Farquaarts. On a visit a few years ago Maud had gone to Farquaarts with Lizzie to watch Lizzie's boyfriend's band: Jake's Blakes. She recalled a pleasant haze of pizza and beer, music and dancing.

According to an attractive black-and-white poster, Fable Mountain Stage Company's production of *Three Sisters* had just closed its month-long run. Maud, impressed with the quality of the poster, wondered what sort of audiences *Three Sisters* had pulled. She would not have thought there would be a market for Chekhov in a town like Marengo. Although perhaps that wasn't fair to Marengo. When some students in her acting class had done a scene from *Uncle Vanya*, Nikos had never gotten around to critiquing their work, just bawled them out for doing Chekhov at all.

"Why not? Why *not*? That you have to *ask* shows why you mangled him, this poor playwright. Why not? Because American actors think his plays are about plot. *Plot!* Americans are addicted to plot," Nikos shouted. "This is so you don't have to think. You don't have to work, to make connections—why is this character behaving in this way?"

Others besides Maud had their journals and notebooks out, pens skidding across the page. "A story is not about *plot*. A story is about *character*. Character *is* plot. Chekhov knows this. This is why actors love to work on Chekhov, although most of them, unless they are very smart"—he tapped the side of his head—"don't know that is why. It is all about inner life." Inner life, Maud underlined so hard the pen tore the paper: Character is plot.

The next production of Fable Mountain Stage Company would be *Charlie's Aunt*. They would finish the season with *A Christmas Carol*.

She dawdled through the aisles of the store. The only interesting cheese she could find was a mild cheddar. There was no "interesting" bread, as her mother called it. What French bread there was came presliced. "A good play is like holding a great hunk of rye in your hand," Nikos said. He held an imaginary loaf in his huge paw and ripped at it with his teeth. "You take a bite, you chew for a while." He did this, gnawing exaggeratedly on air, then stopped, looked at the imaginary loaf, widened his eyes. "Aha! You *get* it! You find yourself! But in America, audiences don't want to find themselves, they want to lose themselves, be taken away from themselves. They want to laugh, but not at the foolishness of their own lives. No, they like pratfalls, humor that is prepackaged, presliced. Humor that won't reflect their own absurdity. How many of us have ever actually slipped on a banana peel? Ha ha ha." He made a big show of laughing, holding his hands to his sides. "But it can mean so much! The slip-ups we all make. Et cetera. But *no!* Don't think about what something might *mean.* Just laugh along with the sound track. Real humor takes some chewing. Then you get it. *Chewing!*" He shook the loaf. "You understand?"

Murmurs, agreement. "No you don't. You want to dance up the aisles. You want to go out singing a pretty little song. A Greek audience, they *like* to leave a play feeling troubled. They go and drink coffee, ouzo, talk until the stars are fading. They go home, they can't sleep, they are worried. We love to worry as much as you love to laugh. We laugh at people worrying, we laugh when things are sad. Because this sadness is a true thing. We recognize it. It's just a different kind of recognition, which is all laughter is."

Maud scribbled: <u>Laughter = recognition</u>.

"The play makes them think about their life. Maybe they change something. Maybe they just drink more." Laughter from the class. "But you Philistines don't want *meaning,* you want to be reassured—that life will give you a happy ending."

Maud pushed the cart up and down the aisles, pausing in front of the cleaning supplies for Comet, a mop—which she would carry home over her shoulder like a boy with a fishing pole—and another packet of sponges. With a flick of her wrist simultaneously flippant and furious, she tossed a box of Tampax, slender regular, into her cart. She would clean her house, as her body flushed away the wasted bloody home, changing that as she'd changed her life, as she'd left L.A.

She paused in front of the apple juice, wondering if Noah would prefer Coke, and if his parents would care in either case. And she should buy beer, in case Lizzie came to visit.

God is in the details. She'd heard the saying before, but it slipped suddenly into focus. An antiquated slide projector, with a recalcitrant focus button, finally made an image clear. God is in the mundane, the specific. God is in the little things, the dots we connect to get us through another day.

CHAPTER 15

LIZZIE

NOTES FROM BENEATH THE MAGNETS ON LIZZIE'S FRIDGE

Heater filters
Call Burt—2 cords oak—DRY
Summer—dentist
closet doors
clean gutters
SAM

"Two! Four! Six-eight-twelve!" a chorus of high voices yelled. "Who do we love besides ourselves? Prairie Dogs! Prairie Dogs! *Yaaay!*"

Lizzie stood with a clipboard on the side of the field, working out positions. Michael Porter, soccer dad for the day, waved his hands at their own motley team, which looked pathetic next to Fairfield's stalwart Prairie Dogs. "Let's hear from you guys," Michael yelled. "Come on, Jackrabbits!"

"Two! Four! Six! Eight!" The voices came high and ragged, too thin to inspire confidence. "Who do we appreciate? Jackrabbits, Jack-rabbits, *yaaay!*"

This effort at inter-team spirit accomplished, the third-grade soccer teams ran towards their respective coaches. The Prairie Dogs waved their hands in the air and whooped. The Jackrabbits, cowed and quiet, crowded around Lizzie. She swaggered her way into a coach's posture: feet spread apart, hands on bent knees, ignoring Michael's wink of approval.

"Peter," she said to a boy wearing green-framed glasses, "you're center. Cory, play left. Doreen, right." She went through the other positions. "Summer," she said, looking down so that she wouldn't see her daughter shake her head. "Summer, this quarter you're goalie. Your job, your whole job, is to keep that ball from getting past you, okay?"

Shoulders hunched, Summer wandered towards the goal. Her shin guards, covered with turquoise knee-high socks, made her look like a diminutive version of a Greek warrior. What were they called, the ancient Greek version of shin guards? Maud would know. She sat on the grass to one side of the soccer field. With Theo on her lap, she looked only vaguely out of place amongst the mothers of the third-graders convening on Fenley Field.

"Summer, close it up!" Michael Porter yelled. Summer shot a glance filled with resentment and woe at her mother and slouched over to stand in front of the goalposts.

Lizzie blew her whistle. The ball dribbled into play. Little feet, little calves, little muscled thighs chased after it. The ball rolled out of bounds, penalty Jackrabbits. A Prairie Dog's father threw it back in, yelling, "Get 'em, Buddy!" Buddy looked like a miniature football quarterback in training. He would grow up to drink too much beer, defend any decent American's right to buy guns, be taciturn and uncommunicative when faced with emotion, and now he was heading straight down the field towards Summer. She stood slack-mouthed as the bodies came rushing towards her.

"Close it *up*! Summer, guard your post!" Michael Porter yelled. Lizzie, loping along the sidelines, seconded: "Come *on*, Summer!" But Summer, dancing back and forth in an agony of indecision and fear, let the ball whisk by. A groan went up from the assembled Jackrabbit mothers.

Summer wiped her arm across her face. Lizzie trotted over to stand beside her.

"I *hate* this game. I *hate* it." Summer's braids were their usual frizzy mess. Reluctant tears stood in her eyes. "I *never* wanted to play it. Why do you make me?"

"It's just a game."

"You've said that sixteen zillion *times*. We have two games left. We've lost every one because of me."

"Not because of you." The rest of the team waited to play ball. Lizzie couldn't have this conversation now. "Do your best, Summer. That's what counts."

"It *doesn't* count."

Lizzie blew her whistle and jogged to the center line. Michael Porter sidled up to her. "Tough when your own kid's screwing up. Like my Mikey, last year. Impossible." A black forelock fell into his eyes. He tossed it back, smiling through dark Irish eyes.

"She's not screwing up."

"Okay, okay." Michael dropped back, holding up his hands in protest. "Just a thought."

At halftime Lizzie dropped to her knees beside Maud, who was holding Theo and chatting with Jane Kirchenberg and Stella Lytton. Maud looked like the dancer she was—erect back, one leg folded under a long jean skirt, the other stretched out to one side. Maud had never had a problem charming people, and already Lizzie could see she had several fans among the women. Their faces were animated as they spoke with her. Lizzie had forgotten how much this difference between them bothered her. "Hi, Jane," she said, "hi, Stella," but was not surprised when the women found a reason to wander away.

Theo spilled out of Maud's lap and into Lizzie's, plucking at her shirt. Lizzie had a bottle in her bag but she resorted to the easy way out, loosening her shirt and giving him a breast. She saw Jane give her a look. *Still nursing. At sixteen months.* Lizzie sighed. "What were those things Greeks wore on their lower legs?"

"Greaves," Maud said. "I was thinking the same thing. All these little Southwestern warriors running around with their turquoise and pottery-red greaves."

"I knew you'd know." Lizzie sounded grumpy, even to her own ears. She looked away from Maud's puzzled glance and adjusted Theo's pull against her breast. In apology she said, "Come for dinner?"

"I have to work. But thanks."

"You sleeping any better?"

"Sometimes."

Before Maud had moved out Lizzie had more than once found her downstairs gulping a double-bagged cup of chamomile tea at two, three, four in the morning, heard her rustling around in the den, saw the light seeping from beneath that door. After she'd moved into town she'd called in the middle of the night, crying, needing to talk, apologizing.

"Five minutes," Michael Porter yelled. "Get those snacks down your gullets, now!"

The kids clustered around Mrs. Porter, who handed out slices of orange, cups of apple juice. Summer stood alone, sucking an orange slice. Lizzie's heart ached: by avoiding her teammates, her daughter convinced herself she wasn't being avoided by them. Theo pulled his mouth away from her nipple and pointed. "Eye."

"Eye," Lizzie repeated.

"I wish I'd played more team sports." Maud bent over her out-stretched leg, pointing, then flexing her booted foot. "But The Parents always had a class to teach, or a lecture to attend. They weren't about to drive me around to softball games. Mom had more time when you got to that age—"

"Yeah," Lizzie said, wanting to interrupt this.

"Maybe because in those two years they'd found some friends who were also parents. Parenting wasn't just an intellectual exercise anymore—"

"Maybe, yes."

"Lizzie," Maud said.

"What?"

Maud let the tone of Lizzie's voice resonate and then shrugged.

"Summer doesn't get a chance to get good at anything." Lizzie changed the subject. "They rotate positions every quarter. It's Michael's idea. The other teams don't do it. I think it's why we never win."

"But I think that's great! They learn that every position is equally important. That's a good thing to know. Going into life."

Lizzie wiped Theo's face with the tail of her shirt. When Maud got going—comparing one thing in life to something else, or to life itself—she found herself getting tired. Compost, ball games, rug weaving. What had it been the other day? That aspen trees are the oldest trees on the planet. "Virtual immortality," Maud told Lizzie.

"What we see as aspens are actually the branches of a larger organism. The actual tree is underground. What we call aspens are its branches sticking up out of the earth." Maud had made a lot out of that one. Interconnection. Communion. Lizzie burrowed in Theo's diaper bag for a cracker. What on earth difference did it make? You lived life or you didn't, some good things happened and some bad, but there was no particular place to put the credit or the blame. Maud seemed to crave an intimate relationship with some higher essence, and worked harder to create it than Lizzie could ever remember working on—or even wanting—any of her own far more temporal ones.

"On the field!" Michael Porter yelled.

Lizzie groaned. "I can't *wait* for this to be over."

Maud gave her a look. "That seems unlike you."

"I *hate* that phrase." Lizzie was startled by the red rage traveling up her throat. "I *hate* it. Mom used to say it: 'You're just not acting like yourself, Lizzie.' I wanted to *scream*, 'Then who in hell am I acting like?'"

Maud laughed, nervously. Lizzie said, "I mean it. It's myself that's doing the acting here, except I'm not acting—I leave that up to you. I'm just being exactly who I am. Who else would I be?"

"Sorry," Maud said.

"Sorry," Lizzie imitated. She blew her whistle and trotted back to the middle of the field. She put Summer left this time, refusing to bend to her daughter's clear appeal to be benched.

The tangle of limbs chased each other up and down the field. Lizzie had a hard time holding her mind on the game and was glad she could count on Michael to keep track of the score. Recently, driving into school, she'd heard a woman on a radio talk show remark, "Well, as they say, the unexamined life is not worth living."

Lizzie had slapped her steering wheel. "Yes," she'd said gleefully to the radio, "but an *over*examined life isn't *being* lived." She'd been thinking of her sister at the time, but the phrase—both phrases—stuck in her head. She looked about now—at the children running down the field, at the trees going yellow and red in the woods next to the park, at the wink Michael Porter threw her, felt the seam of her blue jeans tight against her crotch, and thought about what was in the fridge that she could feed the kids for dinner. At the same time she wondered how one started such an examination. She didn't want to be like Maud, who saw signs in everything—what it meant that she couldn't find a parking space easily, the significance behind the phone company's taking only three days instead of five to turn on her service.

"Go, Summer, *go!*" she heard Maud yell, and realized that the ball was heading toward her daughter.

"Go, Jackrabbits!" she shouted. For a moment Summer came alive, flying into the melee of bodies with something even approaching enthusiasm. But Buddy, the miniature football quarterback, slipped a deft foot into the swarm of limbs, got the ball away from Summer, and kicked it into the net. The Prairie Dogs went crazy. Summer turned her back on the field.

"Play ball!" Michael yelled, stopping Lizzie, who had started towards Summer. Maud was up on her feet, yelling, "Atta way, Summer! Good, good try!"

Mercifully soon, the game was lost and over. They walked to their cars, trailing a sulky Summer. "Why don't you just take her home?" Lizzie said. "Adopt her. She likes you better than me anyway."

"Lizzie, have I done something—"

"Don't start. You keep saying you'll never *catch up*, that everyone got started so long ago, what a mess you've made of things, but sometimes, I've got to tell you, your unencumbered circumstances look pretty damn good." She held up a warning forefinger. "And don't you dare say you're sorry one more time."

⚹

She picked up Hannah and her friend Stephanie from gymnastics on the way home. Their chatter in the back seat made her feel as if she drove a cage full of large parakeets. Summer sat morose in the passenger seat, staring out the window.

Stephanie paused as she was sliding out of the car. "My mom saw an ad about piano lessons your aunt is giving and I get to take them."

"Aunt Maudie?" Hannah said.

Lizzie felt oddly betrayed. Maud hadn't told her.

"Yeah," Stephanie said, excited. "She's an actress."

"I know *that*. I've *seen* her. On TV!"

"I saw her die," Summer said.

"I'm her first student."

"Can I do that, Ma? Take lessons from Aunt Maudie?"

"Perhaps. Would you like that too, Summer?"

Summer folded her arms, pushed her lower lip out.

Lizzie pulled the mail out of the letter box at the head of the drive. Amidst the collection of Christmas catalogues already beginning to arrive, she noticed a blue aerogram with familiar slanted handwriting. "A letter from Grams," she said. Hannah demanded to read it right away. Summer said, "Let me," but without much energy, and went back to staring out the window.

Sara's yellow boat of an automobile was parked between Jeep's car and Sam's pickup in front of the house.

"Sara's here! Can I go see them? Can I?" Summer danced in a panic of desire.

Lizzie raised her hands in submission. Summer raced up the hill. Hannah went into the house, saying, "Hi, Jeep," as she closed the door behind her.

The wind blew Lizzie's hair around her face. She stared up at Sam's caboose. Sam had called it home for at least three decades, had been living there when Lizzie purchased the property. His presence, guaranteed in the sale, made the twenty-acre parcel extremely cheap. Few people visited him. For some years now only Sara ever came, although Summer ran up to the trailer almost daily.

She unfolded the aerogram. . . . *so amazed to hear of Maud's decision. It all seems so sudden. Your father muses that she waited until we were out of the country to "make her move," but I tell him he's making things, as usual, overly significant. (And he wonders where Maud gets her tendency to ascribe deeper meanings to absolutely everything.) Do keep us posted on how she's doing. We've been so worried about her, in spite of our initial disapproval wanting her to be happy with Miles, but hearing so often that she's not. . . .*

Lizzie shoved the letter into her coat pocket. She'd read it later. She stared for a long time at the piles of newspaper in the back of Sara's car and then headed slowly up the hill. Just how much Sara's presence at Sam's encouraged her to put in her own appearance was

a thought she pushed from her mind. The last time she'd seen Sam
was the day Maud had arrived, weeks and weeks ago. She'd spent the
day trying to paint, keeping the door to her studio open, and had begun to seriously think about calling the highway patrol when, late in
the afternoon, Maud had driven up, looking tired and terribly thin.
She'd spent the two nights on the road, she said, and hearing that
Miles had phoned at least six times, she'd walked, slouch-shouldered,
into the house to call him. Sam and Luna had come down to welcome her. Maud got off the phone from Miles, crying. Her long
black hair fell about her face. "You don't want to see me like this,"
she told Sam. And Sam had said, gravely, in the way that made Lizzie
love him so much, "I would always want to see you."

Lizzie knocked on the trailer's screen door. Sara opened the door.
"Hey," Lizzie said. "How is he?"

"See for yourself." Sara stood back to let her in.

During the brief time Lizzie and Sam had been lovers she'd often
visited the caboose. She was amazed how much, fifteen-odd years
later, the place looked the same, if a good deal messier. The piles of
books, *National Geographic*, and other magazines had grown so high
that actual aisles threaded through them. His collection of stones now
completely covered the broad windowsill. Beading projects, along
with strips and rounds of cut leather, still consumed the card table.

Lizzie made her way to the back, where the bed was, and where
she could hear Summer chattering away. Summer was lying across
the bottom of Sam's mattress, her arm around Luna. "Ma!" she said,
startled. "You never come here."

"Lizard!" The way Sam shifted showed it hurt him to move.
"How's my girl?" His voice was slurred. Lizzie noticed, aghast, that
one side of his mouth hung a little lower than the other.

"She's not your girl," Summer said, "I am. And Luna is."

As if to emphasize this point, Luna put her muzzle on Summer's
knee, peering up at her through rheumy eyes.

Sam nodded. "You're right, Summer, as you often are."

Summer relaxed against the back wall of the trailer. Lizzie waited
in the doorway. Sara's presence behind her made her feel flimsy.
"How are you, Sam?"

Sam waved a hand. "And Maud? How's she doing?"

"I think she's fine, Sam."

"She came to watch my soccer game," Summer said. "She has a really loud voice. When she cheers you can hear her in Timbuktu."

"She phones in the middle of the night sometimes, when she can't sleep." Lizzie's mind was whirring, wondering if and when Sam had had another stroke. "We found her a little house in town. Next we'll get her a kitten."

"She has a job!" Summer bounced on the bed. "She's playing the piano. But we can't go see her cuz it's a bar."

"You tell her I'm glad for her." Sam's face was the proverbial road map. Some of the roads became highways when he smiled. He fingered the piece of thin leather around his throat, which had on it, Lizzie knew, a single turquoise bead. It emphasized how scrawny his neck had become. He looked as if he was having trouble breathing. "And how are you doing, Lizard?"

"Doing?"

"Well, it's a little unexpected, I don't doubt."

"What's unexpected?" Summer asked.

"Maud coming," Lizzie said. "But it's fine." If Sara and Summer were not there she would sink to her knees and press her forehead into the mattress. She sat on the bed. "It brings up stuff. I won't say it doesn't."

" 'Mom and Dad always liked her better,' " Sam said.

"That was a long time ago, Sam."

"Whose dad?" Summer said. "Mine or Hannah's?"

Sam pushed with a shaking hand at one of the pillows beneath his head, keeping his face turned towards Lizzie.

"Sometimes I do feel like I want my life back."

She heard Sara sigh. Sam kept his eyes on her.

"That sounds silly." There was another long pause and Lizzie added, "She's so sad."

"Maybe you have a lot of things she doesn't." Again the words were slurred, the meaning sometimes jumbled, and Lizzie had to concentrate to understand what Sam was saying. "And maybe she has some things you don't. But you've caught a little heaven for some time now. Maybe it's time to give some."

"I could give her something," Summer said.

Sara's brown eyes reminded Lizzie of Jake's.

"And we loaned her some furniture," Summer added.

"I'm not sure that's what Sam means." Lizzie stood. "But you're the one that maybe we should worry about. What do you need? What does he need, Sara?"

Sara shook her head. "He won't say. He'd be in terrible pain and never say."

"It's just a cold. Sara's feeding me bark tea and corn pudding, saying the Indian ways will put me right again."

"Sure. Bark tea." Sara laughed. "Try Lipton's finest."

"Don't be such a stranger," Lizzie said. "We eat dinner every night, and we love to have you." Which sounded too formal and barely scraped the surface of what she meant.

Sam lifted his hand in goodbye. His wrist was thin as a twig.

"Come along," she said to Summer, who moaned and fussed but came along. Luna, following her, fell rather than jumped off the bed. Summer squatted beside her.

"Stupid old dog," she said, smooching Luna. "You want to walk us home?"

Luna followed them to the door. "What's happened?" Lizzie said, low-voiced, to Sara.

"It's another BIA, TIA, whatever they're called. I just happened to drop by, he was on the floor." She sounded faintly reproachful. "He won't fuss. You know how he is."

When Sam had his first stroke, two years ago, Lizzie had been with Jake. It was Jake's sister who'd told them about TIAs, short for some impossible string of words. "He'll look bad and his speech will be impaired right after," Sue told her, "and then in a few hours or a day he'll look better. Over time, though, they'll run him down."

"As always, it's 'No doctor, no hospital,' " Sara was saying. "I told him I'd get a medicine man up here, but he's resisting that. He's between the old ways and his own ways and your world's ways. I'm afraid he'll fall between the cracks. No care, no comfort from anywhere in the circle. So here we are. Bark tea." She shook her head.

Summer tugged Lizzie's hand. "You said we were *going*."

"I'll see you Tuesday in class," Lizzie said to Sara, who nodded, benign and solid.

The dog's curve of white tail acted like a beacon, zigzagging ahead of them down the slope in the dusk. Summer skipped up the porch stairs, turning at the door to yell, "Go home, Luna." The dog stared, panting, then headed back up the hill.

Jeep sat at the kitchen table, an open book and a notebook in front of her. Theo had hold of her calf and was bouncing up and down, crooning. Lizzie got herself a beer. "How on earth can you study with him hanging on you?"

"Remember that class I told you I might sign up for?"

"How long has Sara been here? Did you hear her drive up?"

"Couple of hours." Jeep packed up her books. "I'm learning all these things about plants. You have no idea what we've forgotten, or what doctors have replaced with really icky drugs. Tomorrow we're going on a field trip."

She gave Theo a kiss. "Maud called and said thanks for the invite to the game, she loved it, and can she take a rain check for dinner. She wondered if you might want to bring the kids to trick-or-treat in her neighborhood next week."

"Good idea. How's she liking the Garter?"

"She doesn't seem to hate me for hauling her in there. And Barney seems happy." Jeep shrugged into her jacket, an ornate leather belted affair that always struck Lizzie as being too big, and too much, for Jeep's girlishness. "I keep asking her to stay after, have a shift drink with the rest of us, but she's always too tired. She says she doesn't sleep."

"No use asking you if you want dinner." With Theo crooning on her hip, Lizzie took hamburger out of the fridge. "But no, you've got AA."

"I've got AA."

Lizzie walked her out to the porch. Jeep paused, hugging her backpack. "I know you'll think this is corny, but I'm happy." She turned her face to the sky, as if she could feel some radiance aimed specifically towards her. "Thank God."

Lizzie moved restlessly. *Forwhatweareabouttoreceive,* her father, asked by her mother to say grace, would mutter. *LettheLordmakeustruly thankful. AaaMen.* Once, twice a year—Thanksgiving, Christmas. Guests often kept their heads bowed, expecting more than this hurried benediction. She remembered the lowered eyelids, the feeling that there was something surreptitious, even ridiculous, about bringing up God at the dinner table. It was at their mother's insistence, she was certain, that God was invoked at all.

She waved Jeep off and gave in to Summer's pleading to let them watch a video while they ate dinner. She nursed Theo, read the newspaper, kept half an eye on *The Secret Garden*. She supposed this was what she meant when she told Sam she wanted her life back. Evenings such as these had been interrupted by Maud's month-long stay, and by the emotions her sister seemed to swim through on a fairly continual basis.

She brought the girls fruitsicles, put Theo to bed, and started in on the dishes, though it was Hannah's turn. Yes, she told herself, it was nice to have her house to herself again. Although it reminded her of times with Jake. He'd told her once how much he loved these evenings. Respite, he said, from the frenetic activities of rehearsal and performance.

She stuck her head into the den. "Bedtime," she said, but was drawn for a moment by the bright images chasing each other around the screen. She wished she could head out to the Billy Goat Saloon, challenge some bony cowboy to a game of pool. She'd beat him, as she almost always did, or at least used to. And then she would follow up on the promise the game would have offered: provocative leans across the pool table, long haunches, tight rear ends, taunting smiles. She'd go home with him, whoever he was. It had been years, long before Theo, since she'd done that. Before AIDS had made it hard to be spontaneous. Years since she'd gone to bed with someone else so drunk they didn't really remember or care whose lips and body they found some comfort in.

She could smell the bar: the smoke, the beer, the sweat of men who would have come straight from work. The jukebox booked for hours at a time, the speakers blasting, making everybody yell. Smoke swirling above the green felt of the three pool tables, lit by those low overhead lamps where a Coors stained-glass river moved but never went anywhere. She'd bum a cigarette from Cody, behind the bar, and look for a cowboy with legs she could crawl like a ladder from the side, when she got him back to his bed, which would not be made, in a house where there would be a pile of empty beer cans next to the fridge. They'd get it on fast and easy and then she could come home and forget how different Jake had been in every regard. No, she almost laughed, Jake had been no lean cowboy. She never would have dreamed she'd have taken to his muscle and brawn and darkness, liking her men wiry, ropy, concave, and blond. Jake was the opposite of almost all those things. He even made the bed most mornings. He had made her aware of the mess in her own house so that now she could hardly bear it any way but neat. He'd taught Hannah something about table manners and picking up after herself. He'd taught Lizzie a different way of looking at the world. And maybe he'd made it impossible, ever since, for her to want what she'd always thought she'd wanted. But riding her cowboy, making him ride her, maybe she would stop thinking that there was something she could be doing differently than she was, or than she had, or than she should.

"What are you looking at, Ma? You look scary."

Lizzie dropped her eyes away from the TV and found Hannah and Summer staring at her. She looked around at the messy den, at the empty basket for the toys and the toys themselves scattered throughout the room, at the piles of books and scattered leaves of newspaper and videos and blankets and diapers and dishes; you picked things up and there they were, waiting to be picked up again.

"I was just thinking."

"Well, you looked scary," Summer said. "You looked mad."

"Not mad," Hannah said. "Sad, maybe."

The girls discussed the expression on her face. Lizzie pondered asking Maud to baby-sit some night while she hit the Billy Goat. She wanted to feel that power again. Something like her idea of riding a horse bareback through wind, something purple-black and immense and stormy. When this mood came upon her she wished she could be the one to do the prodding and the thrusting. The urge was something that wanted out, the way that men could pump *into* something, pump and thrust and twist until they exploded and were spent.

"Mad!" Summer said, sticking her tongue out at Hannah.

"Bedtime, girls." Lizzie herded them ahead of her, trundled them upstairs to accomplish the nighttime rituals, checked on Theo.

Later she transferred leftover potatoes and a hamburger to a pie tin, covered it with cellophane wrap, and stored it in the refrigerator. Summer could take it to Sam in the morning, before school. She sponged down the counter and started the dishwasher. The sound of its motor filled the kitchen, penetrating even into the den, where she began to pick up toys and straighten the mess. Soon she would be grateful for its homemaking drone. Any moment now she would appreciate the dishwasher's hum, that nighttime, cozy, shut-in, terribly safe sound.

CHAPTER 16

JAKE

the moon's a pale sliver in the dark night sky
a sickle's edge that gleams against the stars
it's a rustler's moon
and he gallops towards the border
someone's going to lose something tonight

Fable Mountain sang its siren song. Took Jake weeks to succumb. Got caught up in solving a software problem. Had to find two days in a row where he didn't have a gig or rehearsal in the evening, arrange to take those days off. Rich Pack called to say something was weird with the propane heater out at the trailer. After a wasted day Jake discovered a faulty thermocouple. Three days later he'd finally tracked down his pack, stored with his sleeping bag, patched with silver gaffer's tape, in Sue's basement. His Ensolite pad, stiff from disuse, was rolled up under their stairs. Finally he was in his Volvo, driving through the brilliant yellow aspens that lined Fable Mountain Pass.

He parked his car at the base of the trail. The path, in his memory a faint marking through rocks and manzanita, appeared ominously worn. Trees nearby seemed faded, jaded, as if people and footsteps and exhaust and admiration had sucked something vital from their leaves. He sighed, heaved his pack up onto his back.

Four hours later, halfway up the trail, he stopped for the tenth, fifteenth time to rest. He was out of shape. He couldn't believe how much. On the steeper bits he had to bend over every hundred yards to ease the stitch in his side. Of course he'd stayed away from the mountain: Memories lurked everywhere. Smells, sounds, blue sky, pines, reminders of his last hike here. Their hike.

He concentrated on the pain of the pack's straps pressing into his shoulders, already wondering how on earth he'd get through the night without a gig, rehearsal, at least his guitar and a beer, TV, to distract him. Off to his right and far below a highway snaked down the mountain. Pale gray ribbon. Colored beads of cars.

In two, out two, in two. He forced himself to breathe in time to his steps. If only the world could be composed of binary systems. Everything would be simpler. Air hit the back of his throat, cool and thin. The sun pressed, warm hands against his face. He stopped again. Far beneath him, gray weather-beaten fences and collapsed roofs of ancient cabins looked like moldering Tinkertoys. Aspens flashed an occasional silver underside, but other than the green of pines most of the trees were canopied in gold. A leaf in autumn is sunlight you could hold in your hand, he thought. It was a spectacular, glorious sight, and he was sick at heart that all the beauty could not make him glad.

In spite of a chill wind, he'd long ago shed shirt and T-shirt. Which led him again to the hike with Lizzie. She'd pulled off her tank top and hiked bare-chested too. Breasts pulled up and out by the straps of her backpack. He'd stepped up to kiss them. Sucked salt sweat off her nipples. Packs off, they found a niche yards from the trail, behind a large rock. Arranging his shorts and shirt beneath her knees, his back against the dirt and granite. Afterward she hiked ahead of him, wearing nothing but her gray socks and hiking boots. They glimpsed a couple a good way off, heading down. Lizzie marched on. He followed, proud of her good looks and her boldness. The woman smiled cheerfully and waved. The man, passing, had examined his beautiful Lizzie in a series of furtive looks.

A strange groan thrummed the back of his throat. With no one around to hear, he let it grow: hum, cry, moan of a cat in heat. But this made him run out of breath again. He stopped, stared down at his boots. Good solid boots. Dependable track in the compact disc player of his mind to skip to. Lots of associations with these boots. Bought them when he was thirty-something, living with Minerva in Nashville—

But there it was: he'd also worn them when he was with Lizzie. Where could he ever live, where could he ever go, that wouldn't have a thousand reminders. What he had done. Had not done. Could have, should have done differently. All those pictures in his head. Pictographs, petroglyphs, painted and pecked into the stone of his memory. A chisel, a hammer, a maul couldn't bang them away.

Hey, bud. Wherever you go, there you are, you know.

Minerva. Laughing in her tinkly way when he'd talk about moving away from Nashville, leaving everything behind, making a fresh start. *Wherever you go, there you are.* It hadn't made sense to him until this minute.

"Shut up shut up shut *up*." He made one boot move, then the other.

He was Marley's ghost, shackled to a clanking jangling chain of wrongdoings, the rusted links and padlocks of happiness he'd known with Lizzie. He'd drag these fetters around forever, into every encounter, every love affair, every gig. Hauling it up this mountain. Hauling it back down. He'd never be rid of it.

He scrambled up the last long hill of shale. Stood on the granite outcropping: Fable Point. He'd made it. He gave himself some credit for that. The sun hovered, briefly halved by the horizon. Late light gleamed on meadow and tree. Dusk layered the valley beneath him. He stared down at pinpoints of moving headlights far below, aware of the earth's turning, moving him away from the sun and into the night. He was turning on it, a speck at the top of a mountain. He shivered, pulled his down vest from the pack and began to collect wood.

He took the potatoes out from beneath the coals long before they were done. He'd forgotten salt and pepper. He ate one anyway, raw, crunchy, unseasoned. The noodles and tuna tasted decent. Desert was a bar of chocolate. Wishing he'd brought a flask of whiskey, he played with the fire with a long stick whose tip he whittled with his army knife.

A rising cold wind drove him into his sleeping bag. He folded his hands under his head, stared up at the flickering wash of stars. Set his mind on rehearsal logistics. Computed electrical outputs of various instruments, the amplifiers that held them. Tangled again with the software problem at work. Pondered opportunities for intelligent life on other planets. Worried if he'd ever sell another song. Fretted about what it meant that he'd had to take a day job. He didn't want to admit he was tired. The deal at work was he could keep his own hours, as long as he made his weekly quota. Even so, rehearsing, playing weeknight gigs—it was arduous.

Not for the first time he wondered if he should just take the band apart. Become the software maven he could see was possible. He was good at it. But, as happened each time he pursued this train of thought, he came back to the same conclusion. He'd built his life around his music. It would do something bad to his soul to abandon it now.

He watched the moon's majestic rise, watched it transform itself from a luminous semiorb into a flawed spotlight aimed at him from the sky. Closed his eyes against its insistent light, a prisoner facing interrogation.

"I'm pregnant, you know," she'd said one morning. They'd made love. He was drowsing, a leg thrown over hers.

His eyes flicked open. He stared at her.

She lay face up. "Yes," she said, nodding as if he'd asked. "I'm certain."

Jake didn't move. The mattress bounced. Lizzie shook him. He smiled, avoiding her eyes. Siamese cat eyes, slanting up at the corners ever so slightly, giving her a perpetual look of intrigue and amusement. "So?"

"That's great!"

She drew back. The smile left her eyes. "I see."

"See what?"

But she only nodded, slowly.

"Liz, I can't—" He stopped. "I just don't have—"

He couldn't think of the appropriate word to describe what he didn't have. *Time* seemed callous, *money* materialistic. *Want* seemed cold—he did want kids. Someday. He wasn't ready, one more thing he wasn't. Considering his advanced age, it was hard to admit that. "The wherewithal." He wondered what that word meant, exactly.

"But I do." She patted him.

Jake rose to face her, both of them sitting cross-legged. He took her hands. "Liz. We don't have to go through with this."

Her fingers went limp within his. A slow disdain entered her eyes.

"Sue can help us out, down at the clinic," he pressed on. "I'm happy to pay for it—"

"It." She slid off the bed and walked to the window. Winter sunlight slipped beneath the curtain, gleaming pale on her pale skin. The thatch of hair between her thighs glinted red. She gazed at him. "You can be such a creep."

He repeated the word with its knife-edged sound. Outrage stirred within him. His head felt triple its usual size. A buffalo, eyes perched on either side of his skull, peering in two different directions so he couldn't get a solid look at the problem. Or a bull in that famous china shop, baffled, infuriated by the chaos created by his smallest step.

"All this time I thought you *knew*."

"Knew *what*?" Nothing about this conversation made sense. He felt absurd, sitting cross-legged and naked on the wet spot. He lurched awkwardly away from its dampness, wrapped the sheet, toga-like, around his upper body. "We talked about this." At least he sounded calm and reasonable. "I asked you to take precautions. You said you were."

Lizzie held the curtain away from the window so she could look outside. "I didn't say I would take precautions. I said I knew when I was fertile."

"But—" This was, in fact, exactly the conversation that had taken place. He felt even more like a bull, baffled, weaving on bloodied sand, watching the picadors ride away.

"It's simple, Jake-o. I want a kid."

"You already have two." He withered under her look. "Look. Liz, I do too. I've told you that." Tumbled tricycles, bales of disposable diapers, piles of doctor bills loomed over him, spun in circles over his head.

"I don't think so."

"Just not at this particular juncture. Not when I'm trying to put this band on the map. I'm barely supporting myself—" He stopped. He was forty. When would this no longer be true? He'd have to get a job. A real job. The kind that paid dependable money. He groaned.

"There's never a good time to have a kid, Jake." Lizzie shook her head at the apparent truth of this. "And I don't need supporting. I've never asked that, I never wanted that."

A shroud of certainty wrapped him in cold, damp folds. He'd never dared to ask—what would the words have been? Throw your lot in with mine, Liz. Walk through life by my side. *Marry me.* It was marriage. Ritualized or not, named or unnamed. Sensing she didn't want that, he'd balanced on the edge of commitment pretending he didn't want it either.

Well, do you, buddy? This is a good time to find out.

Lizzie knelt on the edge of the mattress. "I think we'll have made a beautiful baby." She crawled towards him. He smelled the salt-fish scent of their sex. She nipped his ankle with white teeth, laid her head on his foot, smiled up at him. Her hair pooled out onto the sheet, the nape of her neck exposed, her backbone a mountain ridge in miniature leading to the soft swell of her buttocks.

He had thought of bending down to kiss the array of brown-red curls. He could have bent to her ear and whispered that she was a screwball. That it would be fun. They'd do it together. But he hadn't done those things.

Jake writhed up out of his sleeping bag. What would have been different? he wondered, picking up his whittled stick and poking, hard, at the coals. Would Theo not exist? Or would he be Theo's father in practice as well as in fact? In fact as well as in theory?

He wrapped the sleeping bag around his shoulders, an immense nylon muffler. Found his way by the light of the gibbous moon out to the edge of Fable Point. Stared out into the void, into the heart of darkness beneath him. He could have been less self-righteous. He could have been a willing participant. Could have held her hand during labor, or whatever fathers did. It was overwhelmingly, excruciatingly awful that he had allowed her to go through the birth—and the pregnancy, and whatever else—by herself. He had not been there for any of it. How could he? How had he? He understood why dogs and wolves bay at the moon.

When they'd first met, when she reluctantly agreed to go places and do things with him, he'd been struck at how little faith she had in the usefulness of men. *Except for their sperm,* she'd told him any number of times, one of the many hard-edged, caustic comments she flung about. He'd begun to coax her out of these disparaging remarks. Flattered himself that as the months, and then a year, then two, went by, she'd given him, and by extension men, a more respected—or at least tolerated—place in her worldview. He'd betrayed this utterly. Held the football out, taken it away.

"Lizzie," he whispered. "I'm sorry."

A pair of headlights, two tiny eyes, prowled the road far below. In the immense loneliness he felt at that moment, in the anguish of understanding that he could not pull time back to do this differently, he was glad of this distant company. Sue had wanted to know what had happened. But who—*how*—could he ever, ever tell?

He made his way back to the fire. Coals glowed red and mottled black, tiny cities falling to hoarding marauders.

She hadn't moved when he'd pulled his foot from beneath her cheek, slid off the bed. His body felt like a crude hunk of uncarved marble, one of those Michelangelo statues Lizzie had showed him in a book. Bodies writhing out of stone. At the same time he felt massively horny. Wanted to ravish her, push her up against the wall, make her come. He felt sperm leaking down his thigh. Extricated his boxers from his jeans beside the bed. As he held them out, balancing on one leg, he almost fell over. He caught himself on the edge of the bed, avoided meeting Lizzie's eye. It was the sort of thing that would make them both laugh and then he'd be hard put to recapture the outrage he felt, that he wanted—absolutely needed—to hold on to.

"What are you doing, Jake?" Lizzie sat up. Back curving up from the lilt of calves and thigh. Swell of breast half hidden by the long, straight arm. Blush of telltale tawny red along each cheekbone.

Jake pondered her question as he slid his arms into his shirt, lined up the bottom buttonhole and button. Maybe one of the things that was delicious about making love to Lizzie was the danger of exactly what it was that had occurred. When their bodies entwined it was never just the two of them. Always there was this other, potential third entity in the picture. He felt watched. Oddly protected. Assessed and participatory in a process to which he realized he had, at some point, agreed.

But he couldn't say any of this. "I always thought"—he tucked in his shirt, zipped his jeans—"that I'd be fully involved in this. That when it happened—"

"Couldn't have done it without you."

He yanked the belt tight. His eyes hurt.

"It's a lot more fun that way," she said. "Sexy. Definitely. Making a baby."

She was talking about Blair, who had happily participated in the creation of Hannah. As he now happily contributed to her food, housing, education, clothes. And happily lived two thousand miles away.

"And I miss having a baby around. I love them small, dependent." Her face creased as if something about this statement was not to her liking. Her eyes threw a gauntlet across the space between them. "They haven't figured out yet they can leave."

"Sounds plain old selfish to me," he said. "Just doing what you want."

"Oh it is not selfish," Lizzie said, too fast. She scrambled backwards off the bed, mouth and face wrenched out of shape. "I don't do what I want," she yelled. "I do what other people want all the fucking *time*."

"You didn't *ask* me," Jake yelled back. "Do you *get* that? You didn't even talk it over with me. I *trusted* you. It's such a monstrous—" He pawed the air, looking for the word he wanted. "*Betrayal*. Like you went and fucked somebody else."

For a moment she looked aghast. Then she laughed, a harsh single sound. "Give me a fucking break."

"We had an *agreement*."

"I never agreed to anything."

"You didn't disagree."

"No, I didn't disagree."

Jake slapped the back of the chair, caught it before it fell. He had lost this round. Wonderful, horrible, that she should stand there facing him, fully naked, and admit this. His hands shook as he pulled on his socks and boots.

"What are you doing, Jake?" Her eyes glittered.

"I'm not doing anything. You are." Or, he thought but couldn't say, We are.

She averted her face. Tangle of red-brown curls. He walked towards the door, boot heels loud against the wood floor. She'll call to me, he thought. Before I even get as far as the stairs.

He waited for the whispered "Wait!" The sound of bare feet running, the press of her knees as she leapt onto his back. This had happened once before. Or he could turn back. That, too, had solved a fight. He paused for a long time at the front door, pretending to search in his jacket pocket for something other than his keys. But she did not come, and he did not know how to return. He slammed the door hard.

The air was cold. He cracked ice in a pothole with the heel of his boot as he crossed the driveway. Waited beside his car, staring up at the bedroom window, at the dusting of snow on the peak of Fable Mountain, at the window again. The curtain stayed closed. Finally he opened the door of his Volvo. It creaked, moaned, screamed its protest as he pulled it wide. She must have heard. They'd talked about how human the door's anguished sound was.

He turned the key in the ignition, craned his neck to look up through the windshield. But no face appeared in the window, no hand drew back the curtain.

He turned the car around, headed down the driveway. I'm not doing this, he thought, I'm not. But he had.

He poked with his stick at his flagging fire. The wind sighed, whirled through the trees, drew closer. Battered his hair around his face, shook the branches. He was freezing. He lowered himself back into the depths of his sleeping bag, closed his eyes against the pines that lurched and swayed above him, desailed masts on a ship climbing and descending mountainous waves, heading towards the infinite swirl of the Milky Way.

He had to hope that some insurance through the college helped cover whatever maternity and delivery had cost. He had no idea. Could have asked Sue these questions but hadn't wanted her to ask anything in return. Vague references to commitment, to different points of view on essential things, was how he'd dealt with most of the questions, spoken, unspoken, from those who knew they'd broken up just before her belly began to round.

He did try calling. She hung up when she heard his voice. He left messages on the phone machine. No answer. In a last-ditch effort he'd gone by the house, twice, but neither Lizzie nor Jeep and the girls were home. Left a note. No reply.

Before he left for Nashville he sent her a check for two thousand dollars. A great deal more than he could afford but so much less than he felt it should be—and how could this come down to *money?*— that he almost didn't send it at all. Agonized for days over a letter but in a fit of exasperation finally mailed the check off without enclosing anything else in the envelope. It had been months before the check had cleared.

By then he'd fled to Nashville. On the lam from love.

≍

The sun was high, halo behind feathery pine branches, when Jake finally drew his head up out of its nest of sleeping bag and curled arm. He'd wanted to be up in time to watch the sunrise from Fable Point, had planned to greet the new day, greet the new life he'd come up here to find. Instead, feeling drugged, he'd slept on for hours.

Bare-legged, bare-bottomed, freezing, he sat on his sleeping bag, staring at the ashes of the fire, rubbing his eyes. The effort to stand, pull on pants, sweater, vest, to light the kerosene stove for coffee, seemed insurmountable. But eventually he crouched, shivering, hands held over the tiny bubbles forming on the bottom of the saucepan. His sleeping bag, airing over a branch, looked like a patched purple caterpillar crawling into the tall pine.

He closed his eyes. When he and Lizzie had slept up here, they lingered in the morning inside their zipped-together sleeping bags for a long time. Gazing up, head pillowed on his shoulder, she explained, "The reason why the sky is so pale at these altitudes? Because the air is thinner." Her voice conveyed utter certainty. "You aren't looking through so many layers. There's veils and veils of this cobwebby fabric, one layer on top of another." She undulated her arms above them to demonstrate. "That's what makes the deep blue of, say, tropical islands. Layers upon layers. But up here most of the veils disappear. So you're getting the purest of the blues, the wash on the original canvas." She turned to look at him. "What do you think?"

"I don't know, Liz. Your being fanciful is not something I'm prepared for."

There had been one of those moments, eyes naked with the love they never spoke. Then her face changed, grew sour.

"I'm not being fanciful. My sister is. It's Maud's theory. She came up with it when she was about seven. Mom thought it was so fucking *delightful*, talked about it for years while Dad smoked his pipe and said we'd all heard about it enough already and it wasn't all *that* great. But he was proud."

Voice bitter. Face turned into his arm. He held her, thinking how much there was about his Lizzie he didn't understand, and how much he looked forward to sorting it out. Little by little, like a song lyric you just keep worrying at until it scans and rhymes and adds its layer of meaning:

> *leaning into loneliness*
> *my shot glass full of wry*
> *stood this round and others too*
> *I'm drunk with wonderin' why*

The flame beneath the saucepan, almost invisible in the bright sunlight, barely warmed the water for the instant coffee he'd brought in a plastic bag. He used too much of the powder. The resulting concoction was silty as mud. *Crying like a fire in the sun*, Bob Dylan had written. Exactly how he himself felt. He sat on the very edge of Fable Point, legs dangling over the jutting granite shelf. Rubbed his hands along his thighs, pressed thumbs into his calf muscles, which ached from his scrambles of yesterday. *It's all over now, Baby Blue,* Dylan rasped at him, over and over again, inside his head.

The coffee was undrinkable. He threw it out, restuffed his bag, kicked dirt over the fire, assembled his pack. He'd arranged to stay away from work for two days and nights, but found himself in a tremendous hurry to leave. A number of times, headed back down the trail, he found his mouth twisted into an involuntary grimace, as if he'd smelled something bad. That his face kept adapting of its own accord to this sorrowful, dissatisfied scowl made him realize that he was sorrowful, he was dissatisfied. What had he expected? Revelation? Enlightenment beneath the Piney Tree? Moses on Fable Mountain, arms full of inscribed stone tablets?

He stumbled over a root. His momentum down the path almost catapulted him into the air. One hand scraped along the ground as he struggled to get his feet beneath him.

He stood, breathing hard. Listened to his heart sending the baggage carousel of blood around his veins. Noticed, shocked, that the colorful trees of yesterday were stripped bare. The night's wind had left only an occasional yellow leaf clinging to a branch. All around him was a kind of devastation. He supposed he was lucky it had not been a snowstorm.

Hand to his chest, he felt his heart thump against the skin that covered it. He'd believed Lizzie would not do it. Wanted to believe she had not? Surely there was some trick involved. Underneath her actions there must—mustn't there?—persist a desire to keep him a part of her life. He'd been sending money once a month for a year now, one of the reasons for this "real job" he'd taken. Each month Lizzie returned the check. He deposited the money. Theo's account. But it wasn't enough. Theo would grow up—was growing up!—without him. Whether or not he agreed with its processes, life kept on in its inexorable sweep. The Mississippi in full flood.

You can't step into the same river twice, bud, Minerva had told him.

They'd been separating their possessions, and, holding a footstool they'd bought together against his chest, he'd harshly, unexpectedly, begun to weep. He knew the answer but he asked anyway. Did they really need to get a divorce? She held him against her ample breasts, always such a surprise on that skinny, bony body, and rocked him, silver bracelets clinking. "You can't step in the same river twice."

"That doesn't make any sense," he'd said. Snot ran backwards down his throat. "It's never made any sense."

"There's nothing we can hold on to, love," she said. "Especially if we try. Whoops." She moved a hand as if to grab after something. "There it goes."

The water goes on rolling

he wrote into a song not long after.

> *Down down down.*
> *The river goes on flowing*
> *We can't step in it twice*

Standing on the slope of Fable Mountain, hands on his knees, Jake argued with Minerva. You could step into the river again and see what happened, he told her. You could step into the river knowing it was a different place! He saw her slit her eyes at him. *Maybe,* she said, *as long as you don't need things to be the way they were before. As long as you're willing to let the river do its thing.*

He imagined plastic dolls and an empty gallon bleach bottle, submerged houses with A-frame peaks and a rooster on top, and him swimming after. Swallowing muddy roiling water, one hand held up hailing whoever it was he thought would let him undo the terrible, irreversible damage he had done.

He walked the rest of the way down the mountain, feet treading heavily on the gold and silver coins of aspen and maple. All the leaves would fall, the rain would spot them brown. They would deteriorate and disappear.

He heaved his pack into the back seat of the Volvo. There was more to the metaphor, of course. They would fold themselves into the earth, compost or evaporate, become dust, ground, rain, roots, air, they would return in some form. Would love, too, come round again?

> *Rolling, rolling rolling*

he mourned tunefully as he drove down Fable Pass, hunched over the steering wheel, bulky and baffled.

> *The river goes on flowing*
> *And you can't step in it twice*

Then he tried—it took some rhythmic shifts to get the second line to scan inside the tune—

> *The river goes on rolling*
> *Can you step into it twice?*

CHAPTER 17

LIZZIE

NOTES FROM BENEATH THE MAGNETS ON LIZZIE'S FRIDGE

Lizzie—
Was reading my Electric Code book and found this—thot of you. Gosh.
Wonder why.
    Most modern switchboards are totally enclosed to reduce to a minimum
    the probability of communicating fire to adjacent combustible materials
    and to guard live parts.
See ya around—

                                                                        SPARKY

Lizzie had never run a phone jack out to her studio, preferring to believe that her time there was inviolable. Nevertheless, she dragged the old dial phone, with its long black cord, out to the steps of the main house, where she could answer it if she wanted to. And which, though she pretended otherwise, she always did.

The girls were at school. Theo was down for a nap. She lit a fire in the woodstove and got to work, taking pleasure in the silence, the image she could see forming on the canvas, even the too-cold tubes of paint. As she squeezed a worm of rose madder onto the plate she used as palette, the jingle of the phone made her pause. Brush in one hand, rag in the other, she trotted across the gravel driveway and snatched up the phone on its seventh ring. "Hello?"

There was a long pause. Then, "Hello, Liz."

The smell of turpentine wafted up to her from the brush she held in her hand. She heard in the far distance the buzz of a chain saw, or perhaps someone riding the low, fall-barren hills on a motorcycle.

"Jake," she said. His name, a single syllable in any case, emerged harsh and flat. Lizzie thought, with some triumph, that there was no welcome in it.

"Look. I've been thinking." Jake paused between almost every pair of words. "About a lot of stuff. Theo. And you. I'm— Could I just come over? Talk, maybe?"

"No. I don't think so." Her voice said this. She heard it from a distance. "No, I think not," she said again, and sat on one of the wooden steps. She zipped her down vest up to her chin and stared at Sam's truck, parked across the driveway. In the fields that surrounded her house, tall weeds rustled, emphasizing the silence at the other end of the line. She should just hang up, she told herself.

"I'm terribly sorry, Liz. Does it help at all that I'm terribly sorry? That I want to talk about it? Do something about it?"

"Not particularly." She wondered if he was in the bedroom. Or the kitchen, leaning against the refrigerator. But it would be neither. Since going to and returning from Nashville he'd secured a different place to live. She no longer knew the rooms he occupied. "I'm going to hang up now," she said. "Bye."

The phone's sullen black shape stayed resolutely silent.

She headed back to the studio. After the chill outside it was suddenly too hot. She tossed her down vest into a corner and slid onto the stool in front of her canvas, hooking her toes over a rung. Having given up, at least for a while, on what she mockingly called to herself her Southwestern *Mona Lisa*, she was working on what until a few days ago had been Untitled. Maud had taken one look and said, "Ophelia!" Having been reminded of the story, Lizzie found herself liking the title. A gauzy blue gown, infiltrated with the image of a kachina, was supposed to melt into, become, the water in which a woman was lying. But right now the bleed looked like an amateurish mess. The cloud of pale green hair, supporting cacti, a tumbleweed, a mass of geraniums, looked crude, not delicate and magical as she'd intended. She squeezed some umber next to the rose madder, daubed these two colors together with the tip of a brush.

A knock startled her. Sam stood in the open doorway. His hair, usually a neat plait down his back, hung loose. He was panting, his cheeks a terrible shade of fake-cherry red. The stool scraped as she stood up. "Sam!"

"I heard the phone. Wasn't for me?"

"What's wrong?"

Sam turned away, his lower lip thrust out, as it was when he was hammering, sawing, laying stonework. "Nothing." His face looked blotchy, wrinkled, awful. "You paint, now."

Lizzie put a hand out, but he waved it rudely away. Sam, who was never rude. He stumbled back outside, his shoulder banging once, painfully hard, against the door. He pulled it shut behind him.

"Sam!" She yanked the door open, ran to catch up.

He was breathing heavily, wild-eyed, but his mouth was not sagging to one side. "I shouldn't disturb you. I can't find Luna." He shoved his hands in the pockets of his overalls, took them out, looked at them. "I can't find her. I've called, searched everywhere. I've called—" He passed the cuff of his shirt across his eyes. His skin looked gray, the lines in his face cavernous.

Lizzie put a hand on his arm. He took a step away, shaking his head. "She's crept off to die, maybe. They do that, when it's time. I've been thinking it was her time, hoping, just not yet."

Lizzie climbed beside him towards his caboose. His eyes were red, the tip of his nose red. He stopped, panting. "I just thought— Someone calling because they found her, read her collar." He waved an aimless hand. "You'll let me know."

"Of course."

He peered at her, wild hair, wild eyes, through the wire mesh of the screen door. "Go paint."

"Sam," she said. "Let me fix you some tea."

He shook his head, pushed the door closed.

A cold wind tugged at her hair. She whistled and called for Luna, hanging on the *u* as Summer did.

One of the nights, that first winter when Sam slept over now and again, he hadn't been able to get an erection. "Lizzie, I need some help here," he'd said. She hadn't known what he meant until he guided her hand to his limp penis, his balls soft as kittens. Sam was then well into his fifties, a handsome man, grizzled yet fit, by far the oldest lover she'd ever had. She'd encountered this failing of male sex again, more often as she and her lovers grew older, but at the time it had shocked her. Not so much the guiding of her hand, which other lovers had done, but the admission of need, the sweet request. *I need some help here.*

The wind buffeted her as she held her knuckles poised in front of his door. What must Sam be going through, sitting alone inside the dark musky trailer, without his Luna?

But he'd closed the door firmly. She had learned these were times when he would not be disturbed. She stood, irresolute, and then, holding her mind away from her motives, ran back down the hill, picked up the phone where it sat on the top step, and dialed.

"How'd you manage to keep the same phone number?" she said when Jake answered.

A pause, then, "They hadn't given it away. A year and a half, and it was still available. I asked for it back."

"Come now, before I change my mind."

"I'll be there."

Lizzie carried the phone inside and set it on the counter. She felt beneath her breastbone with her fingers. Her heart pounded, she was breathless, and it wasn't just the run down the hill. It was Jake's "I'll be there." That certain, infallible tone reminded her that she had allowed herself to depend on him as she never had on Blair, and certainly not on Sparky.

It was Sparky who'd pointed out this—failing? attribute?—to her. During one of their final fights he'd shouted, "You're a fucking control freak." He'd been rubbing his fingers over his head, over and over, so his hair stood up all over his scalp. "You have to be in charge. You have to call the shots. 'I'll take care of it, I'll take care of it,'" he mimicked. His stubby hands, permanently stained with grease and oil, stabbed the air. "But no one better offer to take the *slightest* care of you. Oh no, it might leave you vulnerable, it might leave you *indebted* and then where would you be? You and your huge fucking ego. Noooo, that might mean you were just an average, normal person who maybe *loves* someone. Who maybe, once in her goddamned life, might let herself be *loved*."

Her answer had been to tell him to get his fucking car parts out of her driveway.

She got up and slammed shut an open cupboard door. She called for Luna off the back porch, off the front. She started up the hill to Sam's, carrying cheese and crackers, but came back down. The trailer had a force field around it she didn't know how to penetrate. She rinsed a plate, a bowl, picked up a few of the toys that littered the floor. She detoured herself away from the mirror in the bathroom, although she was tempted to rouse Theo so that she could be sporting him on one hip in the kitchen when Jake arrived. Stirring a quickly thrown-together pot of stew, just to complete the picture.

Having thought of and rejected these ideas, she realized anything she might do would feel like acting, and she was not the actor in the family. She retrieved her down vest from the studio and sat on the house steps, hugging herself against the wind, until Jake's Volvo appeared at the end of the long, unpaved road.

He pulled up, nodded to her out the window. She was glad his face was in shadow, that she couldn't see his eyes. He turned the car off. They stared at each other across the gravel drive, laid since he'd last been to the house. She scratched at a splotch of bleach on her jeans.

"You're looking good," Jake said. He tried the door and swore, then looked at her, as if he expected some response. Lizzie had to squint to keep from smiling, watching him climb across the passenger seat and out the other side.

He had showered recently, his hair was wet. He wore jeans, a deep blue shirt, his leather jacket. As he walked closer she folded her arms across her chest. "At least it doesn't screech anymore," she said.

"What?"

"The door," she said. "It always screeched."

"Yes." He stopped at the foot of the stairs. "It doesn't screech. But it doesn't open either." He tried a smile.

Lizzie swiped her hand in front of her face as if a fly were hovering there, although there wasn't one.

Jake's face looked pale and his eyes tight, drawn in. "Lizzie." He sounded as if he was pleading with her.

She waved again at the nonexistent fly, avoiding his eyes. "Luna's lost," she said. "Or dead." Horrified to find tears in her eyes, in her voice, she stood and headed up the stairs. "Want a beer?"

"What's this about Luna?" He followed her.

"What I told you. I don't know more than that."

"Sam knows?"

"He's the one told me." Again the tears swelled in her throat. She pulled two beers from the fridge and jerked their caps against the bottle opener fastened next to the stove.

Jake was taking in the potbellied stove and the flagstone floor. "Looks different around here. Nice."

"Thanks to Southwest Ink."

"You're making a living as an artist, Liz. Good for you."

"Although that's not really art, is it?"

Jake shook his head at her. "Don't do that with me. That's crap." He stepped carefully, avoiding scattered toys on the floor, and examined the dozens of photographs tacked to the wall beside the kitchen table. She was aware that he would be looking for two things— pictures of Theo, and pictures of the companions who would have replaced Jake in these past two years. She sliced a lime, pressed a wedge into each beer, and walked over to stand beside him. With the top of the long-necked bottle she pointed to one of the photographs. "Theo," she said.

He peered at the three-inch-square of glossy color.

Lizzie didn't want to tell him, *he has your hair, he has your eyes.* She probed at his upper arm with a beer bottle. "He's not awake yet."

"Napping." Jake nodded as he said this, as if napping described a complicated passage of childhood, something about which he could say a great deal, if asked. He took the beer, looking dazed. Lizzie led him out to the back porch, where the eaves would protect them from the wind. She did not know why she didn't want to sit with him in the kitchen, in the living room, in the den. They settled into the heavy wrought-iron chairs that Blair, lucky enough to be independently wealthy, had made during his welding period, which had preceded his jewelry business, which had been followed by his decision to move to Hollywood to pursue screenwriting, and from which locale he generously contributed to Hannah's, and the household's, well-being.

Jake squeezed the lime into the neck of the bottle, then sucked on the rind, making a little green grin in front of his teeth. He removed it when Lizzie did not smile, and tossed it into the bushes beside the porch. His forehead gleamed with sweat, though he sat hunched in his jacket as if he were cold. Lizzie found herself with a weird, mean smile on her face. She hadn't known that making him feel uncomfortable might make her feel so good. She clasped her hands around her knees, drawing her legs up close to her body.

Jake leaned forward. "Is there something we can do?"

"Whoa! You don't beat around the bush, do you?"

Jake stared at her, puzzled. Then his face cleared. "I mean about Luna."

Lizzie swigged some beer.

"Should we drive around, look for her?"

"Sam said he'd looked everywhere." Lizzie hugged her knees, hard. At this moment she didn't like herself at all.

"Liz," Jake said.

"It's *Lizzie*. Lizzie Lizzie."

"You're not making this so easy."

"Why the fuck should I?" Her face felt hot. They stared at each other and then across the field around the house. The grasses shifted color, the afternoon wind like a hand running against, and then with, the nap of their high yellow velvet. The buzzing sound floated towards them, louder and then soft. Under that came the rattle of dry stalks of tall grass.

"Goddamn dirt bikes," he said. "Wrecking the hills."

They listened again. "If you've come to talk, talk," Lizzie said.

Jake stared down at the beer, which he held clenched in both hands. He jerked his bottom jaw forward and back several times, lifted his bottle and took a long swallow. "I suppose I deserve this."

Lizzie shrugged.

"When's he wake up?"

"Any minute. Summer will be home soon." Lizzie sucked beer through the lime. "Don't expect her to remember you."

"Jesus, Liz, of course she'll remember me. Hannah too." But he sounded doubtful.

Night after night, for weeks after Jake had left, Hannah had cried herself to sleep, asking for him, wanting to know when he was coming back. Lizzie, remembering, pulled her heels against her buttocks and shook the hair back from her face. Just yesterday Hannah had looked up from cutting construction paper into paper doilies as a present for Maud and had said, "Remember when Jake carried me on his shoulders to the waterfall?"

"Me too," Summer chorused. "Remember?"

Lizzie had said no. Though she remembered distinctly.

"Hannah's got gymnastics. She gets home late."

"I bet she's good at that!"

"Pretty good." Another long silence. Lizzie stared at Jake's profile. That round jaw, the nose that turned up ever so slightly at the end, giving him, despite his most serious efforts, a mischievous, elfin quality. He cleared his throat. "So. Maud finally did what she kept saying she was going to do and left L.A. I hear she's got a place on Emerson?"

"This is the smallest fucking town."

"I was having dinner with Willy and Sue. Some customer told Willy she's working at the Red Garter."

"You come over here to talk about Maud?" Lizzie tipped her bottle to her lips again, though it was empty.

"This is called small talk, Liz. It fills the voids on the way to big talk."

Lizzie showed him her teeth, where she had stored her lime wedge.

He cleared his throat. "I'd been thinking a lot about this. I mean, I always think a lot about you." He didn't look at her. She watched his Adam's apple bounce as he swallowed. "And then when I was visiting Sue—Johnny was watching TV. We ate dinner. None of that's important." He sipped beer. "Johnny's gotten so big. You wouldn't believe it."

"Of course I'd believe it."

"So many changes. He wants to play drums." Jake's eyes flashed, sharing a joke. "You can probably imagine Big Bad Willy's response to that."

Lizzie almost laughed, imagining indeed Big Bad Willy's response to that, but she said nothing, running thumb and forefinger up and down the cool, wet neck of the beer bottle.

Jake watched her fingers, looked away. "Anyway. I took Sue's advice and climbed Fable last week, thought about you, about us, and Theo. And I just feel so rotten, Liz, I can't tell you. I just thought we could maybe—"

"Another beer?"

She headed for the kitchen without waiting for an answer and yanked open the refrigerator door. As she cut two more slices of lime she heard Theo calling. "Ma? Ma!"

She carried the beer bottles out to the table. "Theo's up," she said. "I'll just get him."

As Jake stared up at her, startled, anticipatory, Lizzie saw her son there. Theo had already developed the wide-open, almost black eyes of his father. She pulled away from whatever emotion this stirred in her. "Don't expect him to reach out his hands and say, 'Dada.' "

Jake hovered between standing and sitting, clearly unsure as to whether he could come with her.

"Ma!" Theo's voice left the arena of demand and headed into panic. Lizzie ran up the stairs. Jake, heavy-footed, followed. She was reminded of certain afternoons, with the girls at school, when she'd lead Jake up to the bedroom. He would put his hands on her hips, rocking them back and forth as if in climbing the stairs he was climbing into her.

Flushed, she stopped outside Theo's room. "Stay here for a sec," she said. "Since he's never laid eyes on you, he has no idea who the fuck you are."

She slipped into Theo's room before she could see the response to this register in Jake's dark eyes, eyes that always looked ready for wounding, and which made wounding both difficult and at times gratifying. Theo was holding on to the edge of the crib, rocking violently, about to unleash an unholy yell. Lizzie swooped him up, muttering nonsense syllables, bouncing him until his mouth turned up at the corners. He pointed to his minuscule sneaker in a corner of the room and said, "Ssew."

"Shoe." She lowered him onto the towel-padded bureau she used as a changing table. "Come on in," she called.

Jake paused in the door. With the edge of the diaper she wiped at the poop clinging to Theo's bottom. "Don't be shy." She pushed the diaper into the plastic pail and reached for a diaper wipe. Theo circled his legs in the air. To the tune of "Pop Goes the Weasel" Lizzie sang: "Someone has come to see you, ah-ha. Yes, someone has come to see you."

Jake stepped closer. Lizzie encased Theo's bottom in a new diaper and hoisted him onto one hip. She turned so that they both faced Jake. "Look, Theo," she said, bouncing him a little. "Take a good look at this guy. He sends you money."

Jake held his hand out, palm forward. The gesture looked like one she'd known in grade school, when her class had studied Native Americans and learned to say "How." Theo stared. Lizzie looked back and forth between the two sets of dark eyes examining each other so carefully.

"Hey. Theo." Jake's voice was pitched high. "Hello there, little fellow."

Theo turned his face into Lizzie's shoulder. She bounced him again. "Come on, Theo. Take a good look. You never know when this guy will grace us with his presence again."

"Give it a break, Liz." Jake's voice was low. As if picking up the anger that swirled between the two of them—an ugly red wind filled with pieces of debris, blowing paper, grit—Theo began to cry.

"Oh, great," Lizzie said, although this was fairly usual behavior after a nap until he had nursed. Theo tugged at the neck of her shirt. She sat on the low couch next to the crib and pulled her shirt up, so used to this action—shirt up over the breast, unhooking the nursing bra—that it was only as she exposed the breast, before Theo, butting with his head, fastened onto her nipple, that she thought to look at Jake. He was watching, or rather watching without watching, not knowing where to look.

"Sit there." She pointed with her chin to a chair across the room. "Or you can wait downstairs." She maneuvered Theo's legs and bottom into a more comfortable position and leaned back. Jake lowered himself into the chair. A rectangle of sunlight molded by the window stretched across the floor between them. Theo periodically left off sucking to gaze around at Jake. One foot prodded at the couch, the other waved in the air, landing on Lizzie's shoulder, pushing at her chin. Pudgy fingers pushed her shirt still higher, as if Theo were doing this for Jake's sake, revealing, she knew without looking down, a white dome of flesh, the blue of veins delicate as tracery beneath the skin.

She kept her neck bent and her face averted to hide the heat that climbed her cheek. Jake had been in almost the same position as Theo was now. She'd held him, just so, as he sucked on her breast and moved his fingers within her moistness so that she could come.

"Men are lucky," she said, her voice loud.

"Not necessarily," Jake said quickly, as if he'd been following her chain of thought. "Not at all, in fact." He held his hands pressed palm to palm between his knees. This was a position she remembered as habitual, and unexpectedly dear, making him look thoughtful, careful, too slow for his own good.

"Yes." Lizzie caught Theo's flailing hand. "Men get to return to this. When they're older." Theo's eyes were closed, his red lips pouted over her nipple. She smoothed his hair. "A woman, unless she's gay, doesn't get to do that."

Jake said nothing. Theo let go of her breast, creating a popping sound. He pointed at her. "Eye."

"That's right." Lizzie hugged him. She pointed across the room. "Jake." She would not say "Pa" or "Dada."

Jake wiggled his fingers at Theo, who pushed away from Lizzie. She tugged her blouse down and scooping Theo up onto one hip, walked ahead of Jake out of the nursery and down the stairs. Theo twisted in her arms to look over her shoulder at Jake, who stumbled once on the stairs behind them. She told herself it was fine to ignore the hollow, burned-out look in Jake's eyes, that he had brought this upon himself, but she had to stop herself from turning around and pulling him to her with her free arm.

He insisted on spending some time looking for Luna, and crashed around through the bushes and undergrowth in the field and gulch back of the house, calling Luna's name until Lizzie thought she would go out of her mind. It was clear he wanted to stay until the girls got home, but feeling like a sheepdog, she hinted and nudged and corralled him in the direction of his car. "But poor Sam," he said. "We've got to find her."

"When Summer gets home we'll go looking," Lizzie told him. "If anyone will know where she might be, it'll be Summer." She felt dizzy with confusion. She had called Jake to come precisely because of what he was trying to be—practical, kind. But now that he was here, she wanted nothing more than for him to go away. She stood adamantly by while he climbed across the gearshift, feeling her body shake with something she refused to name.

The car bucked away from her over the rutted, graveled road, the movement curiously reminiscent of making love. It also made her remember times she'd stood waving goodbye on frosty mornings. She didn't want him to look in his mirror and make any connections, so she headed back to the house, whispering against Theo's cheek, "I love my Theo, I love my Theo," until he pulled away from her in protest.

Summer arrived home a few minutes later, having walked in the half mile from the main road where the school bus dropped her off. "I saw Jake out there," she said from the top of the basement stairs.

"Did you." Lizzie, dealing with laundry, shoved her head further into the washer to get at a tiny sock. When she pulled her head out she was confronted by Summer standing with her hands on her hips, eyes shiny with tears.

"What?"

"You made him go away, didn't you?" Summer said. "You made him go away *again*." She turned and ran out of the house, pounding down the stairs. "Luuuna!" she called.

"Summer!" Lizzie yelled. "I need to talk to you." Summer was halfway up the hill. Lizzie started up after her, calling for her to wait a second, to please wait. But Summer didn't stop. "I need to tell you something." Her voice screeched, black crows spewing out of her throat. "Summer! Before you see Sam."

Summer turned to look at her, puzzled. Her face shifted, altered, convulsed into a rictus of comprehension. "Luna!" she cried, and veered off to the right, slipping and sliding downhill through bracken and underbrush, running as if pursued by a monster. Lizzie followed, but Summer tore ahead, a terrible keening rising from her throat. Suddenly she sat, crumpled into a faded denim heap. Lizzie slowed. Summer had her legs drawn up to her chest, her face buried in her knees, an arm flung over her head. Her body shook.

Lizzie squatted beside her. She knew better than to touch her. Summer lifted her head. "Luna's dead, isn't she? *Isn't* she?"

"I don't know. Sam can't find her."

Summer threw herself sideways to the ground, sobbing. "He told me this would happen. He told me. Just not so soon." She pushed Lizzie's hand away. "Let me alone. I *hate* you. You sent him away and now Luna's dead."

The chill wind rasped through sage and tumbleweed. Dusk was upon them. The sun, the season, her very life, Luna's life, dear Sam's life—everything was heading into night, into winter. She put her forehead against her knees. After a long moment she tried, "It's cold, Summer. Let's go home."

Summer's breaths were audible and had a hitch in them, a little hiccup of air. "I'm going to see Sam," she said, scrambling to her feet. She looked down at Lizzie, superior, distant. "I need to talk to him all by myself."

Lizzie watched her clamber back up through the bracken, find the path, head towards the caboose, a silhouette against the light of evening.

At dinnertime Lizzie found a working flashlight, put Theo on her hip, took Hannah by the hand, and climbed up to Sam's to ask him to dinner and to fetch Summer. The merry light that usually gleamed through the caboose window was unlit. When Lizzie knocked and then opened the door, Sam called out he was in bed, trying to get some sleep. Summer, he said, had left an hour ago.

Lizzie felt her heart turn to a granite lump. She met Hannah's wide eyes with raised eyebrows and kept her voice steady. "Can we bring you some dinner?"

"I want to sleep. Leave me alone, Lizard."

Hannah stayed quiet as they headed back down towards the house and nodded when Lizzie told her to watch Theo while she went looking. "You want to call Aunt Maud?" she said as Lizzie found a parka. "Her and Summer took a lot of walks."

"She and Summer," Lizzie said, examining last year's ski lift tickets and a Chap Stick she found in the parka pocket. She felt cold all over, frozen. She was reminded of the time Hannah was three and had fallen backwards off a stool onto the tile floor. In spite of blood seeping from what had, in fact, turned out to be a superficial head wound, she had commanded Hannah to get up and not be such a baby. The memory could still freeze her blood.

"You know how Summer has all those hiding places she won't show anybody?"

Lizzie shook her head. She was biting down so hard on her back teeth that her whole mouth ached. "I'll be back."

The flashlight made the darkness more dark. She finally switched it off, trying to see by the light of a slim moon as she scrambled and called and climbed and slid in and around and through the various bifurcations of the gulch in the acres behind the house. She called for Summer. She called for Luna. Once she called for Jake. It was after midnight when she finally phoned Maud.

Maud, just home from work, arrived within fifteen minutes. She seemed to have a good idea of where to go and had the foresight to suggest that Lizzie bring Summer's red wagon. Carrying flashlights, leaving Hannah with Theo, they set off. It seemed to Lizzie that Maud knew the branches and forks of the gulch as well as she might know the streets of a city. She led them to a secret overhang. Summer called it Narnia, Maud told Lizzie. Summer was asleep, her arms around Luna, who was curled up in a ball, dead.

Maud carried Summer, who wouldn't let Lizzie touch her. Lizzie followed behind, dragging Luna in the wagon. Summer had her arms around Maud's neck, face turned into her cheek. As they stumbled back towards the house Lizzie heard Summer say, "Sam told me it was going to happen. He told me this was one of those times to catch heaven on the fly, that I needed to be grateful for every minute of time I had with her."

"And Luna was very lucky she had you to hug her like that," Maud said. "She went away feeling peaceful, I bet. Sam will be glad of that."

Dragging her sad load behind her, lifting the wagon and its occupant up and over the rough and steep spots, Lizzie wished there were some way to take possession of this incident. Maud, rarely so capable and in charge, held the reins, and she hated herself for being petty enough at this moment to want them back. She wished she had let Jake stay. She wished Luna had not died. She wondered how on earth she would get through what she now had to go tell Sam.

CHAPTER 18

MAUD

What is love? 'Tis not hereafter.
Present mirth hath present laughter;
What's to come is still unsure.
In delay there lies no plenty.
Then come kiss me, sweet and twenty;
Youth's a stuff will not endure.
                    —*TWELFTH NIGHT*

The uniform at the Red Garter was a costume Maud could have worn for a Hollywood Halloween party: satin corset with plunging neckline, push-up bra, high-cut legs. Fishnet stockings, stiletto-heel ankle boots. A red garter high on one thigh completed the outfit.

It had been Jeep, baby-sitting the kids one night for Lizzie, who told Maud they were looking for a piano player at the Red Garter. Maud said she didn't know enough popular songs, but Lizzie and Jeep persuaded her to try. She auditioned one morning. Barney sat in a far corner of the empty bar and said, "You're hired," when she finished. "But just play straight-ahead tunes. No artsy stuff. You look a little artsy to me." Barney gelled his black hair, wore a leather jacket, and spoke quickly. Maud thought he might be putting some of the restaurant's profits up his nose.

Taking a break in the small changing room on the second floor, she stood before the mirror fussing with her antennae—as they had been dubbed—of blue beads, which matched the turquoise of her corset. The door banged open. It was Ginger, whose corset was green. Ginger never moved but sprang, never entered a room but shouldered her way in, never set a glass down but "delivered" it. Her red hair swarmed and curled, her breasts bulged wantonly; her hips were wide, her thighs ample, her calves long. She sat on a bench and unlaced her boots with quick, practiced gestures, then hoisted one foot onto the thigh of the opposite leg. "Goddamn boots!" she said, pressing thumbs into arch and heel. She threw her head back, eyes closed, mouth open in a grimace of pained and ecstatic relief. The gold feather in her hair, surrounded by stiff wires supporting green glass beads, teetered dangerously. She stood up and yanked open her locker, allowing the door to bang against its neighbor. "Shit night," she said, rustling a pack of cigarettes out of her purse. She lit up and lay back on the bench, crossed one ankle over the other, and closed her eyes.

Maud tried to read on her breaks, but found herself obsessed with time. Barney was ruthless on the subject of time cards and breaks. Nine minutes left. *I measure out my life in coffee spoons.* She found herself studying, again, the hand-printed poster that presented Barney's Rules of Conduct.

1) TIME TO LEAN. TIME TO CLEAN. LEAN ON YOUR OWN TIME.
2) THEY'RE WILL BE NO CONVERSATIONS OF A PERSONNEL NATURE BETWEEN EMPLOYEES WHILE ON THE CLOCK. TALK ON YOUR OWN TIME—WORK ON MINE! IF YOU HAVE SOMETHING TO SAY TO EACH OTHER—DO IT AT HOME—DO IT ON THE PHONE—NOT ON THE FLOOR!!!
3) UNIFORMS ARE YOU'RE RESPONSIBILITY. NO RUN STOCKINGS OR DIRTY LEOTARDS TOLERATED AT ANY TIME. NO EXCUSES!!
4) IF YOUR CUSTOMERS DON'T PAY, YOU DO.
5) NO FRATERNIZING WITH THE CUSTOMERS.
6) VIOLATIONS WILL BE PERSECUTED!!!

Ginger had balanced the cigarette pack on her stomach, and it moved up and down as she breathed.

"Hey, Ginger."

Ginger opened one eye, flicking ash onto the floor with a bright orange fingernail. She took another drag and squinted at Maud through the smoke. Maud wished she hadn't bothered her. But Ginger was staring, waiting.

"I particularly like that last rule." Maud pointed. "Just how does Barney do his persecuting, do you know?"

Ginger looked at the sign. With a sinking feeling, Maud wondered if Ginger had ever noticed—or knew about, or cared about—the incorrect use of the word. She changed the look on her face from one of sardonic amusement to a very real interest in how Barney might, if pressed, persecute an erring waitress.

"Well," Ginger whispered, which seemed unlike her. Maud had to lean across the space between the benches to hear. "If he can't get the state courts to agree he has a *right* to fine us for slapping a man who fondles our butts, well, then crucifixion just isn't good enough for us."

Maud laughed, but Ginger's eyes stayed hard. She held a finger to her lips and pointed to a speaker in the ceiling.

"Barney?" Maud mouthed, disbelieving.

Ginger nodded. "What a night, eh? Fucking boots!" she said, loudly, to the ceiling. She closed her eyes again.

Tonight, Maud told herself, as she told herself most nights, tonight for sure she'd stick around and have that after-shift beer with her fellow employees.

Four minutes.

Footsteps pounded up the stairs. Jeep slammed the door behind her. "I hate men," she said. "I just *hate* them."

Ginger kept her eyes closed. "No, you don't," she said. "And you'd better hustle your little ass right back down where you brought it up from. If Barney finds two of us up here at the same time we're in double dutch and it's my break, not yours."

Jeep stuck her tongue out at the intercom system on the wall. "He's talking to Bart anyway," she said. "Bawling him out for overpouring a drink by about a sixtieth of an ounce. And if I stayed down there one more second that shithead at table fourteen was going to have his hand all over my ass again. Fucking men!"

Ginger waved at them as they left. "Good luck."

"Luck I need," Jeep said as they went down the stairs. "It's no good complaining. If we get mauled Barney assumes we're doing something to deserve it. Men. They just assume we want them to fondle our butts. What a privilege!" She stopped at the bottom of the stairs and waved her rear end in the direction of an imaginary spectator. "Oh, please, baby, baby, just put your hands on me. Anywhere, baby. A touch from any old member"—she winked—"of the male sex will do."

She looped her tongue out of her mouth, running it around her lips, which glistened in the dim light of the stairwell. Maud was reminded of the Cheesios audition and at the same time, like a cinematic overlap, of Driver—the color of his bare shoulder, how the light from the fire he'd built in the kiva emphasized the red in his skin. Jeep tugged at the back of her leotard. "They just want one thing. All of them. You know what I mean?"

"Not all of them."

Jeep snapped her gum. "Wanna bet?"

Maud tried to laugh, but the light in the stairwell made Jeep look like something out of the pages of a porno magazine. "How can you be so cynical? At your tender age."

"Try my life." Jeep leaned against the door. It opened slowly, as if moving the wall of sound inside the bar. "Here goes nothing!" She waved a hand and disappeared into the mass of bodies shouting and holding glasses.

Maud waved to Bart behind the bar to turn off the canned music, wove her way through gesticulating arms to the piano, and began to play.

" 'You Picked a Fine Time to Leave Me, Lucille'!" a man shouted, and Maud nodded, modulating chords on her way into the introduction. Voices in the bar joined in on the chorus. She played a few more sing-along types until the voices lost interest, and then sang some Joni Mitchell and Linda Ronstadt. Jeep wandered by and leaned against the piano.

"Barney says don't get too artsy."

"This is artsy?"

"You might try moving your repertoire forward about twenty years."

"Impossible. Does Shawn Colvin count?"

"He says give it another half hour and then you can go."

"Maybe I'll stick around for that after-shift beer."

"I hope you do! It's fun. We've missed you. Bart says maybe you think you're too good for us."

"That's terrible!" Maud said. "Of course I don't."

"He's joshing. I told him it's because you don't sleep and then you're tired. But he says, 'If she can't sleep, she should stay up late with us delightful types. We'll not only bore her to sleep, we'll bore her to *death*.' " Jeep tried to balance her tray on one finger, and caught the pile of cocktail napkins before they spilled off. " 'Time to lean, time to clean.' " She imitated Barney's nasal voice, dabbing insincerely at the piano with her bar towel before she sashayed away.

After Maud punched out and changed she went back down to the bar. Two men sat at the far end, silhouetted against the pink neon outside the window. For a stomach-dropping moment she thought one of them was Miles, until he drawled, "Nice playing, ma'am. Buy you a beer?"

She shook her head. "But thank you."

"So you finally decided to join us." Bart slid a coaster in front of her. "What'll you have?" He was very handsome. Jeep had told her he was part Cherokee. When he smiled, deep crevices ran from the edge of his mouth to the edge of his nostril. Like Driver, though Driver hadn't smiled much. "First one's on Barney."

Jeep appeared beside Maud. "You can have Coors, Bud, Bud Dry, and Miller Lite. The cheapo, American ones."

Bart put his elbows in the little trough on his side of the bar. "Imports, Barney says you buy. You want hard liquor, you don't drink it here."

"Miller Lite," Maud said. Lizzie would have paid for an import rather than drink what she called horse piss.

"I'm just heading up." Jeep patted her bulging apron. "I'll do my checkout and get changed and then I'll be down."

Bart gave her the beer and began to wash glasses. "How you liking it here?"

"It's fine." She wondered what it would be like to date him, what it would be like to go on a date at all. "What I do is so different from what the others do." She gestured at Ginger, who was walking around the almost empty bar picking up glasses. "Easier than that, I think."

"Barmaid's one of the hardest jobs in the world. They put up with a lot of bullshit, keep a smile on their face, and still manage to believe—most of them—in the basic goodness of hu-*man* nature." Bart looked at her. She felt her cheeks go hot.

"Sometimes I wonder if they hold it against me," she said. "I just sit up there playing the piano, while they have to deal with booze and customers."

Bart shook his head. "You're talking about Ginger. She's tough as they come. Pay no attention. She gets paid, they all do, with tips, a whole lot more than you do. Jeep, on the other hand—same job, same hours, same number of men coming on to her—she adores you." Bart expertly fanned a pile of cocktail napkins into a circle. "She's a funny, lonely little thing," he said. "Proof that lousy family life equals lousy love life."

Maud pondered this. Her own parents were still married. To all intents and purposes they seemed to hold each other in deep—if somewhat distant—affection and esteem, but this hadn't translated into healthy marriages, even relationships, for either Lizzie or herself. "I wonder if it's fair to blame everything on family."

Bart stopped wiping the bar. "Ah. So you're one of those transformational types."

"Transformational?"

At a signal from the men sitting at the other end of the bar, Bart moved off. Maud swiveled on her stool to look at who was left in the room: the other waitress, Veronica, had gone upstairs to check out. Ginger was mopping down tables, in a corner a man and woman murmured, and near the piano, two couples laughed boisterously, chewing margarita straws.

"All done." Jeep slid in beside her. "I ended up getting stiffed by table fourteen. Barney made me pay. Bastard. Fifteen-plus bucks. Thanks," she said as Bart set a Coke in front of her. "Just because I told the asshole to keep his paws to himself. Are all men assholes, Bart?"

"I'm glad they've got one," Bart said, and laughed.

It took a moment for Maud to realize what this meant. Jeep took a sip of her Coke and said, "I mean, do you get that shit? Men leering at you and even feeling you and stuff, when you go dancing at the Mine Shaft?"

Bart shrugged. "Sometimes. The difference is that's one reason I go there, you know?"

"We should go to Farquaarts sometime. All of us. Hey, Ginger!" Jeep flagged her down. Ginger paused, her tray resting on a cocked hip. "Let's go to Farquaarts sometime."

"Sounds good," Ginger said, and moved off.

Maud watched her go, black fringe swishing. No wonder men thought of "tail." She turned back to Bart. "What's transformational?"

"What?" He did an imitation of a cartoon version of a dazed bird. "What you say?"

"That thing you said, about being a 'transformational type.' What is that?"

Jeep groaned. "Don't get him started. Bart's had more therapy—"

"Don't knock it till you've tried it," Bart said. He began to wipe down the bar. "You never know what beasties you could stand looking at, little girl."

Jeep shrugged. Bart said, "You allow yourself to be abused, missy, one way or another, and after getting dumped by one asshole you take right up with another." He twisted the towel forcefully, although no water came out, and then slapped its end against the edge of the bar. "Blow, or whatever your biker boyfriend's name is, is nothing to write home about, you know. You were probably better off with Ol' Cowboy Hat himself."

"Forget it." Jeep shoved her empty glass away from her. Tears glinted in her eyes. "And anyway, I've broke up with Blow. Just forget it."

"I will say this." Bart got her another Coke. "Whatever you said to Ol' Cowboy Hat worked. He's been keeping himself scarce. Hasn't been in here in two whole weeks. At least."

Jeep looked somewhat mollified. Bart winked at her. "Transformational psychology," he said to Maud, "offers the understanding that not everything is traceable-backable to some trauma in your childhood. Sometimes we just go through dark nights of the soul. That's what they are. If you take the right attitude towards them they're learning experiences. Or something like that. I may have it all wrong. As Jeep so sweetly pointed out"—he smiled a big false smile—"I've done a lot of therapy."

He stuck his tongue out. Jeep, chin on her hands, stuck out her tongue in return. "Just for the record," she said, "Rich was a bigger shit than Blow. At least Blow had a heart. Maybe I'm making progress."

"*Maybe* you are." Bart's head was in the cooler beneath the bar. Bottles clanked as he stowed Heineken, Bass, Corona. "We'll see, won't we. Now, me?" He stood up, holding an empty cardboard six-pack. "Me, I don't like that transformational shit. I like being a victim, I like to *blame* someone for the mess I'm in." He held his hands out to either side, a crucifixion pose, head lolling to one side, tongue hanging out.

Maud laughed, since that seemed appropriate. Bart bowed. "I gotta restock. Anyone needs me, I'm back in a jiffy."

"Jake's Blakes plays at Farquaarts a lot," Jeep said. "If I can get a sub on a night you're off too, we'll go."

Since moving to town Maud kept expecting to run into Jake. She wasn't sure what to say if she did see him—she'd pried the nasty details of their breakup from Lizzie. She wondered if Lizzie would be okay about her going to see his band. As if Jeep had followed something of this train of thought, she said, "Think we can persuade Lizzie to join us?"

Maud's chuckle was as realistic as she could make it. Bart came back and offered her another beer. "You have to pay this time. But it'll help you sleep, maybe."

"Sure," Maud said, wondering how long a dark night of the soul had to last.

⌇

Maud invited Lizzie and the girls to trick-or-treat in her neighborhood, their own being so far from town. Ever since the episode with Summer and Luna, Lizzie had been cool. She refused to talk about it, but Jeep said it was simple. "Think about it. You knew where to find Summer." Maud hoped the hours of passing out candy on

Halloween would ease the tension, that she could invite Lizzie to
Farquaarts with her new "gang." But the barbed-wire fence Lizzie set
up around herself was powerful. They spent a pleasant if shallow
evening discussing the cleverness of various costumes. The invitation
to Farquaarts was never proffered.

So Maud went alone. The plan was to meet Jeep, Bart, and
Ginger there. As she left her house to walk downtown, Noah waved
to her from a tall stump. Yelling something bloodcurdling, he leapt
to the ground. A lamp fastened to a tree above the dead lawn
highlighted his flying cape and black cowboy boots. He galloped
towards her.

"I got so much candy. Mom's put some of it in the freezer. I
like Summer. Will she come over again? How come you have eye
stuff on?"

Maud watched him jump off his stump for a while, not wanting
to arrive at Farquaarts too early. By the time she got there, the place
was jammed. Shiny tables sprouted pitchers of beer and baskets of
tortilla chips. On a raised stage, the band, leaping and bouncing, filled
every inch of space with sound. She felt as if she were bumping and
sliding her way through that mass of instrumentation as much as
through the maze of chairs and tables.

She recognized Jake immediately, though she'd only met him
that one strained time she and Miles had come to the Southwest. He
was on guitar, head bent over some complicated maneuver of chord
changes. She stood still, struck by how different Jake's performance
style was from Miles'. Miles rarely performed. When he deigned
to do so—"deign" was how Maud felt he thought of it; perform-
ing was beneath him; he was waiting to be discovered through his
recordings—his charm was wrapped in blond aloofness. On stage he
barely touched an instrument, although in fact he played piano, bass,
rhythm and lead guitar, and some horns. For his live performances he
used synthesized backgrounds against which a drummer drummed and
he sang. He seemed untouchable, unreachable; it was terribly attractive.

Jake was short and wiry, dark and intense. He bounded about the
stage as if it were a squash court. As Maud watched he carried his
guitar, trailing a long cord, over to a huge man who bounced before
a rack of keyboards. There were two percussionists—a drummer as

well as a man surrounded by congas, shells and bells, rattles and tambourines. A black man gyrated with a saxophone to his mouth, switching from saxophone to flute as Maud watched. Other horn instruments sprouted beside him, gleaming and glinting in the stage lights. The bass player was female. She wore an impossibly short skirt, and her long blonde hair, a waterfall in the light, swung with her every move.

Jake stepped up to the mike. A deep voice wove its way through the cacophony of chords and percussion.

"Earth to Maud," Bart said, snapping his fingers in front of her eyes. "Earth to Maud." Holding her hand, he plunged through the crowd, leading her to a crowded table. Bart raised Maud's hand in the air as if she'd just won a prizefight: "Maud!"

Ginger moved to make a space for her. A big man with a beard shouted. Maud nodded and smiled, pretending to understand. He reached for her hand. "Ron. Old friend of your sister's!" Like Ron, the other two men at the table wore plaid shirts and the ubiquitous cowboy hat. Their names were vacuumed up in the onslaught of sound.

Ron poured her a sudsy half glass of beer and raised his mug to her, wiggling his eyebrows. "How's Lizzie?" he shouted. Maud nodded enthusiastically. Since she'd arrived in Marengo, Lizzie had introduced her—in a grocery store, a bar, walking down Main Street—to at least a dozen men with whom it was clear she had at one time enjoyed intimate relations. They all seemed to be terrific friends, but Maud's mouth grew dry and her vagina contracted at the idea of entertaining that many cocks inside of her. In the time warp that was Marengo no one seemed to pay attention to the concept of sexually transmitted disease. She thought of her own unexpected night with Driver.

The bass player was seldom still. Ornate cowboy boots emphasized an amazing length of leg between their decorated tops and the fringed bottom of her skirt. She picked her way over the black coils of cording, stopping by the keyboard player, who nodded at something she said, then strutted towards the man on saxophone. He closed his eyes, angled his pelvis forward, and blew a long wail of appreciation. She grinned, swinging her hair. Cheers went up all over the room. She stepped up beside Jake, swinging the bass expertly out of the way to whisper something in his ear. Jake looked at her, then out at the room. He raised a hand from his guitar. For a moment, Maud thought he was waving at them, and moved her arm in a confused way as if to wave back. But he was signaling another time through the chorus. She was impressed with the way the band went right with him in spite of what was clearly an unexpected change in what had been rehearsed. They came to a resounding syncopated finish of drums and chords, a *rat-tat, rat-a-tat*-TAT that pulled half the people in the bar to their feet, clapping and cheering.

The band took a break. Maud took advantage of the relative silence to ask where Jeep was.

Bart shrugged. "AA. She'll be here."

The conversation grew general and loud. Ron poured Maud more beer. "I hear you're an actress!"

Ginger added in her drawl, "From Hollywood."

It would sound stuffy to say the preferred term was *actor*. "You must have sat in hot tubs with all kinds of famous people!" Ron said. The talk turned to the theater company in town, Fable Mountain Stage Company. *Charlie's Aunt* had just opened. Ron pouted. "I keep auditioning but I haven't been cast in over a year. They use only a few locals."

"Not the way I heard it," Ginger drawled. "What about *Music Man* last year? That was all local."

Ron ignored her. "I'm still waiting to hear about *A Christmas Carol*. Auditions were last week. They get all these actors to come in from Denver, friends of theirs, probably, and ignore those of us who've been acting here forever."

Ginger said, "Yeah, and you guys who'd been acting here forever manage to put on a show about once every two years."

Ron shrugged. "Hey! It's expensive. These guys have some kind of trust fund. They use actors that belong to the union. Do you belong to that, Maud?"

Maud found that the stories of her abysmal career could be very funny outside of the context that had spawned them. She was gratified by the laughter she generated when she told the story of pretending that Lizzie's kids were hers during an audition for a Ford commercial. Jeep arrived and asked her to tell the Cheesios story. "Fascinating," Ron said, rubbing his hands together. "You think about auditioning for these guys?"

"You should do that, Maud!" Jeep said.

The idea made Maud feel weary.

The band members made their way back onto the stage. Jake shook his mop of black hair and grinned, holding a fist in the air. The girl on bass sounded a *"Whoo-eee!"* that got the attention of most of the room and made them shout *"Whoo-eee!"* right back. Jake raised his hand. "*One two three* four!" They smashed into a song with a reggae backbeat that made Maud want to leap to her feet and twirl in space. She rocked her shoulders a bit and then stopped; she would rather Ron, or Rick, or Mick, or whoever they were, didn't ask her to dance.

"Hey, Jeep." A man—a boy, really—blond and tall, stood beside the table. He wore a red kerchief around his neck, a cowboy hat pulled low on his forehead.

Jeep's cheek were red. "Hey," she said.

The man looked down at Maud. His eyes were very blue. He jerked his thumb at the mass of swaying bodies at the front of the room. "Dance?"

Ron said, "You beat me to it, numskull. I'm next."

Bart leaned in. "This will be interesting, darlin'."

Maud stood. Jeep said, "Have fun." Ginger shook her head, shifting her eyes away, as if she were seeing something she preferred not to.

Maud followed the narrow hips in their faded jeans through the tables and chairs to the polished wood of the dance floor. He turned to face her. He was tall; she had to crook her neck back to meet his eyes. The faintest glint of blond fuzz ran along his chin, his upper lip. The band pressed, the sax wailed. She looked away from him, feeling a little breathless.

"I'm Rich," he said.

She had a moment's confusion, in which she thought he was telling her his financial status. "Rich," she repeated, realizing this was Ol' Cowboy Hat himself. She wondered if dancing with him would be okay with Jeep, broken up or not broken up.

He began to dance by snapping his fingers and bending and

straightening his knees. His feet, in their shiny, pointy boots, turned in, then out. Maud raised her hands, rolled her hips, feeling awkward in the face of his awkwardness. Yet she was a trained dancer. It was one of the many things she had taken the time and trouble to learn to do, and do well, one of the many things she was ending up doing nothing *with*. This thought made her lift cocked wrists above her head, flamenco-like, and twirl. She touched her right toe down to keep from going around again. Rich looked at her admiringly.

She felt the beer glow in her cheeks. Lights rotating above them made blue spangles on the drum set sparkle. She felt as if she spangled herself, and she smiled at the band, at the blonde bass player, and at Jake, who was standing back from the mike while the saxophonist took a solo. She didn't know if he recognized her, although he nodded in her direction as he played through chord changes.

Maud twirled again. Like some extravagant musical, the first scenes of her time in Marengo had been played against a drab background. But come the first dance number and the stage was transformed. The bleak scrim through which she had been peering suddenly rose to reveal set pieces flying in and out, furniture twirling, the stage itself revolving, lights, color, movement, the flip of skirts, the tap of heeled shoes, arms and legs and mouths in motion, sound pouring from nowhere, from everywhere. Marengo. It was a verb: She was Marengoing. She had come, as others had come, to seek her fortune. When they reached the ends of their ropes, when their stakes tapped out, their lodes ran dry, their streams panned out, this is where they'd come. Maybe here in this town, with its false fronts and dusty dreams, she would finally find her place; she would belong; she would connect.

She twirled again to the last beat of the song. Lizzie would dismiss all this as pheromones. And maybe it was. But something magical, dust in the air, beer, music, the smell of perfume and sweat all around her, made her feel alive, happy. Marengoing. She smoothed back hair that had fallen into her face. "Thanks," she said.

"Thank *you*, beautiful lady." He pushed the brim of his hat up with a finger. "One more?"

CHAPTER 19

JAKE

laser flash
dancers clash
and the lipstick on your sad, sad mouth
a ruby gash
where are you going, girl

On his way to breakfast, Jake ran into Roy outside Joanie's. "We *smoked* last night." Roy held high an open palm. Jake felt like an impostor, slapping five, but Roy kept hold of his hand, manipulating it into various positions. Finished off with one last slap. "How you doing, my man?"

Jake shrugged.

"Pasqual and I were talking last week. You got some shit on your mind it seems."

Jake nodded. Loosed himself from Roy's grip, put coins into the newspaper dispenser. He could imagine. Last week there'd been a Thanksgiving dinner. He'd come late, after eating with his sister and Willy's odd family. Roy, Pasqual, Pasqual's wife, Adela, Santiago and his wife and kids, Randy. They would have used him as some sort of musical theme, taking their riffs. Why he'd left. Why he'd come back. What he and Lizzie were up to. Where Theo fit into things. They would have covered all the permutations.

"Anyway. You wanna talk, sometime, anytime—" Roy's long hands looped through the air, one of his shoulders rising as he pulled a hip back. He snapped a forefinger, thumb up, at Jake. "I'm your man."

"Sure," Jake said. They slapped palms again.

Jake scanned the front page. The right-to-lifers still hadn't left. Sue would be livid. The color photo on the front page showed Kryptonite bicycle locks linking them to each other and to the fence around the clinic. They looked pathetic, heads squished together. The chanting faces of the pro-choicers looked distorted, ugly and mean.

He used the pay phone to call Sue, to put a sympathetic message on her machine. He was surprised to find her home. "You're not working today?"

"The clinic's a zoo. If someone's coming in for something as innocent as a urine sample, they get mauled, hangers shoved in their faces." Sue sighed. "We're taking turns staying out of the thick of it."

"I thought you said they'd all gone home."

"That was *weeks* ago, Jake. *Months.* This is a whole new bunch, from Wichita this time. Why they think they can come in and change things around in a city—a state—that isn't their own . . . It's an extension of the mentality that says a woman can't have control of her own life, her own body. And do you know how many of them are men? It's scary."

"You sound tired."

"Sick of the whole damn thing. I never thought I'd wonder if it's worth it."

"I begin to see Willy's point of view," Jake said. "The country's going to hell—"

"Don't—"

"*I'm* going to hell." He ran the edge of a quarter along the grooves someone had carved with a knife in the wall beside the phone: Y & A FOREVER! "Since I've been back I don't do anything. Can't finish a song. Still haven't unpacked. Four months and I'm still living out of suitcases."

And why do you think that is, buddy?

He told Minerva to shut up.

"Have you had breakfast?" Sue asked.

"Since I've been back?"

"Ha ha ha. Low blood sugar. Culprit of a myriad so-called quote-unquote disorders."

"Yeah, yeah."

"So, have you?"

"Actually, no. I'm at Joanie's. Join me?"

"I can't, Jake-o. I've just stripped the beds. Dishes await, no one's vacuumed in weeks."

Jake felt as little and as disappointed as a boy.

"But the hell with it," Sue said. "A latte sounds great. Give me ten minutes."

Jake hung up. Mortified at how glad he was to have some company. Company he didn't have to explain himself to. Justify himself, or his failures. He stood for a moment next to the phone, surveying who it was he'd have to get by to reach a table. Elmer of Mountain Music, head bent over a newspaper. Joanie herself, perched on her usual morning bar stool, presiding over the cash register. Last week she'd slid into his booth, wanting all the "gory details" of the Nashville debacle. And Tina was fetching a coffeepot, doing her best to lock eyes with him.

Still he stood there, tapping fingers on his jeans to the polyrhythms Pasqual had concocted for "On the Lam from Love." The only song he'd managed to write that whole time in Nashville, one he'd started on his way down there. Even now he could remember the sense of that drive. Shoulders hunched over the steering wheel, foot pressing the accelerator all the way to the floor. The car itself had seemed to hunker into a forward-leaning trapezoid, shaped by the urgency of his need not to get where he was going but to get away. Away from things that swooped and dipped above him as he drove, small cartoon tornadoes with leering faces.

"Jake! Hello! We heard you were back!"

"Hey, Emily. Tom!" He lifted his hand to the couple who had lived next door to him before he'd left. "Hey, Becky! You've gotten so big!"

"We're so glad you're back!" the woman shouted as they were towed out of the café by their daughter. "Come see us!"

He returned the wave of another acquaintance slipping onto a stool at the counter. A booth was empty but he didn't move. Remembered driving down a street in Nashville. Looking for the house of someone who knew someone who might be able to get his tape to someone who knew someone. Was it the width of the street?

Hour of the day? Kids pulling a wagon along the sidewalk? For some reason he'd missed Marengo with a force like compressed air. But as he drove along, peering at house numbers, he knew there was no way he could face the discussion and conjecture that would surround him if he should return. He'd resolved yet again that he'd just have to stick it out, even though he was so depressed he could hardly get up each morning.

Then a song came crooning through the car radio. Travis Tritt, chalking up another love lost to foolish pride. He'd pulled over, put his head back, closed his eyes. Listened to the rest of the corny song.

Apologizing would be so simple. He'd be damned if he'd crawl.

He could apply the lyrics to himself, himself and Lizzie. But that he was moved had to do with Marengo. He had a life there. Things that mattered were already in place. Things he couldn't imagine ever finding in Nashville, things that when named were, like the song, corny, sentimental. So he didn't name them. But he knew he had to go back.

Still, months had passed. Then he met Santiago. Who'd made it easier to return.

And he'd walked the gauntlet ever since. Joanie's was only a concentrated form of it. A song of his hadn't, and wouldn't, ever make Top 40. He'd gotten adept at the quips that allowed him to sidestep the queries, the concern.

He made his way to the empty booth. Waved at Joanie, making change for a customer, talked with Elmer, promising to stop in at Mountain Music, nodded at Tina, who bumped into a table as she told him hello.

A woman sat in a booth opposite, sheets of paper scattered on the table in front of her. Chewed the end of a pen. Composer, creator, working at the endless task of perfecting what seldom seems perfect. Caught up in this thought, he smiled when she looked up. Her own smile leapt back, lighting a face that otherwise seemed to brood. She took a breath, as if she were going to say something, then looked down.

Maud, Jake realized. Maud Maxwell, who'd been dancing with Rich Pack the other night at Farquaarts.

He thought he would try a belated hello. But she seemed self-consciously caught up in her work. He pushed the remains of someone's breakfast to the edge of the table and opened his newspaper.

"Hi, bruth." Sue slid into the booth opposite.

"One of the many ironies in my life," Jake kept his voice low. Maud had looked up to watch them. "Is that I ran away from any semblance of home and family as soon as I was old enough to drive a car. Then, after Nashville, *twice* after Nashville, I come back partly because you're here. Go figure."

"Coffee?" The waitress—he was thankful it was not Tina—held mugs in one hand, the pot in the other.

Jake took coffee. Sue ordered a latte. Leaned across the table. "That's Lizzie's sister." Maud was writing furiously. Black hair fell over her shoulders, looped onto the table on either side of her arms. "I saw them together at Safeway the other day. They were with the kids."

"Why are we whispering?" Jake whispered. They both laughed. The waitress brought Sue's latte. When he thought Maud wouldn't think the laughter was associated with her, he looked again, found her sliding out of her booth. She stood beside her table, huge bag hanging from one shoulder, counting change onto a tip tray. Long skirt, short sweater emphasized a very flat stomach. Turned sideways, she could slip through the crack in a wooden porch. Lizzie had always described her as skinny. To Jake she looked as if she were agonizingly hungry.

She approached them. "Sorry I keep staring. It's just I know who you are. Don't get up." She had a crooked front tooth. He thought about Lizzie's slightly sharp ones.

"Hello, Maud. Good to see you." He took her narrow hand in his. Her clasp was strong, fingers cold. "This place is buggy with sisters. Scuzzy with them. This is mine. Sue."

Sue, as always, was good with small talk. Asked how Maud's house was, where she was working, how she liked Marengo. Maud was impressed that Sue was an RN. "I have such admiration for people who really *do* things for people. Theater, television, is such a playground most of the time." Just before she'd left Hollywood she'd sent away for an application to the Peace Corps. "It was forwarded to me.

But after reading the small print I realized I probably wouldn't get posted to Nairobi, or to some small village in India. I'd be sent to Detroit. Some unromantic, smoggy place like Pittsburgh. So I threw it out. So much for my vocation."

Sue found this funny. Took Maud's phone number. "Maybe we can have a cup of tea one day."

Tears bloomed in Maud's eyes. "I'd love that."

"Tea sounds boring," Jake said. "But I'll buy you a beer. We've both fled tinseltowns. Nashville. Hollywood. We should compare notes sometime."

Maud nodded. Her face looked strained, half-moons beneath her eyes the color of bruises. Jake figured it wasn't a good time to bring up Miles, though he was curious to know, in a competitive sort of way, how his career was doing.

"Well, it's good to see you."

She turned to leave. Jake asked, too fast, "And how's Lizzie?"

Maud's eyes widened, narrowed. Deep brown, different from Lizzie's, which glinted gold and sometimes turned green. "Fine," she said, "fine." They all nodded several times. Jake wondered how much Maud knew. Probably everything. On the other hand, Lizzie was incredibly opaque about her emotions. Any number of times she'd not told him about some crisis in her life until after it had passed.

"Well." Maud adjusted the strap on her bag. Her face looked older than her body, eyes bracketed by bursts of what could be called laugh lines except for the sorrow that seemed to burn there. Before he could think of anything else she was walking away from them, bag bouncing against her thigh.

"Oh, boy," Jake said.

Sue had her hands pressed to her mouth. "Well?"

"Well what?"

"Will she do?"

"Do?"

"Do you find her attractive?"

"Jesus, Suze!" Although his mind had skittered onto and away from the same idea.

She grinned. Hellion. Brat. "Just wondering."

"Well, stop wondering." He rubbed his face with his hands. "I feel half-baked. Nothing's going right. Songs won't come. I hate my job. No, that's not true. But I drag my butt through rehearsal at night when what I've been doing all day is thinking in binary. On, Off. Yes, No. One, Two."

"You know what you should do?"

"Here you go again! I did what you said! I climbed Fable. I even went to see Lizzie. It was a bust. I told you. A complete and total bust. She hates me."

"Ask her if she'd let you have some time with your son."

He grunted, rubbed at the caffeine prickle behind his eyes. "I've been thinking about that."

"Tell her that you'd like to have some normalizing time with him—that should impress her."

"*Normalizing time?* She'll barf. And then laugh. And then she'll hang up."

"It's a thought." She stood and zipped her parka. "I've got to go. The permanent-press buzzer on the dryer is blaring at me across town."

He reached for her wrist. "Don't go yet. I've gone on and on. What about you?"

"Is Willy having an affair? Is Johnny going to be screwed up for the rest of his life by our fights and by his dad's drinking? Did I wind up marrying Pop, God forbid? Is our marriage over? Does anyone ever really love anyone? Does anyone ever really *know* anyone?"

"Sue."

"Maybe I'm imagining. I'll keep you posted." Sue sat down again and leaned across the table. "It's so *tacky*. Some little twit who works at the store. Pert breasts, long legs. She wore halter tops all summer. Frayed jean shorts cut off just below the crotch so there's this nice little wedge of rear visible all the time. Stats were up just because farmers come in to admire her cute little ass while they're buying ten-penny nails." She laughed. "Now she's had to put on some clothes. Why do overalls look so adorable on a little butt like that?"

She tapped fingernails on the table. "The worst of it is realizing she's me about twenty years ago. Maybe Willy wants me to still look that way, but I'm me, you know? We're supposed to love growing old together. I have wrinkles and some cellulite. I have gray in my hair."

"You're beautiful," Jake said.

She shook her head gratefully at him.

"Goddamn men," Jake said.

"Goddamn men. And eat something. Coffee isn't enough."

"Yes, ma'am."

She squeezed his hand and disappeared. Jake ordered eggs, leafed through the paper.

Walking to his car he could smell snow coming, brittle and sweet. He zipped his jacket. They'd had several snowfalls. Soon winter would come in earnest, howling around Fable Valley. Which meant parkas, frosted breath, puddles of water. Meant taking time to warm the car up to scrape the windshield. Meant Lizzie on tiptoe, nose a cold spot pressed against his cheek.

There it was again. The stuck CD playing Lizzielizzie lizzielizzie. He continually had to bump the CD player to some other track, any other track. Shiny book covers in the windows of LodeStar Books. Posters outside Mountain Music. The new lyric he'd jokingly tossed into rehearsal the other day. *You're my muddy, muddy river, I'm a glass-bottomed boat.* Randy had struck up a low bass riff, Santiago had found some satisfyingly heavy blues chords to move under it. They'd jammed on the tune until Randy cracked them up by singing, loudly and off-key, "Yes, I'm floating on your river, baby, horny as a goat."

Lizzielizzielizzie. The evasive ongoing decision regarding the lyric *Love comes back* versus *Will love come back?* What he'd do with the rest of this day, besides go out and hassle Rich Pack about December's rent, overdue again. Any other track in the CD of his mind except that melancholic, discordant, bittersweet one called LIZZIE.

CHAPTER 20

MAUD

*I can suck melancholy out of a song
as a weasel sucks eggs.*
—AS YOU LIKE IT

"He's such an asshole," Lizzie said.

"But so *cute*." Maud sat cross-legged on the Navajo rug in Lizzie's living room. She giggled, rocking back on the heels of her hands. This devil-may-care feeling—Marengoing—had swirled around her since that first dance with Rich. Exhilaration came and went, leaving her at times hung over with a double dose of reality. And Marengoing was like a cocktail, a powerful mixed drink made with Rich and several clear liquors—vodka, tequila, gin, a little sparkling water, and something red, grenadine or cranberry juice. Or maybe it was more like a disease. She was Marengoing when she could least afford it, when she really had to get serious about her life, her future. She had so little time.

Sobriety fell over her as if someone had cracked an egg on her head. The gloomy white albumen of reason fell past her ears, the yolk slid down over one eye.

"Anyway, Rich is not your type." Lizzie pushed a jam-soaked lock of hair out of Theo's sleeping face.

"Type!" Maud laughed. "Who on earth knows what my type *is*? I've tried everything. Nothing's worked."

"You have certainly not tried everything," Lizzie said.

But Maud collapsed backwards, chuckling up at the stained

beams that crossed the ceiling. "And you know what else?" She felt her belly rise and fall, felt her legs stretched out long and lean against the rug, against the flagstones beneath the rug. She had lost weight; she could feel her hipbones sharp as knives when she ran a hand over her belly and her thighs in the night. She found herself in a heightened state that had little to do with eating, a state that was a rejection of something as mundane as food: Marengoing. "You know what else?" She propped herself up on her elbows. "Lizard, he lives in a *trailer.*"

She was suffused with the cliché of it. She was living in someone else's set design, creating her role around someone else's casting: Hadn't Rich practically worn his cowboy hat to bed? She collapsed again with laughter, responding only minimally to Lizzie's "Shh!"

She stopped, however, when Lizzie didn't join in. She watched her sister smooth hair out of Theo's face. She'd learned to shut a portion of her heart against scenes, masques, crèches such as these: a child in Christopher Robin mackintosh and rubber boots running towards his father; a mother at a checkout stand carrying an infant, articulated tendons in her forearm testament to weight gladly and commonly carried. Against these visions of devotion, Maud erected a curtain, storm windows. If she moved the curtain aside for an instant, or cleared the steamed-up window with a knuckle, what she saw could make her pant with longing. She laughed again. "A trailer! My cowboy lives in a trailer!"

"Jake's trailer," Lizzie said. Maud nodded, but did not pursue this. She'd gone to Farquaarts a second time, by herself. She felt clumsy, standing with a beer beside another woman, making small talk neither one could hear over the din of the salsa band. It was for Rich Maud had come, and she was relieved when he arrived, though she pretended to be deep in animated conversation as he made his way towards her. He placed light fingers on her shoulder. Again they danced. He was not particularly graceful, but he was always game for one more.

After Thanksgiving she went a third time, again alone, and when he invited her back to his place, she accepted. She'd had too many beers, was feeling jovial and sexy, a delightful combination: one word implying cherubic rotundity, the other a lean and dark concavity; one word happy, the other passionate. As they walked past the darkened store windows of Main Street, she marked his vehicle a block before they got to it. The red pickup gleamed beneath a streetlight, and as he opened the passenger door for her—he did this with a flourish, doffing his cowboy hat—she laughed.

"What?" he said.

"You have a red pickup!" She put a hand on his arm. He couldn't know she was admiring the choices of the director of this movie, the insights of the props master. "It suits you."

He patted the roof of the truck. "She's new."

As he started the engine, Maud had an image of him clucking to horses. "Giddiup!" she said gaily, holding an imaginary bonnet in place. Rich, who clearly couldn't hear over the roar of the engine, smiled and nodded. She felt a lurch of uncertainty and stared out the window, swallowing convulsively. At a stoplight he put a hand on her thigh. She closed her fingers over his, grateful for this connection.

He stopped to get them a six-pack and then drove miles out of town. They bounced and swayed over deep ruts. The headlights, on high beam, lit an occasional fir tree, a bank of black pines, the snow that was everywhere now. She wondered how a snowplow managed way out here. As she was about to ask, a rabbit darted out and froze in front of the truck. Rich swore, braking. The hand he threw out to hold Maud back touched her breast. "Sorry," he said, curt.

She began to regret coming. She could not walk home from wherever she was in the middle of the night, and it would be diffi-cult, after the expectations she had raised, to ask Rich to drive her. As they bucked along she braced herself with an arm stretched out against the dashboard. A steep slope loomed ahead of them. "Come on, girl," Rich said. The pickup's engine whined as they breasted the hilltop. In the headlights a trailer gleamed. Rich turned off the igni-tion. A dog barked steadily. "Home sweet home."

A collie leapt to greet him. "That's Betsy." Maud held out her hand. The dog growled and backed away. "Now, Betsy!" Rich scolded. "Don't you be jealous."

Maud followed him along a shoveled path that ran the length of the trailer. He paused before opening the door. "It's a mess, beautiful lady. I wasn't expecting company."

The trailer was warm and smelled of wool and cooking and

something tangy, citrusy—a shampoo or soap. This last was a scent she associated with Rich, and she breathed in, grateful for its clean aroma. He rustled in the dark, scratched a match. "I could flick a switch," he said, "but this'll be prettier." The wavering light of a kerosene lantern filled the room. Maud made out a counter, a pile of bowls in a sink. A plaid blanket and sheets were a tangled cocoon of fabric on a bed that took up the middle of the trailer.

"Told you it was a mess." Rich crossed to a small refrigerator, pulling out two bottles from the six-pack before stowing the rest. He held one bottle in the crook of his arm as he twisted the cap off the other. Maud thought of him holding an infant there, curled against that delicate bend of elbow and arm.

He tapped her bottle with his before drinking. Maud poured some of her beer into the sink. "For the gods."

"You're so amazing." Rich pronounced this as if he wasn't sure it was such a good thing to be amazing. Maud sat on the edge of the bed. She moistened the tip of her tongue with beer. She was sobering up fast. "Look, Rich." Silence congealed around them. "Maybe I don't think I can stay here."

Rich tipped his bottle up. His Adam's apple bounced.

"I mean, I could *sleep* here—" This wasn't at all what she meant to say, but she blundered on. "I wouldn't want to make you drive me back to town, but maybe we shouldn't—" She moved her hands in a gesture at once round and deflated. The word *fuck* was too harsh. But the phrase *making love* was inappropriate, hardly what she felt them capable of doing.

Rich blinked several times. "Whatever. Whatever you want, beautiful lady."

Maud gripped the edge of the mattress. So she would be "beautiful lady" to Rich, as she had been "babe" to Miles. She stared hard at her hand, willing back tears. What was she doing? She had slept with, fornicated with, coupled with, Driver, only a few months before, only two nights after leaving Miles. When she didn't really know for certain she was leaving him. And now she was here, ready to lie with, "know"—but surely not mate with—a boy young enough to be her son. What possessed her? To come here? To come to Marengo? To leave her life? She could be lying beside Miles on the couch in their living room, bathed in blue–TV–screen–light, listening to the *thwock thwock* of police helicopters in the skies above L.A.

She gripped the edge of the mattress and the material there more firmly. The slide of the sheet against her hand let her know it was old and had not been washed in some time.

"Maud?" Rich sat beside her, placing his beer bottle on the floor. "You seemed so—peppy. What happened?"

Peppy. She tried to smile at him, at the taut skin above his cheekbones, an aspect of his face she admired, something she loved about him, actually missed when she was away from him. But she was frightened at how easy it was to find things to love about not only Rich but about some of the other men in the last few months she had spoken to, sat with, watched. She found herself in love with the way a pair of eyes wrinkled when they smiled, the way a muscle bulged inside a T-shirt, the way lips shaped the word *Marengo*, the way a knuckle smoothed a mustache. She was entranced with the slant of hips in blue jeans, teeth set crookedly inside a kind smile; the way someone might say, *Yesterday down in Fairfield*, or how a hand might lie upturned and open on a table, fingernails honestly dirty— from digging holes for fence posts, repairing an engine. It astonished her, frightened her, moved her, what it meant, this propensity to love. She had no vessel into which—whom—she could pour this love. What was she to do with it all?

She put a finger against the smooth skin at the side of his eye and drew it down over his cheekbone, down over the soft stubble on his chin, so different—comparisons rose within her—from Miles' rougher version. "I'm just, ah, new." She shook her head. She wasn't new; she'd probably been making love longer than Rich had been alive. She stared at the bottle in her hand as if it were a Tele-PrompTer, as if her lines might scroll up, neat printing against its brown surface, and tell her what it was she was supposed to say next.

With a sudden out-breath, Rich rose. "I'm so rude." He crossed to the slanting shelves above the sink. "A lady like yourself shouldn't be drinking out of a *bottle*." He took her beer and tipped it into a wineglass. "I only have one." He poured his own into a green cup decorated with dinosaurs. Maud recognized a few—Tyrannosaurus rex, pterodactyl—from Theo's plastic collection. She wondered if Jeep had left the cup here. With that thought a multitude of other complications arose within her. She felt like someone in a horror movie, batting at dark shapes that came at her no matter which way she turned, how she tried to escape.

Rich clacked his cup against her glass. "Here's to you," he said, "whatever you want."

They'd kissed then. He pushed her skirt up above her knee, stroked his hand along her calf and thigh. "Such legs," he said, "the legs of a sixteen-year-old." Maud had stared at them, as if they weren't hers. Again she thought of Jeep.

"So," Lizzie said softly. "Did the earth move?"

Hannah was asleep on the other couch, the lavender afghan thrown over her. Summer was spending the night at a friend's.

Maud shook her head. "Pretty disappointing, actually. Too much beer. I got sad."

"Maud, you complicate everything."

"It's true, I do. And talking around the edges of safe sex doesn't exactly *lubricate* matters, does it? I hate condoms."

"Ain't it the truth," Lizzie whispered. "You take all this time and sweet trouble to get everything wet and ready and there's this huge erection staring at you and then he has to rear back and one of you has to roll this *thing* on—"

They laughed. Lizzie put a finger to her lips.

"He called it the 'glove of love,' " Maud said. "Dropped it in the wastebasket."

He'd held it between thumb and forefinger, the opaque sac sagging with its load of semen, all those wasted babies, carried it across the room as if he were disposing of a dead mouse by its tail. He went outside to pee, came back in with Betsy at his heels. When he slid back into bed his body was cold. She moved to hold him but he stayed on his back. "Hot," he said. She rested light fingers on his thigh, which he patted, and then withdrew his hand. Betsy leapt onto the bed. "Night, lady," Rich said, and Maud didn't know which of them he was referring to. He breathed deep sighs almost immediately. She suffered her usual sleeplessness, made all the worse by the fact she didn't want to move for fear of waking him, or Betsy, who slept protectively across his feet.

"You should be warned." Lizzie shook her head. "Things might get a little weird with Jeep."

Maud nodded. She felt sad suddenly, the same melancholy that had gripped her the next morning as she'd waited, shivering beside the truck, for Rich to drive her back into town, watching his shuttered face as he locked the trailer door and patted Betsy goodbye.

"She knows. She was giggling when I sat down after that first dance with him. She winked at me."

"And she tells me she's glad you guys seem to be having a good time. She's trying really hard. But she's hurting."

The Rich to whom Jeep occasionally referred was a dark, mean creature, a troll beneath a bridge disfigured with evil intentions. Not the tall, handsome, sexy-if-distant Marlboro man Maud had come to know.

"She still has a thing for that shit." Lizzie rubbed her hands along her thighs, and suddenly clapped them. "Now here's a thought! Let him get you pregnant."

Maud snorted. "*How to Totally Complicate Life: Five Quick and Easy Lessons.* The best-selling self-destruct book by Maud Maxwell."

"The man doesn't exist who just says, 'Okay, honey darlin', let's make a kid!' " Lizzie used a deep, jocular voice. "You keep moaning about how you want one. Go for it. Grow your own."

The Taos motel room rose up, the smell of rain, the whispered *I can't*. "I tried that with Miles. It didn't work."

"You're not ruthless enough." Lizzie slid to the floor. "Here's what you do. First of all, no rubbers, no caps, no jellies or foams or any of that crap." She checked Maud's face for agreement. "Then what you do, as soon as it's over? You put your feet up in the air."

She hoisted her legs above her, balancing her bottom on her hands. "Put your feet way up there so that none of those little spermies can escape. Then you've got to shake it down, shake it down." She kicked her legs in the air. "That's how I got Hannah, I *know* it. The second Blair and I finished, I knew it would be a girl. I wanted her so badly. This is exactly what I did, and there came Hannah."

Maud put her own feet in the air. Her skirt fell over her face. She batted it out of the way and watched her legs bicycling in the air overhead. "Like this?"

"Bounce a little, shake them down *in* there."

Maud began to laugh. "Shake it down."

"Bounce, Maud. Shake it down."

They laughed so hard Maud had to drop her legs. "Come on, you have to *practice*," Lizzie said. "Give it to yourself as a Christmas present. If this affair lasts that long."

Maud hoisted her feet back up. Tears seeped out of her eyes, down her cheeks. She swiped at them with the hem of her skirt.

Their laughter woke Hannah. She peered at them. "What are you doing?"

"We're shaking it down," Lizzie said. "Want to join us?"

Hannah's eyes gleamed. She shook her head. The blanket capping her black hair made her look like an illustration out of *The Little Match Girl*. "You're being rather loud."

" 'Rather loud.' She is your niece, Maud." Lizzie rolled over to sit beside the couch. "I'm trying to convince Maud to get you a sister before you're too old to enjoy it."

"That wouldn't be my *sister*."

"You're right, Hannah, as usual. How'd I ever get such a practical child? I know, it's Blair, not me." She pulled Hannah to her feet.

"It was fun seeing that play with you, Aunt Maud," Hannah said. "Summer wants to be the ghost of Christmas past, all jolly, but I want to be the ghost of Christmas yet to come." She pulled the blanket forward, hiding her face. Making wind noises, she pointed a shaking finger in Maud's direction, then at her mother.

"Come along, Hannah-hoo. Christmas yet to come has to brush his/her teeth." Lizzie nodded towards Theo. "Would you carry our little Christmas Present?"

Hannah giggled and let her mother pull her from the room. Theo's cheek was mashed into the couch pillow. Maud scooped her arms beneath him, holding his hot body close. *Puh, puh, puh.* Theo made a puffing noise as he slept.

She carried him up the stairs. Lizzie helped her roll him into the dinosaur-decorated sheets of his crib. Maud wished she could always feel as she did at this moment. Her sister had made Theo's body. But

Theo and Hannah and Summer were and always would be a part of Maud. It seemed you could always need something other than what you already had.

She put her hand on the small of Lizzie's back and stared down at her nephew, adoring his open mouth, the Mick Jagger upper lip with a smear of jam upon it, his sticky hair, the abandon of his round limbs, his tiny fists, loosely clenched against a world that had not yet given him too much anguish.

WINTER

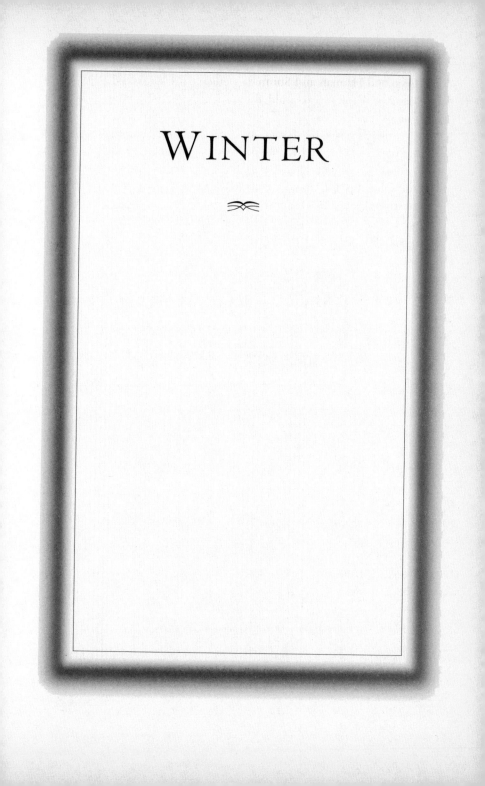

LIZZIE

We need, in love,
To practice only this:
Letting each other go.
For holding on comes easily;
We do not need to learn it.
—RILKE

When Jake called to ask for "normalizing time" with Theo, Lizzie laughed. "Normalizing time?" she repeated back to him in a snide voice. The phrase summoned up visions of a psychologist's office, where adults sat hugging teddy bears and occasionally pounding pillows.

"I'd like to spend some time with him, Liz, where it's natural—whatever the word is. As normal as possible. Given the circumstances."

She wondered if Jake had started to see a counselor. She badgered him with the fact that she didn't owe him anything. He managed, nevertheless, to wrangle an invitation.

Within half an hour Lizzie had finished her first beer and was hankering for a second. She lounged on the couch. He sat opposite, stiff, upright, on the edge of the armchair, hands held in upside-down prayer. Amidst a scattered collection of wood blocks, plastic dinosaurs, animals of the barnyard, Theo squatted on the rug between them. Behind Jake, through the big window, Lizzie watched the sun slip over the edge of snowy mountains. The bright white of the field around the house dulled.

"Cow?" Theo held this up.

"Ask Jake." Lizzie pointed in Jake's direction.

Theo tottered over and placed the wooden cow in Jake's hand. "Moo?"

Jake looked like he might faint. "You're right, it does say moo."

The front door slammed. "Ma!" Summer called from the kitchen. "Ma? Sam won't let me in again."

She careened around the corner, shirttail poking out from beneath a parka that needed a good wash, hair a bristle of red-blonde. When she saw Jake she stopped dead.

"Well, hi there," Jake said, getting to his feet.

Summer squinted at Lizzie. "What's he doing here?"

"How many times do I have to tell you about slamming the door?"

"Visiting," Jake said.

Summer put one foot on top of the other. "I thought you told him to go away."

"He's visiting Theo."

"And I'm visiting you."

"Moo." Theo placed another animal in his hand.

"No, this one goes quack." Jake tried to hand it to Summer. "Doesn't this one go quack?"

Summer grabbed the wooden duck and shoved it at Theo. "Quack, stupid."

"Summer!"

"Wack," Theo tried.

"So," Jake said, "you still run up and see Sam after school?"

"He's been a bit sick," Lizzie said.

"He's not a bit sick, Ma, he's a lot sick. Luna *died.*"

Jake looked shocked. "You didn't tell me."

"That day you were over."

"You didn't *tell* me."

"I'm going upstairs and doing my homework," Summer said, and stomped up the stairs.

Lizzie searched for and found shades of lavender and blue in the dusk outside the window, aware that Jake was fighting a desire to take her to task. She shrugged her inner shoulders. Finally he sighed. "How is Sam?"

"Not good."

After another pause, Jake said, with humor, "So Summer does her homework without being nagged to death?"

It would be so easy, Lizzie thought, it would take so much less effort, if she dropped the load of resentment that dragged at her, and which she had to keep shifting back into place like a loose bra strap or a pair of high-riding underwear. "I'm getting another beer. Want one?"

"I'm still okay, thanks."

As she opened the refrigerator the front door slammed again. "Ma, I got an A!" Hannah dumped her parka, waved a sheaf of papers. "And Mrs. Anderson says could you do car pool next Tuesday and she'll do yours the week after."

Lizzie opened her beer, checked the pot of water heating on the stove. "There's a friend of yours in there."

"Sam?"

Lizzie shook her head. She followed Hannah into the living room.

Jake was on the rug beside Theo. He looked up as Hannah rounded the corner. Hannah stopped. "Jake-o," she breathed, and went towards him like something sucked into a wind. He scrambled to his feet to receive her, bending over the black, sleek head, arms circling her waist. Lizzie watched them with her hands on her hips.

Hannah looked up at him. "Are you here for dinner?"

Jake nodded.

"Could we all eat together?" she asked. "*Please?* Ma? At the round table? Can I dress up?"

Lizzie pondered her.

"Don't laugh. Blair likes it when I dress up. And don't do your grown-up thing and eat by yourselves the way you used to, the way you do with Aunt Maudie. *Please* can we?"

"I guess," Lizzie said.

Hannah clapped her hands. "I'll tell Summer to put on a dress too." She ran up the stairs.

Lizzie lifted Theo onto one hip and headed into the kitchen. "Let's get this normalizing dinner over with." She pulled a bag of mushrooms and some green onions from the crisper. As she slammed the refrigerator door, a Christmas tree, cut from purple construction paper, slipped from its magnet and fell to the floor. "Shit!" she said.

"Sit!" Theo said, waving a fist.

"Right, my man," Jake said, "sit it is." He stooped to retrieve the tree.

"Just toss it," Lizzie said. "The season's over. I've got too many things tacked to the goddamn fridge anyway."

"This must be Summer's," Jake said. "She's got your audacious sense of color." Lizzie did not reply. "Now, Hannah would never have a purple tree."

She dumped spaghetti into the water boiling on the stove. It was true. Hannah's trees would be green, her pumpkins orange, her witches black. Summer's witches had been red, her turkey decorated with purple and pink feathers.

Jake hummed the tune to "How Long Has This Been Going On." "May I help, Liz?" he said. "Hold Theo, maybe?"

"Set the table." She picked forks and knives out of the drawer. "The napkins are in that basket on the counter."

Jake stared down at the collection of silverware askew in his hands. "Lizzie . . ."

Lizzie cocked the hip Theo straddled and raised an eyebrow at him. Jake turned away to place the napkins on the table. She put Theo down. He clung to her legs, crying, "Mami, Mami." She mashed garlic with the flat of a chopping knife, sliced onions, some mushrooms, with a vengeance.

"Sure you don't want me to hold him?" Jake held out his hands to Theo. "Up?"

Lizzie was glad when Theo pressed his face against her legs and cried, "No!"

"Maybe I'll light the candles, then."

"There's plenty of light in here."

"Liz." Jake held out his hands. "I'm trying."

Candles had been Lizzie's ritual, not his. She banged at another garlic clove. She would sauté these vegetables and then dump in some jarred marinara sauce. That was all the effort she would make.

"How about we do it for Hannah?"

Lizzie swiped with the back of a hand at her forehead and lifted

Theo onto her hip. This is our baby, she thought, the statement suddenly encompassing something beyond this simple fact. We made him together. From upstairs Summer shrieked, "Ma. *Ma.* I do *not* have to wear a dress, do I?"

"No," Lizzie yelled back.

"Excuse me a sec, would you?" Jake walked to the bathroom, where he stayed for a long time. Lizzie held Theo away from her, seeing Jake there in the hair, more wispy than Jake's, but as curly and as black. There he was, too, in the dense brown eyes, even in the chin, still hidden in baby fat. But where was she? She hugged Theo so hard he yelped.

Hannah came downstairs wearing a party dress, white socks, and her black Mary Jane shoes. In the calf-length white dress, a ribbon tied to keep her hair off her face, she looked like an illustration out of the volume of *Alice in Wonderland* she'd just finished re-reading. "Where's Jake?" she said, worried.

"In the bathroom."

Hannah climbed up on a stool. "How come you didn't tell me he was coming, Ma? I could have made place cards."

"Wash some lettuce, Hannah."

Somehow she got through the pandemonium of serving the plates and arranging seating. Hannah wanted to be next to Jake, while Summer didn't want to be next to anyone. Jake seemed to enjoy the pasta. Lizzie couldn't stomach a thing. She got up to fetch the Parmesan cheese, then to open a bottle of wine, then again to get the salt. While Theo pounded his hand in the coils of spaghetti on his plate, Hannah told Jake about his vocabulary.

"Everything's a ball," she told him. " 'BA.' "

"Ba?" Theo said, pointing at Hannah's plate. He pointed to the candles. "Ba."

"A candle's not round, Theo," Hannah said.

"It has a halo," Summer argued. "The light looks round."

"Cosmic," Lizzie said, "don't you think? Ball. Circle. The interconnectedness of everything, as Maud would say." She slopped a little more wine into her glass and topped up Jake's, although he had hardly sipped what was already there.

"You know Aunt Maudie?" Hannah said to Jake, excited.

"He met her here, Hannah. Years ago. You remember."

"You know her?"

Jake shook his head. "A little. I ran into her a while back. When I was having coffee with Sue. At Joanie's one morning."

Lizzie set down her glass. Red wine sloshed onto the table. Maud had not mentioned this.

"And I've seen her dancing at Farquaarts."

"With Rich Pack." Lizzie got up to get a dishrag. "I don't approve."

"It is curious."

"Curiouser and curiouser," Hannah said. "Like in *Alice in Wonderland*."

"I don't know him much, except he's always late with his rent," Jake said. "And Jeep's let a few things drop."

"He was a little shit with Jeep." Lizzie's tongue felt too large, her words blurred together.

Hannah said, "Ma! You go wash your mouth out with soap."

"What'd he do to Jeep?" Summer asked.

Lizzie shook her head.

"Ma, *what?*"

Jake said, slowly, "Sometimes, when people love each other a lot, or have loved each other a lot, when they decide to split up, sometimes they aren't very nice to each other."

Lizzie looked at him sharply, but he didn't seem to be aiming this in her direction. Summer rested her chin on the edge of the table. "You mean Rich was mean to Jeep because he *loved* her?"

Lizzie snorted. Jake said, "Not quite like that. Maybe Jeep loved Rich too much, and it started to bother him."

Summer rocked back. "Oh I know *exactly*. Scooter likes me that way and I am *so* mean to him." She giggled. "On purpose I tripped him and when we're standing in line I push the backs of his shoes down."

"Well, then you understand." Jake sipped his wine.

"Or that could mean you like him," Lizzie drawled. "People have funny ways of showing things sometimes."

Jake glanced at her. He chased a few squiggles of spaghetti around his plate.

"Anyway!" Hannah said. "You should get to know her. You'd like Aunt Maudie."

Theo pointed at Jake. "Daitch?"

"Daitch?" Jake repeated.

"We haven't figured that one out yet," Hannah said.

Theo tongued papped carrot onto his lower lip. He pulled at the wad with grimy fingers and examined the blob of food. He dangled it over the edge of the high chair's tray until it fell to the floor.

Jake looked away, swallowing. "Yuck!" Summer said. *"Gross."*

"That's him just being a kid," Lizzie said. "You used to do the exact same thing."

"I *never* did."

Jake pressed a napkin to his mouth, looking so much like a caricature of an offended woman at a tea party that in spite of her efforts, Lizzie laughed. She leaned over and scraped up the food with a fingernail. "You get used to it."

Jake kept his eyes on his plate and nodded.

"I'm never having kids," Summer said. "Ever ever *ever*."

"Why not?" Jake asked.

"Because life is *horrible*."

"Oh, bananas," Hannah said. She patted her hair and adjusted the knot of her ribbon, which peeked out, lopsided, from behind one ear.

"Bananas yourself. I *know* about this. No one cares about *our* future." Summer's voice rose to a shriek. Her braids seemed activated by her vehemence—they stuck almost straight out from the sides of her head. "This country is going to pot and nobody cares about what happens to us."

Jake mouthed "Willy!" at Lizzie, who nodded, aware, once again, that she kept having to stifle a great desire to simply enjoy this conversation.

"Like today," Summer said, "Mrs. Farr tells us that no matter what our parents say Russlimba has it right. We'll probably all die before we grow up because of Saddam, and the Democrats won't let us kill him. And Sally used all the blue paint and Sam won't let me in. *And* Luna's dead. Did you know I ran away?"

"You did?" Jake clearly didn't know whether to take this seriously.

"You didn't tell him, Ma?" Hannah said.

"Killing Saddam has nothing to do with the Democrats." Lizzie gave another piece of cooked carrot to Theo. "And Rush is an uneducated slob."

"Mrs. Farr says everyone will say that. She said someday the world will see he's a clever clever man. Half the world already knows it, she says, and the others will find out soon enough. Clever, clever, she says."

"Oh dear," Lizzie said, looking, in spite of herself, at Jake.

"I did run away, and everyone was all worried," Summer said. "Aunt Maudie came over in her car. She's the one that found me. She said I scared her, that I scared *everybody*."

"I'll tell you about it later," Lizzie said.

"And then *he's* here"—Summer pointed at Jake—"and *then*"— she pointed at Lizzie—"you didn't go to the store the way you said you would and there were no snacks and now we're having plain old spaghetti and I was so hungry."

"Boy," Jake said. "Life *is* horrible."

Summer folded her arms and slumped in her chair. It was clear that by agreeing, Jake hadn't made life any better.

"Jake-o." Hannah folded her hands on the table. "How's your music these days? How's your band?"

Lizzie stared at her in astonishment. Sometimes she didn't know where this creature had come from, with her liking for Mary Jane shoes and her inevitable sense of the polite thing to say. While Jake answered her, Lizzie piled their plates into the sink. She loaded the remaining spaghetti onto a plate. "Run this up to Sam," she said to Summer.

"He won't come to the door," Summer said. "And anyway, his house stinks."

"Summer!"

"It *does*. It smells terrible when you go in there. And I miss Luna." Her voice shook, but she took the plate of food.

"If he won't let you in, leave it outside on the steps. But be sure to tell him, loudly, that we send our love. Put on your coat first."

Summer banged out the door.

Hannah sponged off the table without being nagged. Jake rinsed the dishes and put them in the dishwasher. Theo remained in his high chair, watching the activity in silence, eyes beginning to glaze, eyelids drooping.

Lizzie mopped the counters, wishing Jake would just go home. She didn't want to have the talk he was here to have. When Hannah asked if they could all watch a video together until bedtime she said, "Great idea. It's such a *normalizing* thing to do." Jake put down the sponge, turned to stare at her. She gave him a wide, false grin. "Go choose," she told Hannah, and shooed her into the den.

Jake turned on the disposal as Summer slammed through the door. She was shouting, crying. Lizzie could not understand her above the noise. Jake turned off the motor. Summer grabbed hold of Lizzie's shirt. "He's just lying there. He isn't moving. Right outside the trailer, like he was trying to get here." She pressed her face into Lizzie's belly. "He's dead, I just know he's dead, like Luna."

Jake headed for his coat. "I'll go."

Lizzie wanted to stop him. The ache in the middle of her chest had to do with a confused need to handle this all by herself, while being grateful—horribly, terribly grateful—that Jake was there to handle it with her.

"I'm coming too," Summer said, but Jake was gone.

"No. You need to stay here," Lizzie said. "Watch Theo." She carried Theo into the den and explained things to Hannah.

"You shouldn't leave us by ourselves," Hannah said, her lower lip trembling. "You stay. Or make Jake stay."

"We'll be back as soon as we can."

She pulled her parka from its hook by the door and ran up the trail that had been made by Summer's small steps through snow. No light burned in the dark hump of caboose. A rustler's moon, a fingernail clipping of silver, rested just to the left of Fable Mountain's white hump. The mournful tune from one of Jake's songs snaked through her mind. *Someone's going to lose something tonight.*

Jake crouched by the bricks that served as steps outside Sam's door. Lizzie sank to her knees beside him. Sam was a collapsed scarecrow, a bundle of cloth and bone. "Oh, Sam." Lizzie pressed an ear to his chest.

Sam moaned.

"What should I do?" Lizzie whispered. "What do we do?"

"Door's stuck." She felt the breath of Sam's words against her cheek.

Jake fiddled with the latch, then stopped. "There's no point in taking him in there. He should go to a hospital."

"No hospital."

Again Lizzie felt rather than heard the words. She slid an arm around him. He felt like a sack of bones, as small as, and far more frail than, Summer. "Not unless we have to."

"No hospital."

"Could you find a blanket?" Jake said. He'd gotten the door open.

Summer was right. The trailer smelled of rotting vegetables, of beans or milk gone sour. Lizzie fetched a blanket off the bed and took it out to Jake, then rifled through Sam's closet and drawers to find a sweater, shirt, some socks, some ragged underwear, a pair of ratty overalls. Nothing seemed clean, but she could wash it. In the mildew-encrusted bathroom she picked up his toothbrush. The bristles were worn almost down to the plastic. She put it back in the dirty glass beside the sink. She had plenty in the upstairs bathroom. She found a plastic bag in the kitchen and stuffed the clothes into it. The sink and counter were filled to overflowing with dishes. In a million years no one would call Sam fastidious, but it had been a point of pride to keep his dishes clean, his kitchen tidy. Something was terribly wrong. And where had she been? What had she been thinking?

Jake had managed to work the blanket underneath Sam. Together they maneuvered him into Jake's arms. "He's so light," Jake whispered, to which Sam said, "No trouble."

Lizzie ran ahead of them down the hill. In the living room she swiped the throw pillows off the couch. "Girls?" she called. "Hannah. Summer."

Jake carried Sam through the front door, kicking it closed with his heel, and into the living room, tracking snow. He lowered Sam onto the sofa. "No trouble," Sam muttered.

Hannah and Summer stood in the doorway of the den. Summer had fingers in her mouth, a habit she'd finally lost six months ago. "Fingers!" Lizzie said, too harshly.

Summer took them out of her mouth to ask, "Is he dead?" and put them there again.

"He's sick," Lizzie said. "We don't know how sick." She fetched the afghan that was kept over the back of the couch in the den. "All right, girls. Time to get to bed."

Summer shook her head and watched Lizzie drape Sam with the afghan. "Is he going to die?"

Jake put a finger against his lips and beckoned to her. He hoisted her onto a hip. Lizzie watched her grab on to his shirt and hitch herself into a firmer position. He took Hannah by the hand and on the way up the stairs said in a low voice, "Let's not talk like that. He might be able to hear."

Lizzie picked up Sam's limp hand and tried to check for a pulse. If Jake weren't here, she asked herself sternly, what would you do? You would know what to do. Sam's hand was spotted with age and with purple bruising caused, Lizzie guessed, by skin that had no fat beneath it, skin that pressed right up next to the bone. She put her cheek against the cold, bruised skin. When had he gotten old? "Sam," she said. "Sam."

The fingers moved beneath her cheek. The hand trembled. "Goodbye," he said. "Okay. Go home."

"You are home, Sam. But we have to get you a checkup. We have to see if you're okay."

An expression crossed his face. Irritation at not being understood, at his predicament. She pressed his hand again. She checked on Theo, asleep in the den, and picked up the phone, stood holding the receiver until the nasal recording told her, over and over again, "If you'd like to make a call, please hang up and dial your operator." She hung up when she heard Jake coming downstairs.

"If he doesn't want to go the hospital—" she whispered. "He's always been so clear about that. But what do we do?"

Jake took the phone. "I'm calling Sue."

Lizzie carried Theo upstairs and put him in his crib, then went in to kiss the girls. "Jake remembered where we keep our nighties!" Summer told her.

Hannah reached for Lizzie's hand. "Don't be mad."

"Why would I be mad? Of all things." Lizzie tucked their sheets and blankets in around them firmly. "Sam may go to the hospital. Think good thoughts."

She detoured into her bedroom and fetched the down comforter. As she came downstairs she could hear Jake on the phone in the kitchen. She covered Sam, stared down at the face, such a well-known face, the skin sinking in against the beautiful bones beneath.

It took her a moment to realize that there was another voice in the kitchen. Lizzie went around the corner. Maud stood just inside the door, coat buttoned up. The high collar and muffler made her look like a Victorian woodcut.

"What on earth are you doing here?"

"Hannah called her," Jake said.

"She made it sound like you guys would be gone a while and would I come over," Maud said. "She said she didn't think they should be all alone."

"Alone? They've been alone a zillion times."

"How's he doing?"

Lizzie shook her head. Maud began to take off her coat. Jake stepped forward to help. His hands were long and shapely against its dark fabric.

"You get hold of Sue?" Lizzie asked him.

"She's on her way. The place will be scuzzy with sisters. Including the two upstairs, we'll have a swarm."

"A gaggle," Maud said. "A school, a pride."

This was clearly some joke they shared. Lizzie went back to Sam. Maud and Jake followed. Maud knelt beside the couch and took Sam's hand. Her long skirt fanned out perfectly on the floor behind her. The pose reminded Lizzie of an illustration from *Little Women*, or *Little House on the Prairie*. It seemed to Lizzie that Maud must know what she looked like, must create, on purpose, these pictures, illustrations in the saga of her life.

Jake watched from the same chair in which he'd sat earlier that evening. "Some normalizing time," Lizzie said, using her most dismissive tone. But Jake only nodded.

"Sam?" Maud said.

Sam's eyelids flickered.

"Sam. Jake's sister, Sue—she's an RN?—Sue is coming out here to take a look at you."

"You remember Sue?" Jake said.

"Enough," Sam muttered. "Okay, goodbye."

Maud gave Lizzie an agonized look. Lizzie looked away, watched for the faint rise and fall of Sam's breath in the mound of comforter. The silence was unbearable. She wondered how soon Jake and Maud would fall into bed with each other. She was tempted to say this out loud, try it out as a joke. It was a joke, wasn't it? She wondered how she could think of such a thing at such a moment.

Into the long silence Jake said, "So both you and Jeep are working at the Red Garter."

Maud nodded. "I like her so much. She makes working there bearable. Although they're all a good bunch."

"Maud's boffing Jeep's ex," Lizzie said.

Maud looked faintly, comically dismayed. Jake's eyebrows managed to convey both surprise and disapproval.

"Thanks," Maud said. "Boffing."

"Well." Lizzie tried to fix things. "He's Jake's tenant."

"So he said. Actually, I've been looking for a word like that." Maud was making a determined effort to be cheerful, and Lizzie saw what all those L.A. studio executives must have seen during the auditions Maud had told her about, when she knew she was trying too hard. Skin stretched tight, eyes in a panic, neck muscles protruding, voice high, her excruciating thinness ramified by the tiny space into which she seemed to huddle.

"I've been wondering what on earth the word is. When *fuck* is too harsh and *making love* not—" Maud paused. "Not what's it's about." Now, suddenly, with her dancer's posture—the angle of her defiant torso, the skirt draped over her legs, the length of calf emphasized by a pointed toe—she was a figure of elegance. Maud the chameleon. Crone, goddess, little girl. What turned it on, what turned it off?

"*Boff.*" Jake nodded. "Certainly beats *screw* for a sense of the casual."

"Right. Somehow 'You feel like fornicating?' doesn't sound exactly nonchalant."

"Or 'Let's copulate'?" Jake tried. "And there's *bang*." He didn't meet Lizzie's eye. "As in 'bang away.' "

"Or *bonk. Roger.*"

"*Roger!*" Jake grimaced. "Now that's descriptive."

Lizzie twitched at the comforter. Why didn't they just go do it and get it over with?

"Did. . . ," Sam said.

Jake moved closer. "What's that? What'd he say?"

"D-diddl . . ."

Jake looked at Lizzie, puzzled. She chuckled and squeezed Sam's thin ankle.

"What?" Jake said. "Do you know what he's saying?"

Lizzie rocked back and forth, smiling, shaking her head. The first time Sam had used the word *diddle*, she'd been insulted. They had been lying on a mattress on the floor of what was now the studio, a fire roaring in the woodstove. "Did you have a nice diddle?" he'd asked. She thought he'd said *piddle*. But eventually it became a code word: "Feel like staying over and diddling?" she'd ask. Or he'd say, "Want a little diddle?" It described more accurately what his finger or tongue did before he entered her, rather than the act itself, but the word had its sweet connotations.

At the sound of Sue's car, Jake headed outside. Lizzie followed, running down the porch stairs. Sue's ponytail, worn high on her head, was tidy, even at this hour of the night, and her hug was long and hard. She smelled of soap, or bleach. "It sure is good to see you," she said, "though I'm sorry it has to be like this. It's been far too long."

"Good to see you too." Lizzie found herself light-headed, even nauseated by the faint aroma associated with hospital corridors. It was as if she breathed in the smell of the aftermath of the night Jeep had tried to kill herself, post Rich—all that seeming cleanliness and control masking the chaotic messes life can deal. She took a deep breath of the cold night air. "Sam's inside."

Maud, balanced on the arm of the couch, looked like some black-draped gargoyle. Sue hugged her. "We meet again."

When had all this happened? Lizzie wondered. When had Maud met Sue, or spent enough time with Jake to share a joke?

Sue bent over Sam and folded back the blanket. With deft hands she checked his pulse at both neck and wrist, lifted an eyelid with a thumb, held a palm along his cheek, neck, forehead. Lizzie folded her arms, wishing for an iota of the expertise implied by those practiced, efficient gestures.

"Ma?" It was Summer, at the top of the stairs. She whispered, extradramatically, "Is he going to *die?*"

"Hello, Summer," Sue said, "remember me?"

"Hey, Aunt Sue!" Hannah's voice this time. The two girls descended the stairs.

"Up, up." Lizzie waved both hands. "Back you go."

"Ma."

Upstairs, Theo began to wail.

"Oh great," Lizzie said. "Thanks a lot, girls."

"Want me to get him?" Jake asked. "I'd be happy to."

Lizzie ran up the stairs before he could move. When she came back down, carrying Theo, Summer and Hannah were on the floor beside Maud, who had her arms around them. Jake had put his coat on.

"We'd better take him in for a look-see." Sue folded a stethoscope back into her purse. Her face looked pinched, a line etched between her eyebrows. "I'd feel better about it."

"No doctor." Fretful, Sam moved on the sofa. "Home."

Sue took his hand. "We need to take you where some tests can be run. We'll find out what's best. If it's best for you to be home, we'll bring you back."

Again that look of irritated disgust took hold of Sam's face. He used Sue's hand to pull himself towards her. The darkness visible in the slit between upper and lower eyelid made Lizzie think of the bottom of a canyon at midnight.

"I know, Sam," Sue said. "We'll get you back as fast as we can."

Sam sank back in exasperation, face clenched in pain.

"Is this the best thing?" Maud asked. Tears loomed in her eyes. "Would a doctor come here?"

"He wants to stay *home*," Summer said. "Maybe he wants to do like Luna did."

Sam pointed a shaking forefinger in Summer's direction.

"You called me here," Sue said. The look she gave Lizzie seemed to ask for permission, or even forgiveness. Her nostrils were edged in white.

"Of course," Lizzie said. Theo tugged at her blouse. "Not now, Theo. You need my car?"

"You're not going with him?" Maud asked, clearly shocked.

"We'd best take mine," Sue said. "We bought it for precisely these kinds of—adventures. Would you carry him out, Jake? And Maud, would you run out and lower the passenger seat as flat as it will go?"

"Me too," Summer said, running after Maud. Hannah stared at Lizzie. "You aren't going with him?"

Lizzie thought of fluorescent lights, shiny corridors. Syringes. Tubes. Sam. "No," she said, "Jake is. I have to stay here. With you. And Theo."

"We should *all* go."

Sue helped Jake lift Sam. Carrying Theo, Lizzie followed them outside. A light snow had begun to fall. The windshield wipers of Sue's van pulsed. The heater blew hot air. A combination of exhaust and mist swirled around the car.

"May I come along?" Maud said to Sue. "I'll just get my coat." She sprinted across the driveway and up the stairs as Jake lowered Sam carefully into the passenger seat. "I'll have Sue drop me off at home," she told Lizzie as she came back out. "I'll get my car tomorrow."

"Can I go?" Summer pleaded. "Can I go with him, Ma?"

Lizzie shook her head. "Call as soon as you know anything. No matter how late."

"We will," Maud said, climbing into the back seat.

"I'll meet you there," Jake said.

Sue backed the van and headed down the drive, brake lights flashing, avoiding the worst of the potholes.

"Well," Jake said.

"Well," Lizzie said back. It didn't come out nastily. She shivered. "We need to put the girls back to bed. I need to. Hannah!"

"Why didn't you go?" Hannah said. "Why didn't we all go?"

Lizzie stared after the red flash of brake lights wondering if here too Maud would be better than she was. Summer, Luna. Now Sam.

"Sam needs her, but you need her, too," Jake said. "C'mon. Bed-time." Again Summer went to him, willingly hoisted herself up into his arms. He put out his hand for Hannah's.

Lizzie sat in Theo's darkened room and nursed him, listening to Jake in the bathroom exhorting the girls to brush their teeth.

"We haven't eaten anything since last time." Summer's voice was high and plaintive, ready to dissolve into either tears or anger any second.

"It's a good ritual before going to sleep. You'll feel better, promise."

Lizzie listened to the squeaky spigots, the sound of brushing, of spitting, the murmurs of good night from the bedroom. As she low-ered Theo into his crib Jake appeared in the doorway. Lizzie beck-oned him closer.

"It wasn't so bad, was it, Liz?" Jake said, staring down at Theo. "My being here?"

Lizzie adjusted a fold of blanket. "But you have to decide if you want to be a father to Theo because you want to do that, or if your wanting to be a father has to do with being around me. There's a big difference."

He raised his face to hers. White and shocked. Those dark eyes. But before he could say anything the girls peeked around the corner, ghostly in their long, pale nightgowns.

"You were all tucked in," Jake said.

"Will Sam be okay?"

"We won't know until Sue calls," Lizzie said.

"Wake me up. As *soon* as you know."

Hannah tugged on Jake's sleeve. "I want to tell you something."

He leaned down. She whispered in his ear. "Me too," he said.

Summer pointed at Jake. "Is he staying?"

"Are you?" Hannah said.

"You, young lady"—Lizzie pointed—"are to tell me why you called your Aunt Maudie to come all the way out here when you are perfectly capable of looking after yourself and your siblings. And why Maud? Why not Jeep? She even lives closer."

"I knew you'd be mad." Hannah had her head down.

"Maybe this isn't the time, Liz," Jake said.

Lizzie flared. "So all of a sudden you know all about raising children?"

"I'll be downstairs."

"Night, Jake-o," Summer said.

He left the room. Hannah concentrated on balancing on one foot. "We didn't call Jeep because she's always working."

Summer said, "She *wants* to go to school!"

Lizzie almost had to laugh at the expression on Summer's face. Hannah kept her head bent. "And Maud is family."

"So's Jeep," Lizzie said.

"So's Sam," Summer added.

"It was a very odd thing to do, Hannah-hoo."

"We didn't want to be alone," Summer said, in what was probably the first time in two years that she'd sided with her sister. "And anyway, we think if *you* aren't going to like Jake anymore, then maybe Aunt Maudie will."

"Ah. I see. Off you go. I'll tell you the moment I hear anything."

The pillows were back on the sofa and in the kitchen the kettle began to whistle. "Quite like old times," she said as she sat at the counter. She sounded sarcastic, caustic, all the things he used to try to cajole her out of being.

Jake's look at her was filled with a kind of disdain. He shoved the box of tea bags back into the cupboard. "This has been a rough evening," he said. "But it is awfully easy not to like you when you're like this."

Lizzie felt as if she'd been slapped. "Well, maybe you should try Maud. Hannah's right. You would like her."

"I already do. So?"

"More than you like me, I mean."

Jake stared at her, then, weary, shook his head.

"She reminds me of a wounded doe." Lizzie opened the refrigerator, debated between orange juice and beer, chose beer. "She has these brown eyes that look as if she's barely overcoming this mammoth sorrow in her life. I swear to God that's what got her work in L.A. She even has a name for it: *Bruised Innocence*, she used to call this picture of herself. Years ago. She used to get more work. Maybe the look is more appealing in a younger woman. Or maybe after a while the look stops being innocent."

Jake got his jacket. He let it hang off a crooked finger. She tipped the bottle to her mouth, felt the beer course through her veins, an elixir of clarity. "She's folk music but wishes she were rock and roll. She wants to stand by her man but she wants her independence. She says she wants commitment, children, but she's scared to death they'll cramp her style."

Jake scratched at the back of his neck. His eyes looked red and dull and hooded. "Sounds like someone else I know."

Lizzie shook her head. "Not me. She wears this panic in front of her face like a catcher's mask. I keep telling her, 'Just get pregnant. So what if the guy doesn't know. At least you'll have what you want.' " She looked at the bottle of beer in her hand, wondering when she'd gotten drunk.

"I can't believe you sometimes, Liz. I came out here to mend some fences, not pull more of them down." He moved to the window, although there was nothing to see out there in the darkness but the black shapes of trees and bushes against snow. She had stared out the same window many times at night, waiting, though she would not have been able to say for what.

"I don't want to talk about Maud," he said. "And we should be talking about Sam. But what I wanted to talk about, what I came over to talk about, was you and me and what in hell we're going to do. But it's too fucking late."

"Too late," Lizzie echoed, dazed, agreeing.

"I mean that it's too late at night." He turned to look at her, in his eyes that look of hangdog despair that used to irritate her so much.

Lizzie looked out the window. Their faces were ovals of white in the glass. She thought of Sam, in the car with Maud and Sue, on the way to Marengo. "I should have gone," she said, suddenly appalled that she had not.

"We could use my car. No. I could stay with the kids. You could—" Reflected in the window, Jake's eyes were dark holes. He cleared his throat. "I'd been wondering . . . This will sound absurd. I wondered—" He walked a few steps away and then returned, as if he needed this anonymity, this staring into the darkness side by side. "If maybe you'd be at all interested in trying things again. It's no good, of course. I can see that."

Lizzie shook her head at their reflections. "I just don't think I'm made for this man-woman stuff." This was not what she'd meant to say.

Jake groaned. "What a load of crap."

"Maybe I just don't know how to love steadily, you know? I want a hot, fast burn. You want something different." Somewhere, without knowing, she'd been thinking about this.

"How can you say that?" The anguish in his voice turned it dark. "You have three kids. They require pretty damn steady love."

"Kids are different. They need me, they love me."

Lizzie watched as Jake's reflection turned to her, holding hands out, palms up.

"But you see," Lizzie said, as much to her reflection as to his, "there's no question of them wanting, at least right now, a different mother than the one they have. Or—more to the point—of me wanting anyone different from who they are."

Jake fit himself into his jacket. Lizzie walked ahead of him to the door. Blood hammered at the inside of her chest. She put a hand there to make it stop. She looked forward more than she could say to this being over, to closing the door, to leaning her forehead against the cool glass of the front window after his tail-lights had disappeared.

"Liz. Please just look at me. You haven't looked at me once all night."

"I can't," she said, but she did. And there they were, arms around each other, lips finding home, with the ease and sweetness that had always startled them both.

From upstairs came a wail from Theo. Lizzie drew away. "Some-times I wonder if they're psychic," she said. The wail died to a whimper.

"Psychic which way," Jake whispered. "He does want this, or he doesn't?"

"See, you would like Maud," she said, although maybe what

she meant to say was that he was like Maud. She stooped to pick up a miniature plastic tractor that lay on the floor between them. With some awe she observed her hand shaking, felt a shiver deep within her.

"I should go."

She nodded.

"I'll call from the hospital."

She took a shaky breath. "What if Sam—" She stopped.

"You're shivering."

"I'm fine." She folded her arms across her chest.

"Are you cold?"

She shook her head. "Yes. But go, Jake. Go."

CHAPTER 22

MAUD

Weary with toil I haste me to my bed,
The dear repose for limbs with travel tired
But then begins a journey in my head . . .
— SONNET 27

When Maud invited Rich to dinner he only reluctantly agreed to come. "Just don't feed me dirt food."

"Dirt food?"

"Alfalfa sprouts. Rice cakes. Tofu." He said this last with protruding lips, swinging his hands up in imitation of the name of an oriental defense system. "You eat like that, I bet you do. But don't feed me that shit."

Maud wondered if pasta was considered dirt food. She settled on steak and salad. She also bought potatoes, and splurged on a good bottle of cabernet. Simple enough, she thought as she pushed red candles into candlesticks, nothing he could complain about: It was a he-man, cowboy dinner, and elegant and classic too, wasn't it?

As she was putting the potatoes in the oven a knock startled her. She smoothed her hands over her hair as she crossed to open the door. Rich had not struck her as the sort of person who would be early.

It was Noah, lurking out by the edge of the stoop. He wore gloves and a muffler. His thin parka, clearly too small for him, was frayed at the cuffs and collar.

"Hi, Noah." Maud pulled him inside. "Get in here before we let all the heat out."

She squatted beside him and Noah put his arms around her neck. After a moment Noah said, "Our snowman melted."

"Darn rain." Maud squeezed him. "But it was a good one. Those the shoes Santa brought you?"

Noah shoved a foot out, nodding. The shoes were high-topped, way too big. Maud felt the toes. "Santa's a good guy. Can you run fast in them?"

"Can I!" Noah opened the door and sprinted down the steps. He ran around the lawn two or three times, holding his arms out from his sides, yelling, "Whooo! Whooo!" as he circled. "I can beat anything!"

"I just bet you can," Maud laughed. "Now get back inside. I'm freezing."

He came and pressed against her. "You have eye stuff on again."

"I've invited a friend to dinner. He'll be coming along in his red truck any minute. You want to walk down the street to meet him?"

Noah leapt away from her. "I can race his truck," he said. "I can beat any old red truck!"

Maud took the apron off, lit the candles, and got her mittens and coat. She'd bought red plastic peppers that snapped on over the bulbs of a string of tiny Christmas lights. The season was long over, but she plugged them in every night. They glowed merrily.

That morning an unexpected late February rain had melted much of the snow along the sidewalks and lawns. In the afternoon the temperature had dropped, and now the frozen surfaces touched by the street lamps glinted and gleamed. A deep blue permeated the darkness, draping the street and houses with melancholy. She reached for Noah's hand, wondering if women had children so that they could have someone to love—someone who wouldn't mind the immensity of that affection. Children didn't know, yet, that so much love blazing in one direction could be perceived as shameful, an embarrassing manifestation of need. Children took it as their due, received it without running away. At least at first, she amended, thinking of Summer's battles with Lizzie, of Lizzie's battles with their father, and her own.

"My mom gave me a stirrup gun!" Noah let go of Maud's hand to run ahead of her, backwards. "At Kmart! Pow!" He mimed the motion, sighting into a tree. "Pow!"

"Is this him?" Maud whispered at the sound of an engine. "Is this a red truck?"

Noah looked to see what was coming. "Nah. That's just an old Plymouth."

"How do you know it's a Plymouth? How do you know that already!"

"My dad."

"You want up?" Maud held her arms out, surprising Noah as much as herself.

Noah stared at her speculatively. "Okay."

"You weigh a ton."

"I'm a growing boy." Noah nodded happily. At the sound of an engine he cried, "Put me down! I have to race!"

The red pickup swerved around the corner and slowed. Noah dropped to the ground and bent his knees, putting one hand on the ground in imitation of Olympic runners. Rich rolled to a stop beneath a street lamp. Maud walked around to the driver's side.

"Hey," Rich said, not smiling. Beneath his coat he wore a knit shirt with a collar. It was the first time Maud had seen him in anything other than a T-shirt. She was touched, embarrassed too, that he had chosen to dress up.

"That's Noah," she said. "We came to meet you."

Noah, fists against the ground, flexed and straightened his back leg. "I can beat you," he said. "I bet!"

Rich frowned. "What is this?"

"He's going to race your truck," Maud said. "See, in his new shoes he can beat *anything*."

Rich drummed his fingers on the steering wheel. "You want to ride with me, or you want to watch him?"

Maud stared at his profile, puzzled. "I guess I'll stay out here and watch the race," she said. "Ready, Noah?"

Noah nodded, adjusting a foot, cocking a hip.

"Ready, Rich?"

He gunned the engine. Noah giggled.

"First one to the end of the block. On your marks! Get set. *Go!*"

Noah leapt into a run. Rich took off, tires squealing dramatically. Maud grinned; he was playing the game. But the truck didn't slow. Rich reached the end of the block. Leaving the truck running, he climbed out and lounged against it, waiting for Noah, still halfway down the block.

Noah slowed to a trot and then stopped altogether. Maud jogged to catch up with him. "Pretty darn fast!" she said. "Those are some shoes!"

Noah's chest heaved. He held his mouth screwed tight and blinked his eyes over and over again. Maud whispered, "Stupid red truck!" but Noah just shook his head. She held his hand as they walked towards Rich, who leaned against his truck, hands in his pockets, one booted foot crossed across the other. "Congratulations," she said, dry as she could muster.

Noah squirmed his hand out of hers. "I've got to go home."

"Home?" Rich said.

"Well now, wait," Maud said. "You deserve some cider or something after all that!"

Noah shook his head. His eyes were red. Small wrinkles formed around his lips with the pressure of keeping them still.

Rich wiped a hand across his chin. "Maybe he wants to ride in my truck?"

Noah shook his head. "Naw." He headed up the sidewalk.

Maud followed. "Those are good shoes, Noah." She squatted beside him. "Rich just didn't play the game."

Noah's shrug was a tiny gesture inside the threadbare parka.

"Come see me tomorrow, okay? We'll do more playing on the piano?" But he didn't look back.

Rich slouched by the door, hands in his pockets. "You look nice."

Maud waited until they were inside before she looked at him. "Why couldn't you let him win? Or at least let him think he had a chance?"

"Who's going to beat a truck? He might as well learn early." Rich shrugged out of his coat, looking around the room. She'd draped a shawl over the top of the upright piano, which Miles had finally shipped, replacing the one she'd rented from Mountain Music. The candles and pepper lights cast a cheerful glow. Brie and crackers waited on one of the Portuguese plates, and the wine was open.

"For a moment there I thought you'd tricked me." He coated a cracker with a thick wedge of Brie and pointed the knife at her. "Like maybe you just happened to never mention that you had a kid."

Maud sank onto the piano bench. "He lives next door."

"Yeah, well." Rich dusted cracker crumbs from his hands as he moved around the room inspecting the pictures on the walls. He had to stoop from time to time, squinting. In the midst of her irritation she was aware of what those long thighs in their faded jeans could do to her, the wide shoulders so neatly descending to that narrow waist. She and Rich had seen each other in a vacuum of beer at Farquaarts and a few nights in bed. They had never, not once, talked of past relationships, not even of families. It had been a tacit agreement: To bring these subjects up meant they were discussing, however obliquely, the potential of permanence. To avoid them meant they could go on as they were.

"I was just thinking that maybe you'd been acting, is all," Rich said, turning. "Not telling me something pretty damn important. Like you had a kid or something." Flecks of cracker fluttered on his lower lip.

Maud looked away. What sex will do, she told herself, picking up the bottle of red wine.

"None of that fermented grape juice for me," Rich said. "You got beer?"

"I *don't*. I'm sorry, I didn't think. I have water. Apple cider?"

Rich shook his head and reached for one of the glasses. "This stuff gives me a headache."

In spite of this, he managed to drink more than half the bottle. He liked his steak but barely touched the salad. Maud, frustrated with her inability to take him to task regarding his treatment of Noah, had a hard time thinking of topics of conversation. They had depended on the loud music at Farquaarts or the humming silence they created in his bed to cover these holes. She talked of the Red Garter, babbling to fill the silence.

"You and Jeep must work together a lot," he said.

"Yes." Maud felt her teeth moving up and down on a piece of steak. She swallowed and sat back with her glass of wine in her hand.

"Where were you today?" he finally said.

"Visiting Sam."

" 'Cause I called to cancel."

"You could have left a message on the machine."

Rich put a last bite of meat in his mouth and grinned. His lips glistened. He pointed at her plate with his knife. "Only thing better than steak is pussy. As my father used to say. You going to eat that?"

She forked her steak over to his plate and watched him plow his way through it, thinking of Sam, sallow and thin and pathetic in the backless hospital gown, lying against white sheets with his face turned to one side, those long wrinkles like gashes down his face.

"You visited him yesterday. Why doesn't Lizzie take a turn?"

Maud wondered that herself, but she said, "Every day the nurses say he might be able to go home soon, and every day they say it won't be tomorrow. I just want him to know he's not alone."

He'd had a stroke. One side of his body could barely move. He didn't say much, although his black eyes glinted when Maud babbled on about Hannah and Summer, Theo and even Noah. She'd taken to telling him the sonnets she knew, reciting monologues from all the plays she could remember. Today she'd taken a book of poetry with her, read things to him that she once had used for speech and voice exercises: *Oh sylvan Wye, thou wanderer through the woods.* He listened with his eyes closed. *Turning and turning in the widening gyre.* When she paused, his eyes flicked open, fathomless and black. She hoped that meant he wanted her to continue, since that's what she'd done.

Like Eagle that morning over Salt River . . .

Sundays, too, my father got up early . . .

I have seen them coming with vivid faces . . .

When his eyes finally stayed closed she tiptoed away.

"I read him poetry," she said, and then wished she hadn't tried to explain it. She got up to clear the plates. *Don't grieve. Anything you lose comes round in another form.*

Rich took hold of her wrist. "The little boy, Moses, whatever his name is—"

"Noah."

"Biblical bullshit. He'll survive." He moved a fingernail against the inside of her wrist.

Maud let her hand linger in his. Like a moth and a flame, like a cat having its forehead stroked, she was mesmerized, entranced, against her better will, against her better sense. "I just think you could have played the game," she said. "Noah's not stupid, no child is, he knows he can't beat a car. But why not help him create his fantasy, why not let him enjoy it?"

Rich took his hand away. "He'll have forgotten all about it by tomorrow."

"I don't think so."

"You're one cynical lady, you know that?"

"*I* am?"

Rich nodded, passing a finger back and forth through the flame of a candle.

Maud shook her head. Cynical! "We all find out soon enough the world isn't the way we imagined it." Her father, arguing with her, telling her that *Romeo and Juliet* was certainly *not* about "true love." *Why do you think Shakespeare put Romeo's love for Rosalind in there? Eh?* The eyebrows raised, forcing agreement in a face Maud knew, even at the age of fourteen, he would describe as obdurate. *To prove that young love is fickle. If their love hadn't been forbidden, if Romeo had not been banished, their love would have gone the way of all puppy romances. His point is that Romeo would have moved on as soon as he saw yet another pretty face.*

Maud had argued with him, had gone upstairs to cast herself face down on her bed; ultimately this was a lecture about a "crush" she was herself enduring. But she'd been jaundiced about every produc-tion of *Romeo and Juliet* she'd seen since. To Rich she said, "What's the harm in letting a child believe in dreams? As long as they're able."

"Well, we differ there, lady," Rich said, and she wondered, not for the first time, about his childhood—a father who compared pussy to steak, for example. But there was that agreement of theirs, and she wasn't going to break it now. She found herself kissing his forehead, bestowing a kind of forgiveness she didn't in the least feel and that, to her irritation, he didn't seem to feel he needed. As she drew back from this kiss, aware of the silky feel of his hair beneath her fingers, the citrusy smell of his skin, she was reminded of the last time she'd told Miles she loved him. She had asked him—how appalling it was to remember!—to marry her. Had she really wanted that? *We'll see,* he'd said. *I'm not opposed to the idea.*

She stared at her hand on the nape of Rich's neck. When would she stop acting the part she thought she was supposed to be playing? She felt Rich look at her. She met his eyes. "I think maybe we should stop seeing each other, Rich."

A lock of blond hair had fallen across his forehead. He stared, then shook it back, drained what was left in his wineglass, and stood. "Where's my jacket?"

"In the bedroom." Her hands felt useless, hanging by her sides, but there was nowhere to put them now. "I'll get it."

It was lying across the futon where she'd tossed it. As she picked it up he came into the room, put his arms around her, spoke in her ear, a hot breath that made her knees give. "How about a last one, beautiful lady, just to say goodbye?"

She shook her head, but she did not move away.

He slid his hands beneath her turtleneck; his fingers found and released the button of her skirt. As they stumbled towards the futon she felt hot tears gather at the corners of her eyes. After tonight they would not hold each other again. After tonight they would not dance again at Farquaarts; she wouldn't touch the curve of his face, nor sit beside him again in his red pickup.

He drew away. His face, his hair, picked up a sheen of light from the street lamp outside. "You protected?"

"Yes, Rich."

"I got a condom in my jacket pocket."

"If I'd wanted to get pregnant I'd have done it before now."

"I'm just thinking—this will be our last night and then I'll find out you're p.g. or something." He patted her. "Seeing you with that kid got me scared."

"It's not just a kid I want, Rich." A car, turning at the corner, swerved its headlights through the curtains. She waited for the sound of the engine to fade. "It's more than—it's the whole thing, the whole package."

He blew his breath out.

"Right. It's always been a problem. I wonder why. It seems like such a straightforward, normal thing to want. To want to do it with someone who wants it too." She thought of Lizzie, who'd just gotten pregnant when she wanted to, who hadn't waited for agreement. They stared up at the ceiling, bodies separate, two long burrows beneath the bedclothes. "And it's not going to happen. Not with you, not with anyone. I'm too old."

Rich threw back the covers. "I should go."

"Yes." Her voice was calm, far calmer than she felt.

He sat with his head in his hands, rubbed at his scalp, then reached for his hat, which was on the floor beside them. He put it on, took it off again and looked at it. The ridge of his long backbone gleamed. Maud moved a hand up to her chest to feel the miraculous force in the thudding of her heart. This is the best thing, she told herself, and kept herself from reaching to touch that shining ridge of spine.

He stood up, holding his hat, turned to face her. "Jesus! Two people get together to have a good time. It's not about me being the father of your kids, or taking care of you the rest of your life or whatever the *fuck* it is you want."

"I've never ever brought any of that up. Not once."

"It hangs out all over you. Even your stomach, so goddamn flat, drives me crazy thinking about it, what I should do is poke my dick up there, make it round with a kid." He tugged his hat on, pulled it off, held it in front of him as if covering his nakedness. "I can't believe I even *think* about it," he said. "I hate my goddamn family. Never want to bring a child on this earth. I've got to go." He pulled his pants from the heap on the floor. She heard change roll out, keys land with a *clump* on the floor. "Damn." He crouched, gathering these things.

Maud moved to turn on the light.

"No, don't," Rich said. "Leave it off." He knelt beside her, pulled her face to his, and kissed her. "Goddamn it," he said, and continued to pull on his clothes. Dressed, his hat tilted back, hands shoved in his pockets, he stared at her. His body, topped by the hat, was limned by the streetlight and the darkness. Now and again the whites of his eyes gleamed. Finally he said, "If I get back in bed with you, it doesn't mean anything other than the fact that we're going to fuck, one last time."

She said nothing. The buckle of his belt hit the floor. He slid beneath the blanket, the length of his legs cold against hers. He held her, close, tight, their hearts beating together. "Shit," he murmured.

Afterward she lay face up, staring into the darkness, wondering what it meant that she had given in to the demand of her body, and of Rich's. Let it be, she told herself, let it be. But she skimmed the surface of sleep, afraid, as she always was, that if she dozed she would waken into the sucking dread, the litany that murmured in her head: all the wasted, useless moments of her life, all the things she had done and could not undo, all the curving paths twisting back and back and back. *And knowing how way leads on to way.* She could not make out which was the original wrong fork. No doubt this affair with Rich was just one more. She understood she was an unsatisfied person; she sucked melancholy. She was one of those condemned—condemned by herself!—to live an unhappy life.

And in spite of her efforts to be emotionally distant and disconnected, Lizzie-like, the ivy of her heart had crept its way into the trellis of the unsuitable man who lay beside her. She would have a hard time detaching, spiky leaf by spiky leaf. After she'd spent the night with Rich she didn't want to wash her hair; she wanted to keep the lemony smell of him nearby. She would put the ends of her hair to her nostrils and breathe deeply of his sweat, their sex, whatever it was they created together or he rubbed off, like butterfly dust, onto her skin and hair. She'd never felt this way about Miles. But it wasn't love she felt for Rich, it was lust, or maybe just some terrifying need. She was tempted—as she was almost every night—to rise from the bed and call Miles, ask if she could please come home.

Home. Not that she had one anymore. And she never really had, even in those years with Miles, when everything always felt temporary, endlessly mutable. And now home was a rented house filled with found and borrowed furniture; she owned nothing in the material world. Lizzie had used the money their grandparents left them to buy a piece of land. Maud spent it on piano and singing lessons, on photographs and expensive acting seminars; towards the end of her time in Hollywood she'd invested in silk blouses and a push-up bra. She'd used it to buy time in a recording studio for Miles so that she would feel, as she seldom did, that they were contributing something to each other's lives. But she had neither purchased nor created something lasting. Her few accomplishments were in the ephemeral arts, moments gone, as Nikos said, as soon as they were created. Lizzie had paintings. Lizzie had children. Noah's mother had Noah. Other artists had books, sculptures, photographs—tangible mementos of their aspiration and their effort. But only the smallest measure of her artistry would endure: a patched-together video of her appearances on television, a tape of a song. Even memories were transient, and would endure only as long as the owner of the mind that carried them. Her blood ran only in the veins of her nieces and nephew. Not a wrinkle, a crumb, a tear, a dent would show that she'd put her time in on the planet.

Rich slept curved away from her, blankets drawn high up over one shoulder. The hunch of his back—dark blanket against the darker black of the room—seemed protective. And he was protecting himself. He had to. Who could possibly endure the rush of longing that streamed from her? Just as she sometimes literally sat on her hands to keep from touching him, she also sat on her heart to keep its red from seeping through the bandages, where he would see it, and run from its running.

Her life was a huge and heavy tarpaulin, flapping in the wind, the kind of tarpaulin that might hang over a wedding banquet to protect the cake and canapés from the sun. A few tent pegs held sections of the tarp in place—the pegs of acquaintances, her little rented house, her job at the Red Garter, the sound of Rich breathing beside her. But the big pegs, the flat-topped wooden stumps that held the corners, which needed huge-handled axes to pound them into place, were missing. She had Lizzie, of course, and Hannah-hoo, Summer, and Theo. But where were the husband, love, children, career? Her army green, tattered tarpaulin flapped in a dreadful wind that blew through her life. The noise it made was deep and roaring, a thousand rugs being shaken, a hundred vacuum cleaners left on high. Moments like this, the only tether that remained was the ten-cent aluminum peg of her self, her slim, all-too-malleable belief in her self. And amidst the ferocity of the dry, sand-filled wind that roared around her, even this was being yanked, little by little, out of the arid earth. Soon it would pull free, and she would flap and tumble through endless dark and freezing space.

It was no wonder she clung to Rich, the flotsam that had presented itself to her in this cold, heaving sea.

Block that metaphor, she told herself, some desperate humor asking her to look at the blood red heart and the seas and the tarpaulins and winds and flotsam and tent pegs that she had depicted and then discarded, the crumpled-up sketches of a frustrated cartoonist, around the bed.

The bed she had made and was lying in.

She lowered her forehead to the curve of Rich's bare back and held it there, breathing.

❊

"God," Rich said, stretching, "I could sleep forever."

Maud opened her eyes. Light filtered through the patterned white cloth she'd made into curtains. She'd slept. She thanked the gods for that, an earnest, heartfelt prayer of gratitude. She kept her face turned away from his, afraid of what she knew would be her puffy eyes, the pronounced circles beneath them, the wrinkles around them. *The morning sun when it's in your face,* Rod Stewart mourned in his rattly voice, *really shows your age.*

Rich stretched again and yawned, a huge, generous sound. Maud pushed back the covers. "We should get up."

He stared at her, grumpy. "Right," he said. But he pulled her to him. Maud breathed in the smell of him, of them. "I'll take you out for breakfast at Joanie's," he said. "How's that?"

She felt his cock rise and lift. He took one of her nipples in his mouth. As he sucked she felt the tug all the way into her stomach, into her womb. She wondered what invisible cording, musculature, physiology, psychology, bound the breast and womb together. And she would never know. A baby would never gaze up at her, pulling love from her eyes and milk from her breast. The ancient and familiar ache of tears made her bend her head to kiss the top of Rich's head. His hair was as fine as corn silk, the simile incredibly apt: white-blond, silky and fine. "Richard," she whispered.

He pulled back. The air in the room changed, no longer sweet and slow-moving but jagged as barbed wire. "Richard," Maud repeated, and then realized: For the first time she had called him by his full name. It acted like an endearment. It was as if she'd said *sweetheart*, or even, *I love you*.

"We should go," she said.

"I got lots to do today," he said at the same time, and kicked away blankets and sheets.

She dressed quickly, thinking that she should refuse the offer of breakfast, she should stay in her house, with a jaunty wave say a final goodbye to him from her little doorway. But when she saw the kitchen, littered with dirty plates and a fatty broiler, she changed her mind. She had neglected to put the cheese away. She did this before they left, although he stood in the door of the kitchen, slapping his hat against his knee. As she placed dishes in the sink, he said, "I hope you're not expecting me to do those."

"Why not?" she said, turning on the hot water. "It'll just take a minute."

But she settled for Rich bringing her the empty wine bottle and the glasses off the table.

The phone rang as they were on their way out the door. She let the machine pick up. Rich paused, clearly interested. "This is Chris Daugherty, Artistic Director of the Fable Mountain Stage Company. Ron Bartlett gave us your name. He said to tell you that he's a friend of your sister's and met you one evening at Farquaarts. We are in the midst of casting our next production, *Twelfth Night*, and wonder if you have a P-and-R you could drop by and some pieces worked up you could show us. Please give us a call at your earliest convenience."

She enjoyed the flicker of interest this aroused in Rich. "An actress," he said. "I forget that. What's a P-and-R?"

"Picture and resume." Her mind whirred. The female roles in *Twelfth Night* were all excellent: Olivia or Viola. Maria.

"Let me see."

She had to dig through a file box to find them. He held one between finger and thumb. She waited to hear what actors always heard: *This doesn't look like you*. And yet that black-and-white representation was chosen with such care and indecision, with the help of agents and friends. So much was riding on the choice: Was this the picture that would get you in the door? Was this the one that glowed with all the stuff of which your art and soul were capable, and was it "pretty," too?

"You don't look anything like this," he said. "You look so beautiful." He turned it over. "What's all this?"

Just her history. Black marks on a single sheet of paper representing the characters she'd brought to life from the literary cyberspace they inhabited between manifestations. Hundreds of these—photo, resume, stapled back to back—had been mailed and handed and requested and discarded in the studios and offices of Hollywood. If she was really lucky, she got a five-minute audition out of it. If she was touched by God, she got a job.

"You were on *Search for Tomorrow*?"

"Briefly. Those are the places I've worked, the shows I've done, the classes I've taken, the teachers and directors with whom I've worked."

"With whom," he mocked, handing it back. "Aren't you going to call the guy back?"

"Later, maybe."

On the brief drive to Joanie's, he nudged her knee with his gloved hand. "Can I have your autograph?" But he did not leave his hand there, and he did not reach towards her again. Maud told herself this was good. After all, they were breaking up—if there was anything to break—and being civilized about it: a final breakfast. She stared out her window at the passing neighborhood, the occasional patch of dirty snow, the houses, pathetic in the bright wintermorning sun. Her breath pooled on the glass. She thought of Lear's anguished vacillation of belief, just before he dies, that his beloved daughter, who he knows is dead, might still be alive: *Lend me a looking glass*, he says. *If that her breath will mist or stain the stone, why then she lives.*

Maud breathed onto the glass again and doodled a flower in the mist with a finger. At least Lear had died comprehending his tragic flaw: *Thou art the thing itself; unaccommodated man is no more than such a poor, bare, forked animal as thou art.* His next lifetimes, if he had them, or the spore of his being that would float into the cosmos upon his death, would be infused by this recognition; he died knowing the lesson he'd been put here to learn. *When we are born we cry that we are come to this great stage of fools.* Would she have a similar moment of realization? Would the chronic bombardment of memories of Miles and life in Los Angeles, or the anguish of her long, wakeful nights, lead her to some understanding of, some justification for, the struts and frets of her hour upon the stage? *I live with bread like you,* Richard II says, *feel want, taste grief, need friends. Subjected thus, how can you say to me I am a king?*

Shifting down for a stop sign, Rich asked, "What are you thinking about?"

Maud tried to think of something other than the truth. "Shakespeare," she said, and laughed. "Life, death, God. 'Men must endure their going hence even as their coming hither.'"

"Can't follow you there, I guess," Rich said. Maud grinned at him, a surprising degree of agreement suddenly warm between them. He shifted, wrapped his fingers around the steering wheel. "And I guess I wouldn't want to."

Joanie's smelled of yeast and coffee and heating butter and eggs. Rich made no gesture of connection, walking ahead of her towards a booth at the back, but Maud was aware that appearing at Joanie's first thing in the morning with him indicated rather precisely the nature of their relationship. Why had she not thought of this? She nodded at the man she saw most days behind the checkout counter at the grocery store, and caught the eye of Lynn, a bartender at Farquaarts. Elmer, the gentle owner of Mountain Music, who played mandolin and had a long white beard, lifted a hand. Her first response, when she saw Jake sitting at the counter with a newspaper, was to turn and flee. In fact, she stumbled on an uneven piece of tile and this attracted his attention. "Well, hello, Maud-Lizzie's-sister," he said.

She wanted to respond to the kindness, and the joke in this, but knowing that his eyes would follow her, that he would see that she was with Rich, made her face hot.

"Hello, Jake," she said as her mind sang, *searching for love in all the wrong places.* She wished she could tell him she was out of her head, out of her heart; could he, would he tell her what to do? He was seeing her, as perhaps the whole restaurant, all of Marengo was seeing her, one more horny lady who clogged the arteries of singles bars, someone who was so desperate that she fucked a twenty-three-year-old she didn't like or respect, rather than sleep alone.

"How's it going?" she said, although she wanted to joke that she was robbing the cradle.

"I'm alive," Jake said.

Maud saw a mourning in those brown eyes, eyes the color of espresso. He had lines in his forehead, as well as around his eyes. She wondered what had happened the night she and Sue had driven Sam to the hospital. Lizzie had never broached the subject; Maud knew better than to ask.

He folded his newspaper. "Sue tells me you've been really good about visiting Sam."

She nodded, aware that Rich, who had seated himself in one of the high-backed booths, was looking irritably around its side at her. "I think we should steal into the hospital in the dead of night and whisk him away."

A waitress paused, hip cocked, pot proffered, and raked Maud with a glance. Jake lifted a hand. "No more, Tina, thanks."

"Well," Maud said. "See you." She slid into the seat across from Rich, hoping that the high back would prevent Jake from seeing who her breakfast partner was. Although of course he knew—she was boffing, bonking, rogering Jeep's ex.

"So all of a sudden you're palsy-walsy with old Jake?" Rich jerked a thumb in Jake's direction.

Maud dropped her head in her hands. The gesture was melodramatic, but it felt true. The actor in her went to work, recording that fact. "Don't, Rich. I beg of you, just don't."

"Actresses. So, what're you having?"

If she were the person she wanted to be, she would stand up and leave.

"Maud?"

"Muffin, tea."

He reached for a section of newspaper that had been left on the table. "Eat more than that. I swear to God your hips are like cow bones you might find out in the desert. Put some flesh on 'em. Have anything you want. I'm buying."

He buried himself in the sports section. She found the pages with "Dear Abby" and the horoscopes. A woman in Baton Rouge wrote to tell Abby that her husband, the father of her two-year-old child, had cheated on her, had stolen money from her in order to pay for the other woman's abortion and had been caught and was in jail for stealing but that he'd become Born Again and wanted to come back and should she give him another chance. Abby counseled a very cautious yes, since he'd been Born Again.

The waitress arrived with the coffeepot. "Hey, Tina," Rich said as she filled his cup. "I'll have eggs and hash browns and sausage and toast and a side order of pancakes."

"Jeez-loueeze!" Tina wore neon blue workout tights under her apron. "Big night last night, I guess! You want those sunny side like usual?"

"Atta girl!" Rich grinned. Maud guessed she was being informed that Tina and Rich were not exactly strangers. Feeling unbearably prim, she ordered tea, muffin, no butter, please.

Rich looked up from a long silence and rustled the paper. "You working tonight?"

Maud wondered how they would get through yet another meal with nothing except the Red Garter and Jeep to talk about. She read her horoscope, which told her that she should rearrange her office furniture, that she should not expect her relatives to approve of her romance. She received a jolt of pleasure, as she always did when celestial advice and her own activities lined up, allowing her to believe there might be some order in the universe. She'd been planning to move the card table in the bedroom to a place beside the piano, where she could use it for notes while she was teaching. And Lizzie's opinion of Rich was clear.

"You know Jeep?"

Maud must have looked blank.

"At the Red Garter. Jeep?"

"That's the third time you've asked me that, Rich."

"Calm down. I was just going to ask you something. I didn't mean did you *know* her. Jesus."

Maud stared down at a section of newsprint, telling herself not to apologize. Tina arrived with their food. She put a hand on Rich's shoulder as she lowered his plate in front of him. "Enjoy. And here's your muffin. No butter, like you asked." She dashed off, legs shapely in their blue leggings.

"She's cute," Maud said.

Rich stopped with his fork on the way to his mouth. She could see a mush of toast and egg there. "You are so amazing." He'd stopped saying this as much as he used to, but once again Maud had the feeling that he didn't really find her amazing as much as incomprehensible. He punctured the top of one egg with a point of toast. "So she's working tonight?"

"Probably." She chewed her muffin, dry sawdust in her mouth, and looked at the want ads, pretending she was a hairdresser, a mechanic, looking for a job.

"You got a headache?" Rich asked.

She was massaging the area to the side of her eye, a gesture she'd caught herself doing often recently, a gesture she had come to recognize as an effort to smooth away the wrinkles she felt forming, etching themselves there. "I don't know why I'm here."

Rich pushed his plate to one side, dug in his back pocket for his wallet.

She folded her section of newspaper and added it to the pile on the table. She looked at her hands, clasped together in her lap. She would let this go, she would, although already she mourned it. He would not again give her that sloe-eyed look that meant *let's go to my bed right now*. He would not again thrust into her, giving her some measure of peace with his maleness, his fullness, his weight, and his seed.

He was watching her. "Richard," she said, and stopped. There it was again, his full name, tender as a kiss, implying an intimacy he had not granted and did not want.

A trace of red started up his neck. He rearranged his knife and fork across his plate. "I hate it when they don't take your plate away," he said. "It just sits there and you have to stare at all that crap."

They both looked at the pool of ketchup on his plate, at the smears of yolk and crusts of whole-wheat toast. Maud felt tears welling. She put fingers to the sides of her eyes, pulling them up and out and stared down at the scarred wooden table, at the dissected, uneaten carrot whole-wheat muffin.

Tina brought the check. "Have a great day, you guys." Her ponytail bounced as she walked away.

Maud followed Rich out the door of the café, glad that Jake was no longer at the counter. They stood for a moment gazing up the street, as if they both expected something to come along. She pulled on her mittens, wishing she could ask Rich to take her, as he might take his dog, Betsy, panting beside him in the front seat, wherever he went this day. "Thanks for breakfast," she said.

"Thanks for nothing. What did you eat?"

She shrugged. He looked at her, the sun dazzling on his dazzling hair. "You'll be all right," he said. "You can always go be in a theater somewhere. Look how they found you."

She knew he meant this to be kind.

"Need a ride?"

"I'll walk."

"All right then. See you."

He strolled away. Maud lifted one hand to shield her eyes from the sun and its reflection on a tin roof opposite, which used her tears as an intensifier. His hips swayed high above his heeled boots. He stopped to look at a poster in a window a few stores down, crossed the street, and got into his truck. He drove away without looking back.

'Tis not so deep as a well, Mercutio says when he is stabbed, *nor so wide as a church door, but 'tis enough, 'twill serve.* She remembered the dirty dishes in the sink with a bleak satisfaction. At least she had that to do. And there was visiting Sam. And she guessed she would return Chris Daugherty's call. She started up the street, glad of the twenty minutes it would take her to walk home, while she figured out what she would do to fill her time this morning, her time this day, her time on earth.

When she got home she avoided the blinking light on her machine, did the dishes, swept, scheduled lessons with a new student. Finally she sat in the chair beside the phone and punched the rewind button: ". . . wondering if you have some pieces worked up you could show us."

She wrote down the theater's phone number. Of course she had some pieces worked up. All those years of auditions, she had pieces in spades. *The best actors in the world,* as Polonius would say, *either for tragedy, comedy, history, pastoral, pastoral-comical, historical-pastoral, tragical-historical, tragical-comical-historical-pastoral . . .*

She sat for a moment, watching as a dusty traveling trunk materialized on the wooden floor. She slipped off the chair, kneeling in homage and in joy before the ancient, decal-decorated box, ready to sift through the array of fabrics and textures that awaited her, the jumble of characters she had assembled over so many years.

She tried on monologue after monologue, shaking out the dusty garments, the velvet cloaks and farthingales, print dresses and faded silks, crinolines and scarves, of Imogen, Viola, Hermione; Nora and Irina; Madge and Blanche and Amanda; the ancient loves of her childhood: Anne, of Green Gables; Alice, of Wonderland. The deflated heroines surrounded her, waiting for life. She briefly considered Juliet's poison speech, though she would never again be cast in a role so young; Portia's speech to Brutus from *Julius Caesar—Dwell I but in the suburbs of your good pleasure?;* and the other Portia, who speaks of the quality of mercy. She lifted out fragile Stella; sturdy Macon; anguished and hopeful Salley Talley; bruised Blanche depending on the kindness of strangers. She brushed them off and tried them on, their words rooted in her memory as if she'd spoken them just yesterday. Within three hours of that galvanizing phone call she was ready. She called the theater. It was an Olivia they were looking for. She scheduled an audition for the following day.

≫≪

Fable Mountain Stage Company was located on Sipapu Street, which made Maud think about Driver for the first time in weeks. She pushed through the ornate, gilded, slightly battered double doors of the theater, wondering how his own sipapu was doing, if he'd been digging in the rain.

Chris Daugherty waited in the lobby. Short, balding, he radiated a palpable energy. His eyes were in constant motion, as if he was looking for something else—something a little more interesting, Maud thought—to come around the corner. He introduced her to his wife, Roberta.

"Call me Bobbie." Roberta Daugherty was taller than Chris, her hand cool and firm.

"Welcome to FMSC." Chris gestured around the lobby. The walls were covered with gilt fleur de lis against a faded burgundy background; here and there the paper peeled away from the walls. The red rug was worn through to string in places. He led her into the auditorium, where the carpet and the seats were similarly aged. He pointed at the ceiling. "We've cleaned those up. Maybe an odd priority, but that's what we fell in love with. Bobbie paints."

The domed ceiling was covered with spectacular murals. Red-cheeked cherubs danced, pranced, played stringed instruments, and sang amidst what Maud guessed were the Muses—Terpsichore and all the rest, breasts and upper thighs trailing wisps of gauzy fabric.

"I wanted to start with the Muses and work our way down." Compared to Chris' enthusiastic boom, Bobbie's voice was soft. "Then the carpets, the toilets. It's not practical. But most of the time, neither is art. I like what Thoreau says. 'You have built your castles in the air. That is where they should be. Now put the foundations under them.' "

Chris held a half smile on his lips, clearly anxious for her to finish. "This building's housed some sort of theater for over a hundred and fifty years," he said. "Burlesque, Chautauqua, a silent-movie house. Ever since the silver rush brought people to Marengo."

"Don't you love to imagine who it was first brought culture to a town like this?" Bobbie said. "Who imported the first opera singer, the first ballet dancer? How did they get enough support from *miners* to build a theater?"

"Women," Chris said. "Harbingers of culture." He hustled them down the aisle, apologizing for being in a rush. "I've got a mailing list to deal with, marketing needs to get out."

Black wings of curtain rose high on either side of the empty and well-lit stage. "We appreciate you coming in so quickly. The woman I'd cast as Olivia decided she needed to spend time with her family—"

Bobbie lifted a hand. "Well, she's done five shows in a row with us. As actress, stage manager, props person. We understand she might need some time with her kids and all."

"Rehearsals start in March," Chris said. "Eight weeks, since it's Shakespeare. Nights, weekends, wherever we can find hours. Everyone's got job conflicts. You bring your resume?"

Maud handed him a manila envelope. "I'm impressed you're doing Shakespeare *and* Chekhov in the same season."

"So are we!" Bobbie said.

"*Charlie's Aunt* was a big success last fall," Chris said, opening the envelope. "And we printed money on our production of *A Christmas Carol*. Very successful."

Maud nodded. "My nieces loved it."

"So we hope that the town will swallow some Shakespeare. It is supposed to be a comedy."

Maud watched him scan her resume. "The fellow who gave you my name—Ron?—told me that you guys run a lot of this out of your own pocket."

"Bobbie's great-aunt bequeathed her money with the edict that it be used 'solely for artistic purposes.'"

At Maud's expression, Bobbie laughed. "Exactly. Can you believe it?"

"It's like a plot from the kind of novel I loved as a kid." Maud looked around the theater. "How perfect."

Chris whistled. "You've worked at some amazing places. Ron Bartlett—he'll be Toby Belch, he was Scrooge in *Christmas Carol*—told us he'd only met you once but that you were impressive. Your resume certainly is."

"Thank you." Maud was glad for Ron, who'd been so upset about his casting when they'd talked at Farquaarts.

"Bobbie, look at all this Shakespeare!"

"He's my first love."

Bobbie smiled. "How convenient. He's always there."

Chris looked up. "And he doesn't talk back."

"A little bit square in bed," Maud said. "But very wise. And funny."

"And the directors you've worked with! What on earth are you doing here?"

"Long story. We'll swap them sometime."

"We'll do that. So. Let's see your pieces."

She walked up the set of movable stairs that abutted the edge of the stage. The lights warmed her face, blinding her to Chris and Bobbie sitting several rows back in the semidarkness. She introduced her pieces and began, and discovered that the months away from driving the freeways of L.A. in search of always elusive employment had changed something. She could appreciate—for the first time!—that she had stored technique as well as characters in the disk space of her memory: her choice to sustain the ends of certain lines; to build in pitch as well as volume; to inflect vowels in specific ways; to sink with ease to her knees and rise again; to know when to hold a pause and when to press on for the laugh. All of these were things she had studied, fervently; she had not realized that at some point she might have learned them.

They were effusive, they were kind. "You're probably more right for Viola than I am." Bobbie laughed. "But I've always wanted to play her."

Maud shook her head. "You're so long and thin. Viola's dressing up as a boy will be perfect on you."

Bobbie shrugged. "I'm too old."

"And I'm too old for Olivia," Maud said. "By the time we have the skill it takes to do Shakespeare well, we're all too old. On the other hand, isn't acting about convincing people we are what we're not?"

Maud almost skipped home, delighted that the theater was walking distance from her house. Chris called later that day to offer her the role of Olivia. In addition, he wondered if she would be willing to work with the other actors on Shakespeare's language. "We'll pay you."

Legs looped over the arms of the large chair borrowed from

Lizzie, Maud studied the sheet of paper on which she'd written the particulars of rehearsal time and place, salary. For one moment she caught a glimmer of possibility: in the transitory and amorphous creation that was theater, perhaps she had built something. Perhaps she was building something. Perhaps, as Rich had said, she would be all right.

CHAPTER 23

LIZZIE

As Lizzie left her office on her way to class she was greeted by Cal and his lopsided grin. Clearly he'd been waiting for the sound of her door to open his. "El Toro for a margarita?" he said. "Sweetwaters for a glass of fine wine?"

"Oh, Cal, I've done it again." This time Lizzie was genuinely sorry. "I've got a conference with Summer's teacher. Next time I won't forget. Promise."

Cal followed her back into her office, watched as she pulled out her appointment book. "Can't next week," she said. "The one after?"

Cal nodded. His eyes, angled down at the outward corners, gave him a sleepy, almost hangdog look. She asked if he needed to write it down, but he smiled and shook his head.

Rounding a corner of the corridor, carrying the weekly load of sketchbooks, she came upon Yvette of the beret. Aaron's arm encircled her waist. The solemn curve of her chin and cheek shifted into a smile at something he whispered, and she rose up onto the toes of her black clogs to whisper something back. The whisper became a

226

lingering kiss that traveled from Aaron's ear to his eye, along his cheek, down to his lips. His hand found her rear end and tightened there, pressed her against him with a muffled groan. The hem of her black smock rose up, exposing skinny thighs. Beneath sheer black tights she wore white panties. Not bikini underwear, not satiny, not flowered or colored. Plain practical white, riding up over one buttock.

Blood beat against the inside of Lizzie's ears and at the backs of her eyes. Her arms ached with the weight of the sketchbooks. Young love, she told herself. It wouldn't last. But it was as if the weight of the books she held in her arms echoed some vaster load. What exuded from Yvette and Aaron was all she wanted. That bottomless, thought-less connection was what she waited for, kept looking for. But it never lasted, and what were you to do when it disappeared?

You had a margarita with Cal.

Voices and laughter sounded down the corridor. Aaron and Yvette drew apart. "Well, hello, you two," Lizzie drawled, walking towards them. "You look cozy."

Yvette turned, clearly pleased to see her. "Hello, Ms. Maxwell." Aaron's gaze flicked her up and down. Lizzie felt her chin rise. He knew. He knew why she was wearing her tightest jeans, her heeled boots, her cropped sweater. He was not too young for that. All his male computer chips were already in place and whirring. She turned away.

Hands on her hips, back to the class, she began to inspect the charcoal compositions hung for critique. This hour and a half of class was always hard on the students, although it was where they learned the most—not from what was said about their own drawings, but from being forced to comment on the work of others. Sara, due to model during the second half, arrived just before break. She was accompanied by a man carrying two grocery bags. He wore a Braves baseball cap pulled low, hair in a long braid.

Lizzie told the class to take a break and went to find Sara and her friend in the dressing room. The man in the Braves cap leaned against the wall beside the bags of groceries. "Vegetables will freeze if I leave 'em out there," Sara said. "Lizzie, this here is my sister's husband's cousin's nephew. Or is it my cousin's sister's husband's boy? Something."

He did not look like a boy to Lizzie. His face was a wonder of planes and surfaces. The light from the window, flattened by the steely skies outside, caught on nose, scarred cheekbone, angled brow. "You want to model for me?" she asked. "What do you think, Sara?"

He shook his head.

"I'll even let you keep your clothes on." Lizzie smiled, trying to charm him, but he shook his head again.

"Don't fun him," Sara said. "He doesn't have much in the way of a sense of humor."

"I want to see what they're drawing," he said. "I'll be out there." He went into the studio. His long torso sat oddly on stocky legs.

"My sister's cousin's husband's cousin?" Sara turned on the electric heater, began to get undressed. "We worked it out once. When I'm done here we're going over to visit Sam. You seen him?"

Lizzie shrugged. "Sure." She'd been to the hospital, once, to pick up Theo when Maud had taken him for the afternoon. Sunk into some deep place inside himself, Sam had barely acknowledged her, hardly responded when she kissed him. The skin of his cheek had been leathery and papery at the same time. It had seemed as if her lips would go right on through to the inside of his mouth. Sam kept his eyes closed.

"Lizzie, girl." Sara stopped in the middle of pulling her arms out of the enormous halter that was her bra. "What is it with you? He's been there for over a week."

"It just makes me—" Lizzie pushed her hands apart, as if she might throw them away. "I don't know how to see him when he's like that. I can't bear it."

"And by not seeing him you're going to bear it better? You're a mystery, girl."

Her father had told her the same thing, when the old family dog had been put to sleep. Maud had been hysterical. Lizzie locked herself in her room to paint pictures of seagulls. Seagulls! "But we don't live near an ocean." Her mother, holding one up to the window, clearly trying to draw something significant out of the subject matter. But there wasn't anything significant. How often had she told them that. Lizzie let herself slide down the wall to the floor. Her feet sprawled out along the linoleum. "I'm tired."

"Everyone's tired," Sara said. "Or sick. Seems like the planet's sickness has got to get everyone sick before anybody does anything about it." She pulled the back of her bra around to her belly so that she could get at the hooks and eyes, and then stepped out of beige cotton underwear as large and square as boxers. Her thighs were like tree trunks—thick, brown, sturdy. The muscles in her shoulders and upper arms were taut ropes, bunched beneath the skin. So much flesh. So much skin, so many places that blood had to pump to. Lizzie felt suddenly exhausted by all the work bodies had to go through, every second of every day.

Sara sashed herself into the kimono she lifted from its hook on the wall, shoved her clothes off the chair, and sat. "I went. He didn't want to see me. Told me to get away."

Lizzie was tempted to ask something she'd wondered for a long time: if Sara and Sam had ever been lovers. But something about the solidity with which Sara sat on the chair, staring at her cracked, splayed feet, kept Lizzie quiet. She heard the large clock on the wall tick.

Long time passing. She wondered when the last time was she'd actually heard Maud sing that song. *Where have all the flowers gone, long time ago.*

"I'm trying to get hold of some clan," Sara said. "He's thinking he's all alone in the world. Doesn't know he's making it be that way."

Lizzie felt something shift, the way a lock might give when the dial is spun back to the third number in a combination.

"I'd do anything for him. He did for me." Sara kept her eyes lowered. "Won't let me."

"Yes," Lizzie said. That first winter, when her hands were so cold she couldn't hold matches long enough to strike them, Sam had arrived unexpectedly and built a fire in the woodstove. Kept wood piled outside the door. Brought potatoes and cheese or onions and wine to augment a meal. Held her, the one time she ever cried in front of him, when she was so scared that she wouldn't make it through the winter, that she wouldn't make it through life. What had she ever done for him that was comparable? What had she ever done for anyone that was comparable?

"Sometimes I hate winter," she said. "I have to get more wood in. Already."

"It's a cold one. Except for the rain. Can't make up its mind. Crazy." Sara stood. "How many positions today?"

"Three." They left the dressing room, Lizzie carrying the electric heater. Students returning from break were setting up easels, flipping the pages of their sketchbooks, eyeing the attractive but slightly ominous presence of Sara's relative. He'd taken off the cap and sat cross-legged on the floor in the corner of the room, his back straight, as if he were trying to be a picture of something. All he needed was a peace pipe.

Sara pulled the model's cube to the center of the room. "I put an ad in the paper down on the Rez," she said as Lizzie draped a piece of cloth over it. "To see if anyone might show up to talk about Sam Dunn, Bitter Water clan."

Lizzie plugged the heater into an extension cord, aware of being watched by Sara's sister's cousin's nephew. Sara nodded in his direction. "That's why he's here."

"He's a relative of Sam's?" Lizzie turned to look at him. He made her efforts at civility—such as the smile she now sent in his direction—seem cheap, manipulative. She raised an eyebrow at him, registering this, and turned back to Sara. "So that means you're related to Sam?"

"I'm probably related to everybody. You're probably related to everybody. The point is, someone should take Sam out of that place."

"I guess we can't," Lizzie said. "They don't let you."

"That right?" Sara surveyed her, eyes dark and steady. "They?"

Lizzie moved to the front of the room, pulling her mind away from Sam, lying alone in a hospital bed on this bleak, cold day.

"Three poses." This was the first exam of the semester, and the air in the studio was charged, anticipatory. "Twenty minutes each. What's at stake here, what I'm looking for, as you better know by now, is that first clean line."

She flicked her eyes past Aaron, sought Yvette's. "I'll stress it again. If you get that, the picture will draw itself. Wait until you know before you put charcoal to paper. No flipping to a clean page. No erasing. Begin."

Sara disrobed and took her first pose—slouched over, head bent into encasing arms. Her face and breasts were hidden, her braided hair looped over one broad shoulder. From every angle in the room the pose was excellent. Rodin's *Thinker* gone female and in despair.

Lizzie passed Aaron without a glance at his pad. She paused behind Yvette, fighting with a desire to find fault—she who was young, who had talent, who had a man who adored her, who would be both muse and model, who would not let life get in her way, who would paint and paint and paint.

Yvette gave her a quick, shy smile. Lizzie's presence did not seem to make her at all nervous. Lizzie had to grudgingly respect this. Most students quailed when she stood anywhere near them. Yvette took her time. She tried a few movements in the air in front of her pad. When she finally allowed charcoal to touch paper the upward, curving swoop of black took in the long thigh, the folds of skin of Sara's belly, the bulky line of the bent arm, the curve of skull and the long down-line of braid. The stroke also managed to convey the inherent melancholy in the pose. The authority of Yvette's hand and arm, that unbroken line that delineated and communicated so much, made Lizzie give an involuntary grunt.

She moved on to observe another student, aware that the atmosphere in the room—intent, studious, disciplined—was both a product of, and conducive to, good work. This had been the climate her own favorite mentors had provided, and as a teacher was what she sought to emulate. She felt an upward tilt of her spirits.

She ambled through the easels and stools, aware of being watched by dark eyes from a corner of the room. "That's it," she said. There were several groans and frantic scribblings and the sound of the large pages being turned. Sara rested and then took the next pose. In her face, lined as it was, furrowed with crevices deep enough to sink a dime into, Lizzie saw that the brown eyes that stared without blinking were not necessarily happy, but they were accepting. Resigned. How did one ever get to be that way?

Today. She would go today, visit Sam, talk to whoever was in charge about letting him go.

Again she worked her way around the room. She paused beside

Aaron. He had not yet begun to draw, although Sara had been in this particular pose for almost five minutes. Lizzie waited, standing to one side and behind him, recognizing the acrid odor that he exuded. She had smelled it in the arms of nervous men. She folded her arms, waiting for him to make his first stroke. Aaron cast her an imploring glance. She arched an eyebrow at him and moved away.

For her third pose, Sara lolled against the back of the cube, presenting breasts, belly, pelvis, legs separated, one bent, the other straight. Lizzie watched from a corner of the room, aware of hands flashing in and out from the sketch pads. She thought about the beautiful boy-man who had posed in a similar position for the class last week, a young ski-patrolman. She had enjoyed prowling the room, looking at his body and at her students' renditions of it. Yvette had concentrated on the semierect cock that probed out of tightly curled pubic hair. Then too, Lizzie had felt a grudging respect and affinity for the girl. It was what she would have chosen to draw herself.

Now, standing in her corner, she listened to the long pull and quick scratch of charcoal. One day that beautiful boy-man's pubic hair would be gray, the lovely cock would have a hard time rising. He would have wrinkles deep as Sam's arroyos in his handsome face. He would have age spots, tired limbs, skin that no longer pulled tight against muscle.

She checked her watch. She had stood for ten minutes without moving, as if she were a pose herself. "That's it," she said, and ignored the groans. "Close 'em up, hand 'em in."

She stood at the table at the front of the room as the students dropped their sketchbooks off. Sara disappeared into the dressing room to change. The nephew-cousin stayed where he was. His gaze at her, at the room, at the disappearing students, seemed full of loathing. She resisted the impulse to stroll towards him and ask, "What's your problem?" But as she listened, nodding, to the murmurs and excuses of her students handing in their sketch pads, she thought that after all she would not go to the hospital today. Not when Sara would be there. Or this fellow with his hateful stare. Nor when Maud was there, either. What she would do, tomorrow or the next day, was make some calls, find out how to spring Sam from the hospital. She would bring him home, put him by a window in the living room, where he could look out at the sky, the bare trees, the snow, his trailer. Summer could see him every day when she got home from school. But today she would go home, turn on the heat and lights in her studio, and paint. Seagulls, maybe. Or self-portrait of cactus.

CHAPTER 24

JAKE

the water goes on rolling
down down down
the water keeps on rolling
can we step into it twice?

T he elevator slowed, stopped, pinged. The doors opened. Eleventh
floor, Mountain Memorial Medical Center. Jake stepped out.
Linoleum squeaked beneath his boots. Corridors spoked away from a
central reception desk. He stood in line to ask for directions. Ahead
of him a Native American with a long braid and cowboy hat wran-
gled with a nurse over some paperwork.

Waiting, he stared at passing nurses, at his boots, at patients, visitors. Then he saw Sara, reading a magazine in the lounge area. Last
time he'd seen her he'd been living at Lizzie's. She wore her usual
long skirt, unlaced work boots, man's shirt. She looked up as he
approached.

"Well, now, it's Jake! You visiting Sam?"

He nodded.

"We are too."

Hope flashed like a blast of reverb. "Lizzie with you?"

"Ought to be. Shame on that girl."

Jake agreed. But it would be a betrayal to say so. He'd gotten up
enough nerve to call her that morning, ask if she'd visit Sam with
him. Her machine had picked up. He'd left the message. She hadn't
called back.

"He's down there." Sara pointed. "On the right. Number eleven fifty-six. There are four beds, separated by sheets. He's D."

The Native American, still in heated discussion with the nurse, looked up as he passed the reception desk. Jake nodded at him, sympathetic to the hassles of bureaucracy. Got a long dark look in reply.

The pulled curtains in room 1156 did look like sheets. In the quiet cacophony of sound—televisions tuned to different stations, visitors engaged in chitchat—he recognized Maud's voice:

> *I do not want them in a boat*
> *I do not want them with a goat.*
> *I do not want them in a den,*
> *I do not want them now or then.*

He looked around the curtain. Maud held Theo on her lap, book perched between his legs. Sam had his face turned in their direction, eyes closed. Attached to a wrist were clear plastic tubes connected to bottles attached to various metal contraptions around the bed. Sam's face was leached of color, features drawn in upon themselves, pinched.

"I do not want them, Sam I am." Maud made her voice intense and irritated. *"I do not want green eggs and ham!"*

Theo chuckled. Sam uttered a small sound. Jake pushed the curtain aside.

"Hey, Maud, Theo. Hello, Sam."

Maud's face lit with that surprising smile. She jiggled Theo on her knee. "Look, Theo! It's Jake."

Sam opened his eyes. Jake sat on the edge of the mattress and took his hand. "Salad," Sam said, and then something else Jake couldn't understand. Maud watched Sam with a face full of worry. "We didn't understand that, Sam," she said. "You want to try it again?"

Sam closed his eyes with a look of utter disgust. Jake kept hold of his hand. Theo leafed wildly through the book, saying, "Sam I am" and "Green eggs and ham!"

"Where's your ma?" Jake said.

Theo looked at him. Brown eyes. Maud's eyes. Or, Jake thought with a jolt of pleased surprise, his own. "Ma," Theo said. "Ma?" And then a series of unintelligible sounds.

"I'm having trouble understanding everybody, it seems," Jake said.

"Ma's at school. Having a conference with Summer's teacher."

"Is that bad?"

Maud tipped her head in Sam's direction. "She's been off the deep end lately."

Theo said something that sounded like "Maud read book."

"Next time, Theo. I've got to go. I've got rehearsal."

"Rehearsal?"

"Moon said now," Sam began, and shook his head. His fingers moved inside Jake's hand.

Maud nodded. "I've been cast in a play! Shakespeare, no less."

"Well, congratulations, Maud. I'll have to come see it."

"I hope you do. Sam says I'm storytelling."

Sam nodded.

"Ball." Theo pointed at the light fixture in the ceiling. The *l* was distinct now.

"It's shaped like a ball," Maud told him as she slid the book into a large canvas bag. "Or a circle, really. But it's called a light. Tell Jake where your eye is."

Theo pointed. "Eye. Nose."

"That's Jake," Maud said.

"Dake."

Again Sam's fingers moved within Jake's.

"Which play?" With a thumb Jake smoothed the wrinkled skin. "Not that I'd know. Except *Hamlet. Romeo and Juliet.*"

"*Twelfth Night.*" Maud manipulated Theo's arms into the sleeves of an impossibly small parka. "I'm even getting paid. In L.A."—she said these two syllables with an odd, quote-marked emphasis around them—"most of the time you act for free. 'Showcases,' they're called."

"Same thing in the music world." He was hit with memory. Dark clubs, tables ringing a postage-stamp-sized stage, air thick with smoke. Guitars glittering blue and silver, women in white heeled boots. All those free performances offered up in hope that Producer X or

Record Label Owner Y would be in the audience and grab you. Grab your song. "I'll walk you to your car." He leaned over Sam. "I'll be right back."

Sam's eyes slitted open. "Not the circus." His smile was a rictus.

"Just to my car. See you tomorrow." Maud bent over Sam. His arms went up, shaky, circled her neck.

Jake looked away from this and found Theo staring at him. Chin pulled in, lips pursed, brow furrowed. "Hey, Theo. Don't look at me that way. I'm a nice guy."

Maud tucked her hair into a large front-brimmed cap. She looked like an urchin. "I was telling Sam I'm not sure why, after all this time and agony, I still want to be an actor."

"The moon falls down," Sam said, or something like it, followed by a string of syllables. Because it seemed appropriate, Jake nodded. Maud said, "He'll be right back."

As they left the room Maud handed him Theo. "You carry him." Theo came into his arms, gazed at him, suspicious, then squirmed, looking at everything they passed. Machines blinking red, green, blue, yellow lights. Half-open, darkened doorways. A woman moving her walker, then her feet. Patients in wheelchairs staring into space. Jake, carrying Theo, realized that those they passed would assume he and Maud and Theo were a family. Amazing what the actual, complicated relationship was.

Beside him, Maud took an audible breath.

Coming towards them were Sara and the fellow in the cowboy hat who'd been talking to the receptionist. Maud moved behind Jake, pulling at her cap.

"Is that Maud?" Sara paused. "I didn't know you were here. You leaving already, Jake?"

"I'll be back," Jake said. "Just walking Maud out."

"Maud?" The man with Sara squinted suddenly.

Maud had drifted to the opposite side of Jake. She put out a hand. "Hey, Driver."

Sara said, "You know each other?"

"It is just so amazing to see you." Maud's *so* hit a high note. She smiled without showing her teeth. Skin above her cheekbones flaring red. "This is Driver. I met him when I was driving here. He was hitchhiking. I gave him a ride." She flushed, if possible, an even brighter red.

Jake shook his hand. "Interesting name. We know someone named Jeep."

"It's that kind of a world." Driver stared at Theo with a kind of boggle-eyed amazement.

"Where is that that sister of yours?" Sara said. "She should be here."

"Ah, Lizzie. The teacher." Driver nodded.

Theo patted Jake's arm. "Ah wa ma wa wa ma."

"Theo's right." Maud put a finger out for Theo to wrap a fist around. "We should go."

"Sara knows how to get hold of me," Driver said. "You should do that, looks like."

Maud raised her eyebrows. "Should I?" She held her arms out for Theo, who tumbled into them, talking.

"I'll be back," Jake said to Sara.

They stood in silence at the elevators. Eyes on the changing floor numbers. "Well, that looked intense," Jake finally said.

Maud burst out laughing. First time she'd reminded him, forcibly, of Lizzie. "I probably don't need to tell you some boffing went on there, some rogering." She sighed. "Odd as it was—and it was odd—I'm very grateful to the powers that be for that encounter." She didn't elaborate.

They left the hospital. She handed Theo to Jake, pulled a tiny hat out of her pocket, snugged it down over Theo's ears. Jake blinked against the onslaught of sun, reflected off patches of snow, roofs of automobiles. Maud unlocked her car, dumped her book bag into the passenger seat, squinted up at the hospital windows. "We should get Sam out into this, cold as it is." Closed her eyes to the sun. Jake studied the lines around her eyes. Some delicate as cracks in a china plate, others radiating like a sunburst. "Funny how getting cast in this play makes me feel I belong here."

"Box." Theo bounced and pointed. Jake was aware of an ever-growing drag on his forearm. Wondered how Lizzie did it, holding

Theo on her hip for hours, even cooking at the same time. "Box?" Jake repeated.

"Do you have a minute?" Maud asked. "He likes to play in the sandbox."

"It's freezing."

"He likes it. Just for a few minutes. Then I'll take him back out to Lizzie's."

Lizzie's name invoked a silence. Maud got a plastic pail and shovel out of the car. They climbed a slope of iced-over earth and dirty frozen slush that led to a swing set, slides, an enormous green plastic turtle surrounded by trampled snow. "Plonk him down in there."

"Box!" Theo said happily.

"It's not a box," Jake said. "It's a turtle. A turtle with some very cold insides."

Theo waved a shovel at him and spoke at length. "We have it on good authority," Maud said when Jake looked at her, "that this is a sand turtle."

"No matter. It looks cold and hard and unpleasant." They watched Theo dig. "Tell me about your play."

"I think I'd gotten so used to *not* getting work that I'm still a little stunned." Strands amidst Maud's black hair glinted red. Jake was pleased to witness Lizzie there. "You give an audition all you've got, and when you get home you look for that little blinking light on your machine that might be good news. But it's your agent saying, 'Not this time, hon.' You have to live with yourself afterward, pump yourself back up to size, explain to yourself: 'It isn't you, you're just not what they're looking for.' Your agent says, 'They went blonde with the role, hon.' Or 'They went black with the role.' "

"They say that? They do that?"

"Once they went *male* with the role!" They both laughed. "Or they tell you—this is a direct quote— 'She's wistful but not pallid, Maud, so don't go bouncing in there.' So you tone down the energy, even though it's been drummed into your head that's what you *must* take with you into an audition, and they call to say, 'You just didn't have quite enough energy.' They say, 'You weren't classy enough' or

'You were a little too classy' or 'You're just not pretty enough, you're not sexy enough.' "

"They *tell* you those things?"

"Once I even got 'You were just too pretty, hon.' That's when I decided agents have this list taped to their desk. They're talking to a client. They close their eyes and point—" She demonstrated.

Jake nodded. "Put out by Pick-an-Excuse, Inc."

"Patent pending." Maud looked towards the hospital, intent, as if she could see through walls and windows. "I'll always be grateful to Driver. It took him to snip the umbilical cord that held me to Hollywood."

"Randy, the bass player in my band? Wanted to know why you'd come here."

"Why on earth! On bad days I think I've jumped out of the frying pan of Hollywood into the fire of the Red Garter. Talk about creating your own reality. Now I'm a time-travel Playboy bunny. How is that any different from what I was doing in La-La land?"

"She wondered if you miss L.A." He made his own questions belong to Randy.

"Some things." They watched Theo squat by his pail, sifting sand into it. "Probably like you miss Nashville?"

Observant of her. "As you say. Some things. But I was sick of sending songs out to people who didn't want them. Or wanted to change them so I didn't recognize them."

"Look what they've done to my song, Ma."

"And then there were drugs, especially cocaine, which made me feel smart while I was snorting it, and really stupid the next day. Add whiskey and women—it's like all those country-western songs. Some great people. But I had to get away." He looked up, at a tree with bare branches, at a contrail feathering out in the sky. "And then I went back. You probably know why."

He didn't look at her. After a pause she nodded.

"And now I'm here again."

Theo shoveled sand with vigor. Maud said, "The other day I read that Theodore means loved by God. Gift of God. Something like that."

"Theo." Jake tried the name.

Theo waved his shovel. "No! No home."

"As in theo-logy," Maud said. "Study of."

"Theo-sophy."

"Theo-centric. Do you think Lizzie knew that when she named him?"

Jake pondered this. "With Lizzie you can't know."

Maud's laugh was a guffaw. "Exactly what I thought. I doubt she'd tell me. If I asked."

Jake kicked at a pile of dirty snow.

"She can be frustrating," Maud said. "And I don't know what I'd do without her."

"I called today, asked her to visit Sam with me. But I just got her machine."

"She's being very weird about Sam. But she's always been weird about loss. About losing." Maud knelt beside Theo.

"No home!"

Jake wanted to explore this piece of information he'd just been given. Maud would know! Maud could tell him. But she was dusting sand from Theo's hands, explaining all the reasons it was time to go. Protesting, then resigned, Theo insisted on keeping his shovel as she hoisted him onto a hip.

This is why women have hips, Jake thought, following with the bucket, watching her negotiate the slope down to the sidewalk. To have something those legs, that diapered rear end, could perch upon. The discovery was vast, undeniable. Usually a thought of this magnitude forced its way, sooner or later, into a song.

Hip, lip, trip, his mind began.

Ship. A harbor one came home to?

Maud handed him Theo, opened the car door. He lowered Theo into the car seat, bumping the little head on the edge of the door, struggling to figure how the various straps worked. Theo stayed good-humored, even helpful. "Juice," he said, and let the shovel out of his tiny grasp only when he realized he could not hold on to it and his bottle too.

"He'll be asleep as soon as we start driving," Maud said. "You should do that. Ask Lizzie if you can take him to the park, and then drive him around while he naps. Sometimes I think I'm going to get into an accident. I'm always adjusting the rearview mirror so I can see his face instead of keeping my eyes on the road. Sorry. I'm babbling a lot."

"Not babbling." Jake liked standing here with her in the all-too-rare March sun. "By the way," he said. "I thought of some more words to add to the entry *Roget's* missed."

Maud looked confused.

"*Bop,*" Jake said. "I heard it the other day."

Maud's face cleared. "I thought of some others too. *Going at it.* Not to mention *intercourse.*" Jake made a face and she smiled. "Yes, I thought so too, until I started to think about all the ramifications of the word *course.* Then it's not so bad."

Water coursing down a mountain. A skier, alternating shoulders, slaloming through poles. Jake nodded.

Maud adjusted the rearview mirror. "I don't really stare at him the whole time I'm driving. But look at him."

Theo, blissful, sucked away at his bottle.

"Would you like to have a beer sometime?"

Maud looked at him, surprised, then wary. The glow she'd begun to exude faded away.

Jake gave the top of her car a little slap. "Tell me what to say to Sam."

"I babble. As I have to you today. Or I read to him. He doesn't say much. Sometimes his sentences start okay. Then he gets confused and trails off. You heard him. Usually you can figure out what he's trying to say. But sometimes he opens his eyes and fixes you with a look." She clicked the key back and forth in the ignition. "Sometimes I think a heart attack is about a broken heart, or maybe a tired heart. And cancer is loneliness that's eating away the core of a person."

"Or anger," Jake said, thinking of his father, who'd died of colon cancer. And of his mother, who'd had a breast removed before she died. Jake had never told anyone he thought his father's alternating rages and silences had sucked her insides right out, had dehydrated her love until her heart was dry as sawdust. Another song he'd started. Never gotten past what might have been the hook, or the first line. *he sucked the heart right out of her, he might have done the same to me*

"But I can't quite get what a stroke would be. It has to do with a blood clot in the brain. But the word implies being hit. Something you need to attend to? A mechanism that's frozen up in midstroke? That's been abandoned? He's lost the use of half his body." Her eyes were dark.

She turned the engine on. "I told Jeep I'd have Theo back by three, and I'd better go prep the talk I'm supposed to give to the cast tonight: 'Speaking Shakespeare.' " She put the title in ironic quotes, distancing herself from the thing she could be proud of. Lizzie did this too. About her painting, about her teaching. Irritating quality.

He held up his arm until the car disappeared around a corner of the park. Headed back to the hospital, zipping and unzipping his leather jacket. Lizzie carrying Theo around the kitchen, fixing dinner. Maud hoisting him out of the sandbox.

> *lip*
> *ship*
> *trip*

He tried some lazy rhymes too:

> *sit*
> *fit*

"Ad-lib," he tried, then "Shit."

Impossible. Like the song about his father he'd never finished. But on his way back up in the elevator he kept trying to wrap his mind around a rhyme, an image, a way to slip towards the unexpected, unpredicted beauty of a child on a woman's hip.

⋙⋘

A nurse stood next to Sam's bed. Turned as Jake came in, as if she'd been waiting for him. Sara and Driver stood on the other side of the bed. Driver had his arms folded.

"I must tell you!" the nurse said. Hair drawn tightly towards her white paper cap. Eyes stretched, elongated. "I advise against this in the strongest possible terms. He needs to be monitored very carefully. He's not eating. He's been put on medications—"

"We'll take the meds with us."

Driver was handsome, Jake had to admit, in a surly way. Long hair, jutting nose, black eyes. He looked from Driver to the nurse. "What's going on?"

"We're next of kin. We have papers that prove it."

Jake realized where this might be heading. Where the hell was Lizzie? "Next of kin?"

The nurse held up her hands. "Please understand. I'm not disputing their right. I'm disputing the wisdom."

"Bitter Water clan," Driver said.

"I put a notice in the paper on the Rez, see," Sara said. As if that explained anything.

Sam's eyes were closed. How much of this was he was hearing, did he understand? Jake felt his own jaw tighten.

"It isn't right," the nurse insisted. "He needs to be where we can take care of him."

"You've been saying that for over a week," Sara said. "More. He isn't any better."

"He's better off dying out there, in the living air," Driver said, "than here, where he's breathing death, in, out, in, out, every minute of every day."

The nurse looked stricken. Sara put out a hand. "He's not talking just to you—"

"She works here."

"—but death is in this air," Sara continued. "It's not the best medicine. Not for Sam."

Jake had a sudden, absurd image of his mother's *Reader's Digest*: "Laughter, the Best Medicine." "What about Lizzie?" he said. "Lizzie needs to be consulted."

"Lizzie has abdicated." Driver's tone made Jake want to slug him. "Where is she? Sara's been here almost every day. I've come three times. Where's Lizzie?"

Sara did not meet Jake's eyes. "Once," Sara said. "She has been here once."

"I'm sure there are reasons," Jake said.

Driver folded his arms, a particularly irritating pose.

"She cares. She cares too much. Sara, you know how she is." Maud had just said it. *She's weird about loss, losing.*

Sara bent her head. "I've tried to explain that."

Arms still folded, Driver said, "Interesting way of showing care."

Jake sat beside Sam. Took his hand. "What do you want?"

Sam's eyes slitted open. "Home."

"Where are you taking him?" Jake was troubled that Sara looked so troubled.

"Home." Driver put an edge on the word.

A pinched-faced intern made his way through the curtains surrounding Sam. Driver seemed to know this was about papers. He handed over multiple forms.

"The hospital can not nor will not be culpable," the intern said.

"I've told them," the nurse said, weary.

"He couldn't get much worse now, could he?" Fluorescent lighting accentuated a cluster of pockmarks on Driver's cheek. "What are they doing, these men in white who get paid a million dollars to come through once a day, scribble something unreadable on a chart? Doctors are your gods, drugs another. Money another. Hospitals are where you sacrifice to these deities—"

Sam muttered something. Sara, examining a computer printout, looked up. "Driver. Okay, now."

"And who really benefits?" Driver finished. "Not the ones who are sick."

"That's not altogether true," the nurse protested.

Sara held out the bill. "Two hundred and fifty-six dollars for a foam pad?"

The nurse sighed. "He might get bedsores."

"Two hundred and fifty-six dollars?" Driver seized the bill. "What's it actually cost? Five? And who's getting the surplus on that? Not you. Certainly not me. Not Sam."

"He gets to take it home with him."

This sentence balanced in the air, nosedived towards the floor. The nurse and the intern exchanged a look. Driver shook the bill at them. "Maybe you started in this work because you care. But you have been sucked into this maze."

Sam's hand was cold inside Jake's. Now and again his fingers twitched. Jake cleared his throat. "So where are you planning to take this mattress pad? Not to Lizzie's, I gather. Sam's trailer?"

Sara had her mouth pulled down at the corners. "This is a bad business."

Jake held out his hand for the bill. It was horrifyingly large. Sam, he was sure, had no insurance. "Who's paying this?"

"Send it to this address." Driver pulled a card out of the pocket of his fringed coat, handed it to the nurse. "The government taketh away, and the government giveth."

The intern maneuvered a gurney next to Sam's bed. "You all need to vacate while we get him loaded up."

"Now hold on just a second." Jake's forehead felt bunched and knotted. "Lizzie needs a chance to— Lizzie has to know before this goes any further."

Sara pulled him out of the room. Behind them curtains swished shut. "We're taking him to the Rez," she said. "To my cousin's sister, Maggie. He'll be closer to his own."

"This isn't right, Sara! That isn't his home. Those aren't his people! You're his people, and Lizzie is. *Summer.* This will kill him." He took hold of her upper arm, too hard.

Sara looked away. "But where's she been?"

Jake shook her arm. "Do you want it to be this way, Sara? Do you think this is right?"

Driver spoke from behind Jake. "Lizzie's not clan."

Again Jake wanted to punch him. "Of course she is. The girls practically call him Dad."

"We're the ones came and got him out." Driver's eyes were hard and black.

"Speak of the devil," Sara said.

"Hail, hail, the gang's all here," Lizzie sang, halfway down the hall. Black jeans under a bulky parka made her legs look tiny. "Just got your message, Jake. And here I am!" She hugged Sara, smiled at Driver. "Good to see you again, Sara's mother's-sister's-cousin."

Silence. Jake heard the beeps of medical equipment in the perpetual twilight of the rooms that surrounded them. Lizzie looked from Sara to Jake, put out a hand. "I never did get your name the other day?"

"Driver." He did not take the proffered hand. Lizzie pulled back, eyebrows raised. Flicked a look at Jake.

The intern wheeled the gurney into the corridor. Sam's body a narrow mound beneath a pastel blanket.

"Hey, Sam." Lizzie stepped forward. "You getting some tests done?"

Sam's eyelids fluttered.

"They're taking Sam out of the hospital." Jake kept his eyes somewhere to the side of Lizzie's face.

"How did you do that!" Lizzie's eyes glittered. Jake could not read her face. "I should have known you'd get this handled, Sara! I was coming to ask about it today. And I thought it would be so complicated!"

"Well, sure," Sara began.

"Not sure," Driver said.

"Maybe, Driver, we should—"

"Maybe we should not."

Lizzie looked like a confused puppy. Checking their faces for the bone that was being hidden by one of them.

"You never visited him." Driver had his arms folded again. "Sara tells me he lived on your *property* and you never visited him. And even while he was here, sick and old and maybe dying—"

"What are you talking about?"

Sara made a sound like air escaping from a tire. Sam rolled his head back and forth. Down the hallway, a nurse taught an emaciated young man how to use a metal walker. "Move, balance, step," Jake heard the nurse say. "The balance there in between is important."

"What are they *talking* about, Jake?"

He cleared his throat. "What does Sam mean when he says 'home'? That's the important thing."

"Move, balance, step."

Sara gazed off, down the hall, away from Lizzie.

"Bitter Water clan." Driver shoved his hands in his pockets, rocked back on those silly heeled boots. "He should come to his people."

Jake wished they weren't in a hospital, so he could yell at Driver the obscenities the asshole deserved.

"But we are his people." Lizzie sounded puzzled.

Sara nodded. "Sure, we thought of that."

"What do you mean, you thought of it?"

"That's where he got sick," Driver said.

"He got sick because his dog died." Lizzie's voice was loud. "And what the fuck do you know, anyway?"

"He got sick because he was lonely. Sara's told me how often you visited."

"Summer went up there every day!"

Driver's nod was insolent. "Some company that is."

"She's good company, Driver," Sara said. "That's not the point. He's been lonely, Lizzie. We've discussed how he is. He needs to know he has family. I've thought about this a long time, about what is right." Sara looked miserable.

"What is right!" Lizzie cried.

"We're taking him to his people."

Driver had a real knack. For the third time in twenty minutes Jake wanted to knock him down. He took a deep breath. "Lizzie and her children are Sam's people."

"Clan, then," Driver said. "Tribe. It's a different thing. He needs to be near those of his own blood."

"Blood?" Lizzie's eyes were wide.

"If he's going to die soon—"

"He's *not*."

Only once in the three years they'd been together had Jake seen Lizzie cry. That twisted mouth. Swiping tears from her cheeks. His chest ached. He had never felt more helpless.

"But if he does, he should know he has these things," Sara said. "That he comes from these things."

"He has *us*. *Please*, Sara."

Driver gestured to the slack-jawed intern. Began to walk towards the elevators. With a glance at Lizzie, the intern set the gurney in motion.

Lizzie turned a stricken, awful face to Jake, then ran to catch up. Walked beside the gurney, touching Sam's face, his hand. "Sam. Tell them no."

The intern, looking scared and young, cleared his throat again and again. Jake wondered if he should lie down in front of the gurney, chain himself to it. As if reading this thought, Lizzie ran ahead of them, put her hands out to bring the gurney to a stop. The people in wheelchairs at the sides of the corridors watched in astonishment. "Now you stop this," Lizzie said. Jake could see she was trying to bring her voice under control. "You can't do this."

"But we can," Driver said. "The papers are signed."

The doors of the elevator slid open. The intern, looking embarrassed, turned the gurney so that he was pulling instead of pushing it. Lizzie, holding on, was pulled into the elevator with them.

Sara put a hand on her shoulder. "You need to let go, Lizzie."

Lizzie stumbled backwards out of the elevator. Reached blindly for Jake's arm. "What am I supposed to do?" Shaking. Mouth twisted. "Oh, Jake, what are we going to do?"

CHAPTER 25

L I Z Z I E

NOTES FROM BENEATH THE MAGNETS OF LIZZIE'S FRIDGE

HINTS FROM HELOISE
UNEXPECTED GUESTS?
In a big laundry basket, stash anything that doesn't belong in the rooms
where the guests will be. Hide it in the bedroom closet.
   Kid's room a mess? Close the door!
   Dishes in the sink? Load them into a plastic dishpan and stow it in
the oven.

Lizzie was pondering the cord of wood Bud had dumped outside the house when Maud's white Toyota bumped its way up the driveway. Leaving the engine running, Maud got out of her car, her face white beneath her urchin cap. "Where did Sara and Driver take Sam?"

Lizzie pulled on a pair of work gloves. "Who is that asshole, anyway? Jake says you know him."

"Where did they take Sam?"

"You planning to go fetch him?"

Maud's nostrils were white-edged. Her stare was furious. Lizzie kicked the pile of logs. "I've got to teach this afternoon. Help me get this out of my driveway before it snows again."

Maud turned her engine off. In the storeroom next to the kitchen Lizzie found her a pair of Sparky's work gloves. They didn't speak for some time. Maud tossed the split logs up the flight of stairs, Lizzie piled them under the eaves. Maud was clearly struggling with what she needed to say, and Lizzie found herself glad that verbose Maud was wordless. What would Maud have done against that asshole who'd appeared out of nowhere to lay claim to Sam? How would she have dealt with Sara, who with smiles and pretended wisdom—*you need to let go*—had pulled Sam from her life?

"And I thought I'd never see him again," Maud said suddenly. It took Lizzie a moment to realize she was not talking about Sam. "Have you called Sara?"

"If you're so goddamn interested, why don't you call Mr. Asshole yourself?" Lizzie dropped a log on the pile, kicked it into place. "They were taking him to Sara's cousin's sister's place. Or something."

Maud blew a sibilant breath and began to pitch wood again. Lizzie wished the lecture would just start and be over. She'd been teaching. She'd been busy with the girls and Theo. She'd grown too accustomed to the work Sam did around the place, ordering and stacking wood, getting the storm windows up, making sure the pipes wouldn't freeze, checking the roof, gutters, insulation, and other details so myriad she didn't even know what they were. So the gutters had filled with leaves and overflowed, disastrously. She'd had to order another cord of wood in the middle of winter. Summer's school kept calling her in for conferences. She had to teach, prep, grade. She had no time. Not like Maud, with her piano playing and theater. No kids to bog her down.

"Let's switch. That way I can practice both tossing and stacking." Maud's voice was irritating, falsely bright.

"This doesn't take *practice*."

"Everything is a practice." That bright, cheery voice. "Interesting word, really. Violin players and dancers practice. But lawyers and doctors *have* a practice."

Lizzie uttered a soundless groan, kicked another log into place.

"So maybe the idea behind the word is that you can find what you need to know about life—even your experience of life—in each action you do. Practice. Catch."

In spite of herself, Lizzie felt the heft of log through her leather glove, smelled a faint aroma of resin. But she said, "For God's sake, Maud. It's just something you do."

Maud threw another log, hard. "I'm trying here, Lizard. I'm

freaked about Sam. I'm afraid he's going to die. But you have an electric fence around you on that subject. So I'm trying not to talk about
it. Give me, as you would say, a fucking break."

They tossed and caught, stacked and piled in silence. Lizzie assumed Maud was pondering practice, her tedious practice of making
everything-be-a-metaphor-of-everything-else. Wood, the catching
and stacking of wood, its goddamn relevance to her life, to Lizzie's
life, to Sam's life. Logs. Source of heat. Came from trees. Trees lived,
logs burned, which meant trees died. There was something in that.
She imagined ashes blowing up out of the chimney, settling over the
land to be turned into new growing things. Death into life. But that
led to wondering where on the Reservation Sam might be. She
moved her mind back to wood, the way one used to move a needle
on a record player past a song one didn't want to hear. There was
tossing. And stacking. She liked stacking better. Was that significant?
Maud would find a way to have it be. Fitting things together? Lizzie,
trying to wrap her mind around the concept, grew tired.

Maud, false-bright again: "Someday, when I have a house with a
fireplace, I'll have practiced how to throw and stack wood, and I'll be
ready."

Lizzie shoved a log into place. "So now we get poor Maud's
litany of how she doesn't have anything and I do. How her art
is so intangible and mine isn't. How I have kids and she doesn't.
How I make fucking greeting cards for a living, while she performs
Shakespeare."

Maud dropped her gloves and the piece of wood she was holding
onto the ground and walked to her car.

"I'll give you Sara's fucking phone number," Lizzie called after
her. "You can do what you want with it."

Maud opened her car door, stopped. "Sometimes I think you just
hate the fact I moved here."

"Bullshit." Lizzie yanked her own gloves off, slapped them hard
against her jeans.

"And I'm so grateful I had you to come to. But you seem so mad
at me. All the time."

"I'm not."

"Mad at something. And I don't quite understand why you should be mad at me."

Except that you've taken over my life, Lizzie thought but did not say.

Maud stared into the distance, clearly making a decision. She closed the car door. "Did you know that Jeep's seeing Rich again?"

"She better not be."

"I think she is. From things she's said. Here. You toss. Let me catch for a while."

Even as she was grateful Maud was staying, Lizzie resented her being magnanimous. The wedges of pale wood arced through the air. When they were done, Lizzie fetched the broom to sweep the stairs. "I'll do it." Maud closed her hand over hers on the broom handle.

Lizzie tried to get her hand out from beneath Maud's, but Maud held it there. For the first time in a long time Lizzie was aware that Maud was the older sister. "What?"

"I ran into Jake. At the hospital yesterday."

"Really."

"While I was visiting Sam. He walked me to my car. We talked a little. Theo played in the sandbox."

Quite the little family. Lizzie resisted saying this out loud.

"He mentioned our having a beer sometime." Maud began to sweep. Her hair swung forward, obscuring her face. "This seems rather unmonumental now, with Sam gone, but yesterday I felt very weird. I thought I should talk to you."

"Why on earth?"

"I just thought, I don't know, that you should know."

"Why on earth? I've only not had anything to *do* with him for, like, two years."

"Okay, fine." Maud handed her the broom. "I came to tell you that. I thought it was the right thing to do. And to find out where Driver is. You don't have to bite my head off." She headed down the stairs and got into her car, then proffered a pile of mail out the window. "I picked up your mail on the way in. Letter from Mom. I got one too."

Lizzie reached for the letter on top of the pile of magazines,

catalogues, bills. Their mother's neat handwriting decorated the back
flap, postmarked Oxford, England.

"They're coming."

"Here?"

"For the opening. Of the play." Maud carefully did not say "my
opening" or "my play." Lizzie used a fingernail to slit open the thin
flaps of the aerogram. She scanned the letter, read aloud:

> . . . *so* <u>*glad*</u> *to think of you girls together. Your father is a bit worried
> about Maud's shift in career aspirations, but we are* <u>*delighted*</u> *she's
> found Shakespeare of all things in that town of yours.*

"That town of mine," Lizzie said, shaking her head.

"You should hear them on the subject of Hollywood."

> *She's always been so* <u>*good*</u> *at theatre; television is just a* <u>*sacrifice*</u> *of
> her talents. I don't know how she'll make any money, or actually*
> <u>*maintain*</u> *the career she's been trying to create for so long, but after all
> those sad years in that* <u>*dreadful*</u> *Hollywood, we hope she is happy.*

"See what I mean?"

> *She writes glowingly of all the help you've given her. Your father and
> I are very touched at your generosity and enthusiasm in sharing your
> lovely life with her.*

Lizzie looked up. "My lovely life."

"It is lovely, Lizard."

Lizzie shook her head, went back to reading aloud.

> *We need to come back and sort out the Seattle house before we leave
> again, this time for Singapore. We thought we'd use it as an excuse to
> come see you! Maud will be doing her show and we'll have a chance
> to see your new paintings and the kids. We haven't seen Theo since
> he was three months old! I still carry that wonderful card you sent us
> for your gallery opening in Santa Fe last year.*

"They didn't come for my 'show,' " Lizzie said.
"I know."

Your father is working __hard__, as always. Most days I seldom see him until dinner, but I'm happy enough browsing through bookstores and having tea and scones or sherry and chocolate digestives at little __shoppes__ around town. Sometimes he meets me for a half pint at a pub. I try to get him to play darts but so far he's refused . . .

"They've never come here. But now they come to see you in a play." Lizzie wondered at the sense of hard fury that came over her whenever she imagined her parents coming to visit. She had moved away from them so that they wouldn't be able to pass their judgments on her life, her house, her children, her furniture, her dishes. Her father *galled*—his word—by *the abundance of progeny*—again, his words— and the lack of marriage. When he saw the trailer she could imagine what he'd say—"You call this a studio?"

"They never visited me either. They hate Hollywood. Dad's embarrassed by my acting. He told me I should have been a scholar, that I was wasting my time and my intelligence."

"At least you do Shakespeare. Not like Southwest Ink." She saw Jeep's car coming up the drive. "I'm late. I've got class. Sara's number is in my address book on the counter in the kitchen. Under Roantree." She ran upstairs. Only after she'd stepped into the shower did she realize that things might be a little awkward between Rich's ex- and current lovers. But she did not go back down to facilitate.

She chose to wear a skirt. A short black skirt and a red shirt with mother-of-pearl snaps. Black stockings, her red cowboy boots. She stomped down the stairs into the kitchen.

"Wow! You look real cute." Jeep sat on a bar stool in front of Theo's high chair, holding a spoon full of something orange and gooey. "He's not eating anything."

"He won't eat for me either. It's another tooth."

"There's supposed to be a really bad storm brewing." With her hair scooped up in a high ponytail, Jeep looked about twelve years old. Except for her body. Lizzie ran a hand up the back of her own upper thigh, checking for an extra bulge, softness. At some point, she thought, no matter what you did or didn't do, a body simply started to sag. But this made her think of Sam, and this made her stomp into the kitchen. "Don't leave these open," she said, slamming a kitchen cabinet shut.

Jeep slurped another spoonful of pureed carrots into Theo's mouth. "You never wear skirts. You meeting someone?"

"Shit." Lizzie stopped in midstride, ignoring Theo's "Shit!" She flipped pages of her appointment book and slapped her hand on an open page. "I can't postpone it again. I'll be home late."

Jeep screwed her lips up and off to one side.

Lizzie wrapped a muffler around her neck. "I'll come as quick as I can. I know you have AA."

Making engine noises, Jeep headed the spoon in for a landing at Theo's mouth.

Lizzie paused in the middle of zipping up her parka. "Jeep. You have a date!"

The red in Jeep's cheeks deepened.

"Who's it with?" Lizzie walked over to stand in front of her. "Jeep Sarah-Ann Smythe. Are you going out with Rich?"

Jeep shrugged.

"Are you?"

"He says it's different this time." Jeep got up, tugging at the back of her jeans. "I *knew* you wouldn't approve."

"What's to approve?"

Jeep ran warm water over a cloth and began to wipe Theo's hands and face. "I wanted to talk to you about it, I really did. It happened so fast. He says he's learned things. He says it'll be different. He says he's really changed. He says he learned a lot from Maud—" She stopped.

"Maud? He says he's learned a lot from *Maud*?"

Jeep lowered Theo to the floor and began to wipe down the high chair. He squatted, playing with his animals.

"What on earth would he, could he, *learn*?" Lizzie gathered up paperwork she needed to turn in to the office and shook these. "Ten months ago your heart was broken. You had all these realizations about what had attracted you to Rich, reasons you told me weren't good ones."

Jeep's head was bent, her shoulders round. "He's nicer than I made him sound."

"Jeep." Lizzie did not speak aloud the thought that nevertheless thrummed in the air between them: *You tried to KILL yourself. Because of him.*

Jeep nodded, shrugged, her hands in her pockets. Lizzie swooped towards her, held her hard. "You don't want me hurt," Jeep said into her shoulder.

Lizzie shook her.

"He's changed. He really has."

"Good," Lizzie said, though she didn't believe it. Theo started to cry. Lizzie kissed the top of his head. "Theo's a mess. There goes any hope of weaning him this week. The Orajel is in my bathroom. Rub it on his gums. I'll try not to be more than an hour late. God knows what Cal and I can talk about that long."

Outside, the temperature had plummeted. By the time she dashed across the driveway to her car the fingers with which she held her collar closed were brittle with cold. She shivered as she waited for the engine to warm up. Winter's wind howled around the house. *Prowling,* Jake had called it when the girls used to climb into bed to complain about the noise. In the field beyond, naked branches stretched up towards an implacable gray sky.

She stopped in town to drop the girls' books at the library and then headed up the hill to campus. In the office she said hello to Pat behind the desk and checked her box, which contained the usual assortment of invitations, departmental notifications, flyers. Nothing from Cal.

Surprised, she scribbled him a note and put it in his box: *See you around 5:00 for that long-awaited drink?*

She had scheduled midterm student conferences for the entire three-hour class—reviewing portfolios, discussing progress made, progress that needed to be made. Somehow the first hour and a half inched by. Lizzie wanted to throw back her head and howl when she considered that another hour and a half still awaited her. The idea of a drink with Cal began to hold deep appeal. She would knock back a shot of tequila alongside her margarita. She would cross her legs on the bar stool. She would buy the second round.

Aaron and Yvette arrived together. They'd signed up for the two last slots. Yvette sat outside the studio during Aaron's appointment. "Here you're on the right track," Lizzie made herself say.

"Thanks, Ms. Maxwell," he said when they were done, riding hard on the *Ms*. He swayed towards the door, some inner rhythm lifting him up on the tips of his bulky, round-toed boots, his walk a kind of bebop, ragtime dance. As he disappeared around the corner, Lizzie heard him say in a bad French accent, "You're up, my leetle mushroom."

Lizzie wanted to tell Yvette that she should not allow herself to be anybody's little anything, but instead worked hard to make Yvette realize what was and what was not excellent in her work. When she handed back Yvette's portfolio, the girl held it clasped to her chest, resting her chin on its edge. "Maybe you'll think it's, like, really weird that I'm telling you this." Her eyes grew shiny. "And it's not because I'm ass-licking or brownnosing or whatever. But I just love this class and I'm just really grateful for everything, even how tough you are, not everyone likes that but I do and you're teaching me things the way I always thought it would be but it never was."

Lizzie felt her own eyes burn. "You're doing the work."

Yvette's thin shoulders, sheathed in black, moved up and down. "No," she said. "I mean, I am, but, you know."

As they emerged from the classroom, Aaron, slouched against the opposite wall, straightened, brightened, looking over Lizzie's shoulder for Yvette. Not one glance, Lizzie thought, for her, for her legs in their black stockings, the miniskirt, the red heeled boots.

※

She unlocked her office. A note lay on the Navajo rug. She stepped past it to sit at her desk, putting her head in her hands. She was off track. She needed to paint. She'd let the girls and Maud and her anger about Sam get in her way. Jake prowling around, taking up her energy. *Sam*. She groaned. She needed to get back to tubes of paint and the smell of turpentine, to the safety of a canvas, to the depths of work.

But first she'd take Cal up on that margarita. She wheeled her chair across the floor to pick up the note.

Lizzie—
My turn to call it off. Can't make it today. Sorry.
Cal

She careened out of her office and knocked on Cal's door. As she held out the note to him she saw that her hand was shaking. Cal took in her outfit and looked away, as if something outside the window had all his attention.

"Sure you don't want to hit El Toro for a quick one?"

He shoved his hands in his pockets. "Something's come up, I guess."

Lizzie stood in the hallway feeling like a fool. "Well," she said. "Well. I've certainly done it to you enough."

Cal raised his hands to his hair as if he wanted to pull some of it out. "Something's come up."

Lizzie waved a hand. "I've always got so much to do."

"That's what I figured."

She stood between their two offices after his door had closed. She'd been looking forward more than she could say to sitting in El Toro's squeaky equipales, stirring a short red straw through a mess of crushed green ice opposite a man who found her attractive. She'd wanted to listen to canned mariachi music and know that she could still cast a spell. She'd wanted to dip chips in salsa and know a world existed that wasn't all children, and old men waiting for death, and ridiculously young love. Love love love that never lasted.

The wind hit her like a blast of ice as she stepped outside. Snow swirled and spat through the lights cast by the lamps in the parking lot. She jogged to her car and started the engine. She let it run, deliberating, then used the nearby phone booth to call Maud. "You're there!" she said when her sister answered. "I'm freezing to death in a phone booth but crazy as it sounds I'm dying for a icy, muy grande margarita. I'm buying. I hardly got to see you today."

"Oh, Lizard," Maud said. "I'd love to."

Lizzie flexed her cold knees. Through the booth's smudged glass she watched as teachers and students exited the Art Building, stood for a stunned second at the top of the stairs, then ran to their cars. Cal emerged and lingered on the top step, peering through the blowing snow. Lizzie turned sideways in the booth, hoping he wouldn't see her.

"I called Sara." Maud spoke quickly. "I told her we had to visit Sam, ASAP. She said she'd have to talk to Driver. I blew my top and then had to apologize. But I think she's pretty distressed about all this herself."

"Let's have a drink and talk about it."

"I'd really like to do that, Lizzie."

"But? How will you have a life if you're rehearsing or working all the time?"

"I've decided work is holy, Lizzie." Maud giggled. "Chekhov said it: Work is life. But tonight they're blocking the scene where Viola pretends she's a man and gives Orsino some guy advice." She sounded very merry. "The fact is, Jake's here, Lizard. We're having that beer?"

Lizzie put a second hand on the phone, holding it as if someone might tug it out of her hands. She looked over her shoulder at Cal, who still stood on the steps, peering shortsightedly out into the parking lot. Was he looking for her? Had he changed his mind?

"Lizzie?"

"Well, good for you! You do have a life. I was just thinking you'd like to join me and another teacher here. We're heading out to El Toro, but maybe you can join us some other time. It's fucking cold out here. I'll call you tomorrow." She hung up, wondering where in Maud's house Jake was sitting. Couch? Armchair? Was Maud making dinner? Would they then retire to the bedroom, to the futon Maud had borrowed from her?

She shook her mind away from this, a cat taking its paw out of water, and watched Cal wave at a car pulling up next to the Art Building. He started down the stairs, sliding in his haste. He got in. The car did not immediately drive off.

So ugly duckling Cal had found someone to love him. That someone was greeting him with a kiss. She stayed in the phone booth until the car had driven away.

Her own car was warm. The engine and the heater had been running all this time. Waiting for a light to change, she watched people on the sidewalk bow their heads and shoulders against the sideways onslaught of snow. She hated the darkness, the need for headlights this early, the fact that she no longer had it in her to sashay into El Toro, sit at the bar, and have a margarita by her own fucking self-sufficient self. A man being interviewed on *All Things Considered* asked his listeners to imagine their funeral service: "Who would come?" his high voice queried. "What might they say—your family, your friends, your co-workers—what might they say, were they given a chance to speak?"

Lizzie switched the radio off and drove with the sound of the engine and the wipers and the heater for company. Hannah would cry. And Theo would too, when he wanted to nurse. Summer might sob hysterically, but she would do it as she always did, privately, letting no one know. Maybe Cal would show up at her funeral. Lizzie grinned. He would look somber, but his big buck teeth would part his lips. He would have his new dame on his arm. Sam would come. Surely Sara would bring Sam. Unless he was too sick to come. And of course her parents, her father irritable at the emotion dredged up out of him. They would arrive in a bustle of luggage and perfume, flying in from whatever part of the world Leopold Maxwell's think-tank expertise might have taken him. Her mother would wear dark glasses over her reddened eyes, as she had for days after Kennedy was assassinated. Maud would weep, copiously. And maybe Jake would. Lizzie drove for a while, imagining Jake's response to news of her death.

But what would people *say* at her funeral? What did anyone know about her? Not much. Not like Maud, who already had a bevy of buddies in Marengo, and more, it seemed, all the time. A local stonemason, it turned out when Lizzie'd run into him, took a weekly African dance class with her. The other day Lizzie had been startled to hear her voice on the local radio station, reciting a Shakespearean sonnet—something the station said they would do once a week until Shakespeare's birthday. Even the man at the checkout counter at Safeway knew her—hailed her, not Lizzie. "How's that play of yours going?"

And now Maud had Jake. *We might have a beer or something.*

The snow whirled at her windshield. Lizzie flicked the wipers on high.

Maud hadn't said tonight.

She groaned when she saw that a red pickup sat beside Jeep's boat-like Plymouth in the driveway. She sat in the car, staring up the hill at Sam's empty husk of a trailer.

Even though the front door was closed, music blasted from the house. The kitchen was empty. Lizzie followed the throbbing air into the living room.

The rug had been rolled up. Jeep danced with a tall man in a cowboy hat. They seemed lost in a sensual limbo, their bodies continuously, sinuously connected. Theo, Summer, and Hannah sat in a row on the couch with their mouths open. If she were in any other kind of mood at all, Lizzie thought even as she crossed the room and punched the CD player's power button, she would find the scene amusing.

After the tumultuous pound of music the silence almost hurt. Jeep screwed her lips up. The man put a hand to his hat, as if to keep it from flying away.

"Mami!" Theo slid off the couch and fastened onto her knee. "Mami."

"You must be Rich," Lizzie said. Her voice sounded clipped, brittle.

"Rich Pack, ma'am." Rich put out a hand. His shake was floppy. Lizzie increased the pressure of her own grip to strengthen his. This was Maud's cowboy, she thought, patting Theo's head with her other hand. She'd seen him at bars, but always at a distance. Their lives, even with Jeep as a common point of interest, had never overlapped. And he was indeed a cowboy. The red kerchief knotted around his neck only added to the cliché. *And Lizard, you know what else? He lives in a trailer!* Maud, falling backwards on the rug in laughter.

"We thought you'd be later." Jeep's voice emerged small, scared. She waited to be reprimanded.

"Glad to meet you." Rich still held her hand. "I've heard a lot about you."

"Oh?" Lizzie disengaged her fingers. His eyes mocked her. He held on to her thumb for an extra millisecond. "My appointment got canceled. You're free to go."

Jeep's hair was haywire, her eyes wide. Rich grinned at Lizzie, moving his eyes slowly up her boots, knees, thighs, frankly admiring the legs beneath the skirt.

"What was that music?" Lizzie stepped to the CD player.

"We danced too," Hannah said. "For a little while."

"Mom hates rap." Summer slid off the couch.

"I don't hate anything. Have you two done your homework?" Lizzie replaced the CD in its plastic case and handed it to Rich. "Yours, I presume?"

As Rich took the CD his fingers lingered against hers. She bent over the waist-high music console to write out a check, aware of exactly how much rear leg she was exposing. "I think that's right," she said, handing it to Jeep, who folded it without looking and put it in her back pocket. They both knew the check could have waited for another day; they had a rolling account. Jeep picked up a few of Theo's toys, draped the girls' sweaters over the back of a chair, began to unroll the rug. Rich and Lizzie watched her.

"Don't worry about that," Lizzie said, cocking a hip. "Go ahead and take off. Hasta luego. Hope I didn't foul up any dinner plans."

Jeep kept going with the rug. She looked suddenly plump, messy, in her carefully-torn-at-the-knee jeans. She stood on the opposite side of the room, looking back and forth between Lizzie and Rich. Her blue eyes glistened.

An image of her sister, nun-like, hands clasped at her waist, made Lizzie feel as if someone had just poked her with a pin. All the exhilarated air went out of her. What was she *doing*? She scooped Theo up and buried her face in his neck, making gurgling baby sounds until he began to chortle. She turned on the porch light and shooed Rich and Jeep out of the house. She pretended not to see the hand Rich extended in her direction as he said, "Nice to meet you, lovely lady."

She turned the flame on under the stew she'd made the day before. "Not that stuff again," Summer said.

"Did you like him, Ma?" Hannah hung on her arm. "Jeep *really* likes him."

"Hot dogs, then." Lizzie put Theo down. He began to cry.

Summer jumped around the kitchen, yelling, "Hot dogs! Yay!" Theo cried, "Mami, Mami."

Lizzie banged the frying pan onto the stove. "Shut up! I can't hold you and make dinner too." To Hannah she said, "You have twenty minutes to do some homework. You too, Summer."

Her tone sent them both out of the room without protest. She gave Theo a toy and made dinner. The meal was a quiet affair. Even Summer ate every bite, corn, broccoli, hot dog and all. Lizzie wondered if—what—Maud was feeding Jake. She got herself another beer.

"Aunt Maudie says she never drinks by herself," Hannah said.

"I'm not by myself, am I? I'm with you."

The dishes washed, the girls finished their homework at the kitchen table. Lizzie picked up the living room and, in spite of her resolutions, allowed Theo to nurse. She broke her resolutions every day, but how was a mother to see her child suffer through the trauma of teething and weaning at the same time? She leaned her head back against the couch and closed her eyes, relishing the pull at her left breast. Theo squirmed and released her nipple with a pop, waving at her too-tightly encircling arm. "Okay, okay," she whispered.

A single light burned on a table beside the chair. She stared at her reflection in the window. The white orb of breast emerged from the dark shirt, Theo's head obscuring most of it. One of her hands curved under his body, the other, fingers splayed, cupped his head.

"Ma?" In the window, Lizzie saw Summer's figure in the doorway of the living room, papers in her hand. She watched Summer's approach in the window.

"I can't figure out what I'm supposed to do."

Lizzie took a look at the papers Summer held out to her. Something to do with matching lower-case letters with their upper-case equivalent. She explained this and then watched Summer's reflection cross the room and disappear in the rectangular light that was the door. She heard the creak of the kitchen chair, an irritated murmur from Hannah.

She should get up and close the curtains, she thought. She was letting precious heat out into the cold and storm outside. But she stared at her reflection, listening to the howling prowling outside.

There had been a time when Summer would not leave the room at all without her. She hadn't noticed it as much with Hannah, perhaps, being busy with other aspects of first motherhood, but she had become aware of Summer testing her boundaries, again and again, leaving her mother but never leaving all the way. And when she did extend the compass of her wanderings to include rooms her mother wasn't in, she would always check back over her shoulder, around the corner, a variation on the game of peekaboo.

And then came the day when she hadn't checked. She'd toddled to the door, legs wide around the bulge of diapers, and left without looking back. Lizzie had waited in vain, tears in her eyes, for Summer to peer back around the edge of the door. But Summer had found activity in another room. Lizzie, in a kind of desperation of loneliness, had eventually gone looking for her. Summer had squirmed away from her kisses and shouted, "Down!"

Everyone left, Lizzie thought. She wasn't sure why this would make her think of her mother, bravely having a sherry and a chocolate digestive alone in a shoppe in Oxford, waiting for Leopold to be done with his endless work. Or of Leopold, stooping to get through the shabby, unpainted doorway of her studio to cluck at her paintings.

So they would go, her parents who were gone all the time anyway. The thought raised tears in her eyes. And in a different sense Theo would go. In yet another the girls would go—boys and perfume and secrets. And she no longer had Sam, alone above them in his windswept trailer. She had never paid attention to his being alone, whatever it was Driver had said. He hadn't been alone—he had them. She hadn't felt alone, she only now realized as a gust of wind rattled the windows, because she had him. "Sam," she said, surprised at how still her reflection remained even as the wind howled and blustered around outside. For the first time she knew what Maud meant when she said she had no one to call. She couldn't call Maud because Jake might be there. She couldn't call Jake—which she just might be motivated to do on a night like this—because Jake was with Maud.

And on such a night, with such an emptiness, she had been known to visit Sam. But Sam was not there. Would he ever be again?

And Jeep and Rich were no doubt parked along a road somewhere, the windows all steamed up. Rich would have asked Jeep to give him a blow job. She thought of the car stopped by the steps of the Art Building, that long pause after Cal had practically slid down the steps and before the car had driven away. Amorphous shapes that were Jake and Maud moved on Maud's futon, swelling and melding and burrowing and billowing beneath a feather comforter.

She was startled when Theo pulled away from the nipple. She rotated him to her other breast, wondering how Cal was making out tonight. And Aaron, and Yvette. Everyone had someone. *I'm gonna go eat worms.*

Which is what she'd wanted to yell out the window at Jake the day they'd fought about what was now Theo. "I miss having a baby around," she'd told him when he'd pointed out that she already had two kids. "They haven't figured out yet they can leave."

And then Jake had left.

Sitting on her bed, she listened to him go down the stairs. She heard the kitchen door slam. His feet crunched ice on his way across the potholed driveway. She kept thinking she was going to run to the window and shout, "You going to go eat some worms, buddy?" It would have made him laugh. Summer had played the stupid little tape with that song on it—she'd gotten it from Sparky, plus tape player, for Christmas—so many times that Lizzie and Jake had spent a long, hysterical hour in bed one morning dreaming up ways to mangle, crush, bend-fold-and-mutilate the tape out of existence. *Big ones little ones fat ones skinny ones, I'm going to go eat worms,* they'd warbled in harmony. But in spite of the sound of Jake's car starting up and then idling in the driveway, she hadn't moved. For days afterward she'd held the phrase ready in her head, in case he should call. "You been eating worms?" and then, after the days went by, "How're those worms you've been eating?" and other variations until the phrase no longer made any sense and like some irritating commercial jingle had gone round and round in her head, absurd, inappropriate. By then she was feeling relief, not remorse. No one else would call the shots. She could do exactly as she wanted. She'd had a kid before. She didn't need help. Although, she had to admit, Theo's labor had been hard, fast and fierce. She could have done with a hand to hold until it bled.

I like them small, dependent. They haven't figured out yet they can leave.

What would have happened if Jake had asked her what the hell she meant? She hadn't known at the time. But maybe now, too late, she had some idea. Until Summer, she hadn't known how to love someone through their changes. Until Jake, she hadn't thought she wanted to.

"You just want what Maud wants," she told herself.

Theo's breathing indicated he was asleep although his lips still worked around her nipple. She carried him up the stairs, lowered him into his crib, pulled the comforter up around his chin. All life was a process of leaving, she thought, staring down at him. She couldn't keep having children forever. And what on earth would she do when Theo headed out that door and didn't look back?

M A U D

This is the hag, when maids lie on their backs,
That presses them and learns them first to bear
Making them women of good carriage.
     —ROMEO AND JULIET

"Hold, Toby!" Maud shouted as she ran. Her skirts flared around her ankles. "On thy life I charge thee, *hold!*"

The two men lowered their swords and backed away from each other. A third wrung his hands and whimpered. Toby looked sheepish. His chest heaved. Heavy but nimble, he brandished his sword one last time in the direction of the very handsome Sebastian, who stood to one side, eyeing Maud with admiration.

Maud whirled on Toby. "Ungracious wretch! Will it be ever thus?" She reined herself in from the rest of this scathing diatribe when she heard two claps and an "Okay!"

"That was better," Chris Daugherty said from his place halfway back in the auditorium. "Toby, it's harder for you to stop fighting. Once your blood lust is up, you're hard put to rein it in. Remember. Your swordsmanship is legendary."

Ron Bartlett saluted with his foil and lunged, expertly. "I shall obey." He burped, swerved in the direction of Henderson, playing Andrew Aguecheek, and draped himself over his shoulder. "How now, sot!"

In an effort to keep warm in the cold theater, Maud wore an enormous sweater, and leggings under her rehearsal skirt. She watched

Chris walk towards the stage, checking his notepad. "Sebastian. You're on the right track ogling Olivia. But wait a bit. You're doing it too soon. Sir Toby has accosted you for no reason as far as you can see. You need to answer this assault on your manhood. Let Olivia's charms work on you more slowly."

Peter nodded. Chris had done well casting Peter as Viola's twin brother. Like Bobbie, he was tall, slim, dark-haired; even the length of their hair was similar.

"That's just right, Henderson." Chris pointed at Andrew Ague-cheek. "You obsequious little fuck."

A hoot of laughter came from Bobbie, sitting in the back of the auditorium.

"But you haven't quite given up hope that Olivia may fall in love with you. So you can resent the hell out of this little Sebastian fellow, especially when it becomes clear that Olivia has the hots for him."

Chris turned to Maud. "Sorry we keep stopping. We'll get past this entrance one of these tries. You need to crank up the voltage. Whip Sir Toby with your rage. He's walking on thin ice. He's only here on your forbearance. And keep in mind, Toby—without Olivia's generosity, you have nothing in the world. Except your swords."

"Both of them," Ron cackled.

"Both of them. And that for some reason Maria loves you." Chris leapt up onto the stage. He had studied fencing and broadsword extensively, and held a diploma in fight choreography. "Try this," he said, taking Ron's foil. He demonstrated a deft wrist-cocked, upward-moving block.

Peter was peering at his script. "What's 'Lethe'? At the end of this I say I'm happy to steep in Lethe. It can't be some kind of tea—some kind of water?"

"River of forgetfulness," Maud and Chris answered simultaneously. Chris waved in Maud's direction. "Ask her." Maud went over the script with Peter while Chris finished up with Ron. "Once more," Chris said as he jumped back off the stage. "I know you have to get to work, Maud. This time I'll let it run to the end."

They started the scene again. Maud rode the tide of verse to the end of the speech:

Will it be ever thus? Ungracious wretch,
Fit for the mountains and the barbarous caves
Where manners ne'er were preached. Out of my sight!

Arms extended, she swayed towards Sebastian. "Be not offended, dear Cesario."

Sebastian pulled back, repeating, "Cesario?" Maud finished the rest of her speech to him, stroking his face, making as much of him as she dared, and was gratified when Bobbie's merry laugh rang out. "Good, good," Chris called.

"How runs the stream?" Sebastian said, weaving.

Or I am mad, or else this is a dream.
Let fancy still my sense in Lethe steep.
If it be thus to dream, still let me sleep!

Maud touched his arm. "Would thou woulds't be ruled by me."

Sebastian stared. "Madam," he said slowly, "I will."

Chris clapped again. "Much better. Get out of here, Maud. Hope we didn't make you late."

Maud pulled off the rehearsal skirt and stuffed it, her thermos of tea, and her script into a large bag. On her way up the aisle she paused next to Chris, who was ticking off notes on a pad filled with scribbles. "I need a day and a night off to go visit a sick friend. It's pretty important."

Chris nodded. "Not a problem until we start doing run-throughs next week. Call me at the office."

Maud waved to the men still up on stage. "But there the lady goes," Peter called. Ron tried another burp. Bobbie, studying lines at the back of the auditorium, looked up to say, "Farewell, fair cruelty."

As she walked through the lobby Count Orsino executed an elaborate bow in her direction. His courtiers, waiting to rehearse the first scene, strode about, strutting, posing in the attitudes Chris had drilled into them.

She paused by the lobby doors, reluctant to leave, watching an actor angle a foot just so, another recover fallen juggling balls, another try on a line reading, tell an exuberant anecdote. Beyond them, through the open double doors into the auditorium, gleamed the box of light that was the stage. Chris was the dancing figurine found in a musical jewel box, demonstrating another piece of elegant swordplay.

Outside, the high lamps of streetlights swam in mist-induced halos. She walked to the Red Garter through snowflakes so tiny as to be almost invisible, delicate as confetti against her face.

Green garlands, interspersed with paper four-leaf clovers, twisted along the stairs and balcony of the Red Garter. One of the cocktail waitresses, a new one, moved through the tables. Bart winked at Maud. "Tell those girls to get down here before Barney's wrath erupts."

Maud clocked in and ran up the stairs to the dressing room. Ginger was in the position she took habitually while she was on break: lying on the bench, smoking. Two of the new waitresses, Kathie and Trixie, hired for the crowds that ski season brought, dressed near their lockers. Maud banged her own locker open, stripped out of her leggings and sweater, pulled on the fishnets and boned leotard. As she jostled her way to a place in front of the mirror, she admitted to a sudden chord of contentment. The spraying of hair and the brushing of blush, the shy murmurs of the new waitresses, Ginger's occasional drawled ironic comment took her backstage: the same camaraderie, the same sense of heightened excitement about what the night ahead would bring.

Ginger had one arm thrown over her eyes. Without lifting it, she said, "There's a guy down there looking for you."

"For me?"

"For you."

Applying mascara, Maud questioned her own face in the mirror. It wouldn't be Jake. They'd spent a pleasant evening having a few beers, but they'd mostly talked about Lizzie—surreptitiously, as if she might be in the next room. She watched her eyes widen as she thought about Driver. Had he somehow found out where she worked?

"It's a producer," Trixie said. "He's just discovered you left L.A. and come to fetch you back."

Maud laughed, once, and popped the top off her lipstick.

For some reason Trixie and Kathie seemed to find this response hysterical. Maud was puzzled, but gratified. The two girls, both barely twenty-one, made her feel cool and experienced, a woman with an "attitude." At times they even made her feel wise, as if her opinions about men and life and Hollywood and even breathing were items they would write into a notebook if they happened to be carrying one.

"Maybe it's an L.A. agent," Kathie suggested. A pile of moussed and sprayed hair above her forehead shifted like a tangle of tiny horns with any movement of her head. "Maybe they heard how good you are in your play."

Maud pulled her fishnets tight. "By leaving Hollywood I've cast myself on a dustheap. I'm a cracked plate, a damaged light fixture, a burned mattress. No one wants me anymore." She was touched at the look on Kathie's face. "I'm not putting myself down, I swear. No one follows a career the size of mine. Out of sight, out of mind. If you don't constantly put yourself in their face, they forget you."

"But you were *making* it. You were on *TV*," Kathie said. Trixie nodded.

They looked so much alike—brunette, petite, pretty—that Maud sometimes had to resort to the color of their leotards to tell them apart. She waved her mascara wand at them. "Do you know how many leggy brunettes are invariably waiting in a casting director's office? Do you know how often characters I auditioned for were named Kate, just as the blondes are called Marilyn? They're looking for types: the Kate type, the Marilyn type. That's what's so hard to fathom. They're not looking for you. And you think they are."

"But you don't all look alike."

"I bet we do if you're on the other side of the casting table. If the character breakdown calls for her to be in jeans and a tank top, or in a tailored suit, we all show up in jeans and tank tops, or tailored suits. What does it take to stand out? Tits? Connections? Talent?" She shrugged. "Who knows? Sometimes you know you nailed it, and that's magical. But mostly, on the way home from an audition, you pound the steering wheel. Or drive dully along the freeway with a million other souls alone in their cars. You're just normal. You didn't knock their socks off. And you wonder who did."

Trixie touched the swarm of hardened hair above her forehead. "Well, we still can't believe you just *left*. You had agents and *everything*. As soon as Kathie and me get enough money together we're heading for Hollywood."

"Out with the old, in with the new." Ginger drew on a cigarette, her lowered eyelids a brilliant parrot green.

"Thanks so much," Maud said, a little shocked.

"She's not *old*," Trixie and Kathie chorused.

"And you girls better hustle your sweet little butts or you'll be fired before Ms. Hollywood here has a chance to offer any more of her priceless bits of advice."

Even from the heavily ironic Ginger this comment seemed barbed. Kathie and Trixie fled. Maud thought about asking Ginger what was bothering her, but decided to drop it. She inserted a last hairpin to anchor her antennae. The conversation made her realize how little she'd heard from anyone connected to her L.A. life, in spite of the occasional postcard mailed to agents and friends. She had not disturbed the waters with either her coming or her going. It had been months since she and Miles had spoken.

She turned to look at her own startled eyes in the mirror. Was it Miles who waited for her to emerge through the door marked EMPLOYEES ONLY? Had Miles tracked her down at the Red Garter? Would he place her, fishnet stockings and all, on the back of his Rock'n Roll'n horse, to ride off into a glorious sunset? Curious that it was not an appealing idea.

Rapid footsteps sounded on the carpeted stairs outside.

Ginger sat up. "That'll be Jeep."

Jeep banged through the door. She looked awful. She'd slathered heavy base onto her skin, and her eyes were limned with black, the result—Maud recognized it immediately—of crying over eye makeup and having to replace it.

Maud moved to put an arm around her.

"Don't." Jeep twisted away, banged open her locker, and began to strip.

"Glad you made it, hon." Ginger stood. "You're late, Maud-girl, and so am I." She hefted her breasts in her two hands, wincing. "Wish my period'd get here. They're big and they're sore."

"Don't even talk to me about periods." Jeep pulled on her leotard and turned sideways to the mirror. "Shit! I starve myself and I just get fatter and fatter and *fatter.*"

"You are not fat." Ginger squinted against cigarette smoke as she laced her boots. "Some asshole who shall remain nameless has been feeding you that crap again. Tell him to shove it. If he wants a little boy, no hips, no breasts, he should come out of the closet. You're *perfect.*" Maud watched, astonished, as the caustic and cynical Ginger put an arm around Jeep.

"No," Jeep said, her voice high and tight. She splayed fingers over the pink satin that covered her belly, pushing in. "I sure am not. I keep wanting to be something different. Than what I am. I tell myself and tell myself I'm going to do it differently, I'm not going to get stuck. I wanted to get the hell out of here, I don't want to be stuck. I don't want to be *stuck.*"

"You're not stuck," Maud said.

Jeep rubbed at her forehead, shaking her head. She met Maud's eyes in the mirror. "What the hell do you know." She was in pink, pretty, blonde, curvaceous, Maud in turquoise, tall and dark. "*You* can get out. You waltzed in and you can just waltz right out. But I'm a fly with its goddamn feet stuck on a strip—" She grabbed a paper napkin off the table and dabbed at tears brimming in her eyes. "Just like everybody else in this goddamn town. You even *try* to leave, you even try to get out of the muck, you get *sucked* right back."

"Look. Hon." Ginger mashed her cigarette onto a plate where ketchup pooled next to ancient french fries. "We're all going to have to leave if Barney sees Trixie and Kathie and our other new girl with an *-ie* at the end of her name down there by their lonesomes."

Maud put her arm around Jeep. Again Jeep shrugged it off. "See you down there. We'll have a shift drink later?"

Jeep refused to meet her eyes.

"Come on, girl," Ginger said, "or Barney will have your ass served up with an apple in the crack."

"In a minute." Jeep banged her locker door shut.

Maud followed Ginger down the stairs. "What's going on?"

Ginger turned to look up at her, eyebrows raised. Maud felt herself flush in response to the disdain pouring at her. As if that were the answer to the question, Ginger pushed through the swinging door into the deafening noise in the bar: music, voices yelling over it, clank of glasses. "Your *sweetie*"—Ginger loaded the word with irony—"is sitting at table eight." She disappeared into the mass of bodies lining the bar.

Maud moved towards the piano. Having teased herself with the idea her visitor would be Driver or, more impossibly, Miles, it was a letdown to see the familiar tilt of cowboy hat, the stretch of long legs ending in boots crossed at the ankle. Rich turned. "Hello, beautiful lady."

She'd imagined this meeting a dozen ways, in scenarios that allowed her to cut him dead. "Hello, stranger," she said with an archness she did not feel.

He dropped his eyes to the cleavage her costume afforded, to her crimped waist and the satin triangle above her crotch. Her insides, behind that patch of satin, grew warm: There had been a particularly sweet tangle of limbs, a sideways rope-climbing posture.

She felt Barney's eyes boring into the back of her head. "I can't talk." Maud looked around as Jeep pushed through the swinging employee door. Across the room her eyes blazed. She grabbed her tray off the bar and strode into a crowd of skiers who'd just clumped in. Maud wanted to go to her, tell her it wasn't what she thought, but Barney pushed himself away from the wall. She headed to the piano.

At some point during a medley of up-tempo songs, Jeep dropped a folded cocktail napkin on the piano. Maud looked up, smiling, but Jeep was gone, leaving behind her a swirl of anger. Fingering triads with her left hand, Maud pulled the napkin towards her:

Do you know "As Time Goes By"? We got married fifty years ago tonight, and that's always been our song. It'd mean a lot to us if you could play it.

Maud modulated through a series of chords that would bring her around to the beginning of the song.

A kiss is but a kiss,
A sigh is just a sigh.

Fifty years, she thought as she sang about a kiss being just a kiss.
If she married someone tomorrow, she would be ninety-two—
ninety-two!—before she could say such a thing.

> The fundamental things apply
> As time goes by.

"That last one was a request," she said into the microphone. "Can
you guess which two people in this room have been married fifty
years? That's their song." She swung around on the stool. They
weren't hard to find; they were shining with pride. The woman waved,
mouthing "Thank you." Someone shouted an admiring "Whoa!"
and started to clap. In a minute the whole room was applauding.
"Fifty *years*," Maud heard a woman say at a table near the piano. "Fifty
years!" She was blonde, a touched-up blonde with eyes that looked
tired. She scooted closer to the man beside her, wrapping his arm
with her two hands.

Maud looked to see what Rich's response to all this might be.
He was staring down at his boots. His hat tilted towards her like a
blank face.

Later, Ginger sauntered by and tossed another folded cocktail
napkin. "Your cutiepie said to give you this."

"He is not my cutiepie," Maud said to Ginger's disappearing
back. It was the first time Maud had seen Rich's handwriting—a
child-like scrawl, tiny, untidy letters slanting up the napkin.

> Great ass you've got.
> I had to go, something came up.
> Call me sometime.

"Another song request?" the blonde woman asked. Maud shook
her head. "Ah, a love note!" her date suggested. Out in the crowd
somebody shouted "To Dream the Impossible Dreams" which Maud
played. She rounded out the set as best she could, wondering when she
would hear back about the teaching application she'd sent in to the
college. The month of *Twelfth Night* performances would give her a
hiatus from this job on weekends, but she needed, suddenly, desper-

ately, to know that she would be doing something other than this to make a living.

"I'm going to take a few minutes here," she told the microphone.

Behind the bar, Bart looked like a whirling dervish, reaching a hand high for a brandy snifter stored in the rack above his head, pouring the green froth of margaritas into glasses already on the bar, grabbing a napkin to place under a brandy glass, which he filled with one hand while using the other to deliver the margaritas to Trixie, waiting with her tray. Unwashed glassware filled the waitress station. Bodies three deep waved at him. Maud spotted Rich's hat and his hawkish profile beneath it. Jeep's bent, fishnetted knee almost touched his leg. He reached a hand to touch her, but she batted it away, talking fast. Rich looked at the floor, shaking his head. Jeep stalked away.

Bart waved at Maud, crossed to the CD player, punched on a blast of guitar and drums. Maud made her way through the bodies that packed the bar, ignoring the florid-faced man who said, "Get me a margarita, hon. Double-quick this time." She stumbled on the way up the stairs, unable to erase the moment: the hurt need in Jeep's face, the hand Rich stretched to touch her cheek, the look in Jeep's face as she slapped that touch away.

She went back down before her break was over to look for Jeep, but as soon as she appeared Barney jerked his chin in the direction of the piano. The audience was responsive enough through the next two sets to allow her spirits to rise. She would buy Jeep a soda after work, explain she had nothing to do with Rich's appearance at the Red Garter.

But Trixie, sipping her shift beer at the bar, told Maud that Barney had let Jeep leave early—she'd been feeling sick. Maud decided to call her from home. She changed and clocked out, slipping out the back door of the hotel and heading across the parking lot, past the dumpsters, the shortcut to Main Street. As she passed the heaps of plastic bags awaiting tomorrow's trash pickup, she heard sobbing. She inched around the huge metal bins and found Jeep there, swaddled in a down parka several sizes too big for her.

"Go away," Jeep said as Maud knelt beside her. "Just go away." Her face glistened, a mess of tears and snot and smeared mascara.

The freeze of pavement worked its way quickly through Maud's leggings. "Whatever you think I did, Jeep, I didn't."

Jeep pushed away from her and tried to stand. "You and Lizzie," she said, "you can both just go to hell." Unable to keep her balance, she slid down the side of the dumpster. "I'm drunk," she said. "I'm so goddamn *drunk.*"

Maud put an arm around her. Jeep jerked away from it. "Both of you," she said. "Just fuck off." She swiped at her nose with a large leather mitten and watched the shiny thread of snot that connected her glove to her nostril. "You steal everything, that's all you do, you're *snakes.*"

"I didn't know Rich was going to come in, Jeep. I haven't seen him since we broke up." Maud wondered what Lizzie had done. She shifted her weight so she could crouch above instead of kneel on the freezing pavement.

"No, no, no. Don't go away. *Don't.*" Jeep clutched at her. "Don't go *away,* Maud."

"I'm not going away."

Jeep leaned her head back against the dumpster behind her, sobbing into the sky, an image of absolute despair.

"Jeep, honey, it's cold out here."

"I'm not going inside the Garter. I'm not going in there like this. Barney's going to fire me anyway. No way he believed me when I told him I was sick. He knows I had a few." She buried her face in Maud's parka. "Everything's as bad as it could be. I'm totally strung out on coke from yesterday. Why do I have to *drink* on top of everything else?"

"Let's go home," Maud said. "It's just a little way."

"Home?" Jeep gave a laugh that turned into a sob. "I should just stay here and die. Let the trash trucks take me away. It's what I deserve."

"It's what Rich deserves, maybe."

The mention of his name caused Jeep to wail. Maud crouched beside her again. "I didn't ask him to come in. You have to know that. You guys are seeing each other now."

Jeep shook her head and drummed her heels against the pavement. "No. I *hate* him. Why's Lizzie have to be so right? *Again.* Oh God, I want to *die*."

Maud got Jeep to her feet. Together they stumbled across the parking lot. Jeep paused at a curb, said, "Hold on a minute, sorry," and threw up. When she was finished, she spat several times. Maud helped her kick enough snow to cover the patch of vomit. She managed to walk the rest of the way to Maud's house without Maud's supporting arm.

Maud settled her on the sofa, covered her with a comforter and put water on for tea. "Want me to call Lizzie?"

"*No!* I don't even want to see *you*." Jeep looked about ten years old, huddled on the couch with the quilt drawn up around her. "Here I am sitting in your house when I wanted to kill you." She used the edge of the quilt to mop at fresh tears. "If you hadn't been with him, if he hadn't told me how much better he was going to be. And he was better, sort of. I don't know. I want it to be someone's fault. I want to blame Lizzie for wearing that skirt. She never wears skirts. But it's him, it is. I can't *stand* it. What am I going to *do*?"

Her head went back in a fresh paroxysm of grief, face upturned, mouth open, eyes squeezed shut.

It wasn't just that Rich had shown up tonight, she sobbed, it wasn't that he'd dropped Maud a note. It wasn't just that she'd started drinking again, had smoked dope with Rich a few nights ago, had spent yesterday snorting cocaine and drinking beer and was too embarrassed to call her sponsor, much less go to an AA meeting, and was avoiding her house and not answering her phone in case her sponsor was trying to call. "It's all those things, but the worst thing, the worst thing—" she would say, and start crying again, unable to speak. "It's that, what it is, is . . ."

Maud finally guessed. "Are you pregnant?"

"*Yes.*"

Maud held out both hands to her. "Oh, Jeep."

"It's just that Lizzie, oh God, Lizzie—"

"Lizzie *what*?"

"I was baby-sitting. She came home early. Rich was there and we were dancing. And she looked sexy and I was feeling fat and wearing these jeans that are old and tacky. I could see Rich coming on to her, and I could see she was coming on to him. She *was*," Jeep said, as if Maud had contradicted her.

"So then"—she pulled herself up to sit on the arm of the couch, perching there like some blonde gargoyle, her face a mask of hopelessness—"I thought the only way I'll make Rich forget about her— That's not right. The only way I'd make Rich think about me instead of her, and you, is—" She began to cry again, blurring her words. "Even though I told him I wasn't going to make love with him until I knew for sure he was going to love me better, love me the way I keep *telling* myself I *deserve*—"

She hit her forehead with the heel of her hand several times. "Stupid, stupid, *stupid*. Bart *warned* me. I got all kittenish and disgusting and he pulled over by the side of a road and got into the passenger seat. And you know how sometimes you get in a certain position and it just feels so good you can't stop? You don't want to stop? So I kept saying no but I kept moving against him at the same time. I'd been telling Rich 'no,' so we were both really horny. And then he came. *Inside* me. He was surprised too. I think he was going to just make me come, you know, before I went down on him, he likes that a lot—" Jeep stopped.

"All guys like that a lot."

"They do, don't they," Jeep said, sniffing.

"It's nice when they get you to come first, though." Maud got another wad of toilet paper from the bathroom. "So how late are you?"

"Three days. And I never am. That's why I know."

"Well, it could be that you're just tense. Scared. That's happened to me." She thought of Driver and of the tenuous weeks she'd lived through when she first arrived in Marengo.

"I *can't* be pregnant," Jeep wailed. "It'll be the end of everything I've been working on, everything I want to *change*." Her eyes welled up with tears again. "I don't want to spend nine months of my life, and then the *rest* of my life, caring for a kid whose father I don't even like."

"You might come to feel differently."

"And we got pregnant in a *car*."

This almost made Maud laugh. "Well, if you are pregnant, and you do decide to have it, those feelings might change."

Jeep shook her head. "I have to get an abortion. That's all. I have to."

All the people who want babies and can't have them, Maud thought. All the babies who have no parents and need them.

"I mean, I think of you," Jeep said. "How you keep saying you want a kid, and I've thought—I've thought so *much* in these three days, you can't believe it, my brain is tired—I've thought, okay, Jeep, just have him, and give him to Maud. But can you just *give* a baby away? And anyway, there goes nine months. There goes my life. They'll take away the scholarship. The rules were so intense to get that. They won't give an award to someone whose belly's big as a balloon and *unmarried*. And I don't want to marry Rich. As if he wants to marry anyone. He *hates* kids. He's told me so a hundred times. And after the baby's born I have to take care of it, I won't be able to go to school and I don't have enough money as it is. And if I don't go to school I'll never—" She shook her head. "I'll be stuck, stuck, *stuck*. Just like my mother. I swore I'd never do what she did. I was a 'mistake.' She's told me so many times I ruined her life. And now I've gone and done the same thing. I won't, I just *won't*."

Maud held her. "It'll all work out. Somehow it will."

"I want the life I'd been planning. I was finally being *smart*. But people will call me a murderer."

"That's only one point of view." Maud thought of Jake's sister—how often she must have to witness and give counsel to this.

"They told my mother she'd be a murderer, that God would punish her. All my life she's just *hated* me, told me a thousand times I wrecked her life. On the other hand, here I am, and there's been times, recently, when I've been happy. Would I rather have not been here? You see what I mean? What should I *do*? It's such a mess."

"You didn't wreck her life," Maud said. "And you would never tell a child such a thing." .

"No." Jeep nodded. "I know what it's like. Not to be wanted. It's the worst. So many times I just wanted to die. I was trying to die, most of my life. Once I almost succeeded. Lizzie will tell you. And now for the first time I'm starting to feel like living might be fun. I'm

just getting my feet underneath me. And what do I do to myself?"
She took a huge shuddering breath. "Could I sleep here?"

"I wish you would."

"I need to pee and brush my disgusting mouth." Jeep pushed
back the quilt. Maud got a pillow and some sheets from the bedroom
and made up the couch. From the bathroom Jeep said, "Rich will
think I did it to trap him."

"Well, you know you didn't." Maud joined her in the bathroom,
sat on the edge of the tub. "That was one of the biggest reasons I was
so careful about birth control when I was with Miles. So he could
never accuse me of taking unfair advantage, of forcing the issue."

"Lizzie says if you'd just gotten pregnant with him, he might
have come through."

"Unlike Lizzie, I was too chicken to find out."

"Rich doesn't have to know, does he?"

"That's up to you."

The length of Maud's nightgown emphasized how young Jeep
was. Her face was shiny, scrubbed; her nose red, her eyes puffy. She
pulled the quilt up to her chin. "I look awful."

"No, you look like you've cried. I've looked just like that more
often than I want anyone to know."

"Doesn't it ever get easier?"

"I don't think it gets any easier. I'm beginning—just *beginning*—
to think we can make it easier on ourselves."

Jeep's eyelids drooped. "Will you stay right here? Just till I fall
asleep?"

"Yes."

Jeep mumbled, "Lizzie will be so mad."

"She won't be mad. Or she won't be mad at you. Go to sleep.
'That knits up the raveled sleeve of care.' We'll figure it out. One way
or another."

Smoothing the hair away from Jeep's face, Maud thought how in
some other organization of things she might be holding a daughter.
And that maybe one of the great benefits of being a parent was that
no matter how frightened you yourself might be, you needed to present a world to your child that was good, and safe, and secure. *It'll all*

work out, she'd told Jeep. As if she knew how. Yet just saying things would be all right somehow made things seem like they might be.

Keeping an arm around Jeep, she picked up her book. Maybe one of the biggest myths of all was that it would all be easier if you had a mate. Jeep's mother hadn't had a man who loved her. She also hadn't figured out how to go it alone. As Lizzie had. Maud herself hadn't managed to create a successful marriage, mating, partnership. But it seemed to her that it should be, ought to be more fun, more satisfying, to move through life with someone, a mate.

Mate. Another verb to add to the collection she and Jake were making. *Cor blimey, mate, want to mate?*

Although—watching Jeep, who had fallen asleep almost immediately—she also understood, wholly, that her own void would not be filled with a child. Nor would it be filled by a man. The void existed. In between the pendulum swings of desire for this, and fear of that, was a place that was simply empty. It was also full. For a moment she understood how both could simultaneously be true. Jeep could or could not have this baby. Maud would or would not find the love of her life, or get discovered as an actor, or be hired by the college and become the best teacher the world had ever known. None of these filled the void. The void was always there. The thing to do—so easy to ponder, so hard to manifest—was to live with it, live within it, and to be aware. The awkward weight of Jeep's head against her shoulder, the sound of breath, in and out, the coconut scent of shampoo. This feeling of empty fullness, full emptiness, in the area of her own womb, her belly, her heart.

And somewhere in there, she thought, her arm tightening around a shiver that shook Jeep's body, somewhere at that balanced, still point—before the magnetizing poles of desire and fear drew her, quivering, towards one, then the other—was where serenity lived.

CHAPTER 27

JAKE

lights down the boulevard, shattered suns
our nights held passion, like a hidden gun
but thunder and sunlight fade

On the sidewalk outside Mountain Music Jake ran into Maud. Muffled up against the cold. Wearing that tweed cap that made her look like an urchin. "Hey," he said. "What're you up to?"

"Exercising my franchise." She pointed to the I VOTED sticker on her coat lapel. "This is exciting! Fixing the roads versus keeping the library open on weekdays. Randolf for mayor! Many times in L.A. I didn't turn out to vote. I'm ashamed to say."

"I didn't do much for Nashville politics myself." He wasn't registered in Marengo either.

She pulled a mitten off with her teeth, handed him a piece of neon blue paper out of the Print Rite bag she was carrying.

PIANO LESSONS
—CHILDREN WELCOME—
MAUD MAXWELL
232-3565

"I can mail these. They'll look a little more official than those three-by-five cards I have thumbtacked around. I have six pupils now. Mostly thanks to Elmer."

Maud looked happier. Not so gaunt, haggard. Perhaps she'd even gained some weight. He would not ask. The only wisdom he thought he'd garnered over the years was never to ask that particular question of a woman. It was never taken as a compliment.

"I've never thought of myself as a teacher," Maud was saying. "But it turns out I'm sort of good at it."

He folded the flyer into fours, put it in his pocket. "Listen. Why don't you come by later? We'll have a beer."

Oh, buddy, Minerva yodeled, *what are you up to?*

Looking wary, Maud pulled her mitten back on. "Well, I have rehearsal. Until ten."

The snowy top of Fable Mountain leered, a squashed scoop of vanilla ice cream.

"That's fine."

She perused him with those odd, worried eyes. Face pixie-like beneath the cap. "But let's not talk about Lizzie the whole time. Is that awful? That's awful, isn't it."

"Is that what we did? You should've told me to shut up."

"I can't say I'm not interested. I'm just not sure it's a good thing to do, is all."

"Cozy, cozy, cozy." Lizzie's voice lilted behind them.

Maud's eyes widened, deep brown. Jake turned. Lizzie stood in jeans and parka. "Don't let me interrupt."

"I was just leaving." Maud opened the store's heavy wooden door. Jake heard, "Hello, Elmer. I've got those flyers you suggested," and Elmer's answering welcome.

Lizzie's red ski hat emphasized her small chin. Jake told her he was glad to see her. She nodded. "That was quite a scene there at the hospital." Her eyes mocked, glittered.

Of course. She had always muffled anything that strummed her emotions. "I think about that." He'd thought about it a lot. Aching, sorry. He'd called her. Wasn't surprised that she didn't call back.

Lizzie tucked an escaping curl firmly beneath her hat. "And what are you doing downtown?"

Jake held up his package. "New strings, picks. You?"

"Seeing a lawyer. He's a friend. Trying to find out if what that

Driver guy did is legal. If I can do anything." She shoved hands in her pockets, pulled her chin into her muffler. "We went to see Sam the other day. Maud tell you?"

"You did! How is he?"

"We took the girls. I figure Summer, especially, better know what's going on. He's not improving. I can't think what good it is keeping him down there. But not being family—'clan,' as the asshole says—I don't know what recourse I've got. It's way too little, way too late. But—" She shrugged, grimacing, the feral look of her eyeteeth more pronounced than usual. "You keep leaving messages."

"You keep not answering them."

Maud came back out of the store. "I'm running late."

"See you later," Jake said, but she didn't meet his eye. The wind flapped the hem of her coat as she walked.

"Jeep's pregnant," Lizzie said.

"Jeep is *what*?"

"I thought Maud might have told you."

This was meant to be a jab. "Is it Rich?"

"Of course. She'll lose her scholarship. The biddies on the board will see to that." Lizzie squinted over his shoulder, as if the biddies were behind him. The lines around her eyes, not as pronounced as Maud's, were a fine crosshatch, reminding him of the set of Haviland china Minerva had inherited from her grandmother. A million tiny cracks lacing the porcelain. Lizzie, he thought, a fine china cup. How she would hate that idea.

"It's not much of a smiling matter," she said.

"No, of course not."

"And her godawful mother will have a fit." The tip of her nose was red with cold.

"Want to get some coffee?" It came out, surprising him.

"Not really." But she walked beside him to a small German bakery with wrought-iron tables and chairs, empty. "We've never been in here," he said as they sat. "Together, I mean." She stared, sardonic. A large blonde waitress left her newspaper to take their order. Coffee, yes. Strudel, no.

"What will Jeep do?"

"Abortion, probably."

He shook his head, thinking about Theo. The enormity of his own failings hit him.

"I don't know what you're tut-tutting about. You of all people. Every time a man and a woman make love, seventeen zillion spermies are loosed on the world. A baby is easy to make. They're very hard to raise. I wanted mine, I planned for each of them." Pouring a stream of cream into her coffee, Lizzie waved away his protest. "Let's not talk about Theo."

Jake's throat was tight. He started to speak. Lizzie shook her spoon at him. "A wanted child is a loved child. Like a lot of clichés, that one is true. So is the opposite. I made a choice. Jeep's had an accident. So she thinks about not having it. She's also thinking about having it and giving it to Maud."

"To Maud!"

"It's pretty late for Maud to have one of her own. She cries about that. I've told her to get a cat."

"Hardly the same thing, Liz."

Lizzie licked her spoon with a curled pink tongue. "No midnight feedings, diapers. You can go out when you please. No backtalk. No acne, tattoos, midnight frets about who they're with, where they are, all the things I have to look forward to. But even if Jeep doesn't end up falling in love and wanting to keep the kid, what adoption agency would let Maud have it? Single female, works in a bar. Actress! Teaches piano. Sporadic income, no equity."

"Would she have to go through an adoption agency? She'd make a great mother." At Lizzie's look he amended this. "Not that I know her that well." He pictured Maud, sitting on the couch in his living room later that night, pulled his mind away from the idea of kissing her. Not the first time he'd thought of it. But he hadn't thought he'd think about it while he was with Lizzie. He groaned.

Lizzie looked at him, curious. "What's that about? A drug addict, a derelict, a child abuser can become a mother. But someone who wants a child, who could offer a loving home, has an impossible time convincing the powers that are in charge of these things that they— she—could be a parent." She flagged the waitress for a refill. "I looked into adopting. Thought I'd offer my home to a Guatemalan kid, but am I an undesirable parent! An artist. No husband. Wildly fluctuating income, splotchy financial track record. And so"—she shrugged—"we have Theo."

Again she shook her spoon. "Nope. Don't. Sorry I brought it up. I told Jeep that if she decided to keep it we could add it to the menagerie." Her sharp teeth showed.

"Lizzie."

"Jake," she mocked. Her hair, that unruly extension of her mental processes, messed by the hat she'd pulled off as they sat down, glinted red-gold.

"Let me— Could we—" He stopped.

"What?"

"Could we have dinner?"

"Oh, Jake." She stood, dropped a dollar bill on the table. Her cheeks were red. "Go figure it out with Maud. She's who you want, anyway."

He grinned at her. "Not yet."

Lizzie breathed sharply out, her face pinched. "What does that mean? What does that *mean*?"

The waitress looked up from her newspaper. This did not stop Jake from reaching a hand. "You make jokes about it, Liz. Why can't I?"

She pulled her hat on. It sat too high up on her head, looking absurd. "Because you're not joking."

"But neither are you. Liz!"

But she was gone, snatching up her parka, scraping against a chair as she went by. It toppled, fell. Jake beat the waitress to lift it back into place. Watched Lizzie out the window. She paused at the sidewalk's edge, put a hand up in thanks to a van that stopped to let her cross.

The waitress went back to studying the newspaper. He sat back down. The coffee in the bottom of his cup trembled, little creamy waves, as he lifted it to his mouth.

⚓

At home, he called her house, twice. She was letting the machine pick up. He left no message.

His phone rang a little after ten, as he was putting the new strings on his acoustic guitar.

"I'm calling to find out if this is still something you want to do. In spite of my better judgment."

"Hey, Maud."

"You've changed your mind."

"No."

"I have too. That's fine. Really. I'll see you around."

"Do you have a pen?" he said. "Here's how you get here."

When she arrived, they hung her coat, discussed the rain that had just turned to wet snow, the lashing wind, how the lamb that the lion of March was supposed to have become hadn't showed. Or was it a lamb that was supposed to become a lion? Either way, April wasn't any better. Her face was a mask designed to represent a smile. She pulled off wet boots, wiggled her toes inside thin socks.

"Those are not suitable," Jake said, pointing. "No wonder you say you're cold all the time. Tea? A beer?"

"Tea." Maud followed him into the kitchen, sat at the table while he filled the kettle. "I keep meaning to buy warm things." She pulled a foot onto the opposite knee. They both watched her rub her toes. "Oh! Did you hear? Fixing the roads will probably win, but sustaining regular library hours won't."

"Welcome to Marengo." They talked about this, waiting for the kettle to whistle. Conversation dribbled. "I thought you might not want me to come," she said. Not looking at him. "That I shouldn't come. I keep wondering if I'm entering territory that's still hers."

"We're not going to talk about Lizzie."

Maud changed feet. After a few moments of kneading toes she laughed. "Well, that initiated what they call a strained silence. Maybe I could have both tea and a beer."

She clinked his bottle with hers, got up to pour a dollop in the sink. "To the gods." Carrying the steaming cup and a bottle of beer, she followed him to the living room. Curtains drawn. The apartment banal, bland, depressingly so: brown and dirty beige. No personality. No interesting books. No prints on the wall. No rugs to break up the anemic wall-to-wall carpet. The place felt cheap, temporary. Chilly, though the heat was on.

She sat on the couch. "Not that I'm saying there's territory to enter, really." Another silence, wet and clammy. She laughed. The sound was high, strained.

"You could tell me about rehearsal." He sounded grumpy. Tried again. "Tell me how rehearsal went."

"That's not what you want to talk about."

"Why not?"

Maud considered this, leaned back against the couch. "Okay. It's fine, it's going well. I think we're in good shape for how close we are to opening."

"I'll have to come see it."

"People always say that. But I hope you do." She took a breath, leaned forward, paused, leapt in: "You know what I keep thinking about? This long river of history." She stretched her arms wide, dancer-like. "And I'm part of it. When did people first put on a mask, a costume, pretend to be someone else? It's so *old*. I don't know why this occurs to me now, after all this time. I never understood the phrase 'it's in my blood' quite this way. But it is a kind of family. A clan. I love the actors in this cast because they're good, fun people. But I also love them because here we are in Marengo, as we were in L.A., and in medieval England and ancient Greece and feudal China, doing what we've always done—holding the mirror up to nature."

Animation flickered around her, sparking like some wild electrical current.

"For centuries, acting's been a sinful way to make a living. Maybe because it was in competition with the church, which can also be a kind of "show." Or maybe because there's ego involved—I can see that's sinful. But there are other motives, other reasons. It's so great to discover this again! It's not about finding love and acceptance. Or trying to escape yourself. It's about finding yourself. New things about yourself, and about life. And if it really works, then the audience sees something too—about themselves, about the world. You know—what art's supposed to do."

She collapsed sideways, onto the couch, put her head into the pillows and groaned. "What a pile of clichés." She sat up. Folded her hands in her lap, parody of a schoolgirl. "Any more questions?"

Jake laughed. Her face glowed. Lizzie had told him how Maud

could move from crone to enchantress and back again with tremendous speed. He wondered what it would be like to make love to her. Wondered what Lizzie was doing. What *he* was doing. Maud had asked about territory. He had no answer. He picked at the label on his bottle. "Tell me more."

"I'm boring you."

"You're not, actually."

"You'll be interested in this, maybe. Willy—Sue's husband?—is donating lumber and hardware. He gets a big mention in the program."

"Willy?" Jake would not have expected this. Willy was a notorious tightwad. "How'd you get that to happen?"

"Sue told me to go ask. He was hard to convince. I did a big pitch about the 'Importance of Supporting Art in the Community.' I think the mention in the program did it."

"Good for you."

"He actually got into it. He's even showed up to help build the set a couple of times." Silence moved in around them again. Maud cleared her throat. "Did you tell Lizzie we were getting together?"

He wished he had. He stood. "I'm getting another beer. Want one?"

"Not yet."

"What's your character?" he called from the kitchen.

"You have to come and see," Maud called back. When he returned she said, "I play a woman who's sworn off men. She's in mourning. Then she falls in love. Everyone gets to fall in love, except poor Malvolio."

"To fall in love," Jake mused.

In the long pause that followed, Maud took a pull at her beer. "Did Lizzie tell you about Jeep?"

Jake nodded.

"I looked up the word *abortion*," Maud said. "Comes from the Greek words meaning 'appear' and 'away.' Disappear."

Another long pause, during which they both nodded. Like the plastic animals with loose necks that used to sit in the backs of cars when Jake was growing up.

Maud stood. "This is too hard, Jake. You're being really sweet, and maybe you really are interested in my babble—"

"You aren't—"

"—but I was so afraid of this. Sitting around with you. Your heart a kite tugged by a different string."

"My heart is not— Maud. We don't know each other well enough for you to presume to interpret my thoughts! Please."

Looking chastened, even shocked, Maud sat back down.

"I'm not bored."

"Okay. It's me. Being weird. I do that." After a pause she said, "I could tell you about visiting Sam."

"That's a good topic." Jake picked up his guitar, began to noodle. "When did you go?"

"Monday. We took the girls. We drove for over three hours, then sat around his bed trying to think of things to say."

"Was the radical there?" Jake formed an augmented chord, diminished it, strummed this hard with his pick.

"Was he. Lizzie calls him The Asshole. Capital *T*, capital *A*."

Jake strummed the chord again, adding a sour flat.

Maud shook her head. "He plans to lash Sam's body to the top of a tree when he dies. The old ways. I mean, I respect it, it's just so— Even Sara, calm, serene, let-it-be Sara, she's speechless. Angry. Doesn't know what to say."

"And how does The Asshole know Sara?" Sara's theme was a series of pretty descending notes.

"I told you about Driver hitchhiking when I was on my way here? That night I drove him to his aunt's trailer, Maggie's. That's where they've taken Sam. Maggie—" Maud stopped. "Let's see. Maggie is a major chord: spangling, cheerful, nice and round. I really like her. She makes Sam twinkle, which is as close as you get to a laugh out of him."

She nodded when Jake found an appropriate chord for Maggie. "Maggie, it turns out, is also Bitter Water clan, related to Sara, so Sara is related to Driver. It's so weird. I'm driving from L.A.—*fleeing* L.A.—and I run into Driver. I actually stayed in the trailer where Sam is now sleeping." She smiled at the series of sounds Jake created to accompany her story. "And now all this."

"Lizzie says Sam isn't any better."

"I wish he were. I actually want him to be, so it'll be right that they did what they did. No matter how hard it was on Lizzie, you know?" Jake nodded. "They've had smokes in the hogan with other Bitter Water clan members. There was a ceremony of some kind planned for the evening after we left. Not that they expected us, or wanted us, to participate."

"I understand that."

"I do too! Don't get me wrong. And if I didn't, Driver would be sure I did. All the same, Sam doesn't *know* any of them." She pushed her hands through her hair. "What would we do without family."

Their eyes met, jumped apart. After a pause, he asked, "Want to stay the night?"

Her cheekbones stood out, flaring a dusky red. "Maybe I could have that other beer now."

Jake took the opportunity to go to the john. Had a hard time pissing. His cock was erect. When he got back with her beer she was looking at the spines of the assorted paperbacks lodged in his shelves. An edge of danger, even darkness, vied with the prosaic furniture, the stucco walls. He cleared his throat. Handed her the beer.

"Thanks." Maud pulled a paperback from the shelf. Jake thought of the books he'd seen piled beside the chair and on the piano at her house the evening he'd spent there. *Seven Arrows. Three Pillars of Zen. Necessary Wisdom. Spiritual Materialism.* A large paperback with a lurid red cover, *Spiritual Emergency,* carefully tucked under a newspaper.

She shelved the book. "Part of me wants to say yes. I'm tired. I'd love not to have to go back to a cold house, I'd love to hold. Be held." Her voice shook. "But staying would probably mean we would—sleep together. Whatever the word is. That describes what it is we would do." Maud the crone had reappeared. "I'd like to. It's simple. But then I have to wonder—by now you know I'm like this—*is* it simple?"

Jake dropped on the sofa, head in his hands.

"I've never been good at living in the moment. I always ask, 'But what about tomorrow?' " The couch sagged as she sat beside him. "Lizzie tells me I complicate everything, and maybe I do, maybe I am. But on the other hand, it seems to me that making love with you might be a pretty complicated act."

Jake kept his head in his hands. Watched Maud's slender, arched feet in their opaque black socks. Toes curled. "Lizzie says things are just what they *are*. I have a hard time believing that. Maybe I've been an actor for too long. I'm too used to asking, 'What's this scene *really* about?' I try not to do it. But I do."

"It's exhausting."

"Yes, it is. In this case I keep asking, 'Am I attracted to Jake because I'm simply attracted to Jake, or for some other, ulterior reason? Is he attracted to me, or is it—' " She didn't finish this. Jake swallowed before looking at her. She peered at his eyes, as if there was something specific she wished to see there. "I wonder if we shouldn't stick to a chronicle of the day's events," she said.

After a long silence they both started to laugh. "Maybe it is simple," Jake said. Leaned towards her. She met him halfway. Their lips bumped, adjusted, bumped again. A clinical, lip-to-lip kiss. They drew apart.

Maud took a shaky breath.

"That wasn't so bad, was it?" he asked.

"Not so bad."

He stood. Held out his hand.

※

The phone blared. Jake jerked awake. Had no problem remembering who was in the bed with him. "I had such a dream," Maud murmured. "What a *dream*."

The phone shrilled again. Jake rolled over. Scrabbled amongst the receipts and coins and pens and song beginnings on his night table. "It's six o'clock in the goddamn morning," he said into the phone, ready to berate Randy, the only person he knew who would dare to call him this early. Or this late, depending on what she'd been up to.

A long pause on the other end of the line. "I'm sorry, Jake. Is Maud there? I need to talk to her, real bad."

"Jeep," Jake said. "Jeep, you okay?"

"Is Maud there?"

"Hold on." Jake turned on the bedside lamp. Maud rolled over to look at him. She took the phone gingerly, as if it might bite her. "Hello?"

It took Jake a few minutes to wonder how it was Jeep would know Maud was at his apartment. He had an inkling, however. He put his hands behind his head, settled back against the pillows, and said, "Hoo boy."

Maud nodded from time to time, murmuring agreement. "Of course," she said. "I'll be there as soon as I can."

She handed the phone to Jake to hang up and pulled the sheet over her head. "I need to get up, right now, and I can't bear to face this day. Jeep slept at Lizzie's last night."

Jake waited.

"Jeep went to see Sue earlier this week." The sheet fluttered in front of Maud's mouth. "At the clinic. She scheduled an appointment. But she thought Lizzie wouldn't approve, and didn't tell her until last night. Lizzie's got a mandatory meeting at school this morning and can't take her. So Jeep calls me to ask if I'll drive her down to Farmington. When I don't answer my phone, Lizzie tells her to try this number. I assume Jeep didn't know it was yours until you answered." She pulled the sheet down to check his reaction. In the light from the lamp her skin looked pale blue. Eyes heavy, bruised-looking.

"Was Lizzie there?"

Maud nodded. "I'm sure she was. *Fuck!*" She rubbed her eyes. "And then there's this awful dream. May I take a shower?"

"Of course."

"Jeep asked would you please call Sue, say she'll be late." Maud pushed back the sheet. She still wore her shirt and skirt. "Tell Sue that Jeep did what she was supposed to—didn't eat and all that."

He dialed the clinic. "Sue Knobbler, please."

Maud perched on the edge of the bed, adding details she wanted him to include. She kept her voice low, but Sue demanded, "Who's there?"

"Hmmm hmmm," Jake said.

"Lizzie? No, you'd have said. Is it *Maud*? Oh good lord."

"Quite," Jake said. "Rather." He spoke with an exaggerated British accent, learned from a childhood tape he and Sue had worn out, on which a character had said these and other words hysterically often. "It is a bit, rather, too too, if you ask me."

"Talking about me, are we?" Maud whispered. "I'll just pop off to the shower, then. Cheerio."

When the bathroom door closed Jake said, "It's not what you think."

"Jake," Sue said. "I can't *believe* you sometimes."

"It isn't what you think," Jake repeated. In the bathroom the water ran.

"Well, what on earth could it be? Does Lizzie know?"

His laugh was harsh. "When Jeep didn't find Maud at home, Lizzie told her to try this number. Did she know?"

"Oh, Jake. I don't know what you're up to."

"I didn't think I was 'up' to anything." But he was reminded of Maud's question: *What is this scene really about?*

"Don't be grumpy. Listen. Demonstrators are out there this morning. They'll succeed in driving away most of our appointments. I'm getting hate mail, did I tell you? Phone calls in the dead of night. I'm scared to be at home alone."

"Hate mail?"

"That's par for the course. But I refuse to wear the bulletproof vest Willy bought for me. There are limits."

"Sue!"

"I've been telling you, Jake. Anyway, be prepared for some nastiness. Gotta go."

Jake pulled on boxers, jeans, socks, a sweatshirt, got coffee started. Put slices of bread in the toaster oven. Maud emerged from the bathroom. "I keep remembering bits of this awful dream," she said. "I *think* it's awful. I can't quite tell. Maybe it's good. Is that coffee?"

"Good coffee. I'll loan you a travel mug. I have several, from work."

Maud passed a comb again and again through the long tail of black hair held in one fist, working out snarls. The sight made him blue. Lizzie's hair was so different. Lizzie herself was. And he'd ruined any chance to make it good with her.

"You seem sad." Maud pulled at the strands of hair that had wrapped themselves in the comb. Deposited the wad in the overflowing paper bag beneath the sink. "Disappointed. Sad."

He noisily washed out a Synercomp travel mug. Didn't answer. But she said, "Don't pretend with me. I'd rather you didn't."

There was little he could say that would not hurt her. He put an arm around her, kissed her forehead. Which was what he'd done last night before they fell asleep. Which was about all he'd done. But even if he ever had a chance to say so, Liz wouldn't believe him. And after all, he had intended to sleep with Maud. Couldn't deny it. Had stroked the long curve of her back. Kissed her. She'd been the one to whisper, "I don't feel right about this." Moved a few inches away. "I'm sorry."

He'd told her she was probably right.

There was no stir of desire, even when they shifted positions, found ways to lie with each other. Familiar yet new, as all lovers' positions somehow are. Those few times with Randy, he'd felt he was betraying Lizzie—not because he was sleeping with someone else, but because he found himself in arrangements of limbs he'd thought unique to the two of them. "Should I go home?" Maud had whispered, and he spooned around her, saying, "Just sleep." And they'd slept without moving until the phone had woken them.

The toaster oven pinged. Maud fetched her boots from the hallway, sat at the kitchen table to pull them on. He spread peanut butter on one slice, honey on the other, cut the sandwich in half, wrapped it in a paper towel. Carrying this and a plastic cup of coffee, he followed her into the hallway. She put on her coat. Her face was pale, scoops beneath her eyes like characters in a *Doonesbury* cartoon.

He handed her the sandwich. "This is a hell of a morning after. Wish we had time for a cup of coffee."

"Probably best not."

"Sue says there are protesters. Just walk through them. They don't know whether you're there to get a Pap smear or an abortion." They both blinked at the word. Jake opened the door. The cold hit, a blast of icy air. "And don't you dare be weird with me now. Please."

She took the cup of coffee. "You should be with Lizzie," she said. "Lizzie is being very silly." She looked at him. "But even so, thank you, more than you can ever know, for the fact I slept all the way through a night."

"Someday you can tell me about that dream."

That mirthless smile. "I don't know if I want to tell anyone about this dream."

He watched her maneuver her way down the icy path. "Don't be a stranger!" he called. She turned, nodded, waved. He shut the door, went back to the kitchen. Poured himself coffee. Leafed through a week-old newspaper. "What were you *thinking*," he finally said aloud. "What on earth did you think you were doing?"

But that seemed a betrayal of Maud, who had cautioned both of them. And he could hardly blame it on demon drink. Two beers hadn't damaged his powers of reasoning. What was it Maud had said last night? He scribbled in the margin of the newspaper.

> *some kind of kite*
> *pulled*
> *tethered*
> *tugged by a different string*
> *by a different wind*

A knock sounded on his door. Even as he hoped it would be Lizzie he knew it was Maud, having forgotten something. Nose and cheeks red with cold. Pale forehead tented by hair that fell loosely over her black coat. "I'm not being a stranger," she said. He appreciated that she was trying to be funny. "My car won't start."

❈

Jake turned the defrost knob up to high. Maud fanned her fingers in front of a heating vent. "A few weeks ago it was something to do with the steering column. I was going crazy trying to figure that one out: my steering's going out. Is something wrong with my choices? I have no control? I need to get control but it's going to cost me?"

She waited, as if she expected him to make fun of this. He kept his eyes on the road. Yesterday's melt and last night's freeze made the pavement slick and driving tricky. And he wanted silence. What would he say to Lizzie?

"But then another mechanic told me I just had to be sure to watch the level of steering fluid carefully and I'd be okay. That made sense to me: Be careful with your driving."

"Be careful with your steering, in fact."

"You understand!" Maud cried. "Lizzie just says, 'It's a *car*, things go *wrong*.' "

"It's probably a dead battery." Lizzie would be waiting beside Jeep in the driveway as he and Maud drove up. Arms crossed. Smiling but grim. Had he asked Maud to stay to make Lizzie jealous? Was that what the scene had been about? "You left your headlights on," he said. "You used the interior light to look for something, forgot to turn it off."

"But what's that *mean*? Why would I do that? And then there's this dream. Letting things go? Letting things die?"

"You'll drive yourself crazy with that." Jake sipped at his coffee. "Can I have half of that sandwich?"

Maud unfolded the paper towel, set the sandwich and paper on his thigh. "What's great—you don't know how great this is." She began to laugh. "I think it's *funny*."

"It?"

"The car, the godawful dream, what everything *means*." She laughed again. "I'm laughing about it!"

Jake wasn't sure what the big deal was. Handed her half the sandwich. "Eat. I made it for you."

"So I walk into this room." She stared at the honey-soaked toast in her hand. "It's just a dream."

Jake checked the rearview mirror. The few cars out drove with their headlights on high beam, dimmed when anyone got close.

"I'm with somebody, but that person's also me. You know how that is? Like she's there, witnessing? Anyway, I—we—see this woman sitting there, cross-legged, bent over. I can't see it, but I know that there's a bloody hole in her belly."

Jake made a noise through the wad of peanut butter in his mouth.

"And I blithely say to this person, who's also me, 'Oh, another woman committing hara-kiri.' I say this as if there's nothing to it, as if it's an everyday thing, as if it's a joke. Although I can see that it's deadly serious. And then the bent-over woman straightens up. She's also a version of me. She puts her hands into this hole in her stomach and starts pulling at it, ripping it further open."

"Jesus."

Maud had been storing her own coffee cup on the floor, between her feet. She took a swallow. Jake glanced at her. She stared at the invisible screen in front of her eyes.

"She's, I'm, tugging herself apart. I can see into the hole. There's this wet, pulsating interior. The kind of thing you see in movies when people get miniaturized and travel through bloodstreams and aortas?" Maud replaced her coffee at her feet. "I have time, in the dream, to be very impressed with the visual detail of the thing, the *reality* of it. The pearly pink of the walls of the uterus. Then there's this large tube. At first I think it's guts, a piece of intestine, but then I realize it's actually an umbilical cord."

For the time being Jake stored the sandwich on his thigh.

"So. I'm impressed with the reality of all this, but I'm also hiding, scrunched, horrified, scared, but wanting above all to be cool. That seems to be very important. To not act surprised, even though I'm terrified. And then suddenly it's like the camera, the point of view of the dream, does a big zoom in, into this umbilical cord, which is flapping in the wind, making this horrible noise. It fills the whole of the screen—of the dream. Then I'm watching the girl, but the girl is me, and now she's flushing something down the toilet. And then the camera, or whatever you'd call it, moves in for a close-up and there are all these innards going down the toilet, swirling, bloody and circular, swirling and disappearing. We-ird." This word contained two syllables.

Jake took a large swallow of coffee. "Had Jeep told you her decision?"

"No. But of course abortion was on my mind. Appear away. Something appears and then goes away." She heaved in her seat to face his profile. "Or maybe I felt sleeping with you was doing something to Lizzie—stabbing her? Pulling her innards out? Or maybe us deciding not to make love was putting a knife inside me—I won't have children, I've flushed that hope down the toilet?" She put her hands to her head, held them there. "All these bloody images keep haunting me this morning. But I also feel tremendously relieved, as if I literally did get rid of something. But I can't think what it is." She laughed. "You see why I'm a little obsessed with why my car won't start."

Jake grunted.

The heater was finally making a difference. Maud shrugged out of her coat. "We could have called Triple A. I feel terrible. Because of my car problems you've been dragged into this. I'm so sorry that—"

"Stop it, Maud."

It sounded harsh. Maud said her now predictable "Sorry." They rode in silence through landscape that was dreary: branches of trees and scrub scratching a sky the color of a black T-shirt washed too many times.

"Bare ruined choirs," Maud said. "When yellow leaves, or none, or few do hang upon these boughs." She heaved around in her seat again. "I can't help but run it around. What engine isn't running in my life? What needs jump-starting? What battery's run down? There are a lot of possibilities."

"You are exhausting," Jake said.

"But at least I'm *laughing*."

But when they turned onto Lizzie's road, Maud's voice was subdued. "If Jeep's not waiting, I'll just run in and get her."

"That'd be good." Jake imagined the arch of Lizzie's eyebrows, the lifted chin. He smacked the steering wheel with his gloved hand. "Why am I so goddamn worried? She's done nothing but dismiss me, make me feel like a cad. Okay, I'm a *cad*," he yelled. "I'm an asshole. I could have been better. I fucked up. I feel bad. Real bad. Do I eat shit for the rest of my goddamn life?"

He was driving fast. The car lurched over a dip in the road. He braked, too hard. The car skewed back and forth, went into a skid. Maud reached for the dashboard. Her face a white, aghast blur in his peripheral vision. He turned into the skid, impatient lessons taught to him by his father years ago in an iced-over parking lot. The car stopped at the edge of the road, front end hanging over a ditch. They stared into the white field ahead of them.

Maud said nothing while Jake straightened the car out.

They approached the house. "Since we did what we did, and only did what we did," Maud whispered, as though Lizzie might hear, but her voice was fierce. "can we let it be okay? I don't want us to regret it. Please don't regret it."

"I'm not regretting it."

Lizzie's car was gone. Maud pulled on her mittens, didn't look at him. "I'll be right back."

But she didn't get very far up the stairs of the house before Jeep came out, zipping her parka, breath puffing in the cold. She wore

Lizzie's red ski hat pulled down to just above her eyes. Maud insisted she sit in front.

"Thanks," Jeep said to him. She didn't seem surprised he'd come too. "I know this is a hassle."

"No." He wasn't sure whether he should smile at her. What tone did one adopt while driving someone to an abortion? Funereal? Probably not celebratory, although he wouldn't want to have Rich's kid either. It'd be born wearing cowboy boots. Cowboy hat. And nothing in between but a red kerchief and a well-slung dong. He said, "You tell Rich?"

Jeep shook her head.

Huge flakes of snow whirled towards them. Jake tried to keep his shoulders from hunching with tension. Maud leaned forward into the space between the front seats, told Jeep about the protesters who might be waiting. Jake listened to the following discussion with interest. The pros and cons of the "procedure," as Jeep referred to it. How long it would take. That it was good she was doing it so early. Her insistence that her mother must never know. Or Rich either. What she could and could not expect for the next few days. "I can't wear tampons for at least two periods. But that's petty. I guess. In the scheme of things."

Maud put her arms around Jeep's neck. Jeep's hands came up to hold them. After a silence, Maud began to sing.

> When that I was and a little tiny boy,
> With a hey, ho, the wind and the rain,
> A foolish thing was but a toy,
> For the rain it raineth every day.

The tune was mournful but pretty. After another long silence Jeep took a deep breath. Didn't speak.

"What?" Maud said.

"It's just an idea. Silly."

"Jake's good at listening to silly ideas. He's been listening to mine all morning. Was Lizzie mad?"

"I don't know. I really don't. When she realized I was talking to you she went over and started doing dishes."

They stared forward. The curtain of snow spiraled towards them. Jake said, "What were you going to say?"

"It's just I keep thinking this thing. It's stupid." Jeep pulled her mitten off, put it on again. "I just keep thinking. That if I don't have this baby it gives a chance for Sam to stay alive. Silly."

"No," Jake said. Maud said, "It's not at all silly." He downshifted to stop at a light. They were in Farmington.

Jeep drew a shaky breath. "Not that I think there's only so many spirits on the earth at any one time or anything."

Outside the clinic a dozen protesters, bundled up in parkas and mufflers, waved posters tacked to sticks. Blurred by falling snow, it was still obvious that the signs depicted something pink and bloody. "Oh no," Jeep moaned.

Jake drove around the side of the building and parked. The two women stood and watched without smiling as he maneuvered his limbs and length of parka over the emergency brake and gearshift. He took Jeep's other arm. She looked about twelve years old. Red ski hat perched above frightened eyes. They walked around the corner of the building. The knot of protesters turned towards them.

"Dedicated little fuckers, aren't they," he whispered.

Jeep kept her head down.

About fifteen feet from the clinic doors, one of the men—they were mostly men, as Sue had said—stepped so close Jake could smell sour creamy coffee on his breath. "What're ya doing here? Why would you bring your sweet daughter to a murdering place?" Brown eyes flecked with green. The eyes were nice. The look in them was not.

"Excuse us," Jake said. Jeep made a little sound. Jake slid his arm all the way around her. Maud's arm held her waist from the other direction.

A woman stepped in front of them. Eyes filled with tears. "What if the blessed Mary had aborted her baby?"

Appear and away. "Excuse us," Jake said. "Excuse us."

The woman fell back but another pushed forward. "You'd murder your own child? You'd aid and abet? You'd *help* them invade the sanctuary of the womb?"

"Please let us through," Maud said.

"You call yourself parents?"

A young girl, younger than Jeep but not by much, pushed a poster into their faces. Maud hissed. Jake jerked his eyes away from the sight of chunked-up flesh and blood.

"Jesus H. Christ." Jeep pulled away. "You should be ashamed. Shoving shit like that in people's faces. Have you thought about it? It's pretty damn easy not to think about it, let me tell you, until it hits you between the eyes. Do you think this is easy? Do you think I want to do this? It was a *mistake*. I've cried about it all night, I've cried for three fucking weeks."

Jeep's raised voice caused a tumult. "You never know when a mistake is the *word* of God," a man yelled. Brandishing a poster, he pushed towards them. "Who are we to say the will of God is a *mistake*?" Shoved the poster in Jake's face.

Jake pushed it away. "Don't go poking that thing where it ain't wanted, man."

The man jabbed the poster at Jake repeatedly with a kind of weird glee. "I'll poke it where I want to, *man*. It's a free world, *man*." He hadn't shaved. Eyes small and red, face blotched with cold.

Jake felt rage boiling. "I'm asking you. Get that thing away from me."

"Cool it, Bill," someone said. Others shouted. The door of the clinic opened. A pale, scared face looked out, disappeared.

"Let's not do this." Maud was almost moaning. "Please."

Spittle clung to the corners of Bill's mouth. *"Man,"* he kept saying. *"Man."* Unexpectedly, he backed up, then shoved the stick, hard, like a wooden sword, into Jake's stomach.

Jake doubled over.

Jeep gave a scream. Maud shouted.

"Bill!" a woman shrieked.

Jake could not get a breath. He grunted, gasped, holding his stomach. Wished he could laugh—show he was okay. But couldn't get breath for that either.

"Jake?" Maud bent beside him.

"Stop it, you guys." Jeep was crying. "Just stop it."

He tried to straighten. The man named Bill loomed over him. Flecks of spittle at the corners of his mouth. "You murderer. Murderer of innocents."

Jake grabbed the poster out of Bill's hand. Put the stick across his knee, snapped it in half, dropped the pieces to the ground.

Jeep's gasp was a scream.

"Now, Bill."

Jake felt Maud go stiff. Looked up. Noted with a peculiar mixture of wonder and outrage that Bill held a gun. A little snub-nosed gun whose handle fit his hand neat as a computer mouse.

"Who will suffer the little children if we don't?" He waved it in front of Jake's face. The other protesters backed away. "Put that away, Bill," someone said.

The muzzle of the gun grew, yawned, stretched. A cartoon. More large, more black than was possible. "Hey, man," Jake said. "Let's just cool it." Wanting to laugh.

Hairs sprouted on the knuckle that crooked around the trigger. Lizzie, painting, would be able to find the color blue in the flat black of that muzzle.

Then. "Put that the fuck away." Jeep's voice was thick with tears, but she bellied up to Bill the way a cowboy might a bar. "That make you feel good? Forcing your crap on us with your big nasty gun, your big nasty penis extender." Her mouth pinched, turned down at the corners, as if the man smelled. She looked at the girl, who was clutching her poster, wide-eyed. "You just let him do this? You let men decide what we can and can't do?"

"Women aren't the only ones who care about this," a woman shouted.

Jake managed to stand straight. In spite of his efforts he was still gasping. In the distance came the sound of sirens. "Go to school," Jeep said. "Go get a fucking education."

Jake pulled open the door to the clinic. Maud and Jeep stepped past him. He closed the door, leaned against it with both hands, shutting out not just the wind and the snow and the voices. For a few moments the hate was shut out as well. He didn't think it was only in his imagination that soon enough, like some ooze from a horror movie, he felt it—tangible, pea-green, oily—seeping through the walls, around the edges of the door.

Jeep sobbed. Maud held her. "I'm not a murderer," she said. "I'm *not*."

The receptionist, pale and scared, did her best to look calm, but one hand washed the other incessantly as she told them where to hang their coats. It was quite cold. "Problem with the heat," the receptionist said. "We're working on it."

Jake wondered what meaning Maud would wring out of a heating problem.

Jeep's eyes were red. Cheeks flushed, lips a hard thin line. "We were reading this book last semester," she said. "All that out there reminded me of it. The way everyone liked to go see the killing. How they scrabbled in the street for the red wine, how they liked to attend the beheadings, see the violence and the blood and the guillotine. It's sick."

He was moved when she came to him, pressed her face into his shoulder. Because of the way it made people behave, he thought, one of the greatest of all the great evils had to do with the desire to perpetuate fear. He put a hand around the small blonde head. Felt her tears wet against his neck, wished he could make it all go away.

Sue emerged from the back. If she was surprised to see him, she didn't let on. She took Jeep into her office for a few minutes. When Jeep emerged she was calmer.

"I'm sorry you had to deal with that," Sue said. "Most people go away instead of walking that gauntlet."

"I'm so mad." Jeep's voice shook. "They act like this is something I *want* to do. They have no right."

Sue shook her head. "Actually, they do have a right. I have to remind myself of that a lot these days. Bad as this is, the alternative would be far, far worse."

She excused herself for a few minutes. Jake looked around. This was where his sister came five, sometimes six days a week. Walls a shade of shiny green that reminded him of the nurse's room in grade school. Hanging pots with thick, abundant leaves. Sue's touch, he was sure. What would pro-lifers say of the irony of her nurturing life in plants and taking life from innocent—what was the word Jeep had used in the car?—viables?

This was where he would have come with Lizzie, he thought, if she had done as he'd asked. He leaned back against the couch to ponder this, watched Maud and Jeep leaf through magazines. Tears

seeped from Jeep's eyes. She pushed them away with the back of a
hand, blew her nose on tissue after wadded tissue pulled from the
box on the table beside the couch. Maud kept an arm around her. He
and Maud had been called Jeep's parents. He supposed in some way
they were in loco parentis, which didn't mean—as he used to think it
did—crazy parents. He watched Maud's face. She wanted a child so
badly, yet here she was, aiding and abetting, as the woman outside
had said, the stopping of a new life. He was glad, guilty and glad, that
such a choice would never be his to so ultimately have to make.

And yet he had thought Lizzie should do it.

His face grew warm. So that was the reason he was here. Maud's
peculiar logic had rubbed off on him. In spite of the ironies and the
moral ambiguities and his own lack of conviction in either direction,
his being here with Jeep might balance out something in the cosmos.
He was being here for someone in a way he had not been there for
Lizzie.

He looked around, feeling lighter, feeling as if sunlight had just
come through windows. "Maud," he said.

She marked her place in a magazine with a finger.

"I think I have an idea of why your car wouldn't start."

Jeep pulled another tissue and blew her nose.

"It's just a thought," he said. But he didn't know how to begin to
share it.

And then the door scraped open. He heard Lizzie say, "Just fuck the
fuck off." She slammed the door, then opened it again. "Those are
such nice signs," she said in a high, fake, sweet voice. "Did you make
them yourselves?" She slammed the door again.

Even Jeep laughed. She stood up. "Oh, Lizzie." She tripped over
the corner of the low magazine table. Lizzie sank onto the couch
with the onslaught of her embrace. Jeep burrowed into her lap,
crying.

"Shh, shh." Lizzie smoothed the messy blonde hair and looked at
Jake. "I thought I saw your car out there." She sounded, unexpectedly, as if she approved. She threw her hat onto a chair. "I got to
school and was sitting in this inane meeting and I thought, this isn't

where I need to be. So I was suddenly taken sick, and here I am. You guys can go along now. I'll take it from here."

Maud looked like the proverbial deer caught in the headlights. Eyes wide and startled. Jake thought it was a measure of some distance he had come that he could lean back on the couch, cross one ankle over the opposite knee. "We're not going anywhere without Jeep," he heard himself say. "Without you. Seems to me we're all in this together."

Lizzie shrugged. Leaned over Jeep. "I've decided. We should keep this little baby."

Jeep pulled back, face full of confusion. "No, Lizzie."

"Yes. We'll all chip in to bring it up. If you don't want to be a mother right now, I'll do it, or Maud will."

Jeep shook her head. "We *talked* about all this."

"You can be around just as much as you want to. You won't have to worry about that 'murderer' crap. And Maud wants a kid. Right, Maud?"

Maud moved her head in what was not quite a nod, not quite a shake. Face drained of color.

Sue opened the door that led into the back. "It's finally warm enough back there. Oh my goodness—Lizzie!"

Jake watched his sister, calm and smiling, greet Lizzie. Recognized the gleam in Sue's eye. He'd hear about this later, he could count on that.

Lizzie took Jeep's hand, straightened her shoulders. "We've changed our minds."

CHAPTER 28

MAUD

Last scene of all,
That ends this strange eventful history,
Is second childishness and mere oblivion;
Sans teeth, sans eyes, sans taste, sans everything.
—*AS YOU LIKE IT*

Maud rode back with Lizzie and Jeep. This effort to avoid awkwardness only managed to complicate matters. The logistics of getting her car fixed had to be discussed, and with Lizzie watching, Jake put out his hand for the key to her car: "I'll get your battery charged." Lizzie stalked to her own car and had not said a word to Maud since they'd started home.

From the back seat, Maud could see a rectangle of Lizzie's face reflected in the rearview mirror. Lizzie checked behind them from time to time, but would not meet Maud's eyes.

The wipers hummed and clicked, heaving their loads of snow from side to side. Maud moved behind the passenger seat and put her arms all the way around it, around Jeep. Lizzie glanced over, slid her eyes back to the road again. Jeep held on to Maud's arm with both hands. "This isn't what you want," Jeep said. "You wanted it to be your own."

Maud tightened her hug, remembering how Sue, in the clinic, held both of Jeep's hands and asked, "You sure?"

Jeep had shrugged. "I'm screwed either way. Either way it's a rotten decision."

Lizzie had made *shh*ing noises. Sue spoke urgently. "You have time. You can still change your mind. This is exactly why we call it a woman's right to choose."

But who had chosen? This should not be about what Lizzie wanted, what Lizzie thought Jeep wanted, what Lizzie thought Maud wanted. Maud kept turning phrases over in her mind to address this. But she felt in some morally reprehensible place. *I didn't sleep with him,* she wanted to say. But she had slept with him. *But that's all we did.* She felt gagged. The windows were closed, but Lizzie's hair billowed out around her head as if blown by heavy winds; she gripped the steering wheel with straight arms, managing to look like both an injured angel and an avenging one.

Keeping her arms around Jeep, Maud stared out the side window through the heavily falling snow, at the passing scene of white fields and snow-covered farmhouses. She was enveloped by a wave of icy fear—how could she do it?—mixed with the old anguish—how had she gotten so old without a child of her own? With Lizzie as an example constantly before her, Maud had to recognize that women who really wanted a child went about getting a child, and in spite of her chronic sorrow on the subject, she had not done that. Now the be-careful-what-you-ask-for mantra had worked its magic. But she was too selfish, too used to calling her days her own. She couldn't pay for it: the clothes, the stroller, the doctors. She would have to find a day job, day care, night care: How did one play the piano for a living, rehearse a play, with a child? She would have to abandon these things.

Yet women did this all the time. *We do not know how you may soften at the sight of the child,* Paulina said in *The Winter's Tale.*

> *The silence often of pure innocence*
> *Persuades when speaking fails.*

Like being doused with freezing, then blessedly warm, water, the clutch of fear released. Briefly Maud floated through a blissful scene of motherhood.

"Where's Theo?" Jeep suddenly asked.

Lizzie didn't take her eyes off the road. "Hard to believe, isn't it? Less than three hours ago I dropped him at the Theibeaus'."

Jeep's cheek rested more and more consistently on Maud's arm; she had fallen asleep. This was the time to question Lizzie about the wisdom of what had happened in the clinic with Jeep, to say what had happened—had not happened—with Jake. The minutes ticked by. *I'm not sure Jeep wants to—* The heater blasted hot air. *About Jake, it's not what you think—*

The wipers moved back and forth, back and forth. As they turned onto the county road that led to Lizzie's house, Jeep woke with a sudden moan.

Lizzie reached over to pat her thigh.

Jeep moaned again. "I had this thought. Oh, I don't like this thought."

Maud understood, instantly and precisely. "Sam."

"What if he—"

"I'll go," Maud said.

"We were just there." Lizzie's voice was baffled and defensive.

"But I'll need to borrow your car. Lizzie?"

Lizzie used the rearview mirror to look at her, finally. "Fine."

"My battery's dead," Maud said to those eyes, green like a cat's, eyes defensive and wounded. "Will you come, Lizard? Please? Both of you?"

"Can't." Lizzie pulled the car to a stop outside the house, yanked hard on the parking brake. To Jeep she said, "I'll run you a bath."

><

The week before, Maud had enjoyed the drive to Maggie's place. This time, due to a low fog, and snow that turned to icy rain, it took almost six hours. She was grateful for Lizzie's four-wheel-drive. For most of the drive, she held a one-sided conversation with the invisible companion in the passenger seat about her tendency to meddle in people's lives, and about what had and had not happened with Jake.

No one answered her knock on the door of Maggie's trailer. The Airstream was empty. The bedding, including the mattress, was gone. Smoke rose from the hogan. She had to walk almost completely around the log building before she found the entrance, covered with an army-issue green blanket.

The floor of the hogan was flattened, pounded earth. In the center a fire glowed in a jagged-edged, sawed-off bottom of a large oil drum, surrounded by patterned rugs. Sam lay on one of these, his body a barely visible mound beneath a blanket. Sara and Maggie, hooded with serape-like shawls, sat next to him.

Maud stood in the doorway, holding the blanket aside in one hand. "There you are," Maggie said.

Something inaudible came out of Sam's mouth. Sara leaned close to hear, then nodded. "Get in here, girls, don't let what little bit of heat we've got escape."

"It's just me," Maud began, but Sara put a finger to her lips. "Get in here, Lizzie. Good to see you, Maud. Glad you brought the girls again. Let that blanket down, Lizzie. It's freezing out there. Sam made us take the door out so he could see the sun rise. Go on, Summer. Sit down next to Luna there."

Maud let the blanket fall to behind her. The twilight of the hogan's interior deepened. For a moment she saw her sister, walking towards Sam, sitting beside Sara. Hannah settled in next to Sara. Luna pressed her muzzle onto Summer's lap. Maud moved, finally, into this mirage. She knelt next to Sam. As she took his hand his fingers moved, a trembling effort to pat her, and then were still.

Sara and Maggie watched, eyes dark within the darkness of their hooded faces. Sam's skin was smooth, taut against his bones, made rosy by the fire: beautiful. As her eyes adjusted to the dim light, she made out a standing bicycle against one wall. A large, many-limbed piece of exercise equipment gesticulated beside it. The walls of the hogan were decorated with patterned rugs, interspersed with shiny posters. It took her a while to realize the significance of these posters, and who it was would have put them there: WASHINGTON REDSKINS, CLEVELAND INDIANS, FLORIDA STATE SEMINOLES, KANSAS CITY CHIEFS, ATLANTA BRAVES.

She took in the rest of the hogan: the packed earth floor, shelves of board and brick. Books, potsherds, miscellany. Magazines piled in an orange crate. Stove, unlit; a pail beside it. Desk, typewriter. Clearly Driver's stuff. But where was he? She didn't want to interrupt the quiet in the hogan to ask.

Every once in an impossibly long while the blanket covering

Sam's chest rose, receded. She understood why Maggie and Sara had included Lizzie and the girls, and Luna too. She felt them there; she willed them with all her might to stay. She wondered if there was any point to getting a doctor, and worried that she should call Lizzie to come. But there was no phone, not for many miles, and she didn't want to leave. Time slowed, stopped. She had no idea how long they sat there. She thought she might have fallen asleep, her head nodding onto her chest, when suddenly the room filled with a breathless sense of waiting. Sam took a gasping breath. His eyes opened, stared. His fingers twitched inside her hand, his lips moved. Sara and Maggie's heads were up, eyes open.

One Christmas Maud and Lizzie's father had given them a glossy coffee-table book of medieval and Renaissance paintings. Maud, fourteen, had pored over them, fascinated by the story each painting seemed to tell. In one of them a group of people gathered around the bed of a man in tangled white sheets. His skin was white; his mouth was open. In an upper corner of the painting hovered a gray, wraith-like thing. She had understood, even then, that this was the spirit that had escaped the dying man. This next moment was like that: a presence hovered, benign, in the room, and then something moved, began to dissipate, like mist under sunlight. After a few minutes, there was a very small skin, smaller than Maud would have imagined possible, that had been Sam.

Maud held on to the cold fingers a few minutes longer. Sara unfolded her legs. Maggie said, "Driver's out in his dig, asked us to send you along when you showed up."

"I have to tell Lizzie." Maud felt she should whisper, although Maggie had not. She also had rehearsal, a concern that seemed trivial. Although it was not trivial.

"It's good Lizzie was here," Sara said. "Even if she didn't know she was."

The sleety rain had stopped. Mist rose from the footpath visible beneath the frosted earth. Maud headed out past the Airstream. She followed the snaking path down into the canyon, and then along the river bottom. The journey seemed far shorter than that first time. The ledge was almost impossible to see from where she stood, but a thin column of smoke lifted into the air, pallid against the dark, bulging brow of cliff. She climbed through scattered boulders, slipping and sliding in her thin dress boots—had it been only yesterday morning that she'd put them on at Jake's house?—and walked towards the column of smoke. She stood on the kiva's edge. Driver, wrapped in a blanket, sat brooding over a fire. He looked up. They studied each other.

"He's gone."

Maud nodded.

"You got here in time, then. Your sister come?"

She shook her head.

Driver broke some dry branches, fed these onto the flame. "You can come down."

The rungs were slick. She held her mittened hands to the fire and after a silence said, "It seems like a kiva is the same as a hogan, almost. The shape. Where the fire is."

Driver cleared his throat. "And what it's used for. Though usually people don't die there. That was Sara's idea."

Her mittens began to steam. "And maybe most hogans don't have exercise equipment?"

"It's not a church. It's another room." He shrugged. "I was young. Who knows why Maggie keeps that stuff? Like those posters. I thought I'd discovered the outrage."

"Outrage?"

"You ever seen the little tomahawks on the helmets of the Seminoles? You seen the 'chop'?"

Maud no doubt looked as blank as she felt. "Tomahawks?"

"Never mind."

Maud crouched beside him. "Sara and Maggie pretended Lizzie was there. Luna too. I feel strange about that. Fooling him."

Driver studied the fire. "While your ancestors were building cathedrals, grand phallic symbols of man's hope to touch God by scraping the sky, mine were digging wombs into the earth, hoping to find God by burrowing into her. With similar success." His smile was dry, ironic.

"I should go, Driver. I need to tell Lizzie."

He put a hand out, but it took him a while to speak. "I think I was a little extreme." He cleared his throat again. "It wasn't right. Sam let me know."

Somewhere a bird called, emphasizing how quiet it was. "I'm through with this." Driver gestured around the kiva. "There's thinking now it was cannibalism. That drove the Anasazi to hide out in cliff dwellings. People chasing others, boiling their heads in pots. It's screwed me up for months, thinking about it. I've always believed it was spiritual"—he flashed his wry smile—"if it wasn't drought. But the evidence is there. And all this time I've thought the Ancient Ones were perfect. Enlightened."

"There are terrible people everywhere, Driver. In every time."

"I've had to reorganize. This was not supposed to be a part of my culture. Of our ancestors. Those who would create that kind of fear. Or those who would spend their lives—their entire lives—running from that fear."

"They're not necessarily your ancestors."

He shook his head. "I hate my thesis advisor. I thought this was a crackpot theory, but there's more and more evidence. And I still have the dissertation to write." He scrubbed at his face. "I slept here last night. Sam came this morning. He thinks it's pretty funny you all tried to make Lizzie be in a place she wasn't. But he appreciated it."

Long ago, when Maud's beloved and aged Siamese cat had not shown up for several nights running, after calling and calling for her Maud cried herself to sleep. In the first light of morning an oriental figure, swathed in blue and gold silk, wearing long brass fingernails, had appeared beside her bed. *Don't worry,* this told her. *I am fine and happy.* Maud's grief had disappeared. When she tried to tell others about it, however, she could hear how much like wishful thinking it sounded. Yet she felt a need to drip Sam's dawn appearance through her realism filter, making sense of it as best she could with her occidental, empirical-evidence-needing mind.

She stood. "Lizzie arranged for me to get a baby this morning."

He stared. "How do you mean, 'get' a baby?"

Maud explained. "It sounds preposterous. It does to me. I have about nine months to get used to it. My own sort of pregnancy, I guess. I'm terrified."

"My first thought is, it would not be yours. But Sam made it clear—" Driver interrupted himself, walked a few steps away. The blanket hung off his shoulders; a corner of it dragged on the ground. "Sam made it clear no one can decide for someone else what is family. What is clan." He ran a hand along the kiva wall, looked up at the glowering rock face. "I should talk to her. I'll borrow Sara's car."

"I can show you the way to her house. But then I've got rehearsal. Even in these circumstances—everything depends on everyone else being there."

He looked interested, making Maud realize how much of his time he spent being sardonic, superior. "I did a little of that. In high school. Maybe I could come watch."

"I'll have to ask. But I'm sure it would be okay."

"Sara said you were a storyteller. Sam agreed." He laughed. "I argued with her. An actress is a storyteller? But she made her points. When we forget the stories of our ancestors we have to reinvent the wheel, life after life." He knelt and began to roll up his blanket. "I took this acting class. We did scenes, the teacher liked my work. And then there were auditions for this play. I didn't get the part. I wasn't cast at all. I drove through the cemetery in my pickup, drinking beer and knocking over tombstones."

Maud nodded. "It's awful to want a role that much. It seems impossible that life goes on. But it does. And it's so unbelievable that the play does too—without you. You feel so bereft. Like you've lost something vital."

"They didn't cast me because I'm a fucking half-breed." His eyes flew to meet her own, she was sure, startled ones. His smile was slow, rueful. "Ah. I had you convinced otherwise."

"You had."

He used a stick to scatter the coals.

"I'll say you had." She gave a little laugh. " 'It's in our blood.' All that. Speaking of acting."

"Sara says it's nothing but a chip on my shoulder, and who cares anyway. 'We're all half-breeds,' she says. 'Who isn't?' "

"Scotch-Irish-English-German mutt myself," she said, but he did not smile.

With the blanket no longer draping his shoulders, his hair pulled back off his face into a rubber band, he looked less like a historical cliché. He also looked terribly sad. She was reminded of times— when a role felt particularly right, or the process of the play was particularly good—how hard it was to close the play, to let go of the role.

"I guess I won't be lashing Sam to the treetops," he said as he followed her up the ladder. Surprised to hear a hint of laughter in his voice, she turned to look down at him. He wore what could actually be called a rueful smile. "Just as well. I had a fight with Maggie and Sara on my hands about that one."

CHAPTER 29

LIZZIE

NOTES FROM BENEATH THE MAGNETS ON LIZZIE'S FRIDGE

Fragmentation helps to establish space . . . the object can't be introduced until the space has been created.

—BRAQUE

B y the glow of the street lamp that stroked light across the bedroom wall, Lizzie tried to make out the features of the people in the photographs tacked beside the bed. Beside her, Ken— she was fairly sure that was his name—caught his heavy breath on a snore.

The photographs could have been of family, or of a happy group at a bowling alley or a picnic. Lizzie couldn't tell. She turned her head. The pillow was so thin as to be almost no pillow at all, the cloth coarse with too much soap. He lay face up, teeth gleaming between parted lips. The light striped the blanket at the level of their knees. A click and then a rush of air let her know that somewhere a furnace was pushing heat into the cold rooms of the little apartment Ken— was that his name?—called home.

She peeled back the blanket and slid a foot towards the floor. He rolled over and, murmuring, threw an arm over her.

"Going to the bathroom," she whispered, and lifted the heavy arm. She gathered her clothes from the side of the bed and made her way into the kitchen, where she dressed quickly.

The door banged shut behind her. She stood for a moment, waiting to hear a voice, movement inside. She didn't want to have to think of excuses, she didn't want to have to defend her desire to escape. Although she had every reason—she had to get home to the kids, didn't she? Shivering inside her parka, she looked up and down the street for her car, which was nowhere in sight. She panicked, until she remembered that she'd loaned it to Maud. She was driving Sam's pickup. The beat-up white Ford, with its familiar bent front fender, was parked askew about two feet from the curb.

She started the engine, hunched over the steering wheel as if it had the power to warm her. Kids, she thought, and felt something wry twist her mouth. No, kids had not been a subject that had come up during the hours spent with Ken. They'd played five games of pool. She'd won three of them. Her victory had peeved him, but he'd hidden it well. And after all, it was her good mood that made her take him up on his request for a ride home.

The ancient defroster, running full blast, made no impact on the frosted windows. She got out and scratched at them with a scraper she found tossed behind the seat, remembering and ignoring Jake's injunctions to do each window thoroughly. She wondered about the bets that would have been laid in the Billy Goat after she left—what else had Lizzie Maxwell done besides drive Ken—Ben?—the seven-odd miles to the little house in a row of identical little houses, lit by the evenly spaced street lamps that marched down this quiet, early morning street? She'd wanted something to take the taste of Maud and Jake out of her mouth, the twitch her mind had to do every time she thought about Maud in Jake's bed, Maud in his kitchen, leaning against his counter, drinking his coffee, Maud riding beside him in his stupid car with the stuck door handle.

And so, dressed in tight jeans and her cropped sheepskin vest, Lizzie had sauntered into the Billy Goat hoping for, but not expecting, a long tall cowboy who happened to have a store of condoms in the pocket of his jean jacket.

She let the engine warm before pulling away from the curb. Another of Jake's admonitions. Don't drive a car right away after it has been sitting in the cold. *You could destroy your engine that way, Liz.*

Maud could do something with that, but she didn't even want to try. She drove along the sleeping roads, a lit window here and there testament to someone's industry, or someone's insomnia. Jake.

Beneath a white sheet the languorous limbs of Maud and Jake moved like the tide coming in. She turned the heater up another notch.

They slept in spoons, Maud's body a pale question mark curled within the dark curve of his. Her wet boots slipped against the bare metal of the clutch and brake pedals. The truck swerved, straightened.

She punched on the radio, poked her way from one brief snatch of country song to another, found *Morning Edition* on the classical station. She listened with as much interest as she could muster to a report on a town that had taken vigilante justice into its own hands, then to an obituary of a jazz trumpet player.

Yesterday after Maud had driven away, Jeep would not stop crying. Tears seeped steadily from her eyes. Thinking it was the ordeal of the morning, Lizzie drew the bath she thought would help settle her, made her tea, wrapped her in a quilt. But it was Sam. "What if he dies?" Jeep sobbed. "We should have gone with her. We both should have gone."

Lizzie had pretended she didn't know what Jeep meant. She felt now, as she'd felt then, an odd wonder at herself. Jeep was right. Why hadn't she gone? What was so important that she couldn't go?

Morning Edition played a slow and mournful trumpet piece, recorded by the musician who had died. A commentator began to talk about what was happening on the West Bank.

When Maud had driven them all down to Maggie's place to see Sam, it was as bad as Lizzie had feared it would be. An old trailer served as his sickroom. Small windows let in little light. The paneling was a fake, orangey plywood, the place cold and dreary on that cold and dreary day. Sam lay on a narrow mattress not moving, though his eyes gleamed when he saw her. His face was slack, wan, and gray, the bleak color of morning sky before sun breaks the horizon. She took his hand. His fingers trembled against hers, a kind of constant patting as if he was making sure she was, indeed, there. Sara, full of cheer, came in to feed him. He coughed in the middle of a spoonful of corn pudding, almost choked, a dreadful sound, as if a gob of hard mucus would not dislodge. "Sorry" may or may not have been what he said. The yellow liquid ran down his chin. He dabbed at it with useless, ashamed fingers. Lizzie found herself scrambling to get outside the trailer, sat with her head between her knees until Mr. Asshole showed up. He stepped over her to get into the trailer, where he'd greeted Maud with his brand of laconic enthusiasm, then lectured her, hectored her, on Indian matters. Lizzie heard Sara try to shut him up at least three times. She sat on the cement block that served as the trailer's step for what felt like hours, while inside, Maud carried on in what seemed a betrayal of cheeriness. She'd stared out at the flat landscape, cold and miserable, until Hannah came to get her. As they walked away, Summer asked, "Why is Sam always in a trailer?" Lizzie watched Maud think about this, as if the answer would be revealed by the expression on her sister's face.

The rear window finally began to de-ice. There were no other headlights behind her, before her. She was driving on the moon.

After Jeep had taken her bath, sipped her tea, gotten the rest she insisted she didn't need, she helped Lizzie pick up the house. Lizzie successfully kept them away from the topic of Jake and Maud, but as they folded laundry, Jeep sighed and said, "Nothing happened, you know."

Lizzie snapped a pillowcase. She did not pretend she did not know what Jeep meant. "What couldn't have happened?" Later, after Mrs. Theibeau had arrived with Theo and Summer, Lizzie asked Jeep to stay with the kids. "After you get back from your AA meeting, of course. I feel like kicking back a beer at the Billy Goat. Do you mind?"

It was clear Jeep had minded, and they both knew Lizzie didn't mean just one beer, but when she called around ten to say so, Jeep seemed resigned. She was watching a video, and told Lizzie that Maud had called. "She was at rehearsal. I didn't ask her about Sam. She said she'd call again later."

Lizzie had been pleased that after such a long time her game had not totally disappeared, and it hadn't been hard for Ken—Ben?—to persuade her to come on into his squalid little house with the promise of a beer. Standing in the glaring overhead light of his kitchen,

Lizzie thought about leaving before things went any further. When he backed her up against the refrigerator, straddling her feet, bending his knees to tilt his pelvis against hers, Lizzie knew his kisses weren't going to light any fires. But she let him press the backs of her hands against the cool enamel of the refrigerator door, let him moan, and move his mouth and hips against hers, let him carry her into the dark bedroom and roll her onto the bed. He shook her feet out of her boots, peeled her jeans off, put his hands beneath her T-shirt.

"Wear a condom," she told him. The glow of the street lamp outside the window passed along the rising and falling shoulders, the muscled legs moved against her own. When she finally raised her arms to loop them behind his neck, she felt rough skin and remembered Jake's, smooth as no man's skin had ever been smooth.

The last time she'd made love it had been with Jake. She'd realized this with a kind of horror. "Don't worry about me," she whispered. "You go ahead. I'm not going to make it."

Ken hadn't liked this idea. In the process of thinking about what to do about it he fell asleep on top of her.

Was that what Jeep meant when she'd said "nothing happened"?

She hadn't passed a car since leaving Ken's, but she put on the blinker anyway for the turn onto the county road. His name wasn't Ken. And not Ned. Jeb? *Jed.* That was it—they'd talked about where it came from, his Seventh Day Adventist parents who'd named him Jedediah. "Jed," she said, aloud. And then, comparing the sounds of the names, "Jake."

An image emerged as clearly as if it were a film she'd seen, unspooling before her like the dark road she traveled down. She laughed, a brief, harsh sound. Maud and her metaphors. It was easy to laugh at the hyperbole of them, but the fucking things were contagious.

She'd been sailing around this vast ocean, looking, though she didn't know it, for a way, a place, to put her anchor down. And without knowing it she'd stepped onto the galleon that was Jake. That was part of the picture—a broad, firm boat in the middle of a heaving sea. But she had stepped off it again, still searching, although she hadn't known that's what she was doing. And she had ruined everything, she had crashed and burned—drowned, if she kept to the

metaphor—everything that mattered to her, she was in perpetual free
fall. She floated, drifted, swimming and diving through levels of salty
water, working her way down through an ocean of complexity and
desire, lower and lower, looking for a certainty she'd known once and
would be seeking now forever.

It was foolish and simple to say this strength and stability had
been given to her by Jake. But there it was, foolish and simple. She'd
come to know it too late. The galleon had settled into the sand of the
ocean bottom. Festooned with seaweed, home to brightly colored
darting fish, serene, unmoving. Home.

All kinds of things were wrong with this underwater analogy. It
had to do with drowning, with being submerged, and, given the water
involved, no doubt with sex. And how could a galleon at the bottom
of the sea be considered serene? But these drawbacks did not diminish
the image. The brightly colored fish were the kids, Mrs. Theibeau,
they were Jeep and Jeep's child-to-be, and Maud as a mother. Sam—
but she would not think of him, not now. Sara and Cal and even
Aaron and damn little Yvette. And Jake. All these things that darted
into and out of the windows of her life. Perhaps for the first time she
understood some aspect of her sister's constant mental acrobatics.

Her boots slipped against the stripped brake and clutch pedals as
she brought the pickup to a stop. Her own car was parked in the
driveway. Beside it was Sara's large and battered yellow Chevy. Lizzie
curved her hands over the top of the steering wheel, rested her chin
on top of them, and contemplated what this might mean.

Her boots squeaked on the hard snow that glistened beneath a
low-slung moon. She pressed the front door open and then closed.
The light over the counter had been left on, a piece of paper placed
directly beneath it.

Dear Lizzie—
It's about midnight. I called from rehearsal several times,
but Jeep said you were out. Now I'm here. You are still out.
Sam passed away today.
I wanted to tell you in person. I'm sorry. You were there in
spirit.

Driver is sleeping on the couch. He wants to talk to you.
I love you. I need to talk to you about Jake. Also about Jeep.
See you in the morning. I love you.

M

Lizzie took a shivery breath. She tiptoed through the living room, careful not to wake Driver, who had the comforter pulled over his head. Jeep would be sleeping, as usual when she stayed over, in the den. She wondered where Maud had parked herself and found her in Hannah's bed. Maud was curled around Hannah, their dark hair identical against the flowered sheets.

She checked on Theo, pulled the blanket up around his shoulders. With infinite quiet, she undressed. She ran water onto a washcloth, making as little noise as possible, and sponged herself all over, then slipped between too-cold sheets. She wished for Jake's hard brown body. Even in his depths of sleep, when she painted into the deep hours of the morning, when she was a cold entity invading his cocoon of warmth, he'd wrapped her body with his, saying, "yes, yes, yes."

Light grew along the peaks and ridges of Fable Mountain, as if someone were drawing it with an unsteady hand. She could sleep for an hour, anyway. Hannah's alarm clock in the next room would wake her, as it always did, the irritating four quick beeps in a row repeating again and again. She would be downstairs before everyone woke up. She would make coffee, turn this into as normal a morning as possible. She turned her face into her pillow. Her eyes ached. They felt hot, dry. She hoped Maud had told Jeep. But what—*how*—would they tell Summer?

⊰⊱

But when she woke, the sky, though still gray, was bright enough to let her know she'd slept late. The house was quiet. She took a fast shower and went downstairs. In the kitchen, Maud, her back to Lizzie, was feeding Theo a piece of toast.

"Where's Jeep?"

Maud jumped, turned. "She had the early shift at the Wagon Wheel."

"She know about Sam?"

Maud nodded. "She couldn't stop crying this morning."

"Mami." Theo put his arms out.

"You're fine where you are, Theo." Lizzie poured herself coffee. "I gather you got the girls to the bus on time."

"Barely."

"They know?"

"I think so. Probably because it's odd that I'm here. And because Jeep kept crying. But I didn't tell them."

"And where's Mr. Asshole?"

"He went up to look at Sam's trailer."

Lizzie peered out the kitchen window. Harsh tears pressed at the backs of her eyes. Driver stood halfway up the path, looking up at the old caboose. He wore Sam's jacket. The fringe flapped sideways in the wind.

"He intend to take Sam's stuff? Works fast, doesn't he."

"I don't think that's it." Maud came to stand beside her. They watched Driver continue on up the hill. "I gather he and Sam had some sort of talk."

Lizzie felt as if her lungs were caving in, collapsing in on her heart. "I don't want to talk about it."

Maud went back to Theo, who was banging on the apron of his high chair.

Lizzie pressed the heels of her hands, warmed by the mug of coffee, into her eyes. She had handled everything so badly. He should have known at the end who loved him. Now he was gone. There was no way to let him know that she was sorry. No way to do it over. She would live with her abandonment of him to the end of her days. What penance could she do? What atonement could she offer that would be enough?

She picked up her cup, staring out the window even after Driver disappeared into Sam's trailer. She stepped to one side of the sink so that Maud could run water over a cloth, and listened to Maud telling Theo what a good boy he was, how much toast he had eaten, how his face was a mess, how much he was loved. She thought how much it would mean to Maud if she were to cross the kitchen, hug her, thank her. It was a journey of two steps. She could not make it. The bitterness pressed at the backs of her eyes again. She picked a few dead leaves off the plant in the window, stared up the hill. "What's he *doing* in there?" she said.

Maud didn't answer. After a pause she said, "Another letter from Mom?" Lizzie turned. Maud held out an aerogram.

"I wasn't in the mood to read it yesterday," Lizzie said, taking it from her. "It's probably just about when they're coming." She tore it open. "Details of their plane, blah, blah, blah. Didn't you get one of these?"

"I haven't been home. I went from Maggie's to rehearsal to here."

Lizzie looked at her, seeing the rise and fall of sheets and blankets that was Maud and Jake in bed. "Quite a couple of days you've had," she said. "As far as that goes, quite a couple of nights."

Maud's face went quite pale. "It wasn't like that—"

Lizzie shook the letter at her. "They won't make it in time for your opening. They'll come later."

"I slept in my *clothes*. That's all."

Lizzie assumed that the knock on the door was Driver. But it was Jake who pushed open the door from the mudroom.

"Hey."

Lizzie watched the color rise in Maud's cheeks. "Hey yourself." So she'd kept her clothes on. Had Jake?

Jake took a step towards Lizzie, stopped. "I'm really sorry, Liz. About Sam. Really sorry."

She turned to look out the window again. Of course Maud would have called him. "What is taking him so fucking long?"

"Driver," Maud explained. "He's up at the trailer."

"I had your battery charged," Jake said. "That's all the problem was."

Lizzie turned in time to see Maud squint. "It's a *battery*, Maud," she said, at the same time Jake said, "Whatever else it is, Maud, it's also just a battery."

Only Maud smiled. Jake said, "May I have some coffee?"

Lizzie watched him look for and find the mug he'd always used. "And you'll be pleased to know," Jake said, getting milk out of the fridge, "or maybe you won't care. I used it as an opportunity to get the door on my own car fixed."

Lizzie turned, again, ready to mock him. He was reading the stuff stuck with magnets to the door of the fridge, looked up in time to catch her eye as she recomposed her features. "Good for you," she said. It sounded hollow, but at least, she told Sam in her mind, she was making an effort.

"And I thought, Liz"—his voice was tight—"maybe you'd drive me back to town. We could talk a bit. Nice portrait," he said before she could answer, pointing to paper filled with back-and-forth scrawls that was Theo's latest effort. "Looks just like you."

Maud brushed imaginary crumbs off the table into a cupped palm, studiously not looking at her, and Jake hurried on. "I was all prepared to use Maud's car for the rest of the day, but it took the guy about fifteen minutes. All this time I thought the lock, or even the whole door, would have to be replaced." He jerked a thumb over his shoulder at Maud. "Talking about this stuff with her around is impossible," he said to Lizzie. "Worse than Minerva, and I've told you how bad that was. 'What's this *really* mean?' "

After a long pause, Lizzie said, "It makes life very dense."

"Dense." Looking hugely relieved, Jake nodded and swallowed some coffee. "Sue called. Wants to know if Jeep's doing okay."

"Well," Maud said, with a glance at Lizzie, "she couldn't stop crying."

"She should have called in sick," Lizzie said.

Maud nodded. "But she had the early shift at the Wagon Wheel and didn't want to leave them in the lurch. Then there's class, which she doesn't want to miss, and tonight's the Red Garter, and she needs the money. She said work is good, that it would keep her mind off things."

"Dammit. I told her to call in sick."

"Morning." Driver spoke from the door. "Good morning, Lizzie." He came towards her. Almost she could see flames flickering around him. Certainly his eyes looked as if they could burn something. She stepped backwards, bumping into Jake.

Driver came very close. His Adam's apple worked up and down. "I was wrong," he said. "Taking Sam away. I was very wrong."

Lizzie watched as Maud's face blurred through sudden tears. She felt her lips, and then her eyes, crumple in upon themselves. She could do nothing to stop the sobs that shook her, and was mortified that when Jake's arm found its way around her, she would so utterly let go, mortified that in spite of her best efforts a cry escaped her, then another. Her legs, too, betrayed her. She turned into Jake. If he held her, she would not slide to the ground. She was surprised that tears could be so hot. Surprised at how much snot would drip from her nose. The tears, the snot, the cries she could not stop buried themselves in the black cotton of his sweater. "Oh, Sam," she cried. "Oh, Sam."

⤬

Two nights later, Maud called, very late. "You need to come, Lizard. Jeep's tried to kill herself."

Into Lizzie's silence she said, "Pills, they think."

"But she was doing *fine*." Last time it had been Seconal. What would she have used this time?

"We all thought so. But when I got home from rehearsal tonight there was a message from Ginger. She didn't come in to work and didn't call. Rich came in later. Said he'd talked to her and she'd sounded very weird and stoned and would Ginger go with him to her apartment. So Ginger called me. We went and—" Maud's swallow was loud. "They say we found her in time. They took her to Emergency—"

"Thanks," Lizzie said.

"She'll lose the baby, they said."

Lizzie looked at the phone after she'd replaced the receiver. Such a small physical action to pick it back up—but it felt as if she were about to drive the Indianapolis 500.

"I'll be there," Jake said.

For the second time that day she felt her knees give. She sat on the edge of her bed, face in her hands. And then she went to rouse the children.

CHAPTER 30

JAKE

driving into Vegas
when dawn had cracked the sky
you said you'd never gambled
i said it's time you tried

Jake was back from rehearsal, beer opened, working on the new song, when the call came in. He let the phone ring, using the back of his guitar to hold his notepad.

I'll wait you out
I'll hope you out
I'll smoke you out of your cave of loneliness

He hadn't expected Lizzie. Voice high and tight. Talking fast, as if she could keep something from unraveling.

Halfway down the sidewalk to his car he stopped, went back inside. He'd slid the Button Up! bag with its corny T-shirt so far under the bed he had to kneel to pull it out. The paper sack rode on the passenger seat beside him. He eyed it from time to time. In the hospital parking lot he got out, locked the car, started across the tarmac. Then he went back, opened the car door, shoved the bag under the seat.

Inside the Emergency waiting room Lizzie and the kids sprawled on a row of bright orange chairs. Summer was pulling pages from a magazine, balling them up, tossing them, with success, into a waste-basket across the room. Theo cruised from chair to chair. Hannah sat beside Lizzie. Lizzie stayed where she was when he came through the door, but her eyes flashed green. When he sat beside her she gripped his knee, once. They watched Summer destroy *Family Circle* and most of *Time*. When Jake tried, "Whatcha doing there, Summer?" she pitched one of the paper balls at him, hard.

Maud came through the double doors that led from the waiting room into the hospital, accompanied by a large-boned, red-haired woman she introduced as Ginger. "They say she'll be fine. She vomited up most of the pills." There was obviously more to this. Maud's eyes flashed what could not be said in front of the kids. Hair pulled back, eyes limned with black, beautiful in an austere, almost European way. Her face had a sheen to it. Startled Jake into a memory of his mother, that residue of whatever she'd used to remove makeup after an evening out glistening along cheekbone and forehead.

"She'll have one hell of a hangover," the red-haired woman drawled.

"She's staying with us." Lizzie said this with so much antagonism that Ginger raised her eyebrows.

Theo held out a *Reader's Digest* to Maud. "Read!"

Maud lifted him onto a hip. "Lizard, you need to get your car and bring it up out front."

"I'll get mine," Jake offered. But Lizzie was already on her feet, out the door.

"Read!" Theo shook the magazine. "Goonite Moon!"

"Tomorrow, Theo. It's time to go home."

An orderly pushed a gurney through the double doors. Jeep. White-faced. Eyes closed. Summer stood on a chair to look. Accepted help from Jake to carry her closer. "Will she die too?"

He shook his head, hoping this time he was right.

The orderly rolled the gurney out to the end of the hospital's cement walkway. Maud followed, carrying Theo, holding Hannah's hand. Summer allowed Jake to carry her. Her finger-sucking habit was back. She stared around with bright, glittering eyes, an arm clenched so tightly around Jake's neck that it hurt.

"I've gotta split," Ginger said. She kissed Jeep, whose face glowed a pale violet under the fluorescent lights, and whispered something in her ear. Jeep didn't respond. "I told Rich I'd call him," Ginger told Maud. "Bastard actually seems to give a shit. Phone me tomorrow, Maud, tell me how she's doing."

Summer was heavy in his arms, almost asleep. Hannah leaned against Maud's thigh, Theo asleep against her shoulder. He held out a stick of conversation. "Rehearsal go well?"

She nodded. "First time in costume. That's always exciting."

Lizzie arrived with the car. Jake lowered the passenger seat. Summer and Hannah argued halfheartedly about who would ride home with Jeep until Lizzie told them they'd both ride with Jake. Maud buckled Theo into his car seat. She had an early lesson to teach, too late to cancel. She'd be by as soon as she could in the morning.

Jake let Summer sit in front. Surreptitiously checked to make sure the paper sack was pushed well out of the way of her swinging feet. Through these arrangements and decisions, he knew, as clearly as if Lizzie had told him, that he would be spending the night. He'd be in the queen-sized bed again. He followed the red now-and-again-flashing taillights of Lizzie's car, awed, nervous, aroused. In the back seat, Hannah chattered about school and her favorite CDs. Halfway home, Summer turned to him, interrupting Hannah. "If Jeep dies too then I'm going to make Ma have a funeral where we all dress in black and sing and throw earth on the coffin and cry all over the place."

"Ma doesn't believe in funerals," Hannah said.

"Well, I'll make her," Summer said. "How else do I get to say goodbye? I never get to say goodbye."

Lizzie had left the porch light on, but dawn already pulsed, a gray-white outline, along the peak and long shoulders of Fable Mountain. "No school for you today," Lizzie said as the girls stumbled up the front steps.

"Good," Summer said. "Will he be here when we wake up?"

Lizzie, carrying Theo into the house, either pretended not to hear this or ignored it. "Would you mind sleeping in the study, Hannah-hoo? So Jeep can be close to us upstairs."

Us.

He lifted Jeep from the car. She smelled both medicinal and slightly stale. The gray light turned the pouches under her eyes into enormous black commas. Her eyes slitted open. "Hey, Jeep," he said.

She moved her lips in something too small to be called a smile. Uncomfortable, moved, he kissed her forehead. Carried her into the house, up the stairs, lowered her onto Hannah's bed. The sheets had been pulled back. Lizzie came in and handed him the purple comforter. "Will you tuck Hannah in?" She crouched beside the bed, smoothing Jeep's hair, murmuring.

Hannah had spread sheets on the couch in the den. "Jeep's in my bed, and I'm in hers," she said as Jake covered her with the comforter. "Summer gets to sleep in the room with her, but that's okay."

"You're a good and thoughtful girl." Jake fought the swell of salted emotion inside his chest, talked with Hannah until her eyes drifted closed. He made tea, carried the steaming mugs up to the bedroom. Lizzie was in bed. A high-necked nightgown made her look unexpectedly Victorian.

"My parents are coming."

He handed her a mug.

"To see Maud, really. In her play."

"To see both of you."

"No." She sipped her tea.

He walked around the bed, put his cup on the night stand. A bird called. It was light outside the window. They were behaving as if they'd last gone to bed together just the night before. He sat on the edge of the bed. Moved one foot to push at the heel of the opposite boot. Waited.

"I forced her, Jake." Lizzie stared at her cup. "She didn't want it. You were there, you saw it. This is all because of me. She lost the baby. We almost lost her. And then there's Sam." Her voice broke, eyes flying up to meet his—green, bright, horrified.

He reached for his cup to keep from reaching for her. This would not be a good time to hold her. The tea was too hot. He put his cup back.

"I hate this herbal shit. What is this, Sleepytime?"

He nodded.

"Maud bought it. She drinks it double-bagged." She sipped again.

"And then The Parents have to show up. With all their condescension and judgment. It makes me feel so, so—what's the word?"

"Defensive?"

"Fuck you." This was not said in anger.

He didn't know how he was to proceed. *I will smoke you out.* "I love you, Liz," he said.

She looked at him, nodded, looked away. Her eyes filled with tears. "I keep doing it wrong," she said. "Everything."

"I know exactly what you mean."

She came to him then. Put her cup down, slid across the bed, put a hand on his chest. He picked it up and kissed its palm. She did not laugh. The tears brimmed over, ran down her cheeks. She lowered her face against his neck. Tears hot against his skin. Burrowed in beside him, one leg thrown over one of his still booted ones. He lay face up, stroking her, eyes open, gentle as he knew how to be.

✄

Breakfast the next morning—brunch, really—felt like a holiday. Christmas. Easter. Maud arrived, long before they were downstairs, and made coffee. When he and Lizzie stumbled into the kitchen Hannah proudly showed off some eggy thing baked in the cast-iron frying pan. "It's a Finnish pancake." Maud dusted it with powdered sugar, cut it into wedges, gave them syrup. When that one disappeared she made another.

Summer crept up and down the stairs, checking on Jeep, finally running into the kitchen, whispering loudly, "She's awake. No, I was quiet as a *mouse*, Ma."

Jeep had propped herself up against some pillows, still very pale. "I hate to be such a problem." Blue eyes awash with tears. "Oh, Lizzie, I'm so sorry."

"Don't." Lizzie went down on her knees beside the bed. "We'll talk, but not now."

Jake carried Jeep to the kitchen. Once again reminded how he could be her father. The comforter was spread over the rocking chair next to the woodstove. Hannah and Lizzie folded it around her.

"I got up about fifty times," Summer said, "and put my face real close to yours so I could feel your breath blowing out. You didn't die."

"No, I didn't," Jeep said, with only the faintest emphasis on the *I*.

"Hungry?" Maud asked, but Jeep shook her head. "Not yet. I'm sure I will be, I think I threw up everything."

"Threw up everything," Summer cackled. Climbed on the table next to Jake. "She looks like a purple cocoon."

"It feels wonderful," Jeep said. "Snuggly and warm. Where's that Theo?"

They put Theo in her lap. Maud got a picture book for them. Hannah said, in a reproving tone, "Summer thinks we should have a funeral. For Sam."

"No, I don't. I said we should have a funeral if Jeep died too. Jake! Isn't that what I said?"

Jake watched Jeep, but she didn't seem to mind this. He nodded. "You'd wear a long black dress and throw earth on the coffin and sing and cry."

Summer nodded. "Could we do that, Ma? For Sam?"

"And for Luna," Hannah said.

Jeep picked at the comforter. Lizzie began to stack plates. "Summer, get down from the table. You're not a monkey."

"Tell them the bury-me story," Jeep said to Maud, who was pouring a round of coffee.

Maud looked startled, shook her head. "You want coffee?"

"I like that story. No coffee. I'll have some of that 'herbal shit.' "

Summer cackled again, looking at Lizzie, who shrugged. Maud put the kettle on. Hannah and Summer drenched their already drenched pieces of pancake in syrup. Lizzie caught Jake's eye. "You only live once," she said. Flinched.

"Stop worrying about it," Jeep said. "It only makes it worse."

"What makes what worse?" Summer asked.

"So these friends of mine in L.A. had gone camping," Maud began, sliding into a chair. She aimed this story in the direction of the girls. "They were boyfriend and girlfriend, and they'd been seeing each other for a while. They lit a fire and got into their sleeping bags. They stared up at the stars. You know how it is when you're camping out. They're looking at the big sky above them and talking about how big the universe is and how insignificant they are. They talk about eternity and heaven. Then they say good night and snuggle into their sleeping bags. And you know how the nylon of sleeping bags and parkas makes a kind of loud sliding, *shoosh*ing noise when you settle in? Anyway, the girl—her name is Trish—hears her boyfriend say, 'Will you bury me?' "

Summer gave a hoot of laughter. She had slipped almost onto Jake's lap, chin on her hands, elbows on the table. Hannah was also rapt. Jeep rocked, listening. Lizzie sat with her head on one side, watching Maud with an expression made up of equal parts of enjoyment and resentment.

"Trish thinks, this is pretty weird, but after a pause says, 'Well, okay, if that's what you want.' And he says, 'It sure is what I want.' There's another pause and he says, 'How about you?' And she tells him, 'I don't want to think about it too much. It's so far ahead.' Then after a *really* long pause, when things feel pretty tense, he says, "It'd be nice if you were just a little more enthusiastic.' "

Jake began to smile.

"So Trish says, 'Enthusiastic about what?' And he sits up and says, 'I ask you to marry me, and this is the response I get?' "

Amidst the laughter Summer asked, "Then what'd she say?"

"They had to sort it out for a while. But now they're married, they're happy, they have two beautiful kids. And with any luck at all one of them will bury the other."

"That's what it's about," Lizzie said, suddenly moody.

Jake knew he had to do it now or he would never get up the nerve again.

"Where're you going?" said Hannah.

"Back in a sec."

Outside a fresh wind blew, smelling of wet earth. Clouds roared across the sky. As he sprinted across the driveway he was dismayed to see a huge yellow car lumbering up the road. Sara and Driver. He waved, got the bag from under the seat. "You're just in time to watch me make a fool of myself," he told them. "Come on in."

He waited until everyone had greeted Sara, then Driver. Waited through Driver's taciturn nonreplies. Waited until Sara hugged and comforted Jeep, and Driver was introduced, until they were given coffee and the remains of pancake. Then, with a smile at Maud, he handed the bag across the table to Lizzie.

"A present?" She took it from him as if it were something that might bite her.

Summer was up on the table again, squirming with excitement. Lizzie held the T-shirt up by the shoulders. It fell open with the letters facing out. White block letters against red cloth:

MARRY ME

He'd struggled between using the wimpish uncertainty of a question mark—MARRY ME?—or the more demanding exclamation point: MARRY ME! But she would be the one deciding the punctuation. She stared down, squinting, as if it were hard to decipher the upside-down letters. He was suddenly terrified. It was all wrong to have done it in front of her family. Sara. Driver. He should have taken her out for champagne after all. Or out for a walk. But every other way seemed sentimental. She would have laughed. So he'd had a T-shirt made at Button Up! Mistake. Error. Dolt.

Sara smiled. Driver broke the silence. "Wow, man."

Hannah clasped both hands to one cheek. "Will you, Ma?"

Summer was still sounding it out, sounding it out again. Then she shrieked.

Lizzie, face flushed, turned the shirt to face her. Examined the letters as if they were indecipherable.

"Ma!" Summer said. "Are you going to?"

"Why?" Lizzie said. "What would be the point?"

The queer elation that had inspired him to do this, the devil-may-care bravado that had propelled him through the last few days, that had made him sneak into Button Up!—burglar in a comic strip, Pink Panther on exaggerated tiptoe—continued to work on him. "Because I love you," he said. "Because I already lost you once, even though I'm old enough to know you don't ever have anyone enough to lose them. Because I'd like us to keep company."

"He'd like to bury you," Hannah said. She and Summer shrieked with laughter. "Put it on, Ma!"

Lizzie refolded the shirt. She did this very precisely. Put it back in its bag, sat with her hands loosely folded upon it. Her eyes were warm when she looked at Jake, and she smiled. But she said, "I don't see the point."

"Because," Summer said. *"Because."*

Jake felt his insides turn a slow somersault. Felt the heat of Maud's eyes, of Jeep's. Lizzie gave him another long, gauging look. Turned to Driver. "What are you doing here, anyway? You come to rifle through some more of Sam's stuff?"

THE
SPRING

CHAPTER 31

LIZZIE

NOTES FROM BENEATH THE MAGNETS ON LIZZIE'S FRIDGE

Lizard—

Thought of you when I read this:

> *Living is a form of not being sure. . . . The moment you know how,*
> *you begin to die a little. An artist never entirely knows. We guess. We*
> *may be wrong, but we take leap after leap in the dark.*

> —AGNES DE MILLE

Love you.

M.

Jeep slept at Lizzie's. As did Jake, most nights. They'd carried the old single futon up to Theo's room, where there was plenty of room in the closet for Jeep's clothes. Her textbooks and her collection of music—new joys for Hannah—were piled on shelves that Lizzie pressed Jake into building. Jeep also brought along an assortment of candles, as well as various odd items from her apartment that looked faintly and ridiculously religious, of the Higher Power sort.

Her household had suddenly magnified, and Lizzie found herself having to work to show she minded. Her fortieth birthday turned out to be a pleasant affair, not the gloomy signpost she'd dreaded. She was surprised to find that she was spending more time rather than less in her studio. Jake usually worked at Synercomp during the days, most nights he had either a rehearsal or a gig, and Jeep went to school and to her AA meetings, but one was often there when the other was not. Maud's play had opened. Busy with that and shifts at the Red Garter and teaching piano lessons, she still found time to drop by often. Driver hung around a lot, supposedly sorting through Sam's stuff.

With more time than she'd had in a long while, Lizzie was painting well. Three new canvases in the last two weeks. She'd turned them to the wall, letting them steep before looking at them again. Sometimes she felt Sam was taking care of her in some way. Her contentment, restless though it was, with Jake, and with her painting. The close call with Jeep. The odd way Driver had begun to stand in for Sam, particularly with Summer, bringing her arrowheads and, just yesterday, a stone shaped like a flying bird. Sam as angel. A silly thought. But it occurred to her often.

Late one morning, when Jeep had returned from her morning classes and put Theo down for a nap, she came out to the studio to tell Lizzie that this funeral idea, discussed weeks ago at breakfast, was something Lizzie ought to consider. "Summer keeps talking about it."

"Summer talks about a lot of things."

"Maybe this is one time to listen."

Lizzie began to wash up. This discussion, she could already tell, would leave her feeling pretty dry. "It wouldn't be a funeral. It would be a memorial service."

"Ceremony, anyway. Maud says ceremonies exist for a reason."

"Maud."

"Not just Maud. We were talking about it in my herbology class. Those of us who don't have a group, a religion—it's harder to acknowledge passages, changes. Like deaths. Coming of age."

"What about AA? That's a group, isn't it?" Lizzie shook the wet off her hands. "And I am *not* giving Hannah a First Moon party, or whatever it's called, when her period comes. She'd die of embarrassment."

Jeep shrugged. "Maybe."

"He's gone. We missed it. What on earth good will it do to 'dress in black and sing and cry'?"

Jeep moved to the window and looked up the hill at Sam's trailer. "Is Driver moving in up there?"

"Looks like it."

"Is that okay with you?"

The trees along the road, scattered on the hillside, were still leaf-less. But Lizzie could see the green running just beneath the surface of the bark. She wondered if she could capture that moment, the one just before budding, with paint. "I have a feeling that Driver moving into the trailer would be what Sam would want. Chalk it up as my own little ceremony. My own little funeral service." She scraped with one fingernail at a fleck of paint beneath another.

"He'll have to put in electricity. For his computer. To write his dissertation," Jeep said.

"Yes."

Jeep turned. The light from the window made one side of her face almost translucent, emphasizing the still-obvious circles under her eyes. "I need to say goodbye too, Lizzie. In the night I try. I try to talk to it, to say, 'I'm sorry I poisoned myself, little one, and poisoned you in the process.' I'm not sorry, on one level, but on another I am. I'd like to say goodbye, properly. Maybe this would give me a chance."

Lizzie stared up the hill for another moment. Sam, she cried to his memory. Why don't I learn? When will I ever learn? She took a startled Jeep by the shoulders. "I never *think*. You've come back so quickly from that Seconal excursion of yours that you've made me forget it happened, that there were reasons you did it. I keep thinking we'll talk."

"You make it clear you don't want to talk. So I don't. Not to you."

Lizzie felt as if she'd just been poked hard in the stomach—as Jake described he'd been that day at the clinic. But she nodded. She deserved this. She needed this.

"Sometimes I think it would help. To sing and throw earth. To cry. Wail." Jeep tried to smile. "Dress in black."

Lizzie ran a finger along the window ledge, examined the resultant snarl of dust and cobwebs. "But get Maud to organize it. I don't know what one does at a funeral. I'll do the wake. Afterward. Beer and juice and chips and cookies."

But she found herself doing more. She told Sara about the plan. And Driver. She also went by the Billy Goat and sat at the bar and told Cody. Cody said she'd be there if she could and that Jed said to say hi.

The girls and Maud decided on a Sunday morning. Sunday on general principles, Hannah told Lizzie. It was the day of rest, and that meant all kinds of rest. And they would do it in the morning because Maud had to do her play in the afternoon. Lizzie had requested that this not be something they did while The Parents were in town. She could see Maud arranging this dramatic moment for their benefit. But Maud had thought of that. The Parents wouldn't be arriving until the following Friday. They would stay through the weekend, see Maud's last performance on Saturday night, then fly back home to Seattle on Sunday. Lizzie, wishing they wouldn't come at all, was irritated they were staying such a short time.

But at least the funeral nonsense would be well over and done before they arrived. Rolling a cart through the grocery store, loading it with beer and chips and flour, she decided to make the frittata Sam loved. She hadn't made it in years. She bought eggs, cheese, spinach, potatoes. She would bake ginger muffins, serve strong coffee after champagne and orange juice. She would make the kind of brunch she and Sam had enjoyed, once upon a very long ago time.

That night, as the girls were preparing for bed, they told her Maud had suggested they choose something they loved and give it to someone as part of the ceremony.

"Someone? You mean, anyone?"

Hannah tried to explain. "Well, maybe someone you think Sam would appreciate you giving something to."

Summer shoved back the covers and fetched her snake's egg. She would give it to Driver, she said. Hannah took more time, vacillating between a little ring given to her by Blair or her CD of the Spice Girls. "What will you give, Ma?" Summer asked. But Lizzie had no idea. She told the idea to Driver, expecting him to scoff along with her, as he often did. "A giveaway," he said. "How'd she know about that?"

"It's not like it's a fucking birthday party," Lizzie said, grumpy.

Summer said, "It's a funeral party!" to which Hannah said, in the arch and superior manner she'd started to adopt, "That's obvious, Summer."

Driver shook his head. "What has happened to our ceremonies? They get stolen, pulled out of shape. . . ." But he seemed to run out of steam before he got very far, and shrugged.

Perhaps because of The Parents' impending visit, there was suddenly a lot of cleaning, repairing, planting to do. With spring beginning to push green onto the tips of the leaves of trees, the daffodils beginning to pop by the roadside where she'd planted them years ago, she found herself dissatisfied with the dilapidated condition of the tool shed, the appalling state of the outside stairs. Jake, and Driver too, dealt with her demands with sarcastic humor. The weather cooperated. Day of sun followed by day of rain followed by day of sun. She thought she could hear the earthworms and the moles and the buried roots of things stretching and moving, growing.

✁

The night before the funeral—even Lizzie had taken to calling it that—Maud invited the girls and Jeep to come to the play again and then spend the night. "We'll raid the costume shop," she said. The girls had seen *Twelfth Night* so many times they could act out some of the scenes. They liked the one in which Olivia—Maud, played by Hannah—fell in love with the girl dressed up as a boy. Summer was particularly fond of saying, "Build me a willow cabin at your gate and cry out 'Oliviaaaaa' so that the hills reverberate." She also used "Farewell, fair cruelty," with indiscriminate glee for all partings and goodnights. At breakfast, or whenever Jake would listen, Hannah would tell them, pointing, "Item: two lips, indifferent red. Item: two gray eyes, with lids to them. Were you sent hither to praise me?"

At other times, especially when they could get Jake and Driver to watch, they imitated the duel between the girl dressed as a boy and the swordsman whose name they loved—Sir Toby Belch. Here they traded roles. Hannah played the ineffectual and terrified Viola, whishing a wooden sword around, while Summer, burping and belching, put one hand high behind her head and lunged: "En garde!"

Watching these *Scenes from Mostly Nonexistent American Family Life*, when she sat with Jake, and sometimes Jeep, joined now and again by Driver and by Maud, Lizzie felt almost terrified. It seemed as if she had come through some enormous travail. A pilgrim who'd survived an Atlantic crossing, a pioneer who'd hauled her wagon over the Rockies. It was absurd to compare these enterprises with the last nine months of her own life, but she felt she had endured something, only barely. She didn't know how to let Jake know. She made him sleep at his own apartment sometimes, even though she missed him when he was not with her. At these times she wore his MARRY ME T-shirt to bed. And sometimes she thought about how different it all might be had Maud not come to Marengo.

"En garde," Summer cried, and charged them, sword held high, where they sat together on the couch. Jake scooped her up and tickled her and she laughed with a joy that Lizzie wished she could let herself express.

❋

She layered a casserole dish with sliced parboiled potatoes. She smoothed the spinach, onion, and cheese mixture over the top, then poured over all a dozen beaten eggs. Jake sat at the counter with a cup of coffee, watching. As she set the casserole to bake, she said, "It takes forever to cook. All those eggs."

"I'm in no hurry." Jake took a sip of coffee. As she straightened, pushing hair from her forehead with the back of her hand, he said, "I love you."

She was aware of the window behind her back. The square of landscape it framed included Sam's caboose and the path up to it. She was mindful of their presence as she looked at Jake, at his curly hair, ringleted and dripping from the shower they'd taken together. "Well," she said. "I love you too." She was aware she sounded defensive, almost querulous, with that *too*.

The sound of car horns pulled them outside, carrying their cups, Theo on Lizzie's hip. Jeep's car and then Maud's, followed by the big yellow car that was passed back and forth between Sara and Driver, proceeded slowly, parade-like, up the driveway.

Maud had indeed managed to raid the costume shop. Hannah wore a low-cut, shiny black gown, the hem pinned up so it wouldn't drag on the ground. An enormous black hat swooped marvelously high in the back and low over one eye in the front. Black netting did not hide her smile as she waved. Curiously, Summer had chosen a white dress. Dozens of pastel ribbons fluttered from sleeve and hem as she moved. She wore a small pink and white hat—more suitable for Easter than a funeral, though Lizzie did not point this out. They both carried furled white parasols.

Jeep had borrowed a skirt Lizzie recognized as Maud's—black gauzy material, spattered with small white and red flowers. Maud herself wore a black skirt, pink sweater, white aviator scarf, white hat. In the chill spring breeze, the fabrics billowed and blew around them. Summer, laughing, held on to her hat with one hand, the ribbons of her dress spiraling and dancing around her.

"I have to get my gift," Hannah said. She lifted her skirts, negotiating the stairs with precision, as if she'd been wearing skirts and long petticoats all of her life. She was, Lizzie reflected, her sister's niece.

"Me too." Summer clomped up the stairs with less grace.

Sara walked with Maud. Jeep, looking pale, carried a bouquet of daffodils.

Driver came down the hill from the trailer. With the fringed leather jacket and his lanky, stoop-shouldered walk, he reminded Lizzie, forcefully, of Sam. Her nose prickled with emotion. The girls clattered back out onto the porch. Lizzie stopped herself from asking what on earth Hannah was planning to do with Jeep's portable CD player, which she was carrying.

She went to get her jacket and to check the casserole while Jake strapped Theo into the backpack that would carry him. The girls pranced and ran ahead, a festive, medieval scene. Lizzie particularly appreciated the parasols, which they opened and twirled on their shoulders. Maud called to them, pulled them close to speak to them, and after that they walked side by side, ahead of everyone else, but in step, heads held high, singing "Michael Row the Boat Ashore."

" 'Michael Row the Boat Ashore'?" Jake said to Lizzie.

Maud walking ahead with Jeep, turned. "Well, it's one we all know. We're saving 'Amazing Grace' for later."

Lizzie turned to Driver, walking behind with Sara. "Do you know 'Michael Row the Boat Ashore'?"

Driver shook his head in disgust. "Poor little Indian boys, parents too poor, too ignorant, to send us to camp. I was seven. So some hokies brought camp to us. 'The river Jordan is deep and wide,' " he warbled.

"We don't think so much in terms of milk and honey on the other side," Sara said. "Milk not being something the Ancient Ones had much knowledge of."

"The river Jordan is chilly and cold," Driver sang.

"I thought you didn't know it," Lizzie said.

"I didn't want to know it. Who wants to know that death 'chills the body but not the soul'?"

"Well, there was a request for singing," Maud said, "and this is what the girls chose."

The high ragged voices of Hannah and Summer floated back to them. Maud joined in. The hair lifted along Lizzie's forearms as Jake's deep baritone took up the melody along with Jeep's high voice, then behind her, Sara, and eventually, and slightly flat, Driver.

Summer had chosen the place for the ceremony—a bank above the arroyo that was already beginning to seep with snowmelt, above the place where Summer had found Luna, and where Maud had found Summer.

Maud spread a cloth in the middle of the circle they formed and put a small leather-bound book on it. She nodded to Summer, who put her egg carefully beside the book.

"Wait, wait, wait," Hannah said. She knelt to put her ring on the cloth and then set up Jeep's CD player. Lizzie recognized what she called tinkly-winkly music—George Winston or some other artist from the Windham Hill label, music she liked but pretended not to.

Driver reached into the pocket of his coat and pulled out a leather thong with a large turquoise bead strung on it. He added this to the array. Jeep put her daffodils there, and added a small leather pouch. She had started to cry, although she made no sound. Jake spread his hands. "I'm singing to you, later," he said. "Back at the house."

"And I'm feeding you." They had not planned this, and Lizzie felt a small, pleased jolt of symmetry.

Summer said, "But that's not for Sam."

"Actually, it is."

Summer accepted this. "Now what do we do?" she said.

Maud clasped her hands, self-consciously solemn. "Well, I thought we would remember Sam a bit—quietly if we wanted to, and aloud if we wanted to share something."

"Can I start?" Summer asked. "He was my best friend." She swallowed. Her voice came out high, pinched. "You were my best friend, Sam, and I miss you very much and I hope you are happy where you are, but not too happy because I hope you miss me as much as I miss you. Now I throw some earth."

She scrabbled in the damp soil and came up with a clot of red dirt. She hurled it as far as she could across the arroyo. It landed in the undergrowth on the other side. She picked up another one. "And this is for Luna. I miss you and wish you were here, Luna." She threw this, then wiped her bare forearm under her nose. "Who's next?"

The music was slow, portentous, something with cellos and horns. Jeep openly wept. Lizzie found herself split in two. Part of her was grateful for the upheaval the music was making in her heart. She also wanted to reach down and punch the music off. Maud picked up some earth. It dribbled through her hand as she said, "Once—I had just arrived here and I was feeling terrible about everything—Sam came down to Lizzie's house with Luna. I said, 'You don't want to see me like this.' And he said, 'I would always want to see you.' I've thought about that many times. That it was true, and he made me believe it. It was simple. He said what he meant." She threw the earth. It fell apart in the air, spilling away in the wind that parted it.

"I wasn't as good friends with Sam as Summer was," Hannah said, "but I remember how he helped with my homework and I miss him a lot. I hope he's happy in heaven." Like Summer, she found a satisfying clot of earth and heaved it all the way across the damp creek bed.

"Sam taught me to build the infallible fire," Jake said. "They don't die out, they always burn. My band thinks I'm a genius because at our rehearsals, when we have to warm the building with the woodstove, my fires always take. Thanks, Sam. We miss you."

"Now throw earth," Summer prompted in a whisper.

Jake got hold of a handful of dirt. "Just throw it?" he said. "Not into anything?"

Summer nodded. "We're not putting him in the earth. He is the earth. That's what Driver says."

"Do not stand at my grave and weep," Sara said, putting an arm around Jeep, who sobbed, once, loudly, then bit her lip. "I am not there. I do not sleep. I am a thousand winds that blow. I am the glint of sun on snow."

Jeep took a shaky breath. "I can't help but think that you would have stayed with us if only I'd— And Lizzie, that isn't meant to make you feel bad. I know that really, Sam, you were sick, and that I couldn't have done too much to make you better, but I hope that if there is a place where you can know another spirit, and if my lost baby is a spirit, that you will take care of it. And if you are just particles blowing around, then I hope you will come together in some way and make a beautiful herb, or become the molecules of another human on this earth, or something that is good and brave and wonderful. I'm sorry, little girl or little boy, but it wasn't time to have you. Please, please forgive me."

The strength of Jake's arm was like a safety railing, and Lizzie leaned into it, shivering. At what point had he slipped that support around her? She could smell the soap on his neck.

"Throw earth," Summer whispered.

Jeep gave her a little smile and leaned down and threw earth. Sara followed suit. "Go *on*, Driver, throw," she said. Driver did as he was told.

They stood and looked at the objects arrayed on the cloth while Maud led them in singing.

When we've been there ten thousand years,
Bright shining as the sun.
Amazing Grace.

Summer gave her egg to Driver, and Hannah her ring to Jeep. Jeep divided up the daffodils so that everyone carried one. Maud's book was for Jake—an old rhyming dictionary she'd found in a used-book store. Driver lifted the thong with its turquoise bead and gave it to Lizzie. "This comes from Sam," he said. "A day or two before he died he tugged at it and said, 'Lizzie.' I tried to persuade myself that it didn't belong to you. But it does."

She bent her head to receive it around her neck. Again she was grateful for Jake's compact and solid body close by.

Theo began to cry. "I was going to bury this," Jeep said, picking up the little leather pouch. "But I'll give it to you instead." She hung the pouch around Theo's neck. "He's getting hungry."

"We all are," Lizzie said. "I should get that frittata out of the oven before it turns to stone." As Maud walked by Lizzie reached out an arm and pulled her in, held her close, feeling Maud's heart, or was it her own, pulsing along her veins. Maud's shoulders felt impossibly small, her eyes, as they pulled apart, were wet, dark, shining— reminding Lizzie, impossibly, of a cherry branch, just ready to bud, gleaming with rain.

She was struck by the beauty of the sky, the wind. She remembered how Sam used to say, "You got to catch heaven on the fly, Lizzie. It disappears so fast." He would hold a hand up, as if feeling for wind, then swing it down in an arc, bringing the other hand up to meet it, catching, just barely, an imaginary ball. "Whoosh." She could share this memory, Lizzie thought. Maybe she would after breakfast. Ahead of her, the wind lifted and twirled the fabric of the girls' dresses. Summer had hold of Jeep's hand. Maud carried Theo, her scarf fluttering out to one side as she walked between Driver and Sara, head bent, listening to something Driver was saying. The wind carried the scent of earth and the piney smoke of some-one's burn pile.

Lizzie reached out and took Jake's hand.

CHAPTER 32

JAKE

you send me like a first-class letter
many have tried
but none can do it better

Recently Santiago had reminded Jake that in Spanish, *wait* and *hope* are the same verb. "This is in our bones," he said, flashing that big smile. "To us it is the same—I am hoping for the bus. Or, the other way, I am waiting to win the lottery."

Jake pondered this, sitting at the small built-in booth in the corner of his kitchen. Hope did seem passive. Waiting in the dreary Greyhound bus terminal of the universe. But what could he do but wait. Hope. He could have faith, he supposed. Faith seemed more active. Something you could take part in. Although faith was only a noun. There was no faithing for the bus, just having faith the bus would come.

Ah, Lizzie.

He tapped a pencil against his lips, picked up his guitar from where it leaned against a chair, played through the series of chords again.

i will smoke you out of your loneliness

He wished he could take a torch, a thick, pitch-dripping, black-smoking torch, and explore the paintings on the walls of the dark cave of Lizzie's psyche. But what would he learn from the figures painted in the colors of dried blood, the color of rust? Was Lizzie the running bison? One of the lean figures pitching a spear?

He spent the night with her more than he didn't. Several times now she'd reached for him, taken his hand. He made her laugh. Theo called him Dake. They were doing fine. Nothing to complain about. He didn't know why he had this need to lock it in, make certain it would abide. Nothing could, he knew that. Except the two of them deciding to make it stay, day after day. As far as Lizzie was concerned, a wedding, the ceremony of marriage, didn't have much to do with that. Yet the idea remained. An ancient six-inch rusty iron nail buried in brick. *Be with me, Lizzie.*

> *how do we make it stay*
> *day after day*

Terrible. He made a jangling noise across the open guitar strings.

Her parents had decided to visit. Leopold and Agnes. Jake had laughed out loud when he first heard their names. Tonight they were taking Lizzie and the kids out for dinner before going to see the last performance of Maud's show. Lizzie would drop Theo at a babysitter's. Jake was to meet them at the theater.

"You ashamed of me?" he'd asked. Yesterday morning.

"Oh, for Christ's sake, Jake!" She pushed a pillow over his face, sat on top of him, pummeled him through the down. "You are out of your mind! Why would I be ashamed of you? For God's sake. That is the stupidest thing I ever heard."

She pulled the pillow away, met his eyes for a flashing moment. Stretched her body along the length of his, holding his arms and hands out to the side with her own, keeping her face buried in his chest. Her lips moved against his skin. "We'll go to El Toro, and he'll sit there putting down my entire life. They'll find something wrong with the choice of restaurant, with the fact I want a beer—beverage of the great unwashed and ignorant masses—instead of a glass of the excellent wine he'll order. There will be complaints about the quality of the service, and comments about the one-horse, hick town that

Marengo is. Hannah will do fine. They'll like her. She'll tell them about gymnastics, something they approve of. But Summer has baseball, which she likes better than soccer, and it's the *sport* of the great unwashed and ignorant masses. She'll be a grump and slide under the table and I'll have to tell her a hundred times to sit up. Theo will bang his spoon and make loud noises and drop his food on the floor and make a big mess."

"Well, I won't."

"Won't what?" Her eyes were at their greenest.

"Drop my food on the floor. Make loud noises. I won't even slide under the table. Promise."

She rolled. Pulled the comforter up around her shoulders. Head tiny within the abundance of quilt. "They're just critical people. They can't help it."

"I create software. I play guitar. What's the matter with that? I'll be a bank manager. A loan officer? A dentist?"

"They'd think I'd lost my mind. No, software is good, being an artist is good. . . ."

"But not rock and roll. How about I play classical guitar? Cello in a string quartet?"

"We're grown-up people, Jake! This makes me feel so un-grown-up. Why do I care about this! I don't care about this." She pulled the comforter up and over them, a lavender igloo. "Once Maud dated a man who was a contractor and we convinced him to go take a painting class so she could tell The Parents he was an artist. So that maybe they'd accept him as good enough for their daughter. It didn't work." She imitated some high British voice. " 'Oh, Jim-Bob-Joe-Pete, and what do *you* do?' It's like some nineteenth-century novel."

Jake stayed silent. Unlike Maud, Lizzie never talked about The Parents, as she and Maud called them, and their possible influence on their lives. Lizzie usually stopped Maud in these discourses by saying, "They did the best they could." Maud's mouth would open and shut, fish-like. Jake could see—what response was possible?

It was hot under the down comforter, but he didn't move. "It was awful, growing up under that kind of judgment," Lizzie said. "I thought I'd moved beyond it. I was sure I had. But here it comes to hit me in the face. Just when I'm on the verge of thinking I might be able to sort out this thing called life."

"Marry me."

He felt rather than heard the thud of their two hearts. She pushed up through the comforter, swiping at the curls that tumbled over her face. "Jake."

"Let me make an honest woman of you."

She didn't think this was funny.

"I could give you the T-shirt again. You could pretend to be surprised."

She groaned. "I can just imagine Leo's response. A sloganed T-shirt. *Clothing* of the unwashed and ignorant masses."

"Well, then, introduce me as your fiancé."

" 'This is Jake? Like, Theo's dad? Like, he's my fiancé?' " Lizzie used a little-girl voice, each sentence a question. "You are so old-fashioned. It kills me."

"What's the matter with it?"

"It's a stupid system, Jake, that's what's the matter with it!" She rolled out of bed, yanked open her dresser drawers, pulled on under-wear, jeans. "What's the point? So we can share income? Fight? End up being cold and tense with each other like every married couple I've ever known? And then split up and make life miserable for the kids?"

Jake did not point out that without cursing herself with the disease of marriage she'd been through these scenarios several times. Lizzie seemed to catch his thought. "Look, I've done it—my life with men, my life with my kids—because I see men and women are usually so much bullshit. It never, it seldom, works, Jake. Marriage doesn't work."

"Sure it does."

She shook her head and a finger at him. "That's the danger. Sure, sometimes it does, sometimes you see it. Sometimes, sure, I feel we could." She stopped. Almost panting. Pulled a long sweater on over her jeans. "It's fun being with you right now. I like how you are with the girls and with Theo. But as my friend Cheryl the lawyer says, marriage is just the predivorced state. What if we change our minds? Then there we are. With each other."

"We won't call it marriage! We can call it burriage, like Maud's story. We can call it—" He moved his hands around, trying to find a different verb. "Braiding, meshing, binding, engaging—an engagement!" She shook her head, disgusted. "We could do it differently, Liz. Like Sam's memorial service. We can make it up. We'll call it something else. We won't name it at all. But we'll do it."

She stared at him, lower lip pushed out, as Theo did when he was working with crayons. As she left the bedroom she pulled up her sweater and twitched her rear end at him.

> going to hope you,
> going to smoke you
> going to lure you, love you,
> draw you, haul you,
> pull, press, pluck, tug, persuade, move, urge
>
> lure you, love you,
> let you, get you
> out of your lonely lair

Jake put the guitar down and doodled, imagining Lizzie and her father and mother and the three kids at the big round table at El Toro's. Would Leopold descend to a margarita? Maybe tequila? Or would it be Jameson? Glenlivet? On the rocks. No, a single rock.

"Why El Toro?" he'd asked yesterday, after he showered and came downstairs. "It's not exactly famous for its food."

Lizzie handed him a box of Cheerios and a bowl. "Because if I think about it, I'll get too complex and choose someplace truly inappropriate, or too expensive, or somehow wrong. This way I can say we're going there because the kids love it."

"Will Maud join you?"

Lizzie made a face. "I wish. She could talk all about Shakespeare"—she dropped the *r* at the end of the word, sounding British and effete—"and iambic pentameter and Stratford-upon-Avon, and charm their butts off with her intelligence and knowledge. But she's nervous about them coming, wants to be 'calm.' They've never come to see *my* shows, you know, not even the one at the big hoopla gallery in Santa Fe."

"They were in Australia, Lizzie."

"Whose side are you on?" She'd handed him the milk.

> *but what will I do when I've got you out*
> *out in the noonday sun*
> *what will you do when you*
> *if you*
> *see the light*
> *and discover I'm the one ha ha discover I'm the one*

Jake groaned, got up to sharpen his pencil. The phone rang.

"I'm such a shit," Lizzie said. "I tell Sam I'm going to be better and then I'm such a shit. Will you meet us at Harmony House?"

Jake was silent.

"You made plans." Her voice was flat.

"Of course I'll be there. But I have to put a suit on. Bank manager, you know."

"Don't you dare."

He arrived at Harmony House just after Lizzie. Hannah wore shiny black shoes and a ribbon in her hair. Summer kept her arms folded across clean overalls. Lizzie wore jeans and a flannel shirt. She lifted Theo from the car seat and gave him to Jake to hold. They turned towards the rental car that parked beside her. A tall, gray-haired, hawk-nosed man—he looked almost exactly as Jake had imagined he would—helped a round sparrow of a woman out of the passenger seat.

"Mr. Maxwell," Jake said, putting out his hand, "Mrs. Maxwell. It's a great pleasure."

"Nessie, please." Mrs. Maxwell had given Maud her smile.

"Like the monster in the lake!" said Summer.

Mrs. Maxwell made growling noises. Summer giggled.

"And call me Leo." Leopold shook his hand. His eyes were an amazing shade of blue.

Jake found himself laughing a little. "I never expected this," he said, "but I see so much of Lizzie in your face."

"Except she's a beauty," Leo said.

Lizzie looked startled, then made a dismissive face.

Hannah took Jake's hand. The restaurant was devised around the rooms and decor of an old Victorian house. A smiling host escorted them to a table with high-backed chairs. A high chair was brought for Theo, who banged his spoon on the apron. "He's just like you at this age," Nessie said. "What a little angel. Aren't you, snookums?"

Lizzie, sitting opposite Jake, met his eyes. Hers were filled with a kind of panicked laughter.

"Looks like a nice menu." Leo pulled a pair of glasses from an inside pocket.

"It was Jeep's idea," Hannah said. "She's quitting the Red Garter as soon as a job opens up here. She told me."

"Never thought I'd crave a hamburger," said Nessie, "but I'm just so tempted." She looked up from the menu. "I thought Jeep was going to join us?"

"She'll meet us later," Hannah said. "At Aunt Maud's play."

"'She has AA every night," Summer said.

Jake watched Lizzie's eyes move back and forth between her parents. Leo looked over the top of his glasses at Nessie, who nodded. "Several acquaintances and even some friends have joined that organization. They clearly do important work!"

Lizzie, dangerously, rolled her eyes. Jake suppressed a strong urge to laugh. When the waitress approached, Leo asked for the wine list. "But have a beer, Lizzie. Jake? Anything you like."

"Nothing quite like a good beer!" Nessie said. "We got to quite like our afternoon pint. That's a part of Britain I will definitely miss."

He avoided Lizzie's eyes. He was too close to a certain kind of hysteria. Looking confused, Lizzie ordered a beer, and out of loyalty, Jake seconded the order. They examined the large menus. A silence settled over the table. "How's Maud doing?" Jake asked.

"Nervous!" Hannah said. "She told me her butterflies had never been so bad. She's been going to the bathroom all day!"

Again Lizzie's eyes ping-ponged between her mother and father. Leo looked over the top of his menu. "She told me she's fifty times more nervous than she was on opening night because we're going to be in the audience. Now what kind of parents would make a child feel that way, eh, Agnes?"

Nessie buttered a piece of bread. "Maybe because you usually found something wrong with anything she ever did."

"I was nervous," Leo said. "What if she made a mistake with all those people watching?"

Nessie leaned towards Jake. "He was such a dragon." Her voice managed to both confide in Jake and tease Leo. "So afraid they'd let us down."

"No, no, no," Leo said. "I've thought about this. One does, when your children move far away and don't write you letters and, when they do call, immediately ask to talk to their mother. But what if someone found fault where I didn't, or before I did? They might think I was overly fond. A doting parent. An indulgent parent."

"God forbid," Nessie said.

Summer had her head on one side. "Were you really a dragon?"

Lizzie's strangled syllable sounded vaguely like "No." Leo laughed. "A dragon *and* a monster in the lake. What a household!"

The wine Leo ordered turned out to be an elegant cabernet, though Jake felt that he was wronging Lizzie in liking it so much. But Lizzie sipped it too, pushing her beer to one side. She grew animated, face flushed, as she talked about how her painting was going. When they asked her about the gallery opening they had missed two years before, Lizzie kicked him under the table, daring him to look at her. She was suddenly knowledgeable on issues he'd never heard her talk about before. The skies of Tourneur, which Nessie loved. The canvases of der Koot, which neither of them did. The Rembrandts Nessie had so admired in the National Gallery.

When their meals came, Hannah made them hold hands while she said grace. After all the stories he'd heard from Maud, Leo's aplomb was surprising. He held his glass up towards Lizzie. "Whatever you're doing, Elizabeth, it suits you."

Nessie nodded. "Both you girls."

"Look," Summer said, "Ma's face is all red."

It was red. Lizzie stared down at her lap, then met Jake's eyes, looking mischievous. She stood up, began to unbutton her shirt. "Ma," Hannah said, "what are you *doing*?"

"I have some news." Lizzie waited until they all looked at her.

Jake held his finger and thumb around the stem of his glass. Summer ate the cherry out of her Shirley Temple. "Wait!" Hannah hissed at her. Nessie, sitting next to Theo, quieted the banging spoon by handing him a piece of bread.

Lizzie pulled her arms out of the sleeves of the flannel shirt. She was wearing a red T-shirt. Jake took in the hand-printed block letters:

JOIN ME

BRAID ME

ENGAGE ME

INCLUDE ME

ENJOY ME

BURY ME

She turned around, looking over her shoulder, so he could see his own, MARRY ME.

Jake's insides melted, spilled. A fire burned within him, cascading lights like divers with torches in the night from a high waterfall. "Oh, wow!" Hannah yelled, and clapped her hands. "Join me!" She almost knocked Jake and his chair over in the onslaught of her hug. Ran to Nessie and hugged her, and to Leo, yelling, "Bury me!" Summer suddenly understood the commotion and screeched. Jake got to his feet, watched Lizzie hug Leo, Nessie. She came towards him, her face tilted up to his, laughing, alight.

Leo examined Jake with wary, amused eyes. He put out his hand. Jake took a step, holding Lizzie's, to shake it. "Bury me?" Leo said. For the first time Jake heard that note of disdain.

But Lizzie laughed. "That's where Maud gets it from." She pointed. "From him. There is nothing the slightest bit weird or odd or dark or subterranean about my use of that word," she said. "It is a joke. It is a reference. It is something I knew Jake would understand, and enjoy, and even though I was tempted not to use it because I knew what you might think, I thought it was more important in the life I'm interested in making with Jake that I let him know that I think burying me is a good idea."

Leo raised his eyebrows. "This calls for champagne."

"We should wait until Maud's with us," Hannah said.

Nessie shook a finger. "Uh-oh. You're taking after your aunt. Maud is always telling her father what to do about wine. Bossy, bossy, bossy. Men decide these things."

"Why?" Summer said, and Lizzie said, "Not in my household."

Leo put up his hands in defeat. "Bossiness, on the other hand, comes straight through Nessie. But you're right, Hannah. We'll wait until Maud's with us, after the show."

Lizzie let go of Jake's hand, went back to her place across the table. She worked her stockinged foot up onto his leg. As he ate his meal, he kept one hand around the small curl of woolen toes, aware of the small pocket of warmth where the arch of her foot rested against his knee.

M A U D

So long as men can breathe or eyes can see
So long lives this, and this gives life to thee.
—SONNET 17

M aud blew on the thin strip of glue she'd applied to a false eyelash as Sage, the stage manager, poked her head around the
dressing room door. "Fifteen minutes to places." As usual, Sage wore
her baseball cap turned backwards, her face reflected in the narrow
mirror that ran like a frieze almost completely around the room.
"We're completely sold out!"

Bobbie raised a victory fist. "Our highest single-ticket sales ever!
And for Shakespeare!"

"Your parents are in their seats, Maud. You can stop fretting.
Summer's mad because I won't let her sit up in the lighting booth.
But I've got too much on my mind." Sage checked her watch. "We
are now officially at thirteen minutes."

"Thank you, thirteen," they chorused.

Sage went next door to the men's dressing room to give the same
announcement. Ron Bartlett was singing "What I Did for Love"
to warm up his voice. *"Why can't a woman be more like a man"* vied
with *"Seventy-six trombones led the big parade"* for popularity, along
with shouted suggestions to Bobbie through the wall for various
musicals that Fable Mountain Stage Company ought to do in its next
season.

Maud straddled her chair, leaning close to the mirror, to land the second eyelash. Bobbie sat to one side of her at the shelf-like dressing-table that ran the length of two walls; Lois—the woman playing Maria—sat on the other. Kelly and Rose, who played Olivia's ladies-in-waiting and helped backstage, were upstairs, busy with precurtain duties.

In other professional theater experiences Maud had been pro-vided with a dresser to help her into and out of costume. FMSC could not afford such a luxury. Lois and Maud took turns lacing each other into their corsets, a process that invariably reminded Maud of the few times she'd cinched a saddle onto a horse. She pulled the strings tight at Lois' waist and then worked upward—as one might with a pair of high boots—tugging and tightening each set of laces. As she often did, she pondered how much this fashion contraption had enforced female dependencies: without a servant, a sister, a hus-band, it would have been almost impossible to get into or out of clothing without help.

Bobbie chattered on—she managed nervousness by talking—about season-ticket sales, so far so good, and about the poster, so far so bad, for FMSC's next production, *The Odd Couple*. She brushed pale pink along her cheekbones, describing the casserole she was making for the party tomorrow afternoon, after they'd struck the set and taken the lights down.

Maud stepped into and fastened two petticoats and an under-skirt, then slipped over her head the black dress she wore for the first part of the play. Lois laced her into this, then turned for Maud to do the reverse honors. Kelly and Rose rushed in, frantic. "Full house!"

In the next room, Ron sang, "A hundred and ten cornets right behind!"

"I'm going up," Maud said, unhooking Olivia's black mourning veil from its hanger.

Kelly hugged her. "I'll be your lady-in-waiting anytime." Rose and Kelly reminded Maud of Kathie and Trixie, who no longer worked at the Red Garter. Maud wondered if they'd made it to Hollywood.

Bobbie waved. "See you out there, fair cruelty."

Maud lifted her skirts to climb the backstage stairs. She didn't have an entrance until the third scene, and that only a slow walk in her veil across the stage while Sir Toby Belch cursed her inconsolable grief, but she liked this time alone. She ran lines, practiced tongue twisters, hummed to keep her voice from growing cold. She stood beside the angled bracing and bolts that held the flats to the stage floor. If she peeked through the crack between flats, she knew the white, leonine head of her father would be visible, eight rows back, and beside him the glint of her mother's eyeglasses. She wiped her hands along her dress, wondering if she had time to visit the bathroom once more.

She hadn't seen much of them, though they'd come by to see her house, complimented the life she'd established for herself. "Quite a community you've found for yourself here, Maudie." Her father, nodding, lower lip out in the expression of approval she craved so much. Her mother offered to take her shopping. Maud wanted new cookware instead of a new dress, and as they prowled the aisles of Marengo's elegant kitchen store her mother asked, "Do you hear from Miles?"

In fact, Maud had received a card from him just before the play opened. He was seeing someone else:

> I waited what I felt was a decent amount of time for you to come "home," but we've been silent for months now, and I figure you aren't going to. The thing that both troubles and gratifies me is that with you, without you, life just keeps going on going on. . . .

Maud could hear the beginning of the song he would find out of that phrase. She told her mother about the letter.

"Is that all right with you? That he's dating?"

Maud lifted a soup-sized kettle. "I keep waiting to have some sort of reaction. So far, anyway, I haven't."

"So you won't be going back to that nasty place?" Her mother, holding a saucepan, looked relieved. "Your father and I always felt its values are just so bad, that you'd be infected by them, in spite of your own sweet self."

Maud waited for the familiar sensation, the resistance to judgment that turned her very bones, her musculature, to a tense but

bendable steel: *Don't criticize me.* It had not come. She shrugged. It
had been a part of her life. It was part of what had made her who she
was. There was much to regret, if she wanted to start down that road.
But here she was, going on, going on.

She put her eye to a gap between canvas and wood and peered
out at the rustle and murmur of the audience, waiting—as audiences
had waited for centuries—for the performance to begin, for a story
to be told. The hubbub was loud tonight. She thought she recognized her mother's laughter.

From the audience's perspective, she knew the wood and canvas
flat through which she peered looked like Tudor paneling and a
window. The false fronts upon which much of theater was based
had once appalled her. Now she was conscious of the duty she and
the troupe had ahead of them: to bring alive a world that did not
exist. Theater came out of nothing but thought, and disappeared into
nothing but memory. This concept had once disturbed her. Now it
pleased her. She stood in the warm womb of the theater, aware of the
efficient bustle of preparation around her, turning this thought over
and over like a stone from a riverbed: The amazing effort it took, the
endless desire that existed, to create something out of nothing—
an edifice, a basket, a child, a university, a painting, love, a piece of
theater.

She rocked forward and back on her heeled, jeweled shoes.
Around her the stage crew, in their black clothes, made sure everything was in place. Sage stopped by on her way back downstairs.
"Thanks for the card. I hope we'll work together again too. I'm sure
we will. Chris says he's asked you to direct next season!"

This was news she was holding close. She would tell The Parents
tonight, but she wanted to savor the possibility it offered before she
let it out into the world.

The actors in scene one came up the stairs, talking in the voice
that was not quite a whisper, picking up props that were, after a
month of performances, a little worse for wear: the plate of spray-
painted Styrofoam fruit, the goblets painted to look like pewter, the
curlicued lute for Curio with strings that produced no notes. They
pulled at their tights, yawned, adjusted the hairpins that held their
wigs in place. What spawned this effort, this holy desire, to take one

reality—people, makeup, cloth, wood—and turn it into another, altogether different one? It was all-encompassing. Except on those nights when it seemed like utter foolishness.

The music swelled; the lights dimmed. The audience murmured their way into silence, their seats creaking as they readied themselves. "Have a great one, Maud!" Matt, playing Orsino, squeezed her hand as he went by. She felt the vacuum around her as the actors whispered and bumped their way past her to their places onstage. And then the sound she loved so much: the hum of the dimmers, hung on horizontal poles high above the stage. The hum grew; the lights brightened; the music—a simple string piece—ended. Onstage, Maud knew, Curio would be looking up from fingering his fake lute as Orsino lifted a languid hand.

"If music be the food of love, play on . . ."

They bid The Parents goodbye on Sunday morning, after coffee and bagels at Lizzie's house. Maud had slept in Hannah's bed. A late-night champagne celebration—of Jake and Lizzie's news, compliments on Maud's performance, on her potential new career as a director—had left them all a bit subdued. A chill May wind blew. Jake and Leo loaded the last bags into the car.

Hannah cried as she hugged Nessie goodbye. Summer stood to one side, shivering in short sleeves and overalls. She refused to go inside and get a sweater.

"It was a good visit, darling, a lovely visit." Her mother hugged her. "We're so proud of you both." Her father patted her on the back, told her she'd been "splendid," and to "keep up the good work." They got into their blue rental car and tooled off down the road, Nessie's hand waving until they turned the corner and were out of sight.

"Well," Maud said to Lizzie. "That wasn't so bad."

"You didn't have them for three straight days."

Summer shook her head. "Grandma doesn't like bagels. Crazy."

"Grandpa's too gruff," Hannah said. "The way he looks over his glasses at you. Like you're so dumb."

"But better than I expected," Lizzie said. "Like having friends visit. Jake says people change. Even parents."

The distant sound of a door slapping made them look up at the ridge. "Our roommate," Jake said. Driver came down the hill, carrying something beneath his jacket. He called to Summer. As she ran towards him, he knelt and a black-and-white bundle of fur wriggled out of his coat. Maud felt her heart lurch.

Summer carried it towards them, eyes gleaming. "Driver says it will be half ours and half his."

"What's its name?" Maud said, going down beside Summer and the trembling, quivering, leaping puppy.

"He says we can call it what we want but not Luna."

"Not Luna," Hannah said. "Can I hold him?"

"I'm going to get a kitten," Maud said. "This week."

"Both of Maggie's cats had litters," Driver said. "You'd do her a favor if you'd take one. We can go down together, pick one out. Take two, so they'll have company."

"I'd like that," Maud said. "I'd love that. How's your dissertation?"

"Don't ask. The topic keeps changing on me. Like trying to catch a sliver of soap. I keep thinking I've got it, and then there it still is, floating benignly. Some system you whites have devised. Torturous. I prefer sitting at the feet of a medicine man."

"Maybe it's the same thing," Maud said.

Jake groaned. "Don't get started, you two," Lizzie said.

Summer giggled when Maud stuck out her tongue at them. "Anyway, I've got to go. I'm already late."

Summer held up the puppy so it could lick Maud's face. "Not Mickey," she said to Hannah. "That's a stupid name."

"Why do you have to strike the set?" Jake asked. "Haven't you worked hard enough?"

"Chris made it clear we don't have to. But I want to. It helps get the play out of my system. Especially when I've enjoyed it."

Driver nodded. Maud remembered the story of his tipping over gravestones because he was so disappointed he'd lost a role. "You should audition for them sometime," she said.

"I don't know how."

"Once it's in the blood . . . ," she said. Driver almost smiled.

She gave the girls a hug, kissed Theo. "Congratulations again," she said to Lizzie and Jake. "I'm sorry I missed dinner last night. It sounds very dramatic."

"It was," Lizzie said. "But Jake may back out. He's worried about how Randy will take the news."

"He won't back out!" Summer yelled.

Maud drove to the theater filled with an irritating combination of fulfillment and melancholy. The play had gone well. She'd be directing next season, something she'd always longed to do. The college had called to say that she was short-listed to teach an acting class for the fall semester, which Lizzie said was as good as having the job. But she was itchy, ready to weep. If she hadn't just had her period, she could have blamed it on that. It was the puppy. It was Jake. Summer and Hannah. It was that Lizzie's life had an order and a logic to it that hers did not, would not, never would have.

As expected, she found some peace in pulling nails, carrying lumber, ripping up carpet, using a screw gun to take apart pieces of the set. The afternoon was filled with bawdy repartee, bad jokes, loud music. The radio was tuned to a station that played sixties and seventies rock and roll: "Desperado, you'd better come to your senses." Periodically the entire company burst into caterwauling accompaniment: "I've got a peaceful, easy feeling, I know you won't let me down . . ."

The capable carpenters who'd built the set showed up to help strike it. Men with names like Jim, Harold, Bud, Dave moved things along with a pleasant combination of skill and flirtation. Even Sue's Willy showed up for a while. Maud found herself obsessed with work, irritated when someone made off with her screw gun, glad when she found a steady job: pulling staples out of carpet, sorting reusable screws into empty paint cans. "I really want to know you, my sweet lord," the cast and crew warbled.

Maud went downstairs to clean the dressing room. She tucked the cards stored around the edge of her mirror into an envelope: notes from Ginger, Kathie, and Trixie, Elmer at Mountain Music, Barney—a surprise, and Noah's parents, who had brought him to a matinee. Opening-night cards from the cast, from Summer, Hannah, Lizzie, Bart, the man in her African dance class. She packed her makeup back into its fishing tackle box, rolled up the white towel littered with pencil shavings, powder, blush, and used it to wipe down the dressing table. She threw out a score of dried flowers, most of them long-stemmed roses, perched in tiny paper cups. The radio's wail, mourning that all they were was dust in the wind, made it all the way downstairs.

As the afternoon wore on, more and more of the actors claimed exhaustion or family commitments. Maud stayed on, unwilling—unable—to leave. Bobbie hung in, as did Chris and Ron. When a song from *Jesus Christ, Superstar* crooned its way over the airwaves, Ron used a hammer as a microphone. "I've been changed, yes, really changed," he crooned, eyes closed, swaying. Maud exchanged bad jokes with Dave and Harold and Bud, whose sexuality hung off them like the tool belts they wore. She looked for jobs that would keep her busy, moving around the space as it gradually emptied: props, furniture, set pieces. The blacks—huge wings of fabric—were folded to Chris's precise specifications. It took two people to carry each of the resulting wads to a storage locker downstairs.

The man named Bud climbed a ladder that made an enormous ratcheting sound each time he lowered, moved, and extended it to get at another set of lights above the stage. Using a rope-and-pulley system, she helped him lower the dozens of lighting instruments to the floor, shook out the colored gels, organized the instruments in order of size. Chris told her to get on home, take a shower, get to the party. "We'll finish this tomorrow."

But Maud was scouring Olivia out of her system. Miles, too. She imagined the life Miles was creating with someone else, the bright lights and fancy restaurants, the promise of Hollywood. She thought about her old acting class, about Nikos, about getting out of her head. Although Nikos would have liked her in this play. Funny how much easier it was to get out of your head when you had Shakespeare to rely on. She also brooded—there was no other word—on Jake and Lizzie. Marriage, or joining, or welding, or whatever they planned to call it, while they rogered and bonked and intercoursed away. They had life, capital *L*. With the children, Driver up in the trailer like old times with Sam, even a dog to complete the picture. They were of the world. Their children's children would take a piece of them along. Even Lizzie's art existed when she was done with it. While Maud's was dust in the wind. Or pieces of lumber, screws, scraps of remembered dialogue.

She coiled dozens of thick black electric cables, welcomed the cup of sweet, milky coffee someone brought her, and plunged back in. Swept the stage, sorted through the piles of sawdust for reusable hardware—wing nuts, bolts—and swept the stage again. Tired and hungry, she wasn't sure what she was wringing out of herself, pushing out, sweating out, but she wouldn't leave, she could see it now, until the theater was once again an empty space.

It was almost 10 P.M. when they finished. Chris, dressed up, wet hair slicked back, came into the theater and bellowed at them to get to the party. "We all can't have a good time until you arrive."

"That's your guilt trip, not ours," Bud said. He had crooked teeth, yellow from smoking, a craggy face. "But let's go. I'll douse the lights backstage, meet you in the lobby."

She fetched her coat, her bag. As they headed up the aisle Chris wrapped an arm around her shoulders. "You doing okay?"

She pushed hair back from her eyes. "It's over."

"Yeah, yeah, yeah. Until next time."

They stood at the double doors of the auditorium, looking back at the stage. "If this were Broadway," Chris said, "or maybe a movie about Broadway, right about now there'd be some stagehand coming out with a bald lightbulb at the top of a pole, placing it in the middle of the stage. I've always meant to find out why they left a light on."

"It's a union thing," Bud shouted from backstage.

Chris snapped his fingers in regret. "And I always thought it was to scare away ghosts."

"Or just that the light doesn't go away," Maud offered, but this didn't say what she meant.

"Nope," Bud called again. "Nowadays ghosts pay attention to the exit signs. You guys ready?"

"Ready."

The auditorium lights went out. Then the ones above the stage. Even so, it seemed to Maud that the stage shimmered, pulsed, glowed. Bud came up the aisle with a quick loping stride. As Chris clicked out the lobby lights and held the door for her, as they exited into a night that smelled of new-mown grass, as they walked down the street towards Chris and Bobbie's house, talking easily, even then Maud felt it: the afterglow of that empty space, waiting, waiting, as it always did, and always had, for the incandescence of new life.

ACKNOWLEDGMENTS

For all they have taught and continue to teach me, I extend profound thanks to my students and editing clients.

This book would not have been written without the inspiration and support of my lovely and loving sisters, Tracy and Brett. I also received help, sustenance, and important laughter from Lynne Collins, Liz Davis, Clare Henkel, Susan Stroh, and many others, including Forbesy, Sunny, Kanga, Laurie, and Kate.

For the inspiration her life and her beautiful paintings she gave me, thanks to Dana Porter Biss. And to Tom Lane, man of such song and heart.

To the children in my life I am grateful: my niece, Emma; my nephews, Justin, Nico, and Hunter; and numerous other good friends, including Dylan, Wesley, Emily, Andrew, Zachary, Grace, Alexandra, and Tomas.

God may be in the details, but it takes someone to attend to them. Tom Taylor's ability to see not only the forest and the trees, but the branches, the pine needles, and the ground greatly enriches my life.

Thanks to the American Conservatory Theatre's Advanced Training Program, especially to Bill Ball, Ed Hastings, and Joy Carlin; to the Oregon, Colorado, and Lake Tahoe Shakespeare Festivals, and the Old Globe Theatre; also to Eric Forsythe, the University of Iowa Theater Department, and Iowa Summer Rep. Special thanks are due The Foothill Theatre Company in Nevada City—especially to Artistic Director Philip Charles Sneed and director Lynne Collins.

Thanks to Marilyn Jones and Mitchell Kaplan for the inspiration provided by their marriage proposal, and to Trish and Mark Koopman for theirs.

Wells Kerr gave me, at the age of fourteen, my first dose of and a never-ending love for Shakespeare. Miriam Gilbert, Professor Emeritus at the University of Iowa, underscored the love by sharing, in a semester-long tutorial, some of her monumental knowledge.

I am profoundly grateful to Leona Nevler, my editor at Ballantine, and to my agent, Michael Carlisle.

And to Tom, who lived so much of it with me.

Catching Heaven

SANDS HALL

A Reader's Guide

A Conversation with Sands Hall

Karen Joy Fowler is the author of two short story collections and three novels, the most recent being *Sister Noon*.

Karen Joy Fowler: Among the most memorable things in your book are your characters, including Maud's acting teacher, Nikos. About a third of the way into the novel, he has a tirade about Chekhov. "Americans are addicted to plot!" he says. "Chekhov knows that character is plot." Can you talk about this in relation to your own book?

Sands Hall: Someone once told me that Chekhov gives his characters profound needs and complicated objectives, and that's what creates the story. I chose to believe in this idea, because I didn't start writing the book with much of a plot in mind. I had Maud with her needs, and Lizzie with hers, and then Jake emerged, and then Jeep and Driver, etc., each with their own set of needs. When an actor prepares to play a character, they ask, "What's my objective? Why do I want that; why do I want that now?" I thought if I kept asking myself those questions as a writer, and if I made the needs of my characters large enough, the plot would emerge. Which is exactly what happened.

It's such a complicated DNA-like helix, those two: plot, character—which comes first? I tend to vote for character because it worked for me, and perhaps because I like reading those sorts of novels.

By putting Maud's memory of acting class at that point in the novel, I hoped to ask, or allow, the reader to question something about creating a character, and, as far as that goes, to question what goes into creating a plot. As a culture, we are addicted to plot—which usually means that the life we're reading about or watching needs to get complicated. I remember watching the movie *Rob Roy*, when the nice young man is heading into the dark wood, bringing the bag of silver home to Robbie. The music is somber and scary—everyone in the audience knows he's going to be set upon by the bad guy—and I hunkered down in my seat and whispered, "I hate plot." I don't, of course. What I hate is watching people get killed. But Robbie needed that money desperately, and that excellent movie would not exist if he'd managed to get hold of it only thirty minutes into the story. So: Need.

KF: **With your three point-of-view characters, you managed a very neat—well, dichotomy would suggest two; what's the word for three—trichotomy? Maud is an actor. Lizzie is a painter. Jake is a singer-songwriter.**

SH: I wanted to talk about art, and its place in our lives. Part of Maud's grief—what's driving her—is that she has no children, and of course here she is involved in this transient art form. Acting, like dance, like any live performance, is gone the moment it's created. Maud understands that she will leave nothing tangible behind to show her passage through the world. Whereas Lizzie not only has children carrying on her very blood, she has her paintings: objects one can touch, hang on a wall.

KF: **And Jake?**

SH: Also a performer, his art disappears the moment it's spun into the air. But music can be recorded in a way that a live stage play can't, and of course his lyrics, written down on paper, form a tangible *something* he can carry with him. He bridges the gap between the sisters, literally, and figuratively.

KF: **What Maud does in the outside world affects her interior life, and Jake is just the opposite: everything that happens to him is fuel for his songwriting. But I didn't see the impact of Lizzie's life on her art, or vice versa.**

SH: Interesting observation. One of the things I tried very purposefully to show is that Lizzie, especially in comparison to Maud, isn't prone to self-reflection. I tried to pull out of Lizzie's language— her dialogue, her thought processes—any figures of speech. She doesn't think things are *like* other things, and she speaks in simple sentences—until the night she's driving home from spending the night with someone whose name she can't remember. Then she finally allows herself to mentally explore that complex, under-water metaphor of her life. Maud's thought processes are more complicated, down to thinking in semicolons. She connects so much more than Lizzie does. It's her personality and it's also part of the career she's chosen.

Lizzie disdains Maud's approach to the world, her philosophy that everything is connected to everything else—because she can't find a parking spot, she shouldn't have moved to Marengo, that sort of thing. And part of Lizzie's journey is that she finally begins to realize that she needs to connect, that connections exist. She is as obsessive about not looking beyond the surface of her life as Maud is about searching for meaning. Lizzie's paintings may be a reflection of that—are they turned into greeting cards because they are *pleasing*, but ultimately surface portraits? Her art is a two–dimensional representation of the world, while Maud's art demands, by its very nature, three-dimensionality.

KF: **Like Maud, you are an actor. You're also a director and a play-wright. I've always thought it would be wonderful to hear some-one speak lines that I'd written. You don't get that thrill when you write a novel.**

SH: It's tremendously satisfying to be a director, an actor, an author, and a playwright, and to utilize those very different approaches to a given piece of writing. It can also be a bit schizophrenic. A play-wright is a bit like a wheelwright—a putter-together-of-things. But author implies authority. As Richard Ford has said, an author "au-thorizes" his writing to go out to the world.

And it *is* a thrill to hear your words spoken aloud. To see those black words on white paper manifesting not only into an active scene, but taking place in a room like the one you described, with lights and costumes similar to those you had in mind; perhaps a lit-tle underscoring under the dialogue to emphasize the mood . . . It can be exhilarating. Except when it sends you back to the com-puter for a thorough rewrite. Hearing one's words aloud is a great lesson in economy.

Traditionally there's been great respect for the playwright, but this is changing, largely because of the attitude in Hollywood, where wordsmiths are considered dispensable and changeable. The screenwriter is often seen as a hired hand—not really an artist. It's dreadful. There's a light bulb joke that sums it up:

Q: How many screenwriters does it take to change a light bulb?

A: Does it have to be a light bulb?

In film, the director is considered, ultimately, to be the author of a movie, and unfortunately that mentality is working its way into theatre. The hierarchy is very complicated and very much in flux. I've been fortunate to work with people who understand and appreciate the role of the playwright, and while there's been tricky territory to negotiate, I've gotten to see the plays as I imagined them—in addition to all kinds of wonderful stuff I didn't, I couldn't have imagined. I'm not a set designer, or a costume designer, or a lighting designer, and each of these, and many other elements, including of course the actors and director—not to mention publicity, box office, ushers!—are essential to a piece of theatre. Theatre is collaboration. It's amazing how rarely we come in over-budget, and that we always open on time. You must be willing to accept, change, alter, and admit that someone else's idea works better than yours. It's the free-flowing, dynamic nature that is at the heart of the art.

Like Maud, I don't have children, and theater is a large part of what I do. Some costume renderings, photographs, and a collection of posters are all the proof I have of a lengthy, satisfying acting career. Being able to hold a published book in my hands is a profound experience. I've started to collect old books—I have a few that are over one hundred and fifty years old, and of course there are volumes far, far older than that. Those words, and therefore that author, is still with us in those sometimes brittle pages. As usual, Shakespeare says it well:

"So long as men can breathe and eyes can see
So long lives this, and this give life to thee."

He's talking about a sonnet, of course, and both he and the inspiration for the poem, whoever he or she may be, are long gone. But the words keep both the author's ideas, and the author, alive. It's so simple, and so moving a thing.

Maud's journey is to face that she will leave nothing behind, and that, in fact, no one really does. It's the realization she has when she's holding Jeep, who's cried herself to sleep: nothing is ever going to fill the vacuum, it's always there. All experience is just a breath, and then it goes. And that's the empty space of theater, too. It comes from a bunch of black marks on a page, and no matter how wonderful, high-tech, long-running a production may be, when it closes, it disappears into that same place.

KF: **Speak a little to the issue of family. There's Maud and Lizzie, their parents, Lizzie's children, even Jake and his sister, but with Jeep, and Sam and Driver, something bigger seems to be going on.**

SH: I've always loved Thanksgiving more than any other holiday, because it's the time when family as we know it, expands. Often enough, in my peripatetic life, I've been the orphan invited to someone's table, and those are invitations I make certain to extend to others if I can. Family, especially in our current society, is so much bigger, looser, than the blood ties that traditionally compose it. Sam is the father Lizzie's girls aren't otherwise having. Jeep is a sister, a cousin, and a daughter. Deprived of a decent mother, she looks for one in Lizzie. Driver has to remove the chip imbedded in his shoulder, but he finds his place in the Lizzie brood as well. And the idea of a clan—a group of people that don't know you but take you in if you're blood—has always fascinated me. Sam won't recognize his clan, but for better or worse, they come and find him when they discover they're needed. Maud realizes that theater is a clan.

The names for Driver and Jeep came to me in roundabout ways, but I kept both of them because I wanted to layer in the transitory nature of our society. We're always on the move, as Maud is when the story begins. But when, in the second chapter, we move to Lizzie's world, everything is embedded in the earth—her studio, once a trailer; Sam's living quarters, once a caboose; even the engine Sparky has left in her driveway is moldering in the dirt. She's that settled. Whereas Maud is on the move—at least when she arrives in Marengo.

KF: **Tell us a little more about Marengo and Marengoing, and what you think the town brings to the book.**

SH: I wanted a place that was a frontier to some degree—even though Maud moves east from her west to get to it. I wanted to create a town that would convey a mythologized West—that demented designer's vision of women in the 1890's at the Red Garter, for instance. A world where you might or might not find your gold.

KF: **At the very least it's your second chance.**

SH: Or your last chance. My characters gather in Marengo for their various reasons. They come to this place where maybe dreams happen and maybe they don't, or maybe there's the discovery of a dream you didn't know you had. I went 'round and 'round about keeping the name Fable Mountain, but in the end, I left it. I wanted to alert the careful reader to the idea that this was a fabulous place.

KF: **What does it mean to be a western writer as opposed to an eastern writer?**

SH: I'd be honored to be considered a western writer, but beyond this novel, and my play *Fair Use*, which does tell a large western story, I don't yet know if the West will remain my territory. I suppose the West brings up issues of space. How to inhabit the land, how to tend it. And, I suppose, issues of the original inhabitants of this continent, Native Americans. As well as the species we've succeeded in eliminating from the planet in our greed. Our history there is so foul I can barely stand to look at it.

But foul as it is, and however much we've raped the land, built dams in the middle of Eden, and stolen water from here to keep power going there—we all rest on the fact that these things were done. We have and rely on our electricity, and our computers; we relish our warm houses; we depend on our roads. I suppose being a western writer means taking on the uses and abuses of living on this planet. How can we be responsible inhabitants of the planet earth?

KF: **Do you miss the acting scene in Hollywood that you, like Maud, left behind?**

SH: No. I suppose I'm sorry I didn't succeed at something at which I worked so long and hard, but it was good to realize that it's theatre

I love, and not the world Hollywood surrounds it with. I have friends who do very well in that environment, but I was intimidated by the emphases: to be pretty, to wear make-up all the time (you never know who you might run into), to have the right clothes, to be thin. I've joked that I left Hollywood because I couldn't bear to wear nylons, but it's partly true. I hated feeling like a sausage, squeezed into a casing—and I suppose to some degree that's how I felt psychically.

And I've always had an odd relationship with television. If you don't get into movies in Hollywood, you're doing television—if you're lucky. I grew up in Squaw Valley, in the Sierra Nevada, and at that time it was hard to get any reception over those high mountains. In addition, my parents always urged us towards books. We were not, to put it mildly, encouraged to watch television. I never got in the habit. When I played the character Maya, years ago, on the soap opera, *The Guiding Light*, I never watched myself on the show. At the time, a VCR was beyond my limited budget. I know it sounds odd, but it had been drummed into me that watching TV in the middle of the day meant that one's day—one's life— was at a very low ebb. You were on the way to the devil—heroin was next. My mother and father had a wonderful time watching me—I was on the show for about six months, on and off—but I couldn't bring myself to do it. And there was so much I could have learned.

It took leaving Hollywood when I was in my late thirties, getting one MFA from the Writers Workshop, and a second one in Drama, to reengage my love of theatre. I was given the opportunity to realize why I'd wanted to do it all my life. This novel became, among other things, a way for me to communicate that.

Reading Group Questions and Topics for Discussion

1. Author, Sands Hall, says that in her book, *Catching Heaven,* she wanted to talk about art and its place in our lives. In our busy schedules, has art become a luxury item?

2. The book raises many questions involving the difference between the "high" arts (theater, paintings) and "low" arts (television, greeting cards). Is this a useful distinction to make? Is a painting inevitably more important than a greeting card?

3. Jake's chapters all begin with lyrics, Maud's with lines from Shakespeare. Why are Lizzie's begun with the things that are pinned to her refrigerator?

4. Hall is clearly thinking a lot about family in the book. On the one hand, her definition of family is expansive. On the other, one of the book's obvious strengths is its depiction of the two actual sisters. Is family today a fluid concept? Is blood less powerful than it once was?

5. Do you imagine the strains in the relationship between Maud and Lizzie will be repeated by Summer and Hannah?

6. Maud sees the world as a plotted place. Everything is connected to everything else; at the heart of the universe, is order. Lizzie lives in a more chaotic and random world. Which vision seems most right to you?

7. When Maud leaves Los Angeles, she seems to leave little behind in the way of friends. Yet she connects easily with people in Marengo. Why is this?

8. What does the mythology of the West bring to the book? Hall says the West is a place of second chances. Contrast this to Lizzie's philosophy, expressed in her drawing class, that the most important line you put on a paper is the first one, that everything else flows from the beginning.

9. What does it mean to be a western writer in America? Are the issues and obsessions likely to be the same or different from those the eastern American writer will take on?

10. Lizzie is a prickly character. Do you grow to love her? Do you think she's a good mother? A good teacher? A good friend?

11. Do you think Jake will be a good father?

12. What do you make of Lizzie's relationship with Sam? Why was it Maud, and not Lizzie, in the hogan with him when he died? Or was Lizzie there?

13. What do you make of Lizzie's relationship to Jeep? What does Jeep's pregnancy mean to Lizzie? To Maud? To Jeep?

14. What motivates Driver's change of heart?

15. Hall's three main characters are artists. All are extremely successful up to a point, and all have failed to fully realize their dreams. Which predominates in your vision of these people—their successes or their failures?